PRAISE FOR OBLIVION'S GALAXY

Dylan McFadyen's adept, vivid storytelling in *Oblivion's Shadow* launches you into an enthralling journey of discovering the fate of humanity after a near-extinction level apocalypse. With compelling characters and thoroughly researched technology, McFadyen weaves a space tale that is at once suspenseful, thoughtful, and believable; a remarkable feat that seems so rare. Its intellectuality is tinged with emotion, and its darkness is tinged with hope. It completely surpassed my expectations, and kept me guessing right until the very end. At its core, *Oblivion's Shadow* is an exploration of humanity's strengths—and flaws. I have no doubt that it will captivate sci-fi lovers and skeptics alike.

ATLAS BLAINE, AUTHOR OF *EDGE OF INHUMAN*

The suspenseful storytelling coupled with well-developed characters elevates *Oblivion's Cloak* beyond a typical space opera. If you're looking for a sci-fi novel that marries intricate world-building with an engaging plot, this is the one to choose. *Oblivion's Cloak* is an absolute must-read for fans of the genre.

TWO NERDS WITH WORDS, AMAZON REVIEW

Oftentimes, sequels to great first novels don't live up to the quality, pace and page-turning excitement the first novel did. *Oblivion's Blade* surpasses its predecessor in every way. The characters and relationships continue to develop while scenes of battles, political negotiations among aliens, and the reader's immersion in a far-flung future setting makes it almost impossible to put down.

R MOLTZON, GOODREADS REVIEW

Oblivion's Triumph is entertaining, surprising, with a lot of mystery, unexpected events, action against the backdrop of an exotic science fiction story! It is now with sadness and nostalgia that I close this fascinating novel on an end that I certainly would not have guessed. Congratulations and thank you to the author for this incredible adventure!

SENTINELLE23, AMAZON REVIEW

LESSONS OF WAR

ALSO BY DYLAN MCFADYEN

OBLIVION'S GALAXY

Oblivion's Shadow

Oblivion's Cloak

Oblivion's Blade

Oblivion's Triumph

THE AETHERIAL EMPIRES

A Poor Day to Die

SI VIS ASTRA

The Blade Within

Lessons of War

LESSONS OF WAR

SI VIS ASTRA - BOOK ONE

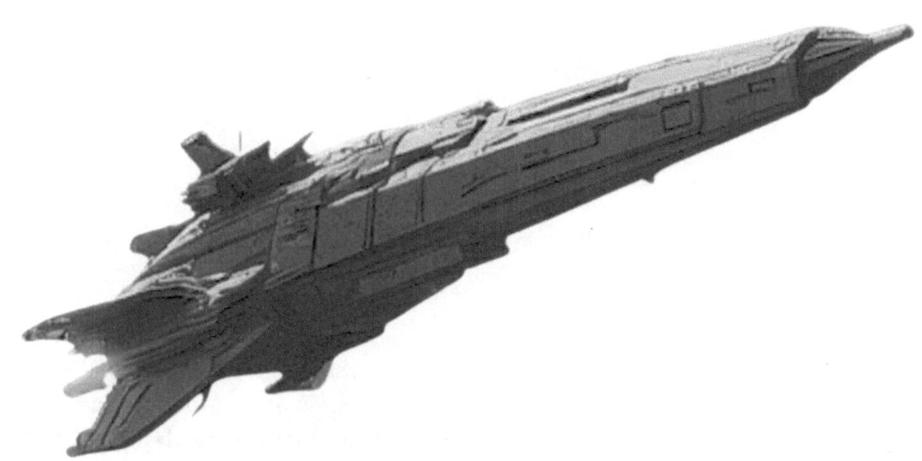

DYLAN MCFADYEN

This is a work of fiction. Names, characters, organizations, places, events, and incidents are either products of the author's imagination or are used fictitiously. Otherwise, any resemblance to actual persons, living or dead, is purely coincidental.

ISBN-13: 9781738314324 (digital)

ISBN-13: 9781738314317 (paperback)

Cover design by the author.

Layout by Gecko Edit.

For all the Kickstarter backers who brought this long-held dream to life,
And for William and Victoria, as is all I have and will ever have.

War is a stern teacher.

— Thucydides, c. 400 BTSY

Si vis astra, para bellum.
(If you want the stars, prepare for war.)

— Admiral Rance "Starbird" Wolfe, TSY 2279

PROLOGUE

"Time to target, five minutes. Drop pattern Delta Four at target-plus three minutes. Full stealth protocols. Confirm."

Commander Sorăna Mirra of the Interstellar Compact Naval Infantry Corps, Long-Distance Reconnaissance Group, flicked her right index finger twice in rapid succession. The muscle impulse triggered her neural implant to send a signal to the tactical AI confirming its drop plan. She twisted easily in the cramped, zero-g environment of the infiltration craft's crew compartment, putting the hardscreen terminal behind her.

"All right, boys," she said, "you heard the machine. Eight minutes to drop. Let's go over it one more time the old-fashioned way."

The other five members of her team floated before her, hands or feet hooked into holds to stabilize themselves. Like her, they were in full armor with their weapons holstered, their faceplates retracted. They might have objected to the redundancy of reviewing the plan the "old-fashioned way," given that they'd already been briefed back at the Fort before departing, *and* downloaded all the relevant information to their implants and their armor's onboard AIs.

They knew better.

"Drop points are here." The Tac-AI displayed the drop map on the hardscreen behind her. Each team member's assigned DP flashed. Each point was separated by a few kilometers, in a wide circle around a redlined central point. "Auto and verbal confirmation once we're down, then we proceed on foot toward the target."

"ROE?" Mirra's second-in-command, Senior Lieutenant King, asked. He knew the mission rules of engagement, of course; but some of the team members might have been hoping they had changed.

"Restricted," she said, to a couple of muted groans. "Only engage when necessary, and when you do, make sure it looks good."

Petty Officer Yamada raised a hand. "And what if the dinos don't give us a choice?"

Mirra tilted her head, just so. "I trust your judgment."

"That's probably a mistake," Petty Officer Demetriou muttered loudly. Yamada punched him in the armor; Demetriou bounced off the hull, grinning.

Mirra allowed herself the slightest smile, then vanished it. "The target is Hakan Nagarra."

A long-distance recon image of a Kyran warlord appeared on the hardscreen, accompanied by several AI composites of him from other angles. Hakan was from the pterochid species, slightly taller than the average human, his razor teeth hidden behind closed lips, a keen and cruel intelligence in his forward-facing eyes. The species' dominant characteristics were their large, dexterous hands, and the brightly colored feathers that covered their bodies.

"Memorize those color patterns," Mirra said, "in case your implants go down, or their ECW's better than intel suggests."

"We're supposed to be able to tell the ugly fucks apart now?"

King leveled a finger at the marine.

Mirra supported her SLT's silent reprimand. She sympathized with Yamada, but the comment wasn't helpful.

"Time to target, three minutes," the Tac-AI announced.

Mirra continued. "Hakan was exiled from Clan Harag for claiming to be the descendant of some mythical Kyran warlord. He's here on Lampshade building a power base; intel projects that given enough time, he may have a shot at making himself supreme hierarch."

"I'll believe that when I see it," Junior Lieutenant Contreras said flatly.

Mirra sympathized with *that* too. The many and fractious Kyran clans uniting under a single ruler seemed an impossibility, if their history was any indication. But even the divided clans remained a threat to the Compact, if a low-level one. Of course, that assessment was relative. Kyran raids didn't feel very low-level to the poor souls caught in them.

"Nonetheless," she said, "Hakan's popular with the warrior castes. Eliminating him and pinning it on a rival clan, in this case Rhyllok, should have them and Harag at each other's throats. Even more than they usually are."

"Amen to that," Yamada said.

Mirra pointed at the hardscreen again. "We get in close, ID the target. Switch weapons over to Kyran plasma mode and take him and his crew out. Then we return to our pods in the chaos, exfil back to the ship, and make the deep space rendezvous. Call sign for this mission will be 'Sigma.' Any questions?"

Warrant Officer Tchaikovsky, the team's Electromagnetic and Cyberwarfare Officer, raised his hand and then thumped it lightly against the hull. "How long will she have on station at full stealth?"

"Sixty to seventy-two hours," Mirra said. "We shouldn't need more than twelve."

Tchaikovsky nodded.

"Don't worry, Tchai," Demetriou said. The ECWO's face twisted as soon as he heard the petty officer's voice, knowing what was coming. "We'll have you back in time for your big date with your boyfriend."

Unwisely, Tchai engaged. "He's not—"

"You should have heard him talking before we left." Demetriou fended off Tchaikovsky's attacks with one hand while grinning at the rest of the team. "I swear to God he's gonna propose."

The team broke into spontaneous applause and congratulations. Tchai floated back and forth, jostled by his comrades, his mouth pressed into a thin line. There was a hint of laughter in his eyes.

Mirra let it unfold. Good to blow off a little steam before the drop. And the team was genuinely happy that the usually buttoned-up ECWO was finding a way to let loose, even if it was with some fleetie officer.

"Time to target, one minute."

"All right, lads, that's it." King clapped his hands. "Pod up. Move, move."

The smiles lingered as the marines clambered through the individual hatches lining the compartment, into their infiltration pods. King lingered a moment, as he always did.

"See you down there?" Mirra said.

"Not if we do it right."

He and Mirra bumped fists, and their faceplates slid closed. She twisted in the air and lowered herself into a cramped infil pod in a practiced maneuver. Then the hatch sealed, and she was alone.

And not alone. No sooner was she in than the Tac-AI fed her status readouts on her team, overlaid with the infiltration craft's position and the dispositions of known and suspected enemy on the surface of the planet below.

With an almost spasmodic twitching of her fingers, she cycled through the information, bringing up one piece here, pushing back another there. Putting the tactical data on her armor's HUD, relegating the team status info to the semiconscious layer of her neural implant, where she'd absorb it as if on instinct. She studied the deployment and compared it to the tracked hostiles and their predicted patrol patterns one more time, deciding whether any last-minute changes needed to be made.

None did. But it cost nothing to check.

There was no audible countdown in the pods. They'd been ready to go the moment they slipped in. The Tac-AI just got them into position, slid into the planet's upper atmosphere, waited a few more minutes to confirm to its own satisfaction that everything was as it should be. Then it launched them into free fall.

The Kyrans had no sensors on the surface or in orbit that could detect them, except by a direct, high-powered lidar ping. And they'd have to know precisely where to aim it for even that to work. At this altitude, with the pods' geometry, there'd be no atmospheric entry burn to give them away. The pods' AI-governed adaptive visual camo was Compact state-of-the-art, meaning that the only sign they'd make during their descent would be a slight disturbance of the air, which should be invisible even to the eyes of the argotids, the Kyran warrior species. The Tac-AI wouldn't drop them close enough to any that would see, hear, or smell the disturbed earth when the pods actually touched down.

Still, the ride was always the hardest part. Trapped in a coffin-like pod, defenseless. Somehow, the chances of detection being vanishingly small made it worse, at least for Mirra. Like if it happened, she'd be embarrassed as well as dead. Not the way she, or any marine, wanted to go out.

She closed her eyes. Except for that nagging dread, the ride was almost relaxing. Only the slightest shuddering, most of the way down. The pods' mass-reduction fields stayed at low power until they were almost on the ground, to limit the possibility of energy emissions-based detection.

That was when the relaxation ended. The fields kicked into high gear and the pod lurched, sending Mirra's stomach into somersaults. Then, just before impact, the artificially lightened pod's compressed air retrothrusters fired, slowing it enough that it came down with a crunch rather than a crash. Mirra's head still clanged against the wall of the pod, but that was what armor was for.

The front of the pod slid open the moment it settled. Despite the all-clear the Tac-AI gave her, she came out walking forward, pulling her rifle from her back and bringing it up as its systems were still engaging. Her swarm of recon and support drones launched from the pod and fanned out around her as she turned slowly, taking in the dark panorama of the alien landscape with her weapon held steady before her.

It was quiet, save for the hum of her drones—artificially piped into her helmet to reassure her they were still out there, since their stealth systems would mask the noise to outside observers—and a strange lowing noise, which rose and fell to a rhythm she couldn't perceive. Her AI told her it was made by a small species of mammalian-analogue that dwelled in the low, thick scrub in this region. They were particularly active at night.

"Glad for that noise," King said on the team comms, as if echoing her thoughts.

"Too soothing," Demetriou said. *"Makes me want to take a nap."*

"Let's hope the dinos feel the same way," Yamada added.

"Don't count on it," Mirra said, ending the chatter. Their squad comms and data were on an internal quantum entanglement comms net—impossible for the enemy to detect, let alone intercept. Their armor would absorb the acoustics. No need for the light-codes and hand signals she'd made them learn back when she was putting the team together, and still had them practice from time to time. Not unless things went very wrong.

So far, they hadn't. Her drop point was as clear as the Tac-AI had said it would be. Her team's were as well. No random Kyran guards or workers stumbling through that the infil craft had somehow missed.

Mirra switched her tactical HUD to an overhead display, a synthesis of the squad net data and the feed from the infil craft in low geosync orbit. She and her team were a constellation of blue arrows arrayed in a circle around their target. They'd all come down within a hundred-meter radius of their assigned drop points. Almost perfect.

"Okay," Mirra said. She looked up; the target buildings flashed on her HUD in the distance, along with suggested paths to reach them. "Let's move out."

Overwatch from the infil craft and Mirra's drones showed no hostiles within two kilometers of her. Still, she moved through the undergrowth deliberately, rifle poised, head on a swivel. Couldn't be too careful.

This planet was deep inside Kyran space, but it was an unimportant outpost. Its Interstellar Compact designation was Lampshade, for reasons Mirra wasn't privy to. The Kyran name for it was unknown. Technically, it didn't fall under Clan Harag's jurisdiction; it had once belonged to a clan that had been destroyed following the war. Now it was claimed by everyone and no one. It was a harsh world, if the intel reports and Mirra's eyes were to be believed. But it was also a lush one, teeming with life, and it had no indigenous sapient population. If it were anywhere else in the galaxy, another species would likely have colonized it and begun developing it long ago.

The Kyrans weren't interested in it—*because* it had no native sapient population. To them, that meant all it was good for was hiding out and doing the sort of business that even the clan hierarchies couldn't stomach.

That was why Hakan was here. *He* was why Mirra was here.

The lack of enemy patrols in her path was just starting to nag at her when her squad net popped an alert. She brought the feed from the alerting team member to the fore of her awareness.

"Sentry spotted," Contreras said just as the data from his armor sensors coalesced in Mirra's vision. She stopped and lowered to her knees so she could assess.

Contreras's sensors outlined the target on his HUD, though it wasn't yet visible through the brush a hundred meters or so ahead of him. From the outline, it was an argotid. A big one, at that, about eight feet tall, with a thick neck and long jaw, its big, clawed hands gripping one of their oddly shaped rifles. It didn't seem terribly alert for threats, pacing back and forth and occasionally sniffing the air. But the clunky suite of sensors grafted to its head would be lighting up the night for it, scanning the infrared and other radiation bands.

"Evade or engage?" Contreras asked.

Mirra thought for a second. Contreras could keep his distance and easily slip past the guard. But when the heat came down, the argotid would probably charge straight at the main compound, and thus straight at Contreras. Besides, it would look more suspicious if they were able to get right into the compound without neutralizing a single sentry. A Kyran kill team wouldn't be able to manage that.

"Sigma Six," she said. "Clone target's transponder."

"Already got it," Tchaikovsky reported. Mirra smiled. *"You're clear, Lieutenant."*

With the argotid's implanted transponder signal cloned, his command would have no idea when he went down. That'd maintain the team's cover until they let hell loose.

"Sigma Three, engage," she ordered.

Contreras stowed his rifle on his back and crept toward the sentry. He kept his right hand slightly back, ready to grab the gun in a moment if needed. His left hand was held forward, his implant projecting an image of it into his mind, and thence into Mirra's HUD, filtering out the adaptive camo that made it invisible to the outside world. A long blade extended slowly and silently from the armor.

Contreras was efficient and precise. He slow-walked right up to the sentry without being spotted, and waited for his moment. The second the Kyran turned toward him, perhaps at last sensing his hunter, the blade slashed through its thickly muscled throat. Then it flashed down, and stabbed repeatedly into the creature's chest, propelled by the armor's powered joints.

The argotid couldn't scream. It flailed, managed to claw ineffectively at Contreras's armor, then collapsed twitching into the brush, livid orange blood gushing from its wounds. The blood sloughed easily off the armor's hydrophobic coating as the blade retracted.

Contreras was moving again while the sentry was still dying. *"Target eliminated. Proceeding."*

"Roger."

Mirra pushed the feed back to her subconscious and kept moving. Perfect execution: quick, silent, and nothing to show it hadn't been a Kyran who did it. Contreras hadn't been in any real danger. The big bastard had no idea what hit him.

Sometimes she almost felt bad for them.

On her squad net, she watched the noose tighten around the compound. She could see it with her enhanced eye now, lit with infrared light: a collection of the squat, brutalist structures the Kyrans preferred. Its tighter-in perimeter defenses would no doubt be formidable. One or two members of her team could still slip through with ease. Probably eliminate Hakan and be gone before anyone else was the wiser.

But then there'd be little doubt who had done it: either the Compact, or the Ciphers. And even if the Kyrans blamed the enigmatic machines, that wouldn't achieve Mirra's broader purpose in being here.

Once the tightening noose of blue dots reached a predetermined, invisible radius around the compound, Mirra called a halt and sank to her knees. "Sigma Six, infil sitrep."

"Hostile sensor profiles stable," Tchaikovsky reported. *"Intrusion nil. Detection probability, 1.4%."*

That high? Mirra could almost hear Demetriou joke.

"Probes in on my mark," she said. "Three, two, one, mark."

With an unconscious command, she launched one of her recon drones toward the compound. The tiny, invisible sphere moved silently through the air. It converged on the target from above with the rest of the team's drones, close enough to peer through the Kyran disruption fields, but not so close that their low power mass-reduction fields would trip the enemy sensors. It would only be a matter of time before they located the primary target.

Mirra tapped a control on her rifle, then twitched out a series of commands. "All Sigma elements, switch weapons to profile K-1."

Silent confirmations came through. Reconfigured, their custom special forces–issue rifles would fire plasma bursts indistinguishable from Kyran weaponry by even the closest forensic examination. All they needed was a target.

Thirty seconds later, they still didn't have one. Mirra frowned. "Sigma team, any targets?"

Negative, came the replies. She opened a private channel to King.

"You seeing what I'm seeing?" her SLT asked.

"Nothing," she confirmed. According to their recon drones, the compound was empty.

"Perhaps they upgraded their signal disruptors?" King suggested.

"Where are the sons of bitches?" Yamada piped in over the team channel.

Mirra switched back to it. "All Sigma elements, hold. Sigma Six, full diagnostic on that enemy sensor net. Anything unusual?"

"Negative. Looks standard issue."

Mirra grimaced. "See if you can crack their intranet. *Carefully.* No trace."

"Roger that."

While the ECWO worked, Mirra turned slowly, scanning her surroundings. The omnipresent lowing of the native fauna seemed to have quietened. She couldn't be sure if that was an artifact of her own building stress, if her onboard AI was filtering out more of the sound to counteract that stress, or if it was occurring in reality. And if the latter, why?

Either way, she didn't like it. Any of this. But her drone feed still showed no enemy anywhere near her. Or near any of her team, for that matter.

Just like it showed no enemy in a compound that was supposed to be packed with them.

"Fuck it. Let's just call in a Starlance strike, slag the whole place."

"Stow it, Yamada."

"Sigma Six," Mirra said. "Intrusion report."

Tchaikovsky didn't respond.

"Sigma Six?" Mirra checked her squad HUD. Tchaikovsky's blue arrow was still there, but he was silent. Her stomach turned to stone. "Sigma Six, report in."

"Tchai, what the hell?" Demetriou added unhelpfully.

"Sigma Three," Mirra said, checking their dispositions. "Get eyes on Sigma Six."

"On it," Contreras confirmed. His arrow began moving toward Tchaikovsky's.

"Sigma Two, push your probe in closer. Right up to the line. Sigmas Four and Five, move to support positions—"

"Demi? What the hell, man, where are you?"

Demetriou's arrow, like Tchaikovsky's, was still on the net. But Yamada, who should have been able to see him, now apparently could not. Mirra spun around, aiming her weapon into the night. There was nothing. Her net still showed clear, no hostiles.

But a second team member dropping off comms couldn't be a glitch, or a coincidence.

"All Sigma elements," Mirra said, "abort. I say again, abort. Proceed to rendezvous Delta. Confirm."

Nothing. She checked her squad net. All her team's arrows were still there. But they were all now motionless.

"Sigma team, report in." Mirra's voice wavered slightly. Still nothing. "Boys! Sound off!"

Silence.

Her eye twitched. On instinct, she triggered her emergency comms override, cutting her armor, her implant, and her drones off from the mission network and putting them under her local control only.

In the same instant, four of her defense drones popped high up above the brush, raced off on four different vectors, and exploded.

Mirra didn't have time to clock whatever threats the drones might have intercepted. All she saw as their explosions lit up the night was the line of Kyran warriors creeping toward her through the underbrush, barely a hundred yards away. A split second later, her armor finally lit up the targets on her HUD.

The drones detonating bought her a moment. She dropped face-first onto the ground just as a storm of superheated plasma bolts seared through the air above her head. She didn't fire back yet; her visual camo might still be effective, and the blazing Kyran plasma bolts her rifle was configured to fire would light her up like a torch. She'd have to—

Roll onto her back to face the new threats her armor told her were coming up right behind her, danger close. An argotid was charging out of the brush, weapon in hand. It didn't seem to see her at first.

Then its terrible head turned straight toward her.

She brought her rifle up and fired a burst, vaporizing the warrior's chest, then twisted around and blasted another Kyran coming at her from her left. The argotid roared as it fell, its own weapon going off into the air.

That might have saved her life. The hail of Kyran plasma fire from the direction of the compound focused momentarily on their dying comrade, turning him to melted flesh before her eyes and lighting the brush around him on fire.

Mirra rose up to one knee, switched her rifle over to standard suppression mode, and swept the Kyran line with a torrent of superfluid projectiles. Two seconds of continuous fire put two hundred rounds downrange. The Kyran firing line buckled, just as another of her defensive drones dove into the center of it.

With the explosion, she got to her feet and ran.

"Sigma team!" she shouted over local EM transmission bands, in the clear. "This is Sigma Actual, report!"

She sprinted back toward her infil pod. Orange-lined enemy were converging on her from both sides. She shot the closest one on the run, two high-caliber rounds putting the warrior down before he could fire.

The one behind her was quicker, and sharper. A plasma bolt caught her in the shoulder. Her armor absorbed it, but she went down, rolling over to fire another suppression burst at the shooter. One of her two remaining drones zipped off and exploded in midair, intercepting some unseen threat. Once they were all gone, she'd be in trouble.

More trouble.

The last of her drones popped up, then back down. It spotted a knot of enemy clustered around her infil pod. She bared her teeth. She could shoot her way through them, but the bastards were all over the pod, from the looks of it. They'd have slagged it by the time she got there. She wasn't getting out that way. If she was right, *none* of them were.

"Sigma team," she said as she took off at a low run, changing her vector. "Anyone who can hear me, head to rendezvous Gamma. I say again, Gamma."

She prayed there was someone out there to hear.

Mirra kept her shooting to a bare minimum. Her active camo and her passive stealth systems seemed to be working. Keeping her alive. Which confirmed what she'd already suspected, why she'd used her emergency cutoff.

The Kyrans had been inside their command net. Tracking them, probably since they made planetfall, if not before. That shouldn't have been possible, but it was the only explanation.

Which led her to another, inescapable conclusion.

As she downed another warrior, she swore revenge, over and over, in the grind of her teeth and the churn of her feet in the alien earth. Not against the Kyrans, who couldn't possibly have done this alone, and who'd earned her enmity decades ago. Against whoever or whatever had served her team up to the vicious bastards. In that moment, she didn't even care why, or how. Whether they were human, alien, or machine. She'd see them dead.

But first, she had to find what was left of her team and get the hell off this rock.

The last of her drones sped off into the night and detonated, a secondary explosion telling its final tale. Mirra's world went darker. The long- and midrange tracks of Kyran enemies turned from clear points to fuzzy blips. Her armor sensors could only do so much.

And that wasn't the worst of it.

She didn't hear the missile that hit her. That was how the saying went, and in this case—as in all the others she'd experienced over the years—it was true. Oddly enough, she did see it. It was just a flash in the night sky. It might have been a star. Might even have been home, wherever that truly was for Sorăna Mirra.

Except that in the instant before it struck, it flashed in her HUD. A warning, but one there wasn't time to respond to. More of a taunt, then. A final insult.

Demetriou would have had a joke about that. Something like—

When the missile exploded, it took the world with it.

ONE

"From where I sit, Captain Hadrian, it appears the Compact has lost control."

Captain Ian Hadrian of the Interstellar Compact Navy leaned back as best he could while sitting on a cushion on an earthen floor. "You'll have to forgive me, Olan Sithelius. I thought we were sitting in the same place."

"At present we are." The diminutive, rodent-like byasian narrowed his beady, intelligent eyes and raised a nimble finger to the sky. "But when we are done, you will return to your ship. I daresay things must appear quite different from that lofty perch than they do to those who remain below."

Hadrian smiled. "Fair point."

"Below" was a semisubterranean meeting hall, lit only by sunlight streaming through windows in the domed roof. The earthen floors were complemented by a round wood table, cut and polished from the stump of some great tree-like flora native to the planet Byas. That was the room's only furniture—the cushion was a provision for Hadrian's delicate human physique. Sithelius was more comfortable on the earth itself, and the meeting's third participant, Jack, had no need of such comforts.

"From your vantage," Hadrian said, plucking a piece of ceremonial food from the central table, "what has the Compact lost control of?"

Sithelius spread his hands wide. "The continent. Perhaps the entire planet, though from *your* vantage, you would know that better than I."

Hadrian chewed the morsel, a leaf of an orange, lettuce-like vegetable the byasians cultivated. The taste was bitter, harsh, yet strangely compelling. At least it wasn't dangerous. The enzyme pills he'd taken before coming down to the meeting ensured he'd be able to digest it. Rather than contest Sithelius's point, Hadrian gestured for him to continue.

"We here in the ocean district," Sithelius said as if delivering a speech, "have always been loyal subjects of the Compact."

You're not subjects, Hadrian thought, but there was no point saying it. He'd tried correcting Sithelius a few times early in his posting here. After a year, he'd learned to save his breath.

"And we have never given you reason to doubt that loyalty. But the same cannot be said for our so-called neighbors in the mountain district." Sithelius made a derisive wave in the general direction of the offending province. "As you both well know, these miscreants, little better than barbarians, have no loyalty to anyone save the machines."

After he said the final word in his own tongue, Sithelius hissed, expelling spit through his front teeth, and then made a protective flicking gesture with his tail. Hadrian had gotten used to *that* too. More or less.

Jack interjected in a soothing, even-keeled voice. "It should be said, Olan, that not all citizens of the ocean district subscribe to the pro-Cipher ideology. Many of them are simply trying to live their lives, as your people are."

"Is that so?" Sithelius sniffed harshly. "It is said that, ignorant fools that they are, mountainers speak openly of their disloyalty in the streets. It is said that each night, mountainer children pray for the machines' return."

Hadrian smiled to hide a grimace at the second spit-flicking. "Surely what children pray for at night doesn't affect you?"

"It does," Sithelius said, "when daily their parents commit provocations and acts of violence against us, in the machines' name." Spit. Flick. "And against *you*, our protectors."

"And weekly," Hadrian added, "we identify and detain the people responsible for those attacks. Sometimes even kill them, when they leave us no choice. What more would you have us do?"

"Is that not obvious?"

Hadrian raised an eyebrow. "Would I have asked if it was?"

"Arrest them."

"Did I not just say—"

"Arrest *all* who speak such treason," Sithelius said, relishing the interruption. "Arrest all who compel their children to utter such odious prayers. It would have been simpler, of course, if the Compact had eliminated the mountainers when you first drove the machines from our world. As *our* packs counseled. But, in your infinite mercy, you permitted them to survive, and now we are left to search for more ... imperfect solutions to the machines' designs."

Some of the latest spits had made it onto Hadrian's deep blue uniform. He wiped the residue off discreetly. "I can't arrest people for talking."

"Talk leads to action," Sithelius countered. "*Violent* action."

"Not always," Jack added. "How are we to know the difference beforehand?"

Sithelius tented his fingers. "My point exactly."

"You're quite right, Sithelius. Talk can sometimes lead to violence." Hadrian pressed on before the olan could relish his conversational victory. "Which brings me back to the reason this meeting was *originally* called."

Sithelius narrowed his eyes again. "That protest was entirely within Protectorate regulations."

"It was, but—"

"And it was intended to express entirely legitimate grievances with the unequal way in which reconstruction aid has been distributed in this district."

Hadrian held up a hand. "We're not here to discuss—"

"My people cannot *possibly* be held responsible for the actions of a few soft-furred foreign agitators."

"So it is your contention that the byasians who attacked our security personnel and killed several bystanders at the protest were mountainers?" Jack said.

"Of course."

"You have proof of this?"

Sithelius opened his hands. "My proof is their actions."

"And if I told you," Hadrian said, "that we had proof they came from your district?"

Sithelius's eyes became suddenly and deeply cold. "Are you calling me a liar, Captain?"

Hadrian raised his hands. There was no more severe insult on this planet. Had he answered yes, Hadrian might well have been attacked by the little politician then and there.

"No. Of course not. I'm simply saying that from where *I* usually sit"—Hadrian pointed at the sky—"things look slightly different than they do down here."

Sithelius stared at him for a moment. Then his eyes warmed once again, and his nose twitched in a rueful smile. "*If* such proof existed, then I would be forced to conclude that some of our youths must have been co-opted, corrupted, by treacherous foreign influences."

"And if they had been," Hadrian said, "they would be unworthy of the protection of your packs."

"Naturally."

"As such, you would have no issues giving us their names, should such information fall into your possession."

"Gladly," Sithelius said. "Any oceaner who acts to bring about the return of the—"

"We can all agree on that," Hadrian said quickly, cutting off another spit-flick.

Sithelius tented his fingers again. "Of course, *were* such names to fall into my possession, and were I to turn them over, there should be no issue if I also turn over a list of provocations and incidents which we oceaners feel have been insufficiently investigated? So that they can be more thoroughly assessed."

Hadrian looked to Jack, who dipped his head in assent. "I don't see why not."

"And," Sithelius said with raised finger, "if they are to be more thoroughly investigated, it stands to reason that you would have no objection to issuing a public statement to that effect?"

Hadrian smiled. "Perhaps a *joint* statement? In which you condemn, in the strongest possible terms, the violence at yesterday's protest."

"Since I was planning such a statement regardless, I would be honored to share the mound with our noble protectors."

"Excellent," Jack said.

"And perhaps those protectors, being so well disposed to us, would care to add a statement pledging to reexamine the distribution of reconstruction funds?"

Hadrian leaned in and smiled thinly. "Let's not push it, Olan."

Sithelius twiddled his tiny fingers beneath his nose for a moment, then flicked his tail in the affirmative.

*

Sithelius and his advisors chittered as they moved into the byasian sunlight. Hadrian stretched his back and rolled his shoulders, glad to be out of the underground meeting hall's cramped quarters. "I gotta tell you, sometimes those little guys give me a headache."

"I don't know. I found it rather engaging."

Hadrian looked up at Jack. "You barely said anything!"

"I meant listening to the two of you argue."

Hadrian snorted. "I'd hardly call that an argument, by byasian standards. They should've given this post to a Free Worlder."

"Captain Tennant *was* a Free Worlder," Jack reminded Hadrian of his predecessor. "Her discussions with the olans were certainly more … thorough."

"Must've been hell on your joints."

"It wasn't pleasant."

Hadrian looked Jack up and down. "I still don't know how you fit into those halls."

The eight-foot-tall insectoid made a show of compressing himself and retracting the upper joints of his limbs into his thorax, then bouncing back to full size. "With practice."

Hadrian caught Sithelius's eye as he laughed. The byasian politician waved with his tail, then scurried off with his entourage while Hadrian was waving back.

"Hell of a way to start the day." Hadrian turned from the meeting hall. A beautiful flower lined path stretched away from the structure toward the landing pad where his shuttle was waiting. It *also* continued all the way around the low, wide hall. "Take the scenic route?"

"Gladly."

Hadrian motioned for their two guards to hang back a little. The marines in their twilight-blue digital-patterned battle armor complied without protest, keeping pace a dozen or so meters behind their charges. Hadrian suspected they'd be glad of the delay themselves. Byas had its issues, but parts of it were quite lovely.

Hadrian took in the impeccably manicured gardens lining the path. "Did you finish that book I recommended to you?"

"Indeed I did," Jack confirmed, nodding in an uncanny imitation of the human gesture. "It was quite fascinating."

"Glad you liked it. Herodotus can be a bit shaky on the facts, but he's a good read. And you gotta give him a break, he was Earth's first historian."

"Are the giant gold-mining ants one of his 'shaky' facts?"

"'Fraid so."

"That is disappointing. For a moment I thought I'd finally found some cosmic kindred, however ancient."

Hadrian chuckled. "Anything else stand out?"

"One thing in particular comes to mind now, given our business here. Forgive me for saying so, but ancient humans appear to have been an astonishingly fractious species."

"Hah! Yeah, we did tend to have our disagreements."

"It's not simply the conflicts." Jack slowed his pace a little as they began to round the meeting hall, and the path back to the shuttle came into view. "Herodotus's use of the term 'race' is shockingly liberal. I find it difficult to understand how a group of people—speaking a related language, with clear indications of shared cultural and genetic ancestry, living barely a few hundred kilometers apart—could be considered effectively a separate subspecies. And for those insignificant differences to lead so often to war ..."

Jack seemed genuinely upset by the prospect. Hadrian was touched. "There's this human psychological concept. The narcissism of minor difference, I think. Basically, the more similar we are to people, the easier it is to see our own flaws reflected in them. Sometimes the response is to attack."

"Not unlike the byasians." Jack glanced toward the distant mountains.

Hadrian's smile faded. "Yeah. Only we didn't have machine overlords tinkering with us for centuries. We came up with it all on our own."

"I wonder if the byasians would have developed along similar lines, absent the Ciphers' social engineering."

"I guess we'll never know."

They headed, somewhat reluctantly, down the path to the shuttle.

"Do you think Sithelius was telling the truth about the attackers at the protest?" Jack asked.

"About them being 'co-opted and corrupted' by machine-loving mountainers?" Hadrian shrugged. "It'd track. Then again, maybe these guys don't see the Ciphers as gods they want to bring back. Maybe they just don't like *us*."

"That, too, is difficult for me to understand. The ICRA is only here to help them build a stable and independent society, after so long under machine domination, after the devastation of the war. When that is done, we will leave. Why would anyone oppose that?"

"Some people just don't like foreigners telling them what they can or can't do. Even for benevolent reasons. Even temporarily."

"No virgonid would ever resist such an effort, especially not with violence."

"I guess you still don't know humans *or* byasians that well."

"I *know* the reasons. I just don't *understand*."

Hadrian smiled. "Maybe that's for the best. But if you *do* want to learn a bit more, and since you liked Herodotus so much, I've got another one for you. If you have time to read, that is."

"Always," Jack said with relish, clicking his mandibles together. "Is this text another history?"

"Another ancient Greek. *The Peloponnesian War*, by Thucydides. My favorite."

"You prefer this Thucydides to Herodotus?"

"Absolutely. I can't tell you how many times I've read it. A lot of people find him kinda dry. You'll love it."

Jack stopped and raised his manipulator appendages to his chest. "I am not dry!"

"No. But people *think* you are."

Jack thought for a moment. "Fair point."

Hadrian grinned.

"Then Thucydides will be my next study." Though Jack's voice was still as mellifluous and bright as ever, Hadrian detected a change in his gait, the way he carried his head.

"You all right, Jack?"

Jack looked up. The shuttle was just a few dozen meters away now. He stopped. "In fact, there was something I wished to speak with you about."

"I got a few more minutes. What's up?"

"It can wait. I would prefer to—"

Jack's head snapped to the side. Hadrian tried to follow his gaze, then a sudden movement from behind them drew his attention. He turned toward it.

"Down!" one of the marines yelled, his armor amplifying the command. The same instant, Jack threw himself over Hadrian. The virgonid's carapaced bulk forced Hadrian into the dirt of the path.

Then, the explosion.

Hadrian didn't see it. Nor did he really *hear* it. He felt it: a sledgehammer blow to his already crushed abdomen, a hard clap on his ears. Pure silence followed. Then a ringing faded in, louder and louder. Something was stinging his face; he opened his eyes, but all he could see was a great mass of greenish brown, and even that was swimming and cloudy.

Someone was shouting, though he couldn't make out the words. For a moment he forgot where he was.

What's on me, why can't I breathe, why can't I BREATHE?

He started to panic, struggling to get out from under the mass crushing his lungs. He pushed up against it while his legs scrabbled against the ground as best they could. The weight became lighter, and he got free. He took a deep and desperate breath, his lungs burning, his ribs aching.

"Sir!" The voice was muffled, but clearer now. "Are you all right? Captain?"

Hadrian tried to shake his head. It hurt too much, and he stopped. There was a great bulk beside him. He placed his hand against it for support. It twitched.

In a moment, all became clear.

"Jack!" Hadrian yelled. His own voice sounded foreign in his ears. He ran his shaking hands over the virgonid's carapace. It was twitching, but otherwise motionless. Bright, alien blood covered it. "Jack, come on!"

"Sir, stay down!" A hand pushed Hadrian down when he tried to rise to get a better look at Jack's head. "*Sparrow One*, emergency medical dust off on my pos! Repeat, EMD on me *now*!"

Hadrian felt something warm on the sides of his face. He ignored it. The ground rumbled again, like another bomb had gone off. He ignored that too. He struggled against the hand holding him down, tried to get a look at Jack's face. It was buried beneath his own legs. "Jack! Wake up, you son of a bitch!"

A blast of wind scoured them, whipped blood off Jack's back and into Hadrian's face. At this, he looked up, wanting to see the second explosion that would kill them. Instead, he saw the shuttle coming down hard in the thoroughfare, crushing floral arrangements, benches, and anything else in its way. The loading ramp was already down.

"Move!" The hand that had been holding him down now dragged him to his feet.

"No!" Hadrian shouted, clinging to Jack's exoskeleton. "No, you can't—"

"We'll get him, Captain, just get on the damn shuttle!"

The marine shoved him forward, kept him from stumbling as he rose, but wouldn't let him stop. Hadrian allowed himself to run toward the loading ramp, looking back at Jack's limp body on the walkway.

The second marine was scanning the horizon with his rifle up; a medic rushed past, two medi-drones following behind him. Belatedly, Hadrian realized the marines had their active camo engaged. Only a shimmering outline projected by his neural implant allowed him to see them. In the middle distance, Hadrian thought he saw byasians scurrying away in panic, but his vision was too blurred to be certain.

Once they were aboard, the marine guided him toward one of the crash seats and strapped him in like a child. Then he returned to the doorway, his weapon raised. Hadrian leaned out to watch. Part of him feared the marine had lied just to get him aboard the shuttle, and they intended to leave Jack behind. He wouldn't allow that to happen.

The medic bent down while the drones did a quick scan. Then he grabbed Jack's body beneath the joints of his legs and lifted. The medic's powered armor let him lift the weight easily, while the drones slipped underneath the virgonid's body and deployed a webbing, going solid and stabilizing the ungainly mass. The strange amalgam moved with unnatural ease up the shuttle's ramp, with the second marine backpedaling behind them. The ramp started to close before she was in the crew compartment.

"Go!" the first marine shouted, and the shuttle lurched off the ground. Its mass-reduction fields gave Hadrian a sick feeling in his stomach. He couldn't bear to look at Jack's mangled body any longer, with the medic and the drones probing his wounds.

He turned his head to look out the shuttle window instead. He saw the blast site; the whole pathway up ahead of them had been blown to pieces. The vegetation around it was on fire. A pillar of black smoke rose into the sky.

Then the shuttle tilted upward and raced toward orbit. In a moment they were over a nearby agricultural zone. The bright orange vegetation seemed to pulse and sway as fields of it blew past. Hadrian watched the roads, the homes, the thousands of byasians fall away into it, until the whole of the planet disappeared into the fire.

TWO

"Jesus, Ian," Lieutenant-Commander Arno Tsegaye said as Hadrian descended the ramp just behind Jack's stretcher. Hadrian hadn't noticed his XO on the landing deck until he'd spoken. "Are you all right?"

"It's not mine," Hadrian said of the blood on his face. He hurried to keep up with the stretcher as the marines hustled it toward the exit. The handful of deck hands on duty filed out of the way, along with their hovering support drones.

"Yes," Tsegaye said, keeping pace right alongside him. "It is."

Hadrian's hand went up to the side of his face and came away bloody. Some of it was virgonid orange. The rest was red. He clamped his hand over the wound, only then feeling the pain. "I'm headed to medbay already. What the hell is going on?"

"Make a hole!" the lead marine shouted as the crew hatch opened. The few crewmembers in the corridor beyond pressed themselves against the walls. The casualty party rushed past them, with the senior officers in tow.

"There've been no other attacks yet," Tsegaye said.

Hadrian winced at a stab of pain. "That's something. Did you pull the ship into higher orbit?"

"Yes, just after—"

"Damn it, Arno!" Hadrian waved angrily at Jack. "He's dying, can't you see that?"

"Standard procedure," Tsegaye said.

Hadrian was already regretting the outburst. "I know, I know."

They reached the medbay. Doctor Stanisław Park was standing just inside, craning his neck to get a look at his patients as they entered.

"Here," Park said, directing the medics to set Jack's stretcher on the right. "And here." He indicated a chair for Hadrian on the other side of the room. Hadrian stayed by Jack's side. The doctor ignored his disobedience. With his left hand, he tapped out a series of commands to his neural implant, while he passed his right hand slowly over Jack. He squinted at some unseen data the sensor suite embedded in his hand was relaying to his optical implants.

"Get her into emergency surgery." Two of Park's bipedal drone orderlies took control of the stretcher from the marines, guiding it toward the back of the pristine blue-white medbay. Hadrian tried to follow; Park placed a hand on his chest. "Sit down, Captain."

Hadrian pointed at Jack. "Doctor, you need to—"

"—perform a lifesaving surgery on the administrator, but not until she's been *prepped* for it." Park guided Hadrian toward the medical seat. "In the meantime, the wounded captain of this ship needs to sit down and submit to an examination, yes?"

Hadrian sighed and sank into the chair.

"ICRA and our marines are already investigating the blast site," Tsegaye said, a welcome distraction. "Bella's scanned all the data we have, and local security are canvasing for witnesses. So far, no suspects."

"No internal injuries," Park reported. "Minor lacerations and contusions, but nothing serious."

Hadrian gritted his teeth as Park lightly prodded his head wound. "Where'd the blast come from?"

"Flower bed, looks like. Along the side of the path."

Park's hand lingered over his head. "Severe concussion, burst eardrums."

Hadrian frowned. "I can hear all right."

"The ringing?" Park asked. Only then did Hadrian hear it, and notice how heavy his head felt. He closed his eyes, and the room spun behind their lids. "I'll give you a shot to help your neural implant treat the concussion, and one of my nurses will treat your superficial injuries. But I'll need to keep you under observation for an hour or two to ensure there are no complications."

Hadrian's eyes snapped painfully open. "Doc—"

Park's eyebrows arched.

"It's okay, Ian," Tsegaye said. "I've got it."

Reluctantly, Hadrian nodded. It hurt.

"Good." Park pressed a micro-injector to his neck. As it hissed, his discomfort only increased, at least in the short term. "I'm heading into surgery, Captain, don't worry. Just try to get some rest. Commander."

"Doc," Tsegaye said.

A nurse appeared beside Hadrian and started prepping one of his ears for regeneration. To his surprise, his head was already starting to clear. Marginally. With that clarity came a memory.

"Jack," he said. "He threw himself over me just before the bomb went off. Like he knew it was there."

Tsegaye nodded. "I saw the feed. Could he have heard something?"

"I don't know." Fresh pain with the regeneration. Hadrian resisted pulling his head away from it. "Jack picked up on it before the marines did. Somehow."

"That could be useful. I'll tell Lieutenant Farris."

"He saved my life." Hadrian glanced at the surgery. Park was stepping in, already wearing a surgical gown. Hadrian caught a glimpse of Jack's mangled body on the table. Then the door closed, and the windows went opaque.

"Thank him when he wakes up," Tsegaye said.

Hadrian took a steadying breath. "Who's got the conn?"

"Hassani."

"You'd better get back to it. Give her our side of the investigation."

"Yes, sir."

"Arno," Hadrian said as his XO was leaving the medbay. "Whoever did this, we *find* 'em."

"We will."

*

TWO HOURS LATER, Hadrian watched Jack through the window of the recovery pod. The virgonid had only been placed there a few minutes ago. He was unconscious. He looked dead.

Hadrian had seen a handful of unconscious people in his time. Most notable in his memory was a classmate that had passed out drunk at a particularly rowdy Naval academy party in his first year. Another was a classmate he himself had knocked out in a boxing match in third year.

He'd felt a curious mix of shame and pride, watching his Free Worlder opponent go down after Hadrian's uppercut landed. His features—pronounced cheekbones and orbital ridges, light gray skin, the product of the extensive cybernetic augmentation that many Free Worlder military personnel preferred—had made him appear almost alien. Somehow, he'd looked more human in an unconscious state, with his mouth hanging open, his amethyst-flecked eyes closed.

He had also looked alive. Hadrian had only seen one dead body up close, that of his grandfather at a funeral when he was young. The final rigidity had been unmistakable. The unconscious people he'd seen had clearly been distinct, removed from death.

With Jack, it was different. The bio readouts on the pod's display panel said he was alive, but that was the only indicator. Hadrian couldn't see him breathing, couldn't see any of the subtler signs of life he'd noticed in unconscious humans. It was a mark of how alien the virgonids were, despite how familiar they, and Jack in particular, felt. Humans and virgonids might have been allies for centuries, and co-citizens of the Interstellar Compact they had created for over a hundred years, but physiologically, at least, a vast gulf would always remain between them.

"Ah, Captain." Doctor Park sidled next to Hadrian, unnaturally chipper. "Feeling better, are we?"

"How is he?"

"Oh, perfectly stable." The doctor's sensor-laden hand appeared next to Hadrian's head. He instinctively jerked away from it. "Hold still, please. Yes, her injuries were quite severe, but fortunately you got her back here just in time. There might have been significant brain damage if you'd waited any longer."

Hadrian felt another pang of bitterness that Tsegaye had moved the ship into higher orbit, jeopardizing Jack's life. He knew it was wrong, that his XO had done the right thing, but he felt it nonetheless. "Why's he still unconscious?"

"Medically induced coma," Park said. Hadrian's head snapped toward him. "Captain, please—" Hadrian sighed and turned back to the window. "Thank you. It's just a precaution, to prevent further brain damage while repairs are underway. Shouldn't be necessary for more than, say, twelve hours."

"Good."

"Of course, it's not *all* good news. Given where the blast struck her, there was significant damage to the gestation sacks. Sadly, a significant number of her embryos were lost. However, given the unique nature of virgonid reproduction, she should still be perfectly capable of—"

"Wait." Hadrian shook his head. He pressed on before Park could insist he stay still. "Embryos? What the hell are you talking about?"

Park seemed confused. "Jack's transitioned. She's pregnant."

She.

Hadrian searched for the words to respond. He didn't know how to feel; he didn't know what to think. No words of consequence could be pulled from that roiling sea, so he simply said, "Oh."

"Yes, looks to be about halfway through the cycle, two weeks along. It's fortunate this didn't occur, say, a week from now. The sacks will be more fully erupted by then, and thus more vulnerable. Even as they are, it was a narrow margin to save the ones we did."

There was something I wished to speak with you about.

"As I'm sure you know, Captain, for standard ratio reproduction, a virgonid technically only needs one healthy embryo; however, the more she successfully brings near to term the greater probability one will survive."

That the embryo *will survive,* Hadrian thought bitterly.

"Excellent work, Doctor," he said, his voice moving to autopilot. "I'm sure h—she, will appreciate that when she wakes up."

"Doubtless," Park said with a smile in his voice. "You've recovered nicely as well, by the way. I assess that you're fit to return to duty. However, I suggest you avoid any strenuous physical activity for the rest of the day."

"I'll try to keep that in mind."

"Since you *have* recovered, you have several communication requests awaiting your—"

"Why didn't you tell me earlier?"

"Because you hadn't recovered yet."

Hadrian frowned. "From who?"

"You have pending communication requests from Admiral Singh and Olan Sithelius," the ship's artificial intelligence answered before Park got the chance. The doctor seemed miffed. Hadrian tried not to smile.

"Thanks, Bella," he said. "I'll respond in my stateroom."

"Of course, Captain."

"And thank you, Doctor," Hadrian said. "Let me know when she wakes up."

"Happy to, Captain—do remember to get some rest!"

Hadrian was already walking out.

THREE

Vice Admiral Rohan Singh's photorealistic hologram peered closely at Hadrian's face. "Good God, Ian. You look terrible."

"Nothing a stiff drink and a good nap won't cure." Hadrian was glad he'd changed his bloodstained uniform before taking the call, if *that* was still Singh's reaction. "Unfortunately, those'll have to wait."

"And the administrator, Jack? He's all right as well?"

"She will be," Hadrian corrected. "She's … pregnant, but Doctor Park was able to save most of her embryos."

"Small mercies." Singh sighed. "This is a major escalation. To target the military *and* civilian heads of the Protectorate administration …"

"We're not certain who the target was yet." Hadrian knew it was a weak caveat, if technically accurate.

"True, it may have been a missed attack against the local leadership. Either way, it's a bad sign. Byas has been the one relatively bright spot in this sector. If it starts to go the way of Ranak, we'll really be in the thick of it."

"How are things out there?" Hadrian asked.

Singh's expression told the story Hadrian didn't want to hear. "I won't lie to you, son, they're not good. Insurgent activity's on the rise in multiple districts. Some people are starting to talk openly, not just about the Ciphers returning, but supporting the insurgencies to make that happen. We're trying to isolate the cells without violating the articles, but it's a fine line to walk. If things keep going the way they are, we might have another Pyria on our hands here."

Hadrian's gaze dropped. He saw the fields of fire rushing beneath the shuttle in his mind's eye. Growing rapidly, smoke rising from them, then clearing, revealing—

"One's hard enough to deal with."

"Indeed," Singh said. "The situation there's growing worse as well. I'm told ICGS is considering increasing the fleet presence, as well as the advisory contingent on the ground."

Hadrian's eye twitched. "Have the Pyrians requested more assistance?"

"Only every day," Singh replied. "One day the Executor says he's behind it, if only parliament would stop dragging its feet, then the next he tells *parliament* we need to be cautious, lest we antagonize the Ciphers."

"The usual."

Singh nodded. "Which is why an escalation on Byas couldn't have come at a worse time."

"We're doing the best we can," Hadrian said. "We could use some reinforcements."

"Well, you'll be getting some. In a manner of speaking."

Hadrian's brow furrowed. "Sir?"

Singh looked to the side, sighed. "Technically I'm not authorized to tell you this, but ... under the circumstances. The minister of defense is planning a surprise visit to Byas, to kick off a tour of the Protectorate worlds. Which I'll be escorting him on. Show the flag."

"Waste of talent."

Singh scoffed. "In any case, he wants to start with Byas because it's *supposed* to be the Protectorate poster child. If the planet turns into a raging bonfire before he arrives, that'll hardly fit the image."

"Politics," Hadrian said with audible scorn.

"Politics," Singh agreed.

That didn't mean they wouldn't do their duty. Hadrian had served with the admiral for long enough to understand that as distasteful as it was, politics were how things got done outside of a CIC. "When's this 'surprise' visit happening?"

Singh's jaw clenched. "One week."

"Son of a bitch."

"Sorry I couldn't tell you sooner."

Hadrian nodded. "What do you need from us?"

"Find the cell that planted this bomb," Singh said. "Dismantle them if you can. If they're planning anything else, stop it. That's your top priority."

A nagging thought navigated its way to Hadrian's lips. "And if we find any evidence of direct Cipher involvement?"

"If they've covered their tracks as well on Byas as they have on Ranak and Pyria, then you won't." Singh's face became graver. "If they haven't ... We'll deal with that when the time comes."

"Yes, sir." Hadrian straightened. "You can count on us."

Singh smiled. "I know, son. Now get some rest. And report back to me as soon as you have anything."

The room felt empty once Singh's hologram disappeared. Hadrian appreciated him using the increased entanglement bandwidth for the personal touch, when an audio or text-only transmission would have satisfied protocol. His old CO always had a comforting presence.

Get some rest.

There was a fire behind his eyes when he closed them.

Not yet.

"Bella." Hadrian sank into the chair next to his carved faux-wood desk. "Put Olan Sithelius through if he's available, please."

"Visual, or audio only, sir?"

Hadrian wanted to answer "audio," but at this range the quantum entanglement communicator wouldn't be necessary. What would his excuse be? "Visual."

"Olan Sithelius coming through now, Captain."

"Thank you."

The byasian's hologram appeared in the center of Hadrian's stateroom, already pacing. Hadrian smiled.

"Ah. Captain." Sithelius looked him up and down, wrinkled his nose. "I see you've recovered. That's very gratifying. And the administrator?"

"Jack's going to make it," Hadrian said, avoiding the pronoun use that might have sparked a conversation he didn't want to have.

"Excellent. Give him my best." Sithelius's tail snapped back and forth. "Let's not waste time, Captain. I'm sure it's not necessary for me to assure you that no oceaner had anything to do with this heinous assault."

"Of course not." Hadrian couldn't rule that out yet, of course, but he was sure Sithelius hadn't been involved. As sure as he could be.

"And I *can* assure you that when we discover the perpetrators, justice will be swift and brutal. Even if the cowards have already fled back to the mountain district, we will not allow them to—"

"Hang on a second, Olan. We don't know where—they could have come from anywhere *else* on the planet. I appreciate any help your security personnel can provide, but if the attackers are located in another district—"

"As they will be—"

"—then *we* will handle it, along with that district's security forces."

Sithelius's eyes narrowed. "This was not just an attack against you, Captain. This was an attack against the very heart of the ocean district, against the heart of *my* pack."

"And I will of course fully acknowledge the important role your pack played in the apprehension of the attackers, when it occurs."

"Very well." Sithelius twiddled his fingers. "And we shall make every effort to discover their identities. In the meantime, I have already forwarded you the names of the miscreants who disrupted yesterday's peaceful protest, as we discussed. I trust there will be no need for increased security measures in my district? Other than those already enacted by my security forces, of course."

"The security of your district is still in your hands, Olan. The ICRA and my marines are simply investigating the blast site and—"

"Because as you know, Captain, local security forces cannot be relieved of their responsibilities except in case of the imposition of martial law, as specified under Section IIIa of the Articles of Protectorship."

"I *am* well aware of that, Olan." Hadrian rubbed his eyes. "I see no reason to impose martial law at this time."

"Ah!" Hadrian heard Sithelius's tail whip. "Then you admit there *may* come a time when—"

"Sithelius, *please*," Hadrian said, a little more brusquely than he'd intended. "Ordinarily I wouldn't mind fencing with you, but ... not now."

Sithelius considered this for a moment, ears twitching. "Of course, Captain. You have a great deal to attend to at the moment. As do I. I will contact you once our investigation has yielded results."

"Thank you, Olan. Good day."

This time, when the hologram disappeared, Hadrian was grateful for the silence. “Now, about that drink.”

“Would you like me to inform Commander Tsegaye that you will be extending your medical rest period?”

Hadrian laughed. “Thank you, Bella, but no. In fact, schedule a senior officers’ meeting for …” He glanced up and to the left; the current time appeared over his vision. “Sixteen hundred. Include Lieutenant Farris. We’ll go over whatever he’s found so far.”

“Yes, Captain.”

Wherever that takes us.

FOUR

"The bomb was powerful enough to vaporize most of its structure." Lieutenant Farris, commander of *Belisarius*'s special marine detachment, threw an overhead image of the blast site onto the holoprojector above the briefing room table. Hadrian winced at the sight. "However, my team's scans located molecular residue here, here, and here. Reconstruction identified the likely trigger mechanism."

The marine commander might have been pulled out of a recruitment ad. He seemed to always have a stern expression on his face, made even sterner by his harsh Free Worlder cyberaug features. His oil-black hair barely peeked out from under the marine officer's cap he always wore, and his light gray skin almost made him resemble a vampire from the stories Hadrian had enjoyed as a child.

A three-dimensional depiction of a lattice-like mechanism replaced the blast site. Hadrian frowned at its familiar pattern. "Is that a flower?"

"Yes, sir," Farris said. "We believe the bomb was buried; the trigger was likely disguised as one of the flowers in that particular bed. It would have been grown rather than mechanically constructed."

"How was it triggered?" Tsegaye asked.

"The reconstruction suggests the flower's petals were sensors keyed to detect specific DNA patterns. In this case, human." Farris turned his serious gaze on Hadrian. "Likely triggered by particles in your breath, sir."

It felt like a violation. Hadrian suppressed a shudder.

"My," Doctor Park said with evident admiration. "That's highly sophisticated."

Junior Lieutenant Nasreen Hassani, *Belisarius*'s Chief Tactical Operations Officer, shook her head. "There's no way the byasians came up with that themselves."

"No, ma'am," Farris confirmed. "The Ciphers used similar devices in leave-behind ops during the war."

"So this could be one of those?" Tsegaye asked.

"Possibly, but it's more sophisticated than anything in our records. If I was to hazard a guess, I would say it was a newer design."

"Machine bastards," Hassani muttered.

"Let's hold the epithets until the end," Hadrian said, though he felt the same surge of anger at the thought the Ciphers had supplied the weapon that nearly killed Jack. Anger, and fear at what it would mean if that were true. "We walked right past that same section on the way to the meeting, two hours earlier."

"Yes, sir. The bomb would have had to be remotely activated after you passed it, or possibly time activated. The likely object was to kill both you and the administrator. Other than planting the bomb in the meeting house itself, which would have been much more difficult, this would have been the best way to achieve that objective."

Anger overcame fear, at least for now. *They came after me. They came after Jack.* "How did Jack know it was there?"

"I'm not sure, sir." Farris looked slightly ashamed. "He seemed to detect the active trigger mechanism a moment before my marines' armor sensors did."

"Virgonids do have an array of natural senses quite unlike anything other known species possess," Park said. "One of these other senses must have somehow identified the bomb moments before it detonated. Possibly by smell, if it had some unique chemical composition. It's fortunate she did, Captain; the damage done to Jack would likely have been fatal to you at that range."

Farris's gaze dropped.

"How and when was it planted?" Hadrian asked.

"An analysis of my sensor data on the area produced the most likely incident," Bella interjected. She played an overhead recording of the pristine blast site, days earlier. "Landscaping work was in progress in this area for most of last week. The precise epicenter of the blast was replanted at 0941 three days ago."

A byasian in a standard work uniform approached the site in high speed. Then the playback slowed. Hadrian watched the worker dig up an apparently healthy patch of flowers and replant it. The new flowers looked perfectly normal. When Bella overlaid a grid of the blast radius, the epicenter matched the new planting exactly. "Did you ID him?"

"His worker's identification was forged. He returned to the capital area for landscaping work for the next three days, until the morning of the meeting. He remained within visual range of the blast site until the meeting was in progress, then abruptly departed."

"Remote activation," Hassani said. Farris nodded.

"Three days ago," Tsegaye said. He gave Hadrian a meaningful look. "The day before the attacks at the protest."

The rest didn't need to be said. It had all been planned. Whoever was behind this knew that an attack on the ICRA at a legitimate, scheduled protest would prompt a meeting between the local district leadership, Jack, and Hadrian. A well-placed bomb could then kill both of them, and potentially Sithelius as well.

Hadrian's hands clenched into fists. "Where's the bomber now?"

"I used biometric data to track him to a local transit hub, at which point he boarded a tram to the mountain district. Security footage then lost track of him. I am scanning local security footage and sensor data on the mountain district to locate him again."

"Request permission to apprehend the suspect once he's located," Farris offered.

"Granted," Hadrian said, "but I want you to include local forces on the op."

"No objections, sir."

"Thank you, Lieutenant." Hadrian took a deep breath, transitioning to the next phase of the meeting. "Now. Obviously this presents us with some new challenges. If Lieutenant Farris is correct, and this bomb was a newer Cipher design, then that means that somehow the machines are getting weapons—or at the very least, schematics and construction materials—onto Byas without our knowledge."

"Could they be coordinating these attacks as well?" Hassani asked, her youthful face hardened by anger.

"Unknown," Hadrian said. "But we can't discount the possibility. Bottom line is, we need to step it up; if these smugglers are out there, we've gotta catch them in the act. And before you ask, no, fleet command does not have any resources or reinforcements earmarked for the Byas system. Not exactly."

Hassani frowned. "Sir?"

Hadrian glanced at Tsegaye. He'd told his XO before the meeting. "What I'm about to tell you does not leave this room. In one week's time, a high-profile delegation will be arriving at Byas for a flag-waving operation. Executive cabinet level."

Chief Engineer Tsung Wei groaned.

"Admiral Singh's ordered us to resolve this situation, if at all possible, before that delegation arrives," Hadrian continued. "Can't have an IC chief minister getting blown up on our watch."

"God forbid," Tsung muttered.

Hadrian ignored the comment. "The admiral will be escorting that delegation. He's promised to bring some extra ships and personnel along, as well as a fresh complement of Sentinel microsats, that he will leave here so we can increase security measures. But until then, we're on our own."

"I've already got our Sentinel complement running double-duty," Tsung said without prompting. "My engineers are putting them back out as fast as they can maintain 'em."

"Then we'll just have to cast a wider net," Hadrian said. "There'll be more holes in it, but that's a price we'll have to pay until the next batch arrives."

"I recommend asking Group Captain Martin to step up combat patrols in the gaps," Tsegaye suggested.

Hassani frowned. "That'll be pretty obvious, won't it? Cipher smugglers would see those fighters ten million klicks away."

Tsegaye gave the junior lieutenant an expectant look. Hadrian watched the wordless exchange with a furtive smile.

"... And they'd try to avoid them," Hassani continued. "Which might make them blunder right into our Sentinels."

Tsegaye pointed at her. Hassani beamed like she'd won a prize, then put a professional damper on the grin just as quickly.

"Good thinking," Hadrian said. "Martin's fighter group is already stretched almost as thin as we are, but if I assure him it'll just be for a week, that should mollify him."

"Send a case of whiskey over to Byas Station," Tsung suggested. "That'll mollify him plenty."

"A *case*? If I had that to spare, I could probably swing us a whole fighter wing." Hassani was the only one to chuckle at that, though at least Farris cracked a smile. "Aside from that, we'll pull into a higher orbit, just outside safe distance for a microjump. That way if we *do* spot anyone who shouldn't be here, we can be on them before they know they've been spotted."

"What if—"

"If you're gonna be jumping my Stardrive within spitting distance of a gravity well," Tsung said, cutting off Hassani's budding question, "I'll want another backup emitter. Tech ops'll have to run an extra diagnostic on the computer system too. We end up a cloud of vapor, it won't be because of *my* engines."

The Chief Electromagnetic and Cyberwarfare Officer looked across the table. His large eyes returned Tsung's incipient glare without apparent emotion.

"The Stardrive computer systems are functioning adequately, sir," Senior Lieutenant Zevran said. "I have multiple diagnostics run on them daily to ensure there are no faults. In the Stardrive, or any *other* system."

"I don't want it functioning *adequately*, son, I want it functioning *exceptionally*." Tsung leaned over the table. "That way my ship, which contains your precious computers, doesn't splatter across the gravity well of that damned planet like a fuc—"

Hadrian raised his hand. "All right, gentlemen, that's enough. I think we can accept it on faith that we'd prefer *our* ship wasn't destroyed in a navigational accident. That said, Lieutenant Zevran, I'm sure your technicians wouldn't mind running an extra diagnostic on the Stardrive, given the commander's concerns?"

"I will find time in the schedule for a *third* daily diagnostic, yes, sir."

Tsung visibly suppressed an outburst. Hadrian nodded. "At least until we get that backup emitter in. Arno, if you could follow up on that requisition, maybe put a little muscle behind it?"

"Of course."

Hadrian gestured to Tsung. The engineer reluctantly nodded,

then sat back in his seat and crossed his arms. He glared across the table at Lieutenant Zevran, who stared right back at him.

"Great," Hadrian said. "Lieutenant Hassani, I believe you were about to raise a point?"

Hassani snapped her eyes away from the silent duel occurring next to her. "Uh, yes, sir, thank you. I was just going to say, if we're in a higher orbit, won't we be out of position to supply fire support to ground operations on Byas? In the event things turn ugly down there."

Hadrian nodded, but for a moment he didn't speak. He saw the field of fire flash in his mind's eye; the moment of silence stretched out, became awkward. Tsegaye's eyes on him prompted him to speak. "Good point, Lieutenant. However, I don't think we're quite there yet. In any case, we'll come in close enough to provide support whenever Lieutenant Farris gets a shot at these bombers."

"Speaking of the ground," Park said just before Hadrian could conclude the meeting. "I would like to take the opportunity of our surveillance period to run additional casualty clearing and evacuation drills. Readiness, as you know, Captain, saves lives."

This time, Tsung and Lieutenant Farris joined Hassani in her disappointment. Fortunately they were out of Park's eyeline—though surely, had he seen their reactions, he would have assumed they were unrelated to his suggestion.

"Quite right, Doctor," Hadrian said. "Thank you. Draw up a schedule and the XO will do what he can to work it in. If that's all … then you have your assignments. Dismissed."

The officers rose from their seats. The hologram above the long briefing room table, showing the projected positions of *Belisarius* and the system's minimal military assets around Byas, winked out. Tsung continued to glare at Zevran; it was hard to read the United Citizen's facial expressions and body language, but he seemed to have already forgotten about his conflict with the engineer. He was first to leave the briefing room.

"Lieutenant Farris," Hadrian called out. The marine stopped. Hadrian waited for the other officers to file out, and the door to close, before he walked over to him. Tsegaye remained seated at the table. "I just wanted to thank you for getting Jack and I back to the ship so quickly."

Farris's eye twitched. "Of course, sir."

"And what happened down there wasn't your fault."

"Yes it was, sir." Farris's expression didn't change.

Hadrian could see arguing the point would be useless. Instead he just nodded, gave a salute. Farris snapped to attention and saluted back much more smartly, then left. Hadrian sighed.

"He's a marine," Tsegaye offered. "Blaming himself when things go wrong is in his DNA."

"I'll take your word for it." Hadrian turned to face his friend, leaned back against the wall and rubbed his eyes.

"You okay, Ian?"

Hadrian nodded. "The treatment worked fine, I'm just tired. Keep thinking about the bomb and ..."

"That's understandable."

"Jack's pregnant," Hadrian blurted out.

Tsegaye seemed surprised. "Was Doctor Park able to save the embryos?"

"Enough of them, yeah."

"Thank God. Jack'll be relieved when she wakes up."

"Should be."

"You're still worried?"

Hadrian remembered where he was, what he was doing. He'd been slipping into an unhelpful reverie. "No, it's just that ... she didn't tell me. And when she noticed the bomb, she just threw herself on me, without thinking. Knowing that she was ... Knowing she might ..." He shook his head. "I don't know how to feel about that."

"Yeah, I can imagine," Tsegaye said. "Speaking of wrangling children …"

Hadrian smiled, grateful for the change of subject. "Tsung and Zevran?"

"I thought they'd have gotten used to each other by now."

It was a difficult nut to crack. Zevran was the next newest member of the crew, after Hassani. He'd come aboard less then a year ago, a few months after Hadrian himself. Conversely, Tsung had been here longer than anyone. The rumor among the crew was that he'd not been assigned, but discovered in the Engineering deck when the ship was commissioned twenty-six years ago, and had been here ever since.

On the surface, that should make things easy. Tsung had seniority and rank over Zevran. Yet he was clearly also the instigator of most of their conflicts. Zevran's attitude didn't help *defuse* those conflicts, but it was difficult to place blame on him for starting them. In as much as their odd verbal sparring skirted the line of discipline, it also hadn't affected their work. Yet.

"I hate to be the one to say it," Tsegaye continued, "but Zevran's not really fitting in."

Hadrian gave a lopsided smile. "Come on, Arno. You know you're the only one Tsung actually *likes*. He's not the easiest guy to get along with."

"Tsung isn't the only one Zevran doesn't get along with."

"Fair enough." Hadrian's smile faded. "Professional" seemed to be the kindest adjective anyone could use to describe Zevran, and then only on a good day. "Condescending," or some entirely less flattering terms, were much more common. "But this is his seventh posting in six years."

"Exactly. He's got issues being part of a crew."

Which was also borne out by the fact that after almost fourteen years in the Navy, he'd only risen to the rank of senior lieutenant.

In contrast, with only four additional years under his belt, Hadrian had command of a battlecruiser.

Maybe that's not a comparison you want to make. Hadrian kept talking to hide his internal discomfort. "He's one of the only United Citizens in the fleet. That can't be easy. What he had to give up just to be here ..."

"I'm not questioning his commitment. But that's not enough."

"He's also a wizard with ECW. All his techs and his former COs say so." *It's the only good thing they* do *say about him.*

"I'm not suggesting we relieve him," Tsegaye said. "I doubt we'd get a replacement even if we did, not promptly. I'm just pointing out that we may have to put him up for transfer when we get the chance."

Hadrian made a face. "I think he just needs a little while longer than most to settle in. I don't think he's gonna be anyone's best friend, but if we give him more of a chance than his last six commanders did, maybe he'll be a big enough asset to make up for it."

Tsegaye raised his hands. "You're the boss."

"Damn right." Hadrian clapped his hands to frighten off intruding thoughts. "All right. You see to the new drill schedules, I'll call up Group Captain Martin and beg for more patrols."

Tsegaye stood. "I can call him."

"Nah. I just got blown up. I'll get the sympathy factor."

"Yeah, speaking of which. Didn't the doctor and the admiral both *order* you to get some rest?"

Hadrian smiled tiredly.

FIVE

"Ian," Jack said, pulling herself up in the recovery bed as he entered. "I'm so glad you came."

Hadrian tried to hide the tinge of sadness that underlaid his relief. He hoped the human facial interpretation algorithms on Jack's implants weren't sophisticated enough to pick it up. Somehow he doubted it.

"Are you kidding?" He took Jack's proffered manipulator appendages in both hands and sat next to her bed. "I came as soon as I heard. Well, as soon as I finished breakfast. Plus I had some admin to do, you know."

Jack chittered. She looked strange in the recovery bed, though it had been reconfigured for her physiology. Hadrian had never seen a virgonid lying down before. They didn't seem like they should be able to bend that way. But then, he was always surprised by the virgonid ability to contort and compress their massive frames.

"How's the doc been treating you?" Hadrian asked.

Jack bobbed her head. "Very well. During my initial observation phase after I regained consciousness, we had a fascinating conversation about the differences between virgonid biology and that of analogous arthropods on Jayu."

Hadrian laughed. Jack tilted her head at him. "No, it's just … I guess I never considered how much Doctor Park would like talking to you. Or *at* you."

"I am grateful to have had the opportunity to be talked at." A silence fell between them. "I am sorry that I did not tell you—"

"Jack, you have nothing to apologize for." Hadrian smiled, though his brow knit. "I'm pretty sure you were about to tell me before you, you know, saved my life."

"Even so. I regret not telling you sooner. My intention was simply to avoid causing you undue distress during an already stressful time."

"I'm the one who should be apologizing, if anything."

"What for?"

"Because, you're carrying children and you almost lost them all, to say nothing of dying yourself, to save me."

"That was not your fault."

"No, but—"

Jack reached out for Hadrian. "I made the choice to shield you from the blast in an instant. I would make the same choice again, even knowing the result *would* be my death."

Hadrian stared at her for a while. "Why?"

"Because you are my friend."

Hadrian had to look away. It was a few seconds before he could speak without his voice cracking. "Then … I really do owe you an apology. Because I shouldn't be anything but happy for you."

"You are." Jack patted his hand. The chitinous digits were abrasive yet comforting. "I know that."

"I am. I'm just not … I've never had a virgonid friend before. I guess this is something I'll have to get used to."

Jack's mandibles clicked in a smile. "It is. My offspring will be eager to meet you."

"And I them. When are you due?"

"In about three weeks."

Hadrian blew out a breath. "And that doesn't … scare you?"

"No. I am excited."

Hadrian tried to share the feeling. "Who's the, uh, father?"

"The contributor-parent is an ICRA sub-administrator on my staff."

"And after you … hatch, he'll take care of the …"

"He and two other virgonids on my staff will form a nurturing pod for the week the hatchling will require to mature, yes."

Hadrian shook his head. "I bet human parents would kill for a week-long maturation period, if what Admiral Singh's told me is any indication."

"Even if that came with a three- to five-year lifespan?" Jack asked with the virgonid equivalent of a smirk.

And if the mother never lived to see her child. "Maybe not. Although I guess the genetic memory thing would take a bit of the sting out of it. Actually I've always wondered how exactly that works. You've been a contributor-parent before?"

"Some virgonids never perform that role, but I have. Two years ago."

"And none of your memories, none of *you*, made it into that kid?"

Jack made a flicking gesture with her hands that said *it depends*. "There is some genetic transfer, though less than there is in mammalian couplings. The contributor-parent's primary role is to catalyze the process; the vast majority of genetic material is provided by the bearer-parent. Still, even the minimal genetic material from the contributor carries *some* trace memory and personality within it."

"That's why your children aren't *exact* copies of you?"

"That, and the fact that their unique experiences will very rapidly make them distinct individuals."

"Right." Hadrian chuckled. "I got to tell you, that's still pretty hard to wrap my head around."

"It was difficult for us to understand your reproductive cycle at first. To simply die, imparting none of your memories to your offspring ... To us, *that* concept is terrifying."

"We're not too thrilled about it either. But I know what you mean." Hadrian thought for a moment. "You said it was difficult to understand at first. Now there's no problem?"

"Of course. Now we understand."

"You *all* understand," Hadrian said. Jack nodded. "I guess that's another difference between us. Each human has to figure everything out on our own all over again."

"Indeed. It's fortunate your long lifespans allow for that possibility."

Hadrian had known most of this already, academically. There was difference between understanding genetic memory transfer, how it enabled the extremely short-lived virgonids to have a complex technological civilization, and being personally confronted with the reality of it.

"Ian," Jack said. "If I may ask, what is your earliest memory?"

It came to Hadrian as if on a breeze. "I remember sitting on the grass, watching a bird fly in circles overhead. I have the vague sense I was waiting for my father to come home, and I think my mother was there. Not sure how old I was. I was too young to talk, I know that." A wave of peace washed over him with the memory; it crashed. "Mostly I remember the bird."

"I have several," Jack said. "The first I formed myself, shortly after I was born. I am watching one of my podmates carve a sculpture out of wax. I am four or five days old. I can't recall the sculpture. I also remember my own gestation and birth, from the perspective of my progenitor. I tend to count that as well, though others choose not to.

"I clearly remember my quingenitor beginning our training for the civil service when the ICRA was formed. I remember my septigenitor fighting in the war, though fortunately those memories are less detailed. Last is the memory I believe to be the oldest. Like yours, it is very imprecise, more of a sense of things.

"I know I am standing in water. There are others with me. There is a light above me, but whether it is the sun, I can't be sure. I'm not certain why any of us are there, but I know I feel content, and safe. We came there for a reason. We're on our home planet. I know it is a long time ago, if only because none of my progenitors has come from Virgon in over one hundred generations."

"Five hundred *years*?" Hadrian said.

Jack nodded. "In fact, based on context clues, I believe the memory is much older. It's not unheard of for my people to have memories stretching back thousands of years, though they are inevitably quite vague. Some claim to remember the unification of the Greater Hive ... though since that occurred more than two thousand generations ago, I find such claims highly dubious. Still, I suppose one never knows."

Hadrian was awestruck. Suddenly his sadness over the looming death of his friend felt unimaginably petty. No wonder Jack and other virgonids felt no fear as their deaths in childbirth approached. How could they, when they were each carrying thousands of years of living memory along with them?

"That reminds me," Hadrian said. "I have a present for you."

"Ian, that wasn't necessary."

"Jack, you're having a kid, *and* you saved my life." Hadrian handed his present to her. "The absolute least I can do is give you a book."

Jack gingerly accepted the bound rectangle of paper pages. She read off the front cover. "*History of The Peloponnesian War*, by Thucydides. We discussed this on Byas."

"I thought you could read it while you were recovering."

"Doctor Park is releasing me in less than two hours."

Hadrian smiled. "Well, then you can finish it in your free time. What little you get."

Jack turned the book over in her hands. "This is your personal ... unit?"

"Yeah. It's an antique, couple hundred years old. It was a gift from my dad when I went off to the academy."

"He is a history teacher, correct?"

"Professor, at the University of Eos."

Jack stared at the book. "Ian, I cannot accept this. It clearly has great personal value."

"Why do you think I'm giving it to you?" Hadrian pushed it back when Jack tried to return it. "I'm serious. You saved my life. I can't ever repay you for that. Especially now that I know you'd have been sacrificing hundreds of generations of history to save my sorry human ass. At least let me share this tiny fragment of mine with you."

Finally, Jack drew the book back in to herself. "When you put it that way, I accept. With gratitude. I will find the time to read it."

"I'm glad."

"And perhaps in the future, my offspring will be able to return it to you."

"No, no, that's *your* family heirloom now. They'll need something to remember me by."

"No. They won't."

Hadrian's smile did a poor job of hiding the tear forming in his eye. "Well. I look forward to talking to you, or them, about it. Once you finish it."

"As will we."

The silence between them now was more comforting than anxious. But while Hadrian did feel better, somehow there was still a pain he couldn't shake. Something even deeper that the impending death of his friend had touched upon.

Whatever it was, he wouldn't get the chance to ruminate on it now. "Captain Hadrian to the CIC. Captain Hadrian to the CIC."

Hadrian looked up. "On my way, Bella."

"We'll speak again soon," Jack said.

"Count on it."

Hadrian glanced back over his shoulder as he was leaving the medbay. Through the slightly frosted window of the recovery unit, he could see that Jack had already opened the book.

SIX

"Captain on deck," Tsegaye said as Hadrian entered the Command Information Center.

The three-tiered CIC was the nerve center of the ship. On the upper deck were the section chiefs' workstations: ECW, Tactical Operations, and Engineering, plus Helm and Navigation. As usual on first watch, Zevran occupied the ECW station, Hassani was at TacOps, and Ensign Keitel had the helm. Commander Tsung, though he could technically do most of his job from the CIC—and though regulations as written *required* him to, at least some of the time—was never there. A rotating cast of junior officers filled the post instead, an arrangement which had been in place when Hadrian took command, and which Tsung had wordlessly made clear would not be changed.

The smaller mid-deck just below the helm station contained only a few acceleration seats, which officers without specific stations, or guests and observers, could use when the ship went into high-g maneuvers.

Most of the action in the CIC took place on the lower deck, the "command pit." At the center was the Holographic Command

Interface, a large multifunction terminal used by the command officers to parse the vast and varied information collected by the ship's sensors and communications. Tsegaye, having the conn, stood next to the HCI looking at a detailed tactical projection floating above it. Ringing the three sides of the command pit facing away from the upper deck were a series of secondary crew stations, where the enlisted command personnel in ECW, TacOps, and Engineering worked. On the wall opposite the upper deck was a large hardscreen, which currently showed an overhead view of a byasian village.

Hadrian descended into the command pit. "What have we got?"

"We've tracked down the bombing suspect," Tsegaye said.

"Where?"

"Remote village in the mountain district." One of the dome-shaped houses on the hardscreen flashed red. "Bella used his ID to pick him out in her old sensor data and track him to this house."

"When'd he get there?"

"Yesterday. He hasn't emerged since."

Hadrian fixated on the glowing house. "Alone?"

"There's a low-level jamming field around the house," Lieutenant Hassani explained. "I can detect movement and heat signatures inside, but I can't determine how many individuals there are. Could be one, could be ten."

Shit. "Doesn't look that big."

Bella altered the tac projection above the HCI to show a wireframe of underground chambers spreading out from the small aboveground earthen dome. "Several of these chambers appear to have been excavated recently."

Hadrian sucked his teeth. "What kind of jamming?"

"Just enough to hide the details," Hassani said. "Nothing so powerful we'd detect it without looking straight at it."

"Sophisticated," Tsegaye said.

Cipher, Hadrian thought. "Can you get through it?"

"Negative," Hassani replied.

"I am attempting to compensate algorithmically," Lieutenant Zevran offered. "However, the diffusion pattern is shifting at random. I'll be able to manage some additional resolution with the motion sensors, but it will be imprecise."

Hadrian closed his eyes for a moment, shook his head fractionally to clear a memory the phrase had dredged up. "Bella ... Go back through all your sensor data on this area, see if you can track entrances and exits from that building."

"Yes, Captain."

"What's the situation on the ground?"

Tsegaye brought up some additional information on the tac projection. "Local auxiliaries are already moving in to establish a perimeter, ETA eighteen minutes. Lieutenant Farris's marines are also en route, ETA fourteen minutes."

"Okay." Hadrian took a quick, deep breath. "Bella, put me through to the marines."

"Farris."

"Lieutenant, this is Hadrian. What's your plan?"

There was a pause. *"Once we're on-site, we'll wait for locals to set up a perimeter. If we can get more resolution on the feed from* Belisarius, *that'll be ideal; if we can't, we'll send in some microdrones. Either way, once we've got a clearer picture, we'll go in and grab him."*

"Understood. Stand by." Hadrian turned to the upper deck. "Lieutenant Zevran, any progress?"

"Some. The diffusion patterns are much more advanced than I anticipated. This is likely the best I can do."

The tac projection zoomed in on the target house. Fuzzy yellow spheres appeared on the wireframe of the underground chambers, moving back and forth with little apparent pattern. "I estimate between three and six individuals inside."

"My analysis estimates between three and five," Bella added.

Hadrian nodded. "You get that, LT?"

"Got it, Belisarius, *thanks. I don't suppose you can figure out what weapons they have in there?"*

Hadrian glanced up at Hassani; she shook her head. "Sorry, no such luck."

"That's all right, Captain. We'll make do. I'll inform you once we're ready to go in. Farris out."

After that, it was a question of waiting. The local security forces moved with more efficiency than Hadrian was expecting. He hadn't directly observed an operation like this on Byas in months. Clearly as unrest had increased, the ICRA Security Force constables and their local counterparts had gained some valuable experience. In the more restive mountain district, at least.

Farris split his force into three teams. The first, a seventy-thirty mix of marines and local byasian and ICRA security, would approach the building's main entrance. The second team, composed entirely of marines and led by Farris himself, would approach a partially hidden utility entrance around the rear, heading directly into one of the new excavations. A third entirely byasian team would maintain a wide perimeter and watch for suspects trying to slip through the net via unseen escape routes.

"Sound off," Farris said, and began receiving check-ins from his element leaders. The tac projection switched to a four-picture split: one large image showing the overhead from *Belisarius*'s sensors, and one helmet-cam feed from each of the element leaders, including Farris.

The sensor picture clarified, somewhat. There was definitely one individual in the aboveground portion of the structure, with at least three in the underground chambers, and a potential fourth and fifth. Their exact positions beyond that were still difficult to determine. Marine microdrones had detected trace signatures of explosives but hadn't been able to get inside the structure to determine whether there were any present on-site, or if they had been moved.

All-in-all, not an ideal intel situation. But Farris seemed comfortable with the ambiguity. *"Okay. E-1, move in on my mark. E-2 will move at T+30 seconds. E-3, keep your noses to the ground."*

"Roger, Lieutenant," the byasian leader of Element Three confirmed, judging from his camera angle taking the order literally.

"E-1 ... mark."

One of the helmet cams rushed forward, then stopped to cover another part of the element as they bounded ahead. The target building still wasn't visible through the thick brush that characterized the foothills, except as a red outline on the marine's HUD.

At exactly T+30 seconds, Farris's helmet cam started forward too. His team had managed to get closer to their entrance without risking detection; if all went well, both assault elements should hit their entrances at the same moment. The marines' armor was on full stealth, and they should be completely invisible to any native observers. Unless, of course, those observers had Cipher sensor tech.

Hadrian watched the camera feeds intently. Restlessly. It was hard watching others go into danger when you yourself were safe thousands of miles above. Particularly when you were the one who'd ordered them into it.

That's not all it is.

Hadrian pushed the thought from his mind. Now wasn't the time. The target structure and its utility entrance finally came into view through the brush. Both elements came to a halt about a hundred meters from their breach points.

"Drones out," Farris ordered. A cloud of microdrones and stealthed autonomous combat units launched from each of the assault leaders and hovered forward at low power. In their wake, the assaulters crept closer to the structure. Hadrian watched the blips indicating the tiny recon bots as they closed in on the target.

The coordination was perfect. They reached the main and

utility entrances at the same time and wormed their way in through any cracks they could find. As they did, they crossed the invisible barrier of the jamming field. For a brief moment, more data flooded in, relayed by a string of drones through the jamming field and back to the marine operators.

Then there was a blue-white flash on the drones' sensor feeds, and they all went dead. Shorted out by a defensive energy surge.

"Breach, breach, breach!" Farris ordered. The marines were already on the run. He and the E-1 leader fired breaching charges from their rifles. The target doors vaporized, leaving clouds of smoke and wood particles behind.

E-1's combat drones went through first, followed by the team leader himself, crouching to get through the small door. *"ICRA-SF! On the ground, now!"*

There was one stunned byasian in the main aboveground area. It looked like a perfectly normal byasian living space, cozy, well kept. The door breach hadn't even disturbed the furniture, giving that part of the raid a surreal quality. The byasian moved slowly but didn't resist, going face down on the ground with his paws spread out. The E-1 leader directed one of his byasian personnel to secure the resident, and continued through the structure, weapon tracking.

Farris reached his door a second or so later. He leaped down through the portal after his own drones, landed in a crouch, and moved out of the way so the rest of his team could jump down, which they did in good order. Definitely not their first raid.

"ICN marines!" Farris shouted into the cluttered, dimly lit underground chambers. *"On the—"*

The flash and rattle of old-fashioned, chemical gunfire was unmistakable. Hadrian flinched at the sound. Farris grunted as bullets pinged off his armor. He swung his rifle toward the muzzle flashes and returned fire just as his armor's sensors resolved a clearer picture of the basement.

Three two-round bursts from his repeater blew the byasian shooter to bits. The chamber they were in was wide and low. Long tables ran through the center of it, piled with scraps of metal, wood, and plastics. Construction materials. Farris's armor didn't ID any of it as explosive.

"ICN marines!" Farris repeated, sounding angrier. His armor repeated the command in harsh-sounding byasian. *"Throw down your weapons and get on the fucking ground!"*

Above, E-1 searched for an entrance to the basement to back him up. Farris's team fanned out through the underground chambers in pairs, looking for the other suspects. Farris turned down a corridor; another muzzle flash greeted him. He staggered backward with bullet impacts. His teammate fired past his head. The superfluid rounds punched clean through the earthen wall the shooter was sheltering behind, killing him.

"Fuck!" Farris spat. Hadrian checked his vitals. He seemed uninjured. Combat drones sped through the corridors, looking for additional threats to engage. They found none in the chambers ahead.

"Lead!" an unseen marine said over team comms. *"I've got something over—"*

Hadrian jolted at the explosion. The feeds from Farris and the E-1 leader disappeared. The byasian perimeter commander's feed became pure chaos, then went dark. Bella enlarged the feed from her own sensors. Hadrian almost wished she hadn't.

"What in the name of ..." Tsegaye said.

The target structure, and the entire surrounding area, was gone. In its place was a geyser of earth and debris hundreds of meters high and growing. The crater the blast had created was just as wide. Seismic ripples tore through the nearby village. Half the security forces manning the perimeter were dead, the rest wounded or status unknown.

"My God," Hassani said, breaking the silence that had fallen over the CIC.

Hadrian couldn't tear his eyes from the devastation. "Bella. Get security and casualty response teams there, now."

"Yes, Captain."

The debris started to fall.

"What in the hell is going on?" Hadrian whispered.

SEVEN

Commander Sorăna Mirra crawled through the muck around the landing site, her belly pressed into the sucking earth. Her armor's adaptive camo was still active. But after three days alone on this hellhole planet, she'd learned not to rely on it.

It had saved her life; she had to give it that. The armor had kept her from being blown to pieces by the missile that landed near her that night, though she'd still been knocked unconscious. When she woke the following evening, she'd found herself buried in mud. That, and the adaptive camo, had kept the Kyrans from finding her. Bought her just enough time to slink away before the bastards came back to do a more thorough search of the area.

They hadn't stopped hunting her. But after a judicious detour, a couple of sentries killed with her blade, and a well-placed explosive on a timer, they were mostly hunting in the wrong place. Mirra had worked hard to give the impression that she was trying to circle back to one of her team's landing pods.

After the detour, she'd gone in the opposite direction.

That meant she hadn't been able to confirm most of her team's deaths, let alone recover their tags. She'd only seen one of them, from a distance. King, she thought, from where he'd been lying. Some of the others might still be alive, taken prisoner. She doubted it, but she'd likely never know. Nor would she really know, for sure, if that was her closest friend lying there, half-melted by Kyran plasma. That stoked the fire of her hatred all the more.

Revenge would have to come later, though. She didn't even have a rifle—wrecked in the explosion. Just her blade, her sidearm, and her armor. It'd be enough to get away, nothing more. And that only if her luck held.

Nor would she get her revenge against the trigger-pullers. Not all of them. There were far too many, for one. And she was never coming back to this godforsaken planet. Not if she could help it. In the depths of the cold night, she'd entertained fantasies of bringing an ICN squadron back here to turn the wretched ball to fused glass. Fantasy was all that was.

Besides, the Kyrans were tools. Brutal ones, but only tools. She'd had time to think, wallowing in the muck and hiding in the brush the last three days. The Kyrans hadn't organized the ambush against her team. They didn't have the capabilities to do what she'd witnessed that night. Only one of the Compact's adversaries did. The machines had made use of the brutish Kyrans to do their dirty work before, and that must be what had happened here.

Why, was the question. The Compact and the Ciphers weren't at war—not officially. The insurgencies the machines were clearly arming and instigating in the Protectorates notwithstanding. What reason could they have for arranging a highly sophisticated ambush of a spec-ops team all the way out here? Unless there was something on this planet they didn't want the Compact to find. Or unless Hakan, the target of this botched mission, was important to them somehow.

Mirra intended to find out. And when she did ... Well. Maybe sending a fleet back here to annihilate the place wasn't a total fantasy after all. Either way, she needed to get off this rock first. And she'd finally found her way to do that.

She'd been watching the landing site for most of the last day. The Kyrans were using all means at their disposal to search for her: teams combing the ground, aerial drones, and patrol craft. This site was host to one of the latter. It had taken off to make sweeps twice since she'd been here, coming back to land in the same spot each time. Sloppy. They clearly didn't think much of her.

They had just returned an hour earlier and seemed to have settled in. The craft was small, a two-seater with its own complement of recon drones. It was built in the typical Kyran style, all hard angles and blade-like edges, making it look more like a fighter than the glorified police cruiser it was. In addition to the two pilots, members of the argotid warrior species, there were two ischeronid worker ground crew, bulky and dull-eyed, with long, downcast snouts and broad head plates. They had mostly finished tending to the craft now; one was lounging at the side of the clearing, munching lazily on some of the thick brush, while the other was still tinkering with something on the ship through an opened panel.

One of the argotids was aboard the ship, the other on guard, patrolling the perimeter. And not particularly diligently. Still, Mirra needed to be careful. She was outnumbered, and while the ischeronids were engineered to avoid violence, they could be dangerous when cornered.

She needed to take out the patrolling warrior first. She crawled forward at a glacial pace, letting the argotid make several circuits of the landing site while she watched. There was a pattern to his movements, but he stopped at seemingly random intervals to sniff the air, literally and with the suite of sensors embedded in his head. Mirra's armor was on full passive stealth, with all its communications and active reconnaissance systems shut down and heat being internally recycled, so she should be functionally invisible. But moving too quickly through the mud or the brush would reveal the presence of *something*, if his motion detectors were well attuned.

Her heat had been recycling for a while, now. Sweat was starting to build up on her brow. She picked a spot near the edge of the site and waited for the warrior to make another pass. Once he had moved around the other side of the craft, Mirra shimmied quickly forward to get into position just at the edge of the clearing. Both the ischeronids were visible from this spot. Now it was just a question of waiting a little longer.

She had her sidearm unholstered and her blade extended when the patrolling warrior came back around. The tensest moment came as he walked the perimeter toward her, vicious-looking head darting back and forth, plasma rifle held at a low ready. He was still a few meters away. If he spotted her now, that would likely be that. She'd die right here without ever finding out why.

He didn't spot her. The argotid walked right up to her, paused briefly a meter or so away, then continued past like there was nothing at his feet.

The moment he'd passed to her left, she struck. She slashed at the back of his left knee with her blade, severing the tendons even as she rose into a crouch. The warrior roared in alarm and tried to turn toward the attack as his leg buckled. Mirra punched the blade into his side, piercing armor and ribs and turning the roar to a bloody wheeze when it withdrew.

The two workers turned toward the sound. They would have seen the warrior struggling and spurting blood, assaulted by an invisible assassin. The only indication she was there the warrior's blood sloughing off the hydrophobic skin of her armor. It must have been terrifying for the docile workers to look upon.

Good.

As she plunged the blade at last into the warrior's brain, she activated her armor's short-range signal jammers. None of the Kyrans would be calling for help. Then she aimed her pistol over the back of the dying warrior and fired. A beam of searing, blue-red light leaped from the weapon, burning into the chest of the worker lounging by the brush. She swept the maser beam up through its neck and skull, and the creature fell twitching into the mud.

The other worker let out a pathetic, warbling cry, dropped its tools, and fled for the illusive safety of the brush. Mirra fired. The maser beam struck the ischeronid in the haunch, but it kept running, fueled by fear. She kept the trigger depressed, swept the beam up—

"What is this?"

Her armor translated the snarling Kyran dialect, preserving the harsh alien intonation. She spun toward the craft's boarding ramp. The other warrior was descending rapidly.

"I told you to keep your rotten mouths shu—"

The pilot had only a moment to see his death. But he did. Mirra saw it in his eyes, just before her maser beam burned them out.

While the pilot's body was tumbling down the ramp, Mirra finally let the other warrior's corpse go. She stepped over it and followed the fleeing worker. A gesture-command reactivated her active recon systems. They found no other threats. It would be some time before the other Kyrans realized anything was amiss here. Hopefully enough.

The ischeronid had kept running after being shot, but hadn't made it far before collapsing. The hulking beast was still trying to crawl away to safety when she caught up to it. It must have heard her approaching, as it rolled over onto its back to face the threat. Its tail twitched weakly, all it could do after being shot rather than whipping back and forth in a vain effort at defense. Its large, watery eyes darted, searching for its attacker. But Mirra was invisible again, the blood and mud having all slid from her. And the worker had no suite of sensors that could pick up the heat she was gratefully allowing to vent from her armor.

She watched it like that for a moment, safe and unseen. The terror in the beast's eyes was not so alien. It was no threat to her. Not physically. But the moment her jamming was out of range, it would be able to call for help. The few extra minutes' warning that call would give the Kyrans might make the difference between her stolen ship escaping or being shot from the sky.

The pity the helpless creature's eyes elicited pricked at her, but only for a moment. Grim necessity would not be pierced by it. She raised her weapon and fired, a single shot burning out the ischeronid's brain. It never knew what killed it.

All the mercy it deserved.

She jogged up the patrol craft's ramp. The controls were all labeled in Kyran script, but her implants translated it before her eyes. She'd trained to fly similar enemy craft in situations just such as this. Had even had to do it a few times, during the war. It all came back to her quick and easy.

If not comfortably. The interior of the craft was designed for an entirely different physiology. All she could do was perch on the edge of the pilot's seat and do her best to wrangle the large, ungainly flight controls. Her armor would compensate for some g-forces, but without the proper seating for a human body, she still wouldn't be able to push the craft to its maximum acceleration until she reached a safe distance to activate its FTL systems. That was likely for the best, however. A patrol ship shooting off at maximum speed would set off alarm bells she didn't want ringing until it was too late.

The ship lurched and rattled when its primitive mass-reduction fields activated and she eased it off the ground—a product of its shoddy tolerances, her rusty flying skills, or both. Mirra got it straightened out easily enough. She pushed the throttle forward and the controls up without looking back. She'd left nothing alive behind her.

She made sure to activate the craft's IFF system. That would probably buy her another minute, maybe one or two failures to respond to the queries that were about to start coming in, asking why the ship was lifting off ahead of its assigned schedule and without orders. A minute or two was all she needed, unless the planet's orbit had filled up with Kyran warships during her extended stay. If it had, she was already dead.

The first query call came in a little later than she was expecting, and by then she knew she'd make it. The sky was already turning twilight-colored, the stars visible above the day. The craft shuddered every now and then, definitely a result of shoddy engineering. She corrected her earlier assessment. She'd make it, *if* the damned thing didn't fly apart when she activated the FTL. Its range would be short, its FTL more of an escape system than a means of long-range interstellar travel. It should still be enough to get her where she needed to go.

A minute after she failed to answer the second query call, the Kyrans tried to remotely deactivate the craft. She'd plugged her armor's ECW systems into it, which would keep them out for maybe another two minutes. If Tchaikovsky were here, the margin would have been a lot bigger. Her lips curled at the pain, at the knowledge she was leaving all his killers alive on this hellhole.

*Not all of them. Someone'll pay for it. Some*thing.

A minute later, the craft's attack alarms started buzzing. Its brothers and sisters were launching from the surface to intercept it, or else vectoring in from their patrol routes. They'd shoot it down without a second thought.

But only if they reached it. Seconds later, the light on the FTL panel started blinking. They'd cleared safe distance.

Without hesitation, Mirra pushed forward the levers. The mass neutralization component of the drive whirred to life, and she lifted marginally off the uncomfortable pilot's seat, gravity's embrace withdrawn. She'd already laid in the coordinates for the rendezvous site. Once she was certain the field wasn't about to sputter out of existence, she pushed forward the stick and the craft went superluminal, leaving behind the nasty little world where her boys had died.

Mirra let out a long breath and retracted the faceplate on her armor for the first time in three days. The stale, alien air inside the Kyran shuttle wasn't the first free breath she'd have liked to take, but it was better than not taking one at all. She gave herself a few minutes to float in silence before the controls while the craft made microjump after microjump, inching further and further into the black between stars. The hum of its engines was guttural and uneven. Something in the hull rattled periodically. It matched the harsh, black metal aesthetic of the interior.

There was nothing comforting about her escape vehicle. There was little enough comforting about having escaped, having survived, when her boys hadn't. When she hadn't even been able to retrieve their bodies to send home to their families. Nadia and Anatoly, Alistair King's wife and son, would never get the chance to say a proper goodbye to him. Nor would they have recognized his body if they had.

Their faces flashed before her eyes, over and over. Alive, as she'd known them. Dead, as she imagined them. The only friends, the only family she'd known for years. Gone, in an instant.

The moments she took were not for silent relief but silent promises.

I swear to you all. I won't let them get away with this. Whoever or whatever they are, and whatever they want. I'll ruin them all.

EIGHT

Hadrian swirled the bourbon in his glass for the nth time without taking a drink. He swiped at the image floating before his eyes. The explosion at the compound replayed, then froze, overlaid with data points indicating the power of the blast and the estimated epicenter. He studied them, as if they would tell him anything new. Then he switched back to the feed from Lieutenant Farris's armor cams, just before the explosion.

"Lead! I've got something over—"

The moment of annihilation played in slow motion. It couldn't tell Hadrian anything he didn't already know. He sighed, swirled his bourbon one last time, then set it on his side table and slumped in his chair.

These were the first people he'd ever lost under his command. To enemy action, at least. There was one rating, Andrejsson, who'd been killed in an accident on Hadrian's first independent command, the old corvette CF-1578B. Nicknamed "Mighty Maude" by generations of her crew for some long-forgotten reason. That death had hit hard, given it was one out of a crew of only fourteen. Even so, his fellow officers with war service under their belts had told him that the first losses to an enemy would hit harder still.

Hadrian knew now they'd been right. It was hard to accept that someone had deliberately killed his men and women, and that the perpetrators of that act were already dead, some by their own hands. The people who'd ordered the bombing might well be forever beyond the reach of justice, if that was even what killing them would be.

It had been hard to announce the deaths to the crew. Hadrian was dreading the memorial service he'd scheduled for tomorrow evening, a fact for which he was quietly ashamed. Speaking for the dead marines was the least he could do, in addition to it being his official responsibility as their surviving commanding officer. Just as Jack was slated to speak for the dead ICRA personnel, when she returned to the surface.

Hadrian felt guilty about that too. The ICRA security had gone there under *his* orders, not hers. He almost wished he'd simply ordered an orbital strike against the compound once it was identified. At the time, a raid had seemed the best option; it had given them a chance of taking some of the perpetrators alive, collecting valuable evidence even if they couldn't. In retrospect, blowing the compound to bits from orbit would have left them as they were now, except that nineteen men and women under his direct or temporary command would still be alive.

His officers and the ICRA-SF were combing through what little data they had, looking for any kind of evidence that might have survived the massive explosion, which might in turn point to connected insurgent cells. So far there was nothing, which meant there likely would *be* nothing. The bomb had wiped the bastards' tracks.

Hadrian resigned himself to working on his remarks for the service tomorrow. That finally prompted him to take a drink. The rich, smoky liquid provided only a momentary respite; Bella provided a better one.

"Captain, Ensign Coleridge wishes to speak with you."

Hadrian opened his mouth, then frowned. "Ensign …"

"Samuel Coleridge, sir. The astrophysics advisory officer."

Hadrian was already nodding as she said the name, and silently chiding himself for his forgetfulness. *Crew of a hundred and twenty, and you can't remember every officer's name?* "Of course. Put him—actually, strike that. Why don't you send him over here?"

"Of course, Captain. Summons issued."

Hadrian was standing by his desk a few minutes later when the door alert for his stateroom chimed. "Come in."

The hatch opened. Ensign Coleridge poked his head through. "Captain, sir?"

"Yeah." Hadrian waved him forward. "Come on in."

Coleridge looked back into the hall, then gingerly stepped over the threshold. He was a young man, probably in his early twenties, with dark skin, a short mop of curly hair, and intelligent, nervous blue eyes. His uniform jacket looked ill-fitting, like it had been hastily pulled on in addition to being a half size off. Hadrian did now remember the young officer, realizing with some embarrassment that they'd only met once before, when Coleridge had been assigned to *Belisarius*.

"Sorry to intrude, Captain," Coleridge said. He spoke with a pronounced accent which Hadrian couldn't quite place.

"It's usually not an intrusion when you're responding to an invitation."

Coleridge squinted. "Yes. Of course. My apologies, sir. And thank you. For the invitation. It's, um … a very nice room. Very traditional."

"Thank you." Hadrian glanced around his stateroom. "I've always liked the wood aesthetic. And it's me who should be apologizing. I try to have all the officers here every once in a while, but you seem to have slipped through the cracks."

Coleridge shook his head with exaggeration. "Oh, no, sir. That's quite all right. Toiling in obscurity rather suits me."

"Fair enough." Hadrian pointed at his bar cabinet. "Can I get you a drink?"

"Ah, sadly liquor does *not* suit me. Sir."

"Probably for the best. If you don't mind my asking, your accent—is it ... English?"

Coleridge smiled. "Yes, sir. I'm from Luna, actually, but my family is ... also very traditional."

"Right. Please, have a seat."

Coleridge took one of the armchairs across from Hadrian's, gingerly. He sat in it for a long moment before embarrassment flashed once again across his face. "I did ask to speak with you for a reason, of course, not simply an unwelcome social call."

"Not unwelcome, but go ahead."

Coleridge pointed at his eyes, then Hadrian's. "May I?"

"Please."

"Bella, could you—" The images that were in Coleridge's mind became a shared holoprojection, floating between the two men. "Thank you, darling."

Hadrian's and Coleridge's eyes went wide at the same moment, though not in the same way. The color drained from the ensign's face. He cleared his throat, and tried to meet Hadrian's gaze, with some difficulty. "Um. Toiling in obscurity as I do, I often have no one to speak to on a regular basis. Except the ship. Some degree of familiarity is to be expected."

"Of course." Hadrian hid his smile, with some difficulty.

Coleridge took a deep breath and indicated the images Bella had conjured for him. "I've been studying yesterday's bombing, and the one from a few days before. I know I wasn't specifically instructed to, but as an astrophysics officer stationed around the same rather ordinary star for the last eight months, I've had little else to do. I hope that wasn't presumptuous."

"Bella wouldn't have shown you anything you weren't authorized to see."

"Indeed not," Coleridge said with an almost loving smile. "I'm not an expert on explosives, or counterinsurgency operations, by any means. That said, I have noticed something quite strange about these explosions."

Replays and data from the bombing at the meeting hall rose to the fore of Hadrian's perception. He saw himself and Jack caught in the blast in one of the images. He winced.

"I noticed it first in the data from the bombing that targeted you, sir. But I wrote it off, for reasons I'll explain in a moment. It wasn't until I studied yesterday's explosion, and saw it again, that it became significant."

Data from the blast that killed the marines came to the fore now; then both were overlaid with a diagram of an unfamiliar compound.

"What am I looking at?" Hadrian asked.

"Ignicite, sir. It's an incredibly volatile element."

"I've never heard of it."

"It's also incredibly rare. It was only discovered seven years ago, and it's still poorly understood. Hence why even Bella didn't understand its significance."

Hadrian frowned. "Not to question your findings, Ensign, but the blast yesterday was caused by an antimatter bomb, not a chemical explosive."

"Yes, sir. It most certainly was." Coleridge switched back to the meeting hall bombing. "But the blast which targeted you *was* caused by a chemical explosive. An antimatter device of the same mass would have destroyed the entire pathway and likely the landing craft as well."

Hadrian's eyes tensed. "It also would have set off every bomb detector in the capital district before it was planted."

"*Yes,* sir." Coleridge pointed at him. "Precisely. *That's* why the ignicite is significant. It was discovered so recently, and until now had never been used to produce explosives, that explosives detection software is not programmed to search for it. Most bomb detection *hardware* can't even pick it up."

"Then why didn't they use more of it?"

"A theory? They thought the bomb they used would be enough to eliminate the target, and they didn't want to give away their trick too early. Moreover, it almost worked. The traces of ignicite I found in the data on that bombing were so minuscule, Bella and I wrote them off as a sensor error."

Hadrian swiped back to the newer images. "So the ignicite you found in yesterday's explosion was picked up before the blast?"

"Right again, sir. I found it in the data Lieutenant Farris's marines collected while they were clearing the compound. In *significantly* larger quantities. I suspect the insurgents were building a number of ignicite bombs in that compound. Probably much more powerful ones."

So the marines' deaths probably saved a lot of lives. Hadrian's gaze fell. *Hope that can bring some kind of comfort to their families.* "You said this was a rare compound. How rare?"

"Well, ignicite is only created by a unique natural process." Coleridge brought up another series of images, scientific diagrams Hadrian could barely decipher. "It requires a particular combination of other chemical compounds in sufficient quantities, subjected to extraordinary pressure, and exposed to a constant bath of intense neutron radiation. That's actually why I knew about ignicite—astrophysics is my vocation, at least in the Navy, but particle physics has always been my first love, so to speak. Actually, after my service, I hope to—"

Hadrian held up a hand. "Apologies, Ensign, I'd gladly discuss that with you another time." He pointed at the data. "Can ignicite be produced artificially?"

Coleridge blanched again. "Sorry, sir. In theory, it could be. However, the processes for synthesizing it, let alone the equipment necessary to effect that synthesis, do not yet exist."

In the Compact. "Could the Ciphers have the ability to do it?"

"It's possible." Coleridge's eyes widened fractionally, then calmed. "However, it would likely be much more efficient to simply harvest the ignicite from one of its few natural sources and smuggle it to Byas."

"Where are these sources?"

Coleridge opened his mouth.

Hadrian held up a hand. "Actually, hang on. How do you feel about public speaking?"

Coleridge's eyes widened anew.

NINE

"There are three locations in the galaxy where ignicite is known to occur naturally," Coleridge said. Images of the star systems in question floated above the briefing room table. "Or, rather, two known locations, and one suspected."

The young astrophysics officer had done fairly well so far, Hadrian thought. He'd gotten off to a shaky start, much as he had in Hadrian's stateroom earlier, exacerbated by the larger audience. But as before, once he got into his element, things moved along smoothly. The senior officers were paying close attention now. Hadrian was, too, though this was his second time hearing it.

Coleridge indicated each of the systems in turn. "The first location, where ignicite was initially discovered, is in the Association of Non-aligned Systems. The second is in the Compact; and the third, suspected location, is in Cipher-controlled space."

"So you think that's where the bombs came from?" Hassani asked.

Coleridge made a noncommittal face. "Possibly. The location is only *suspected* to have naturally occurring ignicite because from a distance it appears to have the appropriate conditions—tectonic activity, atmospheric composition, neutron star. But we don't know for certain that the necessary chemical elements are all present on or below the surface of the planet in question, due to a lack of close observation. For, um, obvious reasons."

"Still." Hassani leaned over the table. "If the machines wanted to smuggle untraceable explosives into the Protectorates, wouldn't it make sense to do it from a source they control?"

"In one sense, yes, but in another ... As I mentioned, ignicite is *highly* volatile. Particularly when being transported in large quantities, even in ideal ultrahigh-pressure conditions. At any given moment, the possibility of a containment failure and explosion would be small. But the potential Cipher-controlled source is over fourteen hundred light-years from Byas."

"Lot of chances for something to go wrong," Hadrian said. "Hence why we think a closer source makes the most sense."

"The Association world?" Tsegaye asked.

"Closer still." Hadrian brought one of the systems to the fore of the projection.

Hassani frowned. *"Ours?"*

"CAS 47988c-VI." One of the moons of the third planet in the system expanded to the center of the projection. It looked a thoroughly inhospitable place, cloaked in a noxious atmosphere, with the occasional burst of magma from an active volcano punctuating the gloom. Coleridge pointed at the moon. "This little character has ideal conditions for the occurrence of ignicite."

The projection made the atmosphere more transparent, highlighted veins of the substance in orange spiderwebbing beneath one hemisphere. "In addition to the perfect surface and subsurface conditions, the particulars of the moon's orbit, and that of its host planet, means that one hemisphere is almost always facing the star, giving it a near-constant bath of neutrons without a gas giant in the way to slow any of the little fellows down. Consequently, there are massive quantities of ignicite below the surface. In fact, many of those explosions you're seeing are not volcanic eruptions, but ignicite deposits detonating."

"But how are the Ciphers able to steal that much of it from Compact space?" Hassani asked. "Right under our noses?"

"Well, until ignicite was discovered," Coleridge said, "there was no Compact presence in CAS 47988. Though it was technically within our claimed space. Only after the discovery did we set up a research outpost orbiting the moon, about five years ago. That's still all we have there. It's virtually defenseless. Surprisingly, military intelligence didn't anticipate the strategic significance of a large source of untraceable explosives."

Tsung laughed out loud. Most of the other officers, even Doctor Park, smiled wryly. Coleridge looked confused.

"It's not surprising at all, Ensign," Tsegaye explained.

"Oh." Tsung theatrically wiped away a tear. "Kids."

"In any case," Hadrian said. "47988's only thirteen light-years away."

Tsegaye pointed at the tiny research station orbiting the moon. "If that's all we've got in-system, the Ciphers could have a whole extraction operation running under full stealth and we'd never know it."

"A permanent outpost is improbable," Zevran said, the first words he'd uttered in the meeting. "Too great a chance of incidental discovery. More likely, they'd send temporary missions in whenever they need a new batch of material. Likely the same platforms that extract the material also smuggle it into Byas, and potentially other systems."

"Talk about under our noses," Tsung muttered.

"Exactly why we need to investigate, ASAP," Hadrian said.

Tsegaye frowned. "Ourselves?"

"We're the closest capital ship to that system," Hadrian said.

"And Admiral Singh did order us to track down the smugglers," Hassani added.

Tsegaye nodded, though Hadrian could see he had more to say.

"Who knows." Hadrian stood. "We might just catch them in the act, or find some concrete evidence they've been there. Even if we don't, the researchers might be able to give us some more information."

"When do we leave?" Hassani asked.

"Tomorrow. Just need to drop the administrator back off on the planet and get things organized for our absence. We'll conduct the service for our marines en route."

Hassani nodded. "And maybe get them some payback."

"Maybe," Hadrian said, though he doubted it. And feared what it would mean if they *did*. "Okay. That about covers it. Ensign Coleridge, thank you for the briefing. Very informative."

"Ah. Yes." Coleridge stood up and brushed the front of his uniform. "My pleasure. Sir. Sirs. Ma'am."

Hassani laughed. Coleridge might have blushed.

"All right. Dismissed."

The officers rose and filed out of the briefing room. Save one.

"You know," Hadrian said, "one of these times you can actually leave with everyone else. I can turn out the lights on my own."

Tsegaye squinted. "You sure?"

Hadrian's smile faded. "You don't think we should be going?"

"I just want to make sure we're going for the right reasons."

"What are the *wrong* reasons?" Hadrian asked, though he already suspected the answer.

"If this has anything to do with what happened at Pyria—"

"Damn it, Arno, not everything is about that," Hadrian snapped. Tsegaye held up his hands. Hadrian took a breath. "Sorry. Truth is … with everything that's been going on, it has been on my mind."

Tsegaye stood up. "Mine too."

"But listen. Hassani's right, Singh ordered us to investigate this. With this VIP bullshit coming up, no one else is close enough to chase down this lead in time."

"And if something happens while we're gone?"

"How many fire support missions have we launched since we've been here?" Hadrian made a zero with his fingers. "We're not fighting a full-blown insurgency down there, not yet. A UMAX shot isn't going to help against a bomb hidden in a flower."

"Granted."

"Any support needs ground forces might have, the orbitals and Group Captain Martin's fighters can handle."

"True."

Hadrian's eyes narrowed. "You just wanted to make sure *I'd* thought of that too."

"That *is* my job."

"Yeah, and you're very good at it." Hadrian pointed at him. "Speaking of which, I think maybe *you* get to be the one to tell Martin he'll need to pick up our slack while we're gone."

"Do your job, get punished for it," Tsegaye said with a shake of his head.

"Welcome to the Navy."

"Did you already bribe him with that whiskey?"

Hadrian grinned. "No. Sympathy factor got me through the last one, so I decided to save it."

"Ah. A *benevolent* dictator, at least. Did you already tell Singh the plan?"

"He's my next call."

Singh's hologram appeared shortly after Tsegaye left, seated at the briefing room table, meaning he was likely seated at his own desk on the *Spruance*. Hadrian could see it now, in his mind's eye.

"Ian," Singh said in a tone that felt like home. "Any news?"

Hadrian gave him everything Coleridge had come up with. By the end of it, Singh's bright demeanor had dimmed.

"Damn. Right under our noses."

Hadrian nodded. "It also occurred to me—you should have your bomb-sniffers on Ranak reprogrammed to look for this stuff, if you can. You might need to get some samples to train them on, but if it's being used here ..."

"The moment we're done. I'll send your report to Admiral Nakatomi at Pyria as well," Singh said. Hadrian glanced away at the mention of his old fleet CO. "I'll also dispatch a squadron to 47988 immediately."

"Actually, I was thinking *we* could look into it. It's right next door; we could get there in half a day, standard time, have this all wrapped up before the VIP visit."

Singh sat back to think for a moment. "All right. Permission granted. Get over there and check it out. But you be back to Byas by the 9th. If you find any leads that'd take you out of range of that deadline, report them to me and I'll have another ship follow up. Clear?"

"Perfectly," Hadrian said, then hesitated. "And if we do find the Ciphers there?"

"They'd be in violation of the treaty. Demand their surrender."

"They've never been keen on surrendering."

"No, but under the circumstances, it needs to be attempted. And in the likely event they refuse ... you're authorized to use any means to defend your ship and the Compact. But it'll be down to your judgment when that line's been crossed. Fortunately, that's a judgment I know I can count on."

In his mind's eye, a fire spread. "Thank you, sir."

"I'll leave you to it, then. You'd best be on your way as soon as possible."

"Yes, sir. Just need to make arrangements for force dispositions in our absence, and drop the administrator off on Byas."

Singh smiled. "Glad to hear Jack's recovered. Give her my congratulations, please."

"Will do, sir."

When Singh's image disappeared, the feeling of home went with it.

TEN

"Downfall, I say again, Downfall. This is Sigma Actual at RO Beta-Three. I am in a captured enemy craft, broadcasting friendly IFF. Once again, Downfall. Please respond."

The Kyran shuttle had given Mirra just enough jump capacity to get within range of the recovery beacon. Her signal would take hours to reach it, then would be relayed instantly via quantum entanglement communicator to the recovery team, if they were even still waiting for her out there. Then, hours more for a reply to reach her—or, she hoped, less for the recovery craft to Stardrive to her location.

Mirra sat back in the uncomfortable Kyran seat to wait. There was nothing else for it. She couldn't get appreciably closer to the beacon on thrusters, and her armor's onboard QEC was only entangled with the comms core on the infiltration craft they'd dropped from. Long gone by now, self-destructed to keep it out of enemy hands.

She took the time to sleep. She hadn't gotten any on the ride out, alert for potential interdiction, however unlikely. But now, even if the Kyrans—or the Ciphers—found her, there was nothing she could do. Unless they decided to board the little shuttle rather than simply vaporizing it. If they did, she'd be better off well rested.

A beeping alert snapped her out of an unpleasant dream—not about Lampshade, but New Eden, decades ago. A quick check of her implants told her three and a half hours had passed. Not long enough for a reply signal to reach her.

And there was the recovery ship, floating in space a few hundred meters away. Which meant they'd not only still been on station, but close by. That should have filled her with relief.

It did the opposite.

"Sigma Actual," a woman's voice said over the shuttle's hijacked comms, *"this is Gamma Six-One. Provide confirmation."*

Mirra closed her eyes and gave her implant the transmission command. She pictured the series of images that constituted her side of the key—feather, bird, cat, bowl—which then transmitted to the recovery craft for verification. If someone had attempted to, say, extract her implant and copy the memory key, its end quantum state would have shown signs of tampering due to wave function collapse. Her craft would then have been blown from space.

"Confirmed. Prepare for extraction."

Now, finally, Mirra let out a relieved breath. Yet something still tugged at her as she creaked out of the Kyran pilot's seat and moved toward the docking hatch. More than the agonizing pull of the bodies of her men, left behind on enemy soil.

She had her helmet sealed when the shuttle's hatch opened. Just in case the seal wasn't perfect, she told herself. But when she saw the officers waiting for her were unarmored and unsealed, she kept her visor down. She just made it transparent, so they could see her face.

The officers were both human, a man and a woman. The woman was a lieutenant, likely Terran based on her lack of visible modifications. The one who'd spoken to her over comms. It took her a moment to realize that she recognized the man.

"Captain Zeiss," she said, unable to hide her surprise.

Zeiss smiled. He was tall, with the greenish skin and abnormally large eyes common among United Citizens. He was one of the few in the service, and the even fewer in Interstellar Special Operations Command. He'd only been assigned as her interim detachment CO a week ago. And this was probably the last place she'd have expected to see him.

"Mirra," Zeiss said when the airlock cycled closed behind her. "Thank goodness you're all right. We thought your whole team had been wiped out."

"They were," Mirra replied. "Sir."

"Damn shame," said the lieutenant.

Mirra eyed her warily. Her ID wasn't coming up on Mirra's implants, even though she'd hooked back into the network via the recovery craft. That wasn't unusual for members of ISOC, but it was odd that neither she nor Zeiss had identified her verbally, even by codename.

"I'm so sorry," Zeiss said, visibly concerned. "What happened?"

No ID on him either. Of course, they knew each other. He didn't *need* to ID himself. "Shouldn't that wait for my debriefing?"

"The lieutenant and I will be conducting it. We may as well start now."

"In the airlock?"

Zeiss smiled again. Mirra didn't like it. "You're still wearing your armor, Commander. You've probably been in it for a few days. I'm sure you'd like to get out of it."

She did. And she didn't. Both the officers were wearing their sidearms. Again, not unusual for ISOC. Again, it burned at the back of her neck.

"Why were you still on station?" she asked. "SOP is to bug out once contact is lost for twenty-six hours."

The officers glanced at one another. Zeiss spoke. "We'd almost given up hope. It's a good thing we didn't."

"We thought you'd be grateful," the lieutenant said.

Mirra stared impassively at her. "I am."

"How did you survive when the rest of your team died?" Zeiss asked.

"Luck."

Zeiss chuckled. "There has to be more to it than that."

"I'll be glad to tell you about it, sir. During the debrief."

"Which we can start as soon as you take off your armor."

Mirra stared at him. "What are *you* doing here, Captain?"

Zeiss's smile faded. But it was his fingers that did it. They twitched, on his right hand. Not like he was going for a weapon; like he was sending a message.

By the time she saw the shadow moving at the end of the hall, she'd already made her move. She grabbed the lieutenant by the collar and dragged her in front of her, her eyes widening further, just before the figure at the end of the hall fired a maser pistol. The beam burned through the lieutenant and seared into Mirra's chest plate, denuded of a fraction of its power. The Terran cried out in pain as she died, the sound mingling with the damage alarms in Mirra's helmet.

A danger indicator flashed on her HUD, a pistol being aimed at her from the right. She raised her arm up over her helmet. The second maser beam burned into her shoulder, vaporizing armor plates and severing connections.

Mirra let go of the dying lieutenant, spun on the ball of her right foot away from the second maser beam, and extended her arm blade. She stepped in as she turned and slashed, severing Zeiss's arm just below the elbow. The pistol and the hand gripping it fell to the deck. Mirra cut off her CO's scream with a powered punch to the sternum, sending him reeling into the wall.

The third attacker kept firing. Mirra sank to one knee, held her left arm over her face, and drew her own pistol. The enemy's maser beam burned into her arm, aiming for her head. As she was still descending, she fired back, starting at center mass and sweeping the beam up. There was a yell from the end of the hall, but not as pained as she'd have liked. The shooter was armored too. He staggered back, alive.

He kept shooting, trying to sweep the beam across her body. She dropped onto her side and it went high, into the airlock door behind her, just as molten armor started fusing to her skinsuit. She swept her own beam low, and found something less protected. The shooter wailed in agony as his legs were severed at the ankle, and he too collapsed to the floor, firing wildly. From the ground, Mirra fired a concentrated burst at his head until the shooting stopped.

She lay there breathing for a few moments, until she was sure he wouldn't get up. Then she tried to. Her armor whined and protested as she forced herself to her knees. It didn't have much life left in it. With effort, she pushed herself to her feet, then triggered the emergency release. The front plates of the armor separated, then popped off. Her skinsuit tore where it was fused to the melted armor, immediately started to regrow itself. She stepped out of what remained of the shell, and it too clattered to the deck.

A whimper drew her out of her momentary pause, her relief and guilt at having survived yet again. She drew her knife from its sheath on her belt and knelt in front of the wounded Zeiss. The captain's implants had stanched the flow of blood, but his face was still pale from shock, and he was gripping the stump of his severed arm with a haunted expression in his large eyes.

"Why did you sell us out?" Mirra asked him. Zeiss looked on her with fear, but didn't answer. Mirra held the knife up to his neck. "Why!"

Zeiss seemed about to answer, for a moment. Then his breaths came in short gasps, his big eyes widened and rolled back in his head, clouded. He slumped against the wall.

Mirra stared at him uncomprehending for a moment. She hadn't punched him that hard, or at least she didn't think she had. Indeed, a quick scan using her implants showed only minor internal injuries, some blood loss from the severed arm, but nothing fatal. And yet, Zeiss was dead.

Total nervous system shutdown. Mirra looked into his dead eyes. *Implant suicide.*

ISOC field operatives were all able to trigger that protocol in the event of capture and torture. But there was no indication that Zeiss had done anything of the kind. Perhaps Mirra had missed it ... or perhaps the protocol had been triggered automatically.

Or remotely.

Mirra snapped up her dropped sidearm and rose to her feet. The recovery craft was small and typically had a crew of two. But there had already been a third. There might be more. She cleared it carefully, first checking the other two bodies to make sure they were dead. No need for implant suicide there.

It took only a few minutes to ensure the rest of the craft was empty. She ended at the cockpit. Every second that ticked past on her way there was nerve-racking. The protocol might have been *very* remotely triggered, from light-years away via QEC. If this hadn't been an isolated betrayal by a few rogue officers.

She was lucky again, in that she reached the cockpit and cut the craft off from the networks without a self-destruct activating. But she doubted she was so lucky that *these* were the only traitors responsible for her team's death.

There must be more, she thought, sitting silently in the pilot's seat for long minutes afterward. *Someone higher up than a captain. Someone with access.*

But why? Why us?

The answer hit her like a high-caliber round, right in the chest.

Baton. It has to be. Fucking Baton.

Another face flashed before her eyes, this one unfamiliar.

Human, or it had appeared to be. Its expression had been human enough, when she shot the life out of it. Surprised.

Whatever it was, it was clear she and her men hadn't been meant to see it. That was the only thing she could think of, the only thing out of the ordinary that might have led to what happened on Lampshade.

But that still didn't answer the question *why*.

She promised herself, and her men, that she'd get some answers. Before she killed the bastards.

Then she checked the craft's navigation logs.

ELEVEN

"So," Hadrian said, taking a sip of coffee. "What's the verdict on Thucydides?"

Jack walked alongside him through the corridors of *Belisarius*. "Excellent, illuminating. Frustrating."

"How so?"

"The concept you mentioned earlier, the narcissism of minor difference. It seems at play here even more than in Herodotus. The two states involved in the titular war have so much in common. They worked together to defeat a common existential enemy just a few generations earlier. To see them then fight so mercilessly against one another, when they could have accomplished so much more together ..."

"That's human history for you," Hadrian said. "There's the occasional war that needed to be fought, where the bad guys are pretty clear cut. Most of them, though? A lot more like that one."

"That is very sad."

"I hope it's not ruining the book for you."

"No, not at all." Jack brightened. "Your prediction was quite right; I do prefer Thucydides to Herodotus. I can't imagine who would find him *dry*."

Hadrian laughed. "I feel the same way about you. It's been nice having you aboard for a few days. Even under these circumstances."

"Agreed. I appreciated the rest."

They reached the landing bay, where the ICRA shuttle was waiting to take Jack back to Byas.

"I guess you'll have a lot to catch up on when you get back," Hadrian said.

"Indeed." Jack raised her copy of *The Peloponnesian War*, which she'd been cradling in one arm. "But I will still find time to finish this. I'm even taking the time to have a party, two days from now."

Hadrian's eyebrows shot up. "A party?"

"Yes."

"*You?*"

"Yes. To celebrate my upcoming birth. My virgonid colleagues are hosting it for me."

"Ahh. Like a baby shower?"

Jack's head bobbed back and forth. "More or less."

"Sounds nice." Hadrian thought for a moment. "Damn. Sorry I'm gonna miss it."

"Don't be. Virgonid parties are somewhat more … subdued than most humans are used to."

"Not *everyone* in the Navy spends shore leave intoxicated, you know."

Jack chittered. "Of course not."

"Well. I'll look forward to talking more about the book when we get back. I should have warned you, though, it ends on a bit of a cliffhanger. Thucydides died while he was writing it."

"Did no one else take up the work from him?"

"Actually someone did, another historian. Xenophon. He wrote a book called *Hellenica* that picks up right where Thucydides left off."

Jack was visibly relieved. "Then I will begin that as soon as I'm finished with this. Was Xenophon Thucydides's offspring?"

Hadrian's smile became sad. "In a way."

"Ian." Jack placed an appendage on his shoulder. "I will still be here when you get back."

"I know. And I am happy for you, I promise. With the last few days, I'm just tired."

Jack nodded toward the mug in Hadrian's hand. "You're aware there are other substances far more effective at battling fatigue than caffeine."

Hadrian winked. "None that taste as good."

"I would be a poor judge of that."

"If nothing else."

Jack stopped, turned her chitinous bulk back toward him. "There was one other thing I wished to mention. Regarding Thucydides."

Hadrian raised his mug to her.

"He seems to have had a very dim view of human nature. Understandable, given the times in which he lived. Yet he dedicated his history to a very distant posterity."

"That's right." Hadrian took a sip. "Well. Back then, as bad as things got, no one really thought the world could ever end. Not at man's hands, anyway."

"Yet *civilization* might have ended. The arts of history, and even writing itself, might have been lost. The Greeks were certainly aware of that possibility, were they not?"

"They were."

"Then," Jack said, "I believe that dedication indicates a core of hope in his work, however faint."

Hadrian smiled. "I suppose it does."

*

"CAPTAIN ON DECK," Tsegaye announced when Hadrian arrived in the CIC a few minutes later.

"At ease," Hadrian said, patting the helmsman on the shoulder as he passed him on the way into the command pit. "Status?"

"Administrator's shuttle is away," Ensign Keitel replied, checking the readouts on his hardscreen. "Clearing *Belisarius* safety perimeter in three-zero seconds. *Belisarius* clearing Byas gravitic threshold in … five minutes."

Hadrian finished the last of his coffee and set the mug on the HCI. Bella dispatched one of her maintenance drones to pick it up. "Confirm course and heading."

"Course laid in for CAS 47988." Byas and the destination star appeared above the HCI. An icon representing *Belisarius* orbited Byas; then a red parabolic arc appeared between her and the glowing blue neutron star. "Estimated flight duration, 12.4 hours Interstellar Standard Time, 6.2 hours ship's time."

"Very good." Hadrian nodded to his XO. "Proceed, Commander."

"All stations, secure for Stardrive," Tsegaye ordered.

As Bella repeated the command throughout the ship, an ephemeral thrill ran through Hadrian. He'd made FTL trips hundreds of times before, of course. But previously, *Belisarius* had only made two microjumps to the outer system under his command. This would be his first time taking her out of the Byas system. She was by far the largest vessel he'd ever commanded, and though she was an older Mark II *Starbird*-class battlecruiser, she was still one of the fastest ships in the ICN. How could he *not* feel a thrill?

"Navigation," Tsegaye said, "confirm Stardrive calculation efficiency rating."

"Efficiency rating alpha confirmed, Commander."

For all that, this might have been one of the countless drills they conducted, the officers and crew seemed so calm. Even so, some of them must feel the same excitement he did. He thought he detected a hint of it in Hassani's voice when she made her confirmations. Zevran sounded almost painfully dour, but that was no surprise.

The strange thing was Tsegaye. Hadrian might have thought he'd share the sense of excitement at the journey, however short it might be, whatever circumstances it was occurring under. Yet there was instead a hint of concern in his voice, likely undetectable to the rest of the officers.

Maybe the circumstances are bothering him more than I thought.

"All sections report secure for Stardrive, Captain," Tsegaye said a moment later.

Or maybe it's not the circumstances that are taking us away. Maybe it's the ones that brought us here.

"Very well," Hadrian said, pushing such thoughts away. "Make the CIC secure."

The command crew engaged the safety restraints at their stations. Hadrian and Tsegaye moved to their acceleration seats on the mid-deck and strapped themselves in. Bella had long since cleared away any loose items in the CIC, and throughout the rest of the ship. The crew chiefs reported their stations secure, and in adherence to ancient protocol, Tsegaye repeated their confirmations to Hadrian.

"Activate Stardrive," Hadrian ordered. Seconds later, his brain told him the deck had disappeared, and he was in free fall. Training and experience kept his physiological panic response in check until his neural implant could kick in and alleviate the symptoms.

"Stardrive activated," Ensign Keitel reported. "Baseframe decoupling nominal. Recoupling to metaframe."

From their perspective, nothing changed. But from an outside frame of reference, *Belisarius* would now appear fuzzy, warped, heavily redshifted. She should; with her mass neutralized, and isolated from the effects of gravity, she was now also decoupled from the layer of space-time that "normal" matter inhabited. Vital, if she wanted to violate the normal laws of physics by traveling faster than light.

"Metaframe coupling nominal. Bearing confirmed. Ready to execute jump sequence."

"Execute," Hadrian ordered.

A hum built up in the depths of the ship as her massive engines' prefire capacitors welled with restrained power. The hum reached a crescendo.

Then came a moment of eerie stillness.

Then, *Belisarius* leaped from the Byas system. Inside her, the stillness persisted. Popular media always made the jump to FTL seem an epic, almost violent thing. Yet for the people making the trip, the result was somewhat anticlimactic. Even on the hard-screen, showing the external view, there was no dazzling visual display. The field of stars simply coalesced into a single blazing point of blue-white light in front of the ship. The rest was pure blackness. Hadrian had been bitterly disappointed the first time he'd experienced it, on the shuttle to the naval academy sixteen years ago, after having been raised on a diet of space action dramas and games. Only on subsequent trips had he come to love the experience, demonstrating as it did, in its own quiet way, technology of almost unfathomable power and sophistication.

After a few seconds and a few dozen microjumps, the nav computer determined that all systems were functioning normally, and the ship was not in danger of striking a particle of space dust at several thousand times the speed of light. Even *mostly* decoupled from the baseframe, as they were, at these titanic velocities such a collision could be fatal.

"Stardrive all-clear," Keitel reported on the computer's behalf.

"Sound all-clear," Hadrian confirmed. He unfastened his restraints and pushed gently off from the acceleration seat. He floated over to the HCI, gripped the handrail that surrounded it to anchor himself. Tsegaye joined him there a moment later.

"Three hours until the service," he said. The mention of it dampened Hadrian's excitement. "Want to go over anything?"

Hadrian sighed. "I already know what I want to say, but it couldn't hurt."

*

PRACTICING HELPED. Tsegaye suggested some minor changes that Hadrian found helpful. He hadn't conducted such a service in years, since Andrejsson was killed in that accident, and the circumstances of this one were very different.

He struck a somber and purposeful tone, focusing on keeping the memory of the fallen in mind as they hunted for answers rather than vengeance, the intention of their mission to prevent more unnecessary loss of life rather than strike down those responsible. It was understood that justice of that kind might not be possible, if the ultimate perpetrators were who, or what, they suspected.

It went as well as it could. After the service proper, the officers gathered for a short wake, at which memories of the fallen were shared. With the four survivors of the marine contingent left behind on Byas, there were few of those to go around, but it was tradition, and it still helped. After that, only an hour ship's time passed before *Belisarius* reached its destination.

Hadrian had never seen a neutron star up close before. Still hadn't, technically, since seeing it on the CIC's hardscreen from tens of millions of kilometers away was functionally little different from seeing it in a recording from thousands of light-years away. Still, there was something different about knowing he was sharing the strange and powerful star's gravity; that if he were out in space with it now, without layers of active and passive shielding between them, its radiation would kill him instantly.

Not that present circumstances gave him much time to dwell on its terrible majesty.

"All stations report integrity condition bravo, stealth condition two," Tsegaye confirmed once *Belisarius* had decelerated from Stardrive.

"No hostile contacts," Hassani reported from the TacOps station. "No anomalous detections at the target site."

"Give me an active scan," Hadrian ordered. "Level three followed by level one. Bella, raise the research station."

Hassani used *Belisarius*'s sensors to sweep the day-side surface of the target moon with active scans, first at a lower, faster resolution to look for anything obvious that passive detection might have missed, then at a slower, finer resolution, to find anything doing a better job of hiding. Initially, they seemed to be alone in the system with the tiny research station orbiting the moon. But that could change in an instant.

"I have a Doctor Narin, head of research, responding to our hail," Bella reported.

"Good." Hadrian circled the HCI toward the fore of the CIC, leaving Tsegaye to deal with the ship's operations for a moment. "Put her on screen, solo projection return."

A moment later, an image of a middle-aged Free Worlder behind a desk in a fairly unremarkable administrative office appeared on the hardscreen. She had her dark hair pulled back. Both she and her office looked well put together, as far as scientists and their workspaces went. In return, she would be getting a projection of Hadrian alone, likely standing before her desk.

"Good morning," Doctor Narin said, looking and sounding somewhat surprised. "I assume you are ..."

"Captain Hadrian, *Belisarius*. Pleasure to meet you, Doctor."

Narin snapped her fingers. "Yes, of course. We got your message, although it was rather vague. I'm afraid other than tidying up a bit, we haven't done much to prepare for your arrival. We don't get many visitors out here, let alone from the military."

"I do apologize for being cagey, Doctor," Hadrian said. "I'll explain everything once I'm aboard. Is there any issue if I take a shuttle over ASAP?"

Narin's eyes narrowed momentarily. Hadrian imagined she was somewhat *more* concerned now that he'd neglected to explain their visit over local comms. "Feel free. Our loading dock's always open. When should we expect you?"

"Say about ..." Hadrian ran a quick calculation, the flight time to the outpost from their projected position plus the time needed to ensure the area was more or less secure. "Thirty minutes?"

"Perfect," Narin said with a somewhat forced smile. "See you then."

"Seems pleasant enough," Hadrian said to Tsegaye once the channel had closed.

"You're going alone?" Tsegaye said.

"Why not?"

"I'd prefer if you'd take a couple armed ratings with you."

Hadrian raised his eyebrows. "Seriously?"

"Well, I'd *prefer* marines, but we left them behind."

"It's three scientists on a backwater station," Hadrian said. "I think I can handle it."

"And if the Ciphers have compromised that station?"

That gave Hadrian pause. He glanced up at the HCI projection. "TacOps. Anything suspicious yet?"

"Negative returns on the level three scan," Hassani reported. "Level one in progress. So far, negative also."

"Just because they're not here, doesn't mean they haven't *been* here," Tsegaye said.

Hadrian was already nodding. "All right, but I don't want to scare these poor people any more than we're already going to. I'll bring a couple ratings, and they can wait on the shuttle in case I need them. Meanwhile, I'll wear my sidearm. Happy?"

Tsegaye tsked. "Maybe if you were a better shot."

"I'm a better shot than *you*."

"Low bar."

TWELVE

Doctor Narin's gaze dropped to the pistol at Hadrian's hip the moment the airlock opened. Her eyes widened. Hadrian was glad he'd told the ratings toting combat armor and rifles to stay in the crew compartment, out of sight.

"Captain," Narin said, recovering herself. "Pleasure to meet in person."

Hadrian shook her cold hand. "Likewise. And again, I apologize for the intrusion."

"Not at all. The occasional visitor helps break up the monotony. Follow me, please."

Hadrian let her lead him through the cramped but clean off-white corridors of the tiny station. "It's just the three of you aboard, correct?"

"That's right," Narin said over her shoulder. "Myself, plus a virgonid, Doctor Allen, and a melakeen, Doctor Tharik. Tell you the truth, it's nice to see a human face in the flesh for a change."

Hadrian glanced through an open door as they passed. It looked like a disused lab of some kind, the equipment covered, the lights off except when they passed by. "Three species sharing one station. That's gotta make accommodations difficult."

"Not so much as you might think." They reached Narin's office, and she ushered him in. It looked much as it had on the viewer, tidy, with only a few personal items visible on the desk and the shelves behind it. It was smaller than he'd thought. "The same species ratio is maintained every rotation, so the quarters, stations, and whatnot are each designed specifically for us. At least we all breathe more or less the same air. If a xirān wanted in on the deal, I daresay *that* would make things complicated."

Hadrian smiled as he took the one seat across Narin's desk. Designed for a human, thankfully. "And how long have you been here, Doctor?"

"Well, the station's been online about five years, since shortly after ignicite was discovered out near Oronam. I was in the second rotation to come on, in the second year. Then I was out, and now I've been back about three months."

"One-year rotations?"

"Initially. Now it's down to six months, thank God. Although even that … Let's just say I doubt I'll be accepting a *third*."

"I can imagine. And what sort of work do you do here?"

"Studying ignicite—oh. My apologies. Anything to drink, Captain? Water, tea?"

"Coffee, if you have it."

"We do, but …" Narin winced. "I wouldn't recommend it."

"Thanks. Tea, then."

"Good choice." Narin continued while the station's service drones filled the order. "Where was I? Yes. Studying ignicite, for what that's worth. Trying to determine precisely how it's created, whether we can synthesize it, whether we can stabilize it. What applications it might have if we could. Truth be told, never mind *my* not coming back for a third rotation. I'm not sure the station will still be operational in a year's time. We may have exhausted all the salient research possibilities by then."

"I noticed the disused lab back there."

Narin nodded. "About a quarter of the station's dark at any one time. Am I to take it that this is a ... security audit of some kind?"

"In a manner of speaking." Hadrian grappled with how to phrase the rest for a moment. "*Belisarius* is stationed at Byas. Ignicite was recently used in a couple of insurgent bombings there."

"My God," Narin said. "Was anyone hurt?"

"Yes, a number of our people were killed."

Narin shook her head. "I'm so sorry, Captain. Is there anything we can do to help?"

"Well." Hadrian cleared his throat. "We have reason to believe the ignicite may have come from ... here."

Narin's confusion turned rapidly to pale-faced fear. "Captain, I can assure you, none of us would *ever* knowingly—"

"No, no." Hadrian held up his hands, chiding himself for his mistake. "I didn't mean to imply that you had anything to do with it, of course. We think it's possible that hostile actors have compromised this system."

"Hostile actors?"

"The Ciphers. Potentially."

The fear returned. "But we haven't seen ..."

"No. You wouldn't have. If we're correct, they could have been coming here under full military-grade stealth and extracting the ignicite, and you'd never know it."

Narin breathed out, slumped back in her chair, and stared into nothing.

"We haven't detected any evidence of them yet," Hadrian continued. "But then, it would be fairly trivial for them to cover their tracks. At least I can tell you there aren't any here right now."

"But if they've been here before, they could come back."

"Yes."

"Are you staying here, to protect us?"

Hadrian's expression was answer enough. She deflated further before he could clarify. "We have a time constraint with our primary mission. If we don't find any evidence here, we'll have to try and pick up the trail elsewhere."

"What should we do if they come back after you're gone?"

"The same thing you've been doing—nothing," Hadrian said. "I'm requesting military reinforcements be sent here, but in the meantime, it's best if you don't know who's coming and going. If you can't detect them, they have no reason to interfere with you."

Hadrian regretted using the euphemism, seeing Narin's reaction. "That's not much comfort, Captain."

"I am sorry." There was an awkward pause. "In the meantime, if there's anything else you can think of that might help us, anything suspicious that's happened recently ..."

She hesitated for so long it seemed she wasn't going to answer. He was about to make his final apologies and excuse himself when she spoke up. "I hesitate to mention it—in part because if I *don't*, you might agree to stay longer, but ... you're not the only military visitors we've had recently."

"No?"

"About two weeks ago, a military vessel arrived in-system. Much smaller than yours; I'm not sure of the type. They ID'd themselves. Just the essentials. They didn't call ahead, like you did. I asked them if we could do anything to assist them, and they informed me we could stay out of their way."

Hadrian had a sinking feeling. "What did they want?"

"Ignicite." Narin shrugged. "They sent some drones down to the surface of the moon, they were down there for a while. They came back up, and the ship left. Didn't even signal goodbye."

"And they didn't say what they wanted it for?"

Narin shook her head. "I assumed it was to conduct their own research. Though what for, I couldn't imagine. Until now."

Hadrian rubbed his beard, stared into the top of Narin's desk. "I don't imagine they said where they were headed."

"No. But I do know where they came from."

*

"Harrington's Haven." The spire-shaped station floated above the briefing room table. Bella rendered the red dwarf star around which it orbited as a tiny point of light in the background. The station was several kilometers tall, with ring sections at regular intervals, each studded with docking ports and berths for ships. Hadrian indicated one of them. "We even got a berth number."

"The shifty bastards gave her all that?" Tsung asked, skeptical.

Hadrian shrugged. "It was in their IFF ping. Standard information. They either forgot to scrub or they didn't care to. Probably the latter."

Interstellar Special Operations Command forces weren't known for making mistakes, at least as far as covering their tracks went. Nor were they known for sharing information with their regular force brethren.

"What would ISOC need ignicite for?" Hassani asked.

"Perhaps they're making their own undetectable explosives?" Coleridge suggested. "Given the reputation some of them have, such things might be rather useful."

"True, but I think Doctor Narin was right," Hadrian said. "I think they were here to conduct their own research. Which, given the timing, can't be a coincidence."

"Suggesting they already knew about its potential as a covert explosive?" Doctor Park said.

"Suggesting it had already been *used* as an explosive," Tsegaye corrected, "and they knew about it."

"And didn't warn anyone," Park concluded.

Tsung scoffed. "Black ops assholes."

Tsegaye and Hadrian shared a look. Hadrian sent him a text message via implant: *Later.* "Either way, they probably know something about it we don't. Maybe they've even got a line on who, or what, has been smuggling it into Byas."

Hadrian keyed Bella to switch the holo to a navigational display. "Harrington's just over a half-day IST from here. Given the lateral course, it's also about a day's journey IST from there back to Byas. Enough time for us to go check it out and make it back by our deadline."

"That's great." Tsung sat back in his chair. "What makes you think the sons of bitches will tell us anything?"

"If we share what we have with them, it might convince them to give us *something*," Hadrian said. "If not, at least we tried. We didn't turn up anything concrete here. I'm not willing to go back with a lead unfollowed when it's within our time radius."

No one seemed entirely satisfied with that, least of all Hadrian himself. Yet there was more to the shadow that followed him back into the CIC as they made their preparations to leap back to Stardrive, chasing the next thin lead. Something that only he and Tsegaye shared.

Maybe we'll finally get some answers.

And not just about the bombings.

THIRTEEN

"Welcome to Harrington's Haven," a pleasant, disembodied female voice announced. "ICDF personnel, please report to your assigned muster points. Everyone else, enjoy your stay."

Mirra followed everyone else. It was an eclectic group debarking from the civilian liner she'd bought passage on, after ditching her stolen recovery ship in the Sang-je system. She'd considered taking the stealth ship all the way here and trying to sneak in, but quickly decided against it. For one, the little ship wouldn't have made it here without stopping to refuel, and she had no idea how she'd have managed that. For another, even if the ship weren't detected by the ISOC presence on the station, *she* certainly would have been when she tried to sneak in through an airlock.

Instead, she'd decided to smuggle herself aboard right under their noses, disguised as a civilian. She'd had her official false IDs loaded up during the mission, of course. She'd purged those shortly after seizing the traitors' recovery vessel, since they were almost certainly compromised. Instead she used one of her own, which she'd had generated off the books. Just in case.

Fortunately, it had been trivial to find a ship bound from Sangje to Harrington, filled with traders from Jayu, and cadets from the Space Warfare Officer School heading to their first assignments. And, with several retired military personnel, like she appeared to be, on their way to private sector work in the Protectorates, or just sightseeing, reminiscing.

She'd chosen the latter excuse, partially because there was some truth to it. Would make it easier to lie, if it came to that. She remembered Haven being rapid-constructed between November and December of '83, to serve as a secret forward operating base for the Tenth and Virgonid Second Fleets in their invasions of Byas and Embra. She hadn't joined the campaign to liberate what became the Protectorates from the Ciphers until later in '84; by then the station had already doubled in size. That was the last time she had been here, having been deployed mostly to Kyran space and Pyria since she moved from marine reg force to LDRG.

Stepping off the transport now, she was taken aback by what she saw, even more than she had been seeing the massive spire-shaped station from the liner's windows. It was many times bigger than it had been when she'd last visited, and entirely different in character. Back then, it had been a grim, utilitarian structure, the only color coming from the occasional cheeky holosign or banner put up by its military denizens.

Now, it was bustling, alive with colors and sounds of all kinds. The main docking ring where she'd landed had looked huge from the outside, but she'd expected it to be more compartmentalized, as it would have been during the war. Instead, it was completely hollow, with docking and commercial decks ringing both the outer wall and the central spire, each of their promenades largely open to the central space. It felt even more vast from inside than it looked from outside, creating a sense of grandeur and scale Mirra had rarely experienced outside of battle. That she should find it here, in what she'd expected would be a distant backwater, disturbed her.

In another stark contrast to her last visit, the military was decidedly in the minority. Of the hundreds of people in her immediate vicinity, only a dozen or so were in uniform, not including the occasional security guard or MP. Most of the civilians she'd ridden here aboard ship with were from Sang-je, or elsewhere in the Free Worlds Republic, not so unfamiliar to her even after decades in the military.

Here, they represented the full spectrum of Interstellar Compact citizenry: Free Worlders; tall, green or blue-skinned United Citizens; insectoid virgonids in their many shapes and colors; quadrupedal, primatoid melakeen; even an aquatic xirān, wearing one of the complex locomotive exoskeletons they needed to traverse the world of the air-breathers. Plain-looking Terrans were barely noticeable in the heterogeneous throng. To the naked eye, Mirra would have no trouble blending in.

Still, as she moved into the crowd, she had to be careful. The after-market biometric hoaxers she'd installed on her implant network *should* keep even high-end analyzers from identifying her —unless the station's security systems decided to focus on her specifically. Even the best spoofing software couldn't fool a combined AI-operator analysis, not from a military-grade ID system. To avoid suspicion, she'd have to avoid doing anything overly aggressive or unusual. At least until she had no other choice.

For now, that shouldn't be a problem. She'd checked the publicly available station map on the journey here and located the berth the recovery ship had launched from. It was military, but not specifically tagged as ISOC. That was a strategy they often used; standard military berths attracted virtually no attention, while special forces ones invariably did. When they didn't use military berths, they tended to use civilian ones, and civilian craft. Always best to hide right under people's noses, if you could. A lesson she'd learned well.

As such, the berth in question was on a military ring of the station, but one that was partially open to the public, with various shops and restaurants which both civilians and off-duty military could patronize. Still, the people using the berth weren't fools. There were no cafés or other businesses directly across from the access points to the berth where she could post up and keep watch on the comings and goings. Even if there had been, she had no idea how long she'd have to wait to get the intel she needed. If she sat at the same café, hour after hour, day after day, right across from a military berth, she'd get picked up in no time.

However, she could pass by the berth without raising any suspicion. It was located between a shopping area and the hotel where she'd rented a room for the week. Not by coincidence.

To make it look good, she had to stop and buy something at one of the shops once she'd taken the lift to that ring. She'd decided on clothes, since in terms of civilian attire, she only had what she was wearing. That decision had been easy; deciding *what* to buy was not. There was only one clothing store on her route from the lift, past the berth, to her hotel. She hadn't been shopping for civilian clothes in years. Still, she assumed she would find something inoffensive fairly easily.

Her hopes were dashed the moment she stepped through the shop's doors, which greeted her with a melodic chime and a cloying male voice saying "Good morning, Sandra. How may we delight you today?"

It was impossible to hide her sneer at the voice. She could only do her best to wipe it from her face by the time a human attendant, Terran by the looks of her, approached a moment later, beaming as Mirra imagined the owner of the disembodied voice would have.

"Good morning!" the attendant repeated. "Are you looking for anything in particular?"

Mirra smiled tightly, swallowing her instinctive response of "Not if what you're wearing is any indication." The attendant, "Adana" from the name popping up on Mirra's implant, was clad in a dress rather more revealing than Mirra had ever worn in her life, its colors fluid and changing, its shape gently but constantly undulating, as if in a light breeze in low gravity.

The other patrons in the store—she assumed they were patrons, though none of them seemed to be actively shopping—were dressed much the same way. Many had extravagant body modifications as well: bright purple skin; prehensile hair; long, extra-jointed fingers. Adana seemed to have gone for a more naturalistic look. Mirra caught the attendant briefly eyeing her own clothes—plain, well-fitting pants and shirt with a black leather jacket—with pity.

"Perhaps," Mirra said as a compromise. She glanced around the shop. Its floor was dotted with seating, some of which was occupied by other customers. Its bright colored walls were covered with decor, changing images, and mirrors. But something was missing. "Where are the clothes?"

Adana laughed lightly. "We have fabricators in the back. Once you select an outfit, they'll print it to order for you."

For a moment, Mirra's hope was kindled. "Can they print anything?"

"We have our proprietary patterns and fabrics," Adana said, snuffing it out. "But we have a wide selection, I'm sure we can find"—another pitying glance—"*something* that will suit you."

"And how do I try it on?"

Another light laugh, and Mirra decided she firmly disliked the pleasant young woman. "Right this way."

Adana led her over to one of the mirrors. As they approached, a primitive HUD appeared over the mirror, showing Mirra the options available to her. She internally chided herself for her obvious naivety. The last civilian clothing shop she'd been in was some archaic hole-in-the-wall on Horizon, which she'd visited with the King family on leave a few years back. They'd actually had prefabricated clothes on racks, and little rooms you could go into to try them on. Somehow she'd internalized that experience as though it were common, instead of the deliberately vintage exception.

Even with the more limited selection, she'd found clothes she *liked* in that place. After politely dismissing the attendant, it immediately became clear she wouldn't be so lucky here. She cycled through dozens of options—tops, bottoms, entire outfits—each of them displayed holographically on the mirror with perfect fidelity, as if she were wearing them. She could even instruct the image of herself to turn around so she could see the outfits from the sides and back.

It certainly was handy. Though, given how revealing some of the outfits were, she was thoroughly put off by the level of detail and accuracy with which the display program was able to model her body. The program told her the hologram was subjective, so none of the other patrons would see it. Of course, when she drilled into the terms of use, it was clear the data was being used to train various display, demographic, and sales models.

Such is life. Civilian *life, at least. And I sometimes wonder why I don't go back.*

Finally, she settled on the least offensive combination of clothes she could find. She considered just buying anything and tossing it once she got to her hotel, or simply never wearing it. But that in itself would be suspicious, and might result in her being singled out by the security AIs. So she picked out one of the few long-sleeved shirts in a solid color, with old-fashioned motionless fabric, that didn't show *too* much extraneous skin around the neck and midriff, and a similarly "plain" pair of pants. In the latter case, she selected the option not to include any randomized holes or tears in the legs, which, of course, came with an extra cost.

At least the outfit printed quickly—and, she was assured, would fit perfectly.

"If they don't," Adana said as she was paying, "you can return them at any time and have them reprinted at no cost."

"Thank you," Mirra said with another tight smile. "You've been very helpful."

Adana beamed, exactly as she had when Mirra entered. "My pleasure. Come back anytime!"

Mirra mentally shook off the saccharine shadow of the store as she exited. She could only hope the visit had done its job. The berth was right around the bend of the ring from the shop, and there were no innocuous places to pause for more than a few seconds on her way to the hotel. If the visit had somehow aroused the suspicions of station security, then what she was about to do would certainly be detected.

Only one way to find out.

Like all the other military berths, the one she was interested in was not marked. She had programmed its location into the nav components of her implant network, and when it came into view on her right, against the outer hull of the ring, a highlight of the entry points flashed on her vision. She gave it only a momentary glance, like any civilian might when surveying a new area, but otherwise avoided looking directly at it. She chose her course through the promenade so that she would have to move to her left to avoid a small knot of civilians walking the other way.

The maneuver brought her almost in contact with the inner wall. She didn't even slow down as she brushed a microdot against the wall with her little finger.

A second later, the image from the dot appeared above her left field of view. She smiled internally. The placement was perfect. Both entry points to Military Berth 17-A were perfectly in view.

FOURTEEN

Harrington was a bare and lonely system. Its red dwarf star burned dim against the dark, its lone planet a ball of lifeless rock in a distant orbit; beyond was a sparse disk of debris which had never quite managed to coalesce into a world. Like CAS 47988, the star and system had only had an alphanumeric designation in all the years it had been known to conscious beings, until Group Captain Harrington of the Naval Engineers arrived, twenty-four years ago, to build the only point of life this star would likely ever host.

Belisarius had taken up a stable position near the station. Hadrian had been here once before, just over a year ago, with Tsegaye. When they'd transferred from their old command, *Marissa Tavukcu* at Pyria, to take over *Belisarius*. The memory was not a happy one, despite being a step in the fulfillment of a lifelong dream. Seeing the station again, Hadrian briefly worried that history was in danger of repeating itself. The hail they received shortly after their arrival did little to dispel that concern.

"Belisarius," the man in the voice-only transmission said, *"this is Major Dayan, Planetary Assault Corps. Welcome to Harrington."*

Hadrian smiled so it would sound in his voice. "Major; Captain Ian Hadrian. I didn't realize the PAC was so desperate for work, if they're assigning officers as greeters."

The major's chuckle didn't sound forced. *"Hardly. I received a flag that you made an inquiry to station control about a particular military berth ... 17-A. Is that accurate?"*

"It is."

"May I ask your interest in that berth, Captain?"

Hadrian shared a glance with Tsegaye. "It relates to an investigation we're conducting into insurgent activity on Byas. We believe a ship possessing vital information relevant to that investigation may have docked there."

"I see," Dayan said calmly. *"I may be able to assist you with that, Captain, but I'd rather have that conversation in person. Can you come aboard Haven?"*

"Of course. Myself and a couple of officers can be there in thirty minutes."

"Actually, it'd be better if you came alone. You're the only officer aboard with security clearance sufficient for what we'd be discussing. Unless, of course, your officers would be happy to do a little shopping?"

This time, Hadrian's smile was genuine. "I'm sure they wouldn't mind, but we don't have time for them to draw lots. I'll come down myself."

"Perfect. Feel free to dock at 17-A. My office is right around the corner. See you then."

"Seems pleasant enough," Hassani said once the channel had closed.

Keitel scoffed. "Don't they always?"

"PAC?" Hadrian asked quietly.

"SWB," Tsegaye responded. "If we're lucky. CRTG if we're not."

The PAC's Special Warfare Brigade was largely tasked with advising and supporting local forces on worlds like Pyria, Sukat, and some of the other Protectorates, as well as conducting the occasional direct operation against hostile forces. Like other special forces units, they fell under ISOC's jurisdiction, but in Hadrian's experience, they were among the least cloak-and-dagger of the bunch.

The PAC's other spec-ops unit, the Clandestine Reconnaissance and Tactics Group, was another story. If Major Dayan was with them, this trip was likely already a dead end. That being said, there were other reasons for Hadrian and Tsegaye in particular to hope it wasn't the SWB on the other end of the line.

"Either way," Hadrian said, "it's worth a shot. I'm not gonna be giving him anything he doesn't already have, and we might get something useful in return."

Tsegaye sighed.

Hadrian frowned. "You don't agree?"

"It's not that. I could go with you. Whatever he says, we've got the same security clearance."

Hadrian put a hand on his shoulder. "I need you to stay here and—"

"—keep an eye on things," Tsegaye said in unison with him. "You know, one of these times *I'm* gonna be the one who gets to go ashore, and *you're* gonna stay here and keep an eye on things."

Hadrian winked at him as he walked out.

*

MIRRA WATCHED AND WAITED for five days before making her move.

As it turned out, the comings and goings of Military Berth 17-A were frequent, and tame. She saw several officers and enlisted enter and exit the berth on the first day of observation. Most of them seemed to go about the station as normal. A few went to and from a bank of military offices a short distance from the berth.

The traffic was too heavy for her to follow each of the

personnel, and without longer-term observation, there was no way to tell which, if any of them, might be involved in the conspiracy that killed her men. Maybe if she could get into those offices … But doing that would immediately blow her cover. She'd have to keep that as a last resort, whenever she was ready to leave the station and not come back.

In the meantime, she decided simply to watch, and wait for something out of the ordinary to happen. For four days, nothing did. The same personnel came and went at more or less the same times, going to more or less the same places. One of the enlisted even went to the same clothing store Mirra had visited under duress on her first day. She pitied the poor man.

She was just considering checking out a few of the recreation spots the officers frequented for potential clandestine meeting sites when, on the fifth day, the pattern changed. A military shuttle docked at the berth around midday station time, which in itself was nothing unusual. The difference was who came out after the docking procedure was finished.

The first man was one of the officers she'd been tracking: Major Carter Dayan, PAC according to his official ID. Dayan was a Free Worlder of middling height and strong build, thirty-one years old by his ID and about the same in appearance; he had dusky skin and buzzed blond hair beneath the officer's cap he always wore. He was often smiling, which rang Mirra's alarm bells. It reminded her of Captain Zeiss.

The second man was the unusual one. For starters, he was wearing a rich blue naval uniform as opposed to the PAC green most of the berth's other visitors wore. The silver buttons, epaulets and piping marked him out as an officer, which his official ID confirmed: Captain Ian Hadrian, thirty-seven. Terran, from Eos. He had a close-cropped beard and well-groomed short hair with a sweep in the front, both auburn in color. Tall, medium build from the looks of him.

Mirra switched on the audio feed from the microdot, instructed it to focus in on the two men for the brief interval they'd be in view.

"... for all the secrecy, but you understand," Dayan was saying. *"The brass can't take a shit without giving the plumbing a security clearance."*

"I remember that one," Hadrian replied. *"No, it's all right. I don't mind the excuse to get off the ship for a bit. Maybe I'll hit one of the malls afterward—if you don't mind falsifying the meeting records so it looks like it went on for an extra hour."*

Dayan laughed. *"Least I could ..."*

The two men moved out of sight, and Mirra lost the audio. She hesitated, sitting on the edge of the bed in her hotel room. The conversation had been innocuous. It could have been a cover, in case anyone was listening; in that case, this Hadrian might be involved in the conspiracy as well. Or it might have been genuine, in which case the naval officer's visit might actually be official. Surely Dayan, if he *was* involved in the conspiracy at all, must sometimes engage in legitimate operations.

But something in the way the two men had been talking, particularly in the way the Navy captain had carried himself, told Mirra there was a third option. That her shot at some answers had finally come.

She was on her feet and hustling out of the hotel in seconds, fast as she could without setting off station security's attention algorithms. She'd have one opportunity to do what she needed to do, and she wasn't about to miss it.

Dayan and Hadrian came into view as she rounded the station's central column less than a minute later. They were heading, as she'd expected, to the offices Dayan and his men used. Based on their relative speeds, she would pass by them maybe twenty seconds before they reached the doors.

She glanced at Hadrian, without looking at Dayan, then quickly looked away. He hadn't noticed her yet. He was actually quite handsome, she realized, but in the conventional sort of way that she found completely unappealing. Like a composite they might feature in a Navy recruitment ad. Still, it would make it easier for her to execute her plan without arousing suspicion.

Mirra corrected her path so that she would pass the duo on Hadrian's side, then made as if she was paying attention to one of the flashing personalized holo-advertisements up ahead of her. At the last moment, she used her peripheral vision to guide her into him, careful not to pull her step so that the impact would seem genuinely accidental.

"Oh!" she said, briefly gripping his upper arm as they collided. "Sorry!"

Hadrian smiled easily back at her. "Quite all right."

His striking green eyes lingered on hers for a moment, then each continued on their way. Dayan had barely glanced at her. As she was walking away, she looked back, pointedly studying his body with her brief glance as if she were checking him out. Hopefully, that would provide a suitable justification for the station AIs to drop the attention on her that the collision had doubtless attracted.

Hopefully, they would also not detect the second microdot she had placed on his uniform sleeve, just under his left arm. Either way, she'd wait to remote activate it until she was fairly certain the two men would be inside the offices, preferably after they'd sat down to talk. That should get it past any scanners keyed to detect active listening devices.

The first microdot she'd placed used a tightbeam graviton pulse transmitter to send her information. Given that it harnessed gravitons from the station's own simulated gravity field and operated on low power, it was nearly impossible to detect from the station's background noise unless an analyst knew right where to look. But inside the military offices, such a signal would be detected almost immediately, and in any case was likely to be jammed by a blanket transmission dampening field.

So Mirra had placed her one QEC-based microdot, entangled directly to her neural implant, on Hadrian. Like all entanglement-based communicators it was untraceable and unjammable, but given its minute size it also had a limited bandwidth before it used up all its entangled particles. She'd only be able to get audio from it, and only a few minutes' worth at best. All the more reason to wait to activate it until she was reasonably sure she would get something from it.

She picked the café nearest the offices, ordered a black coffee and the blandest looking pastry they had, and sat down as if she were simply people-watching, counting down the seconds in her head until she could do it for real.

FIFTEEN

Hadrian sipped the steaming coffee he'd been offered carefully but appreciatively. It was of a better quality than the standard-issue stuff brewed aboard *Belisarius*. Not up to the standard of his personal stash from his home planet Eos, or of Tsegaye's from Ethiopia, but not so far behind either. Certainly not acid enough that he wished he'd asked for sugar as well as cream.

"Thanks," he said as he took his seat. "Where's it from?"

Dayan sat on the opposite side of the desk, his back facing the entrance. The room was small, spare, its only adornments a hard-screen on one wall, and a dynamic art panel on the other. "No idea. Don't actually drink the stuff myself."

"I'll try not to hold that against you."

Dayan laughed, then clapped his hands lightly together. "So, Captain. I have to say I was surprised when your ship showed up here. More so when I got that flag. How do you think my berth fits into this investigation of yours?"

Hadrian took another sip. He'd known it would go this way, however pleasant Dayan seemed. He'd have to give up just about everything they'd found up to this point, and only then hope that Dayan would return the favor. Acceptance of that fate kept his own demeanor equally pleasant.

"There've been a number of bombings on Byas recently. That's nothing new, but the composition of the bombs is. We detected a compound called ignicite in several of them. I'd never heard of it, but fortunately my astro advisor had. We proceeded to the ignicite research facility in CAS 47988, suspecting that hostile actors might have infiltrated the system and stolen it right from under us, then smuggled it into Byas for use as an untraceable explosive."

Dayan listened intently, showing no surprise at any of the revelations. "I see. And our berth?"

Make me say it, will you? "The head of research there informed us that about two weeks ago, a military craft—likely ISOC—arrived in the system, retrieved some samples of ignicite, and left. Its IFF ping showed that it departed from Harrington's Haven, Military Berth 17-A."

"Of course." Now, Dayan showed a little disappointment. Perhaps the failure to scrub the departure point from the craft *had* been a lapse in protocol. "Well, Captain, as I mentioned before, I am involved in a highly classified operation here. But based on what you've already discovered, there are certain things I can read you into. I will, however, have to ask that anything we discuss here remains between us and your superior officers."

Like I'm not gonna tell Arno. "Not a problem."

"For starters, as you probably already guessed, I'm not reg force PAC. I'm with Special Warfare. Over the last few months in our operations on Pyria, we've been encountering bombs that had somehow been smuggled into high-security areas with full-spectrum explosives detection. That sound familiar?"

Hadrian nodded. "One of them tried to take me and the ICRA administrator out in the middle of a capital district."

"You're lucky it missed you. We took some VIP losses before

we figured out the ignicite connection. Your astro officer deserves some kind of science medal for that."

Hadrian chuckled at the thought of pinning a medal on the awkward young ensign's chest, though he agreed with the sentiment.

"We collated data with our other units on Sukat," Dayan continued. "Turns out ignicite bombs are being used there too. Like you, we also determined that the most likely source was 47988, hence the mission I dispatched there to collect samples for our own study."

"Turn up anything?"

"Nothing useful yet, except better detection protocols."

Hadrian sipped his coffee again; the thermal mug was doing an admirable job of keeping it hot. "Speaking of which—"

"I do apologize," Dayan interjected. "If it had been up to me, we'd have sent out a warning to theater and system commands as soon as we figured out what was going on. But ..."

"Orders," Hadrian said.

"Orders. ISOC thought we'd have a better chance of catching the machine bastards in the act if we kept knowledge of it quiet."

So they think it's the Ciphers too. Not that there are many other options. "Turn up anything on *that* score yet?"

"I'm afraid I'm not at liberty to say. However, I can tell you that we've deployed a covert detection system to 47988. You can rest assured that the next time the Ciphers, or whoever it is, come back for another grab, we'll stop them."

Hadrian didn't need to ask what "stop them" meant. He could only hope that the machines had as little interest in another general war as the Compact did. *Then one of their black ops missions being quietly taken out by one of ours might not kick the whole thing off.* "I suppose you've got everything handled, then?"

"We do." Dayan stood. "Hopefully this doesn't make your little excursion feel like a waste of time."

"There's something you could do to help with that."

"Name it."

"Since I'm read into this operation now," Hadrian said, standing as well, "maybe you could see your way to passing along any intel you come across regarding future attacks on Byas? And those detection protocols you mentioned, of course."

"I don't see why not. I'll pass the request up the chain as soon as we're done here."

"Thanks. And for the coffee," Hadrian said. Then he simply stood there, looking down at the still-hot mug. He felt his brow knitting.

"Something wrong?" Dayan asked.

Hadrian shook his head … then ignored the voice inside it telling him to leave things alone. "I guess I do have another question."

"Shoot."

"You said you have covert observation set up in 47988?"

"That's right."

"Then why were you surprised when we showed up?"

Dayan smiled. "What do you mean?"

"Well, you would've seen us arrive there, from Byas, then head here. I'd have figured you'd put two and two together."

Dayan nodded silently for a moment. "We did. Actually, I'm afraid the surprise was … a bit of a put-on. In case it turned out you knew less than we theorized you might."

"Of course," Hadrian said. "Cloak-and-dagger, right?"

"Exactly."

Lying.

Hadrian tried and failed to push the thought from his mind. His hackles were up. He couldn't grasp the significance of it, but something felt ineffably wrong.

Did they really "forget" to scrub the launch-point data from their IFF? And since when do ISOC ships send standard IFF pings anyway?

He shook his head. It was probably nothing, just special forces–induced paranoia. And even if it wasn't, he wasn't going to get anywhere talking to the smiling major about it. "Anyway. Thanks for the debrief, Major."

"My pleasure. You know"—Dayan put up his hand, and Hadrian paused in the process of rounding the desk—"my CO's pretty on the ball with this op. I can run that request up for you right now, probably get a response within a couple minutes. Maybe get her to release some extra intel in the bargain. As thanks for your cooperation."

"Oh," Hadrian said, surprised. "Uh. Sure, that'd be great."

"Perfect. It won't take a minute, if you want to just wait here."

The hackles rose again. "Actually. I should be getting back to my ship. I know I was talking about that shopping break, but I don't want to make my XO jealous."

"Of course." Dayan's smile returned, but didn't quite reach his eyes this time. "But really, it'll just be a few minutes. If you want to sit down, enjoy your coffee."

The major's hand twitched, and something in the room changed. Hadrian might not have noticed, if he hadn't been about to send a signal back to *Belisarius*. Except that now, he couldn't. It gave him a moment's pause. He was using the direct QEC circuit, and everyone knew those transmissions couldn't be jammed or intercepted.

But the devices that sent them *could* be disrupted locally by a powerful enough EM field, specifically attuned to dampen communications tech. Like the one it seemed Dayan had just activated.

Hadrian's hands tightened. "What the hell are you doing?"

"Sit down, Captain." The smile was completely dead now.

"You first."

Dayan sighed and hung his head. "Okay."

The door behind the major opened. Two men in black

uniforms entered—hard men with killers' eyes. Special operators. Hadrian froze.

"Take him," Dayan said tiredly, waving them forward.

The two operators headed for Hadrian, each rounding a different side of the table. He had nowhere to go except over it, right into Dayan's waiting arms. For a moment, he tried to convince himself that this was all a mistake. He'd stumbled into some top secret operation. He'd be taken away and questioned, and once everything was cleared up he'd be released. Resisting would only make things worse.

Then the man on the right reached out for him.

Hell with that.

Hadrian flipped the lid off his coffee and threw it into the operator's face. It wasn't scalding, but it was hot enough. The man yelled in surprise and pain and threw his hands up over his eyes. At the same time, the other operator quickened his pace, coming around the left side of the table.

Hadrian spun around and threw all his weight into a scything right hook, catching the surprised man in the bridge of the nose and staggering him. He followed up with a series of kidney blows and then landed an uppercut square on the burly bastard's chin, like he was back in the ring. The operator's head snapped back, and he slammed into the wall and slid down it, the whites of his eyes showing.

By that time, the first operator had recovered. He threw his arms around Hadrian from behind, trying to get him in a choke hold while Dayan, snarling with anger, came over the table. Hadrian pulled his legs up and kicked at the table, sending Dayan tumbling, and pushing him and the operator holding him back into the wall.

Once they were pressed against it, Hadrian slammed his heel down into the bridge of the operator's foot. The man held his scream, but it gave Hadrian an inch of breathing space. He used it to yank away and elbow the big man in the face, again and again. He felt teeth and cartilage crack under the blows, and ignored the stabbing pain in his elbow as he pulled out of the operator's grip and hauled back his left hand for a knockout punch.

It never fell. His left arm was hooked at the elbow and yanked back. Before he could react, Dayan's fist slammed down into his solar plexus. In an instant, he felt like he was dying. There was no breath in his lungs, and he wheezed desperately for air, all other concerns made irrelevant by his instinct to breathe.

Dayan took advantage to lever him down onto the table, face-first. He barely felt the pain of the blow, his chest and lungs were in such agony.

"Get the injector!" Dayan yelled. Then he kicked at the operator who'd taken the uppercut. "Get up, for fuck's sake!"

The dazed operator rose shakily to his feet. The other was cursing through what sounded like a splintered nose and broken teeth. Some part of Hadrian was still conscious enough to feel grim satisfaction at that.

"Come on!" Dayan shouted.

Hadrian tapped a new reserve of strength when the broken-faced operator came into view holding a medical injector and smiling bloodily down at him. He heaved away from the table, vowing to struggle to the last, however futile that might be.

Utterly, it proved. Dayan pressed him back down with little effort. "Could have done this the easy way, Captain. But you just had to—"

The door opened. Hadrian heard it, but couldn't see it. The operator with the injector spun toward it, holding it up like a weapon. Clearly they hadn't been expecting more guests at this party.

Dayan confirmed that a moment later when he said, "Who the fuck are you?"

The new guest's answer was the searing sound and blue-red

light of a maser pistol firing. Something heavy toppled to the floor behind Hadrian. Injector-operator charged at the door and out of Hadrian's view while the pistol was still firing. The maser beam cut off, replaced by the sounds of a brief and violent struggle. This ended with the cracking of bone, a man's agonized scream, and a slicing sound, followed by a spray of arterial blood splattering across the table, droplets of it warm and repulsive on Hadrian's cheek.

At the same moment, he was hauled to his feet, one arm held painfully up, the other pinned back. The world spun. He felt Dayan's hot, anxious breath on the back of his neck. The world resolved slowly. Someone was standing in the doorway, pointing something at him. When Dayan yelled, the voice was sharp and loud in Hadrian's right ear.

"Stand down, or I swear—"

The maser fired again, a burst of less than a second. Dayan went limp and crumpled like a doll. Hadrian barely managed to avoid falling with him by falling *forward* and stopping himself on the table. He stayed like that, breathing heavily, for a few seconds, waiting for a killing shot to come.

When it didn't, he looked up.

The woman who'd bumped into him on the promenade was standing there, incongruously dressed in a colorful, quasi-revealing civilian outfit. She was tall, about his height; her skin had a grayish tint, and she had the pronounced facial features of a Free Worlder with extensive military cybernetics. Her eyes were flecked with amethyst, contrasting with her tightly pulled black hair.

She had a bloodied knife in one hand, and a pistol pointed square at his head in the other. And she asked the question he wanted to.

"Who are you?"

SIXTEEN

Mirra started moving before the feed was cut.

She clued in that Hadrian was about to get himself black-bagged the moment he asked about the covert observation post. Dayan had obviously been lying to get the captain to drop the issue and go home. In truth, Mirra was surprised Hadrian had figured it out, even belatedly. Fleetie officers usually didn't have the minds for that kind of thing. Or for much else, in Mirra's experience.

At that point, she had two options. Wait for the unfortunate captain to be killed or sedated, then hope Dayan and his cronies would move him so she could follow them—perhaps to someone higher up the chain of this conspiracy. Or, she could blow her cover and intervene, saving Hadrian from whatever fate awaited him, and hoping against hope that she might capture Dayan alive. Or, at the very least, that the Navy captain might know more than he was letting on.

Logically, she should have chosen the first option. Even as she hustled down the promenade, she couldn't say why she hadn't.

Maybe it had been something in Hadrian's eyes, or his voice. Or she'd just wanted a little more visceral payback.

Maybe both.

In any case, she was here now, the maser pistol she'd stolen off the phony receptionist in the front of the offices pointed at the captain's head. He was breathing hard and painfully, from some kind of sternum injury. By the looks of the other three men in the room—or what was left of them—he'd put up a much better fight than she'd have guessed he would. Based on when the transmission had been cut off, she'd expected that he'd be unconscious by now. If he was alive at all. That he wasn't simplified matters, as far as questioning him went.

His green eyes twitched at her question. "Captain Ian Hadrian—"

"I can read your ID. Who are you *really*?"

Hadrian shrugged with his raised hands. "Just what it says on the box."

He showed no signs of deception that her implants could detect. She hadn't really expected him to; it was fairly obvious now he wasn't a part of this conspiracy, whatever it was. Not knowingly. "And what are you doing here?"

Hadrian let out a short breath, frustrated, like he was about to explain something he already had a dozen times. Mirra cut him off. "I heard Dayan's explanation about the bombs. Why are you on *Haven*?"

"You were listening?" Hadrian asked, then his eyes slackened. "When you bumped into me, on the promenade?"

Mirra nodded.

"The system he mentioned," he said. "The research station there said two weeks ago, a military ship showed up to take samples of the ignicite. They sounded like ISOC. Their IFF ping to the station said they'd come from here."

"Impossible," Mirra said. "An ISOC ship would never log that data in its IFF system in the first place. Is that really what the researchers told you?"

"Why would I lie about that?"

"If you were involved."

Hadrian gestured around the bloody, corpse-strewn room.

"All that means is that you got too close to something," Mirra said. "It doesn't mean you're innocent in this."

Hadrian sighed. "Yes. That's really what she told me."

"Did she provide you the data from the station logs?"

"Yes."

"Then there are two options. They set *her* up. She set *you* up."

"That's great," Hadrian said. "Now that we know we're on the same side, you wanna stop pointing that thing at me?"

"How do you know we're on the same side?"

Hadrian's eye twitched. "I guess I don't. You still haven't told me who *you* are."

Mirra glanced at the pistol, then lowered it and tucked it into the back of her waistband, under her jacket. She kept the knife in her other hand. "Sorăna Mirra. Commander, LDRG."

Hadrian lowered his hands, though at the mention of her unit, the comfort the answer brought him seemed to evaporate. "Nice to meet you. And what brought *you* here, Commander?"

Part of her wanted to unburden herself. The other remembered what had happened the last time she'd talked about her team to a seemingly sympathetic officer. "It's personal."

Hadrian glanced at the bodies decorating the room.

"What's your ship?" Mirra asked.

"Belisarius."

The name was familiar. "Battlecruiser?"

"Yeah," Hadrian said. He seemed confused that she recognized the name.

"You should get back to it." Mirra nodded at Dayan's semidecapitated body. "Before his superiors find out what happened and take steps."

It was a moment before Hadrian seemed to realize what "take steps" meant. His eyes widened. "Who else is involved in this?"

"I don't know." Now, Mirra wiped her knife blade off on the man with the injector, then sheathed it. "That's what I came here to find out. And since I blew my only lead saving *you*, you'd best not waste it by waiting around here to get killed."

She spun on her heel and headed back out into the main area of the office.

"Wait." Hadrian followed her out. She heard him slow when he left the room, likely seeing the bodies of the other two men she'd left in the reception area. "Where will you go now?"

Mirra sighed, started searching the bodies for any useful items. "Two options. Get out of this office, wait for the suppression field to come down, then see who shows up to investigate once they realize what's happened. Disadvantage of that, I have to wait around here, and legitimate security might show up before more conspirators can.

"Otherwise ..." She looked over a personal device in the "receptionist's" pocket, then tossed it. "Go to this research station you mentioned, and see who set up who. If I can get off *this* station before my cover's blown."

"I can help you with that."

Mirra looked up at him. "That wouldn't be wise."

"Why not?" Hadrian stepped over to her. "Look. This is the second time in a week someone's tried to kill me. Now you're telling me they might come after my ship. I'm not about to walk away from that. What I *am* gonna do is go back to that research station and get some goddamn answers."

Hadrian pointed at her. "*You* obviously know more than you're telling me. I need more information, you need a ride, and we're headed to the same place."

He opened the hand pointed at her, held it in place. Mirra stared at it for a moment, then up at him. *No signs of deception.*

That wasn't what made her mind up. Again, she wasn't sure what did, even as she took the outstretched hand and used it to pull herself up.

SEVENTEEN

"Ian, what happened down there, we lost ... Who's this?"

The officer waiting for them on the hangar deck was Hadrian's XO, Mirra assumed from his uniform. His dark skin was lined with less age even than Hadrian's, and the stubble on his cheeks did little to offset his soft features. But his deep brown eyes betrayed a thoughtful intelligence. Right now, they were regarding Mirra with understandable suspicion.

"Oh, this is Sarah," Hadrian said, putting an arm around her shoulder. She made herself smile in response. "Friend of mine from the academy. Would you believe it, haven't seen each other in thirteen years, and we just run into each other down there. Sarah, this is my XO, Arno Tsegaye."

"Pleasure," Mirra said, shaking Tsegaye's hand.

"Yeah," Tsegaye said. "That's something."

"Isn't it?" Hadrian gestured for the exit, and guided Mirra toward it. Tsegaye reluctantly turned to keep up. "Bella, I want you to cut the ship off from all external networks immediately."

"Confirm, Captain," the ship replied. "*All* networks?"

"Confirmed. Emergency authorization Hadrian Alpha."

"Yes, Captain. Emergency network severance in progress."

Tsegaye grabbed Hadrian's arm. "Ian, what the hell is—"

"Not now."

The ratings working the hangar deck watched them leave, clearly not buying the "old friends" routine. Mirra didn't pay them much mind. She had known the ruse wouldn't work, but it might prevent any uncomfortable questions being asked, at least for a while.

"Network severance complete," the ship reported.

"Conn, this is the captain," Hadrian said as the trio moved into the corridor. "Set course back for CAS 47988, maximum Stardrive velocity, immediate execution."

A woman's voice responded after a short pause. *"Roger that, Captain, laying in course and securing for Stardrive."*

At least they're prepared to follow his orders, Mirra thought. *Without question, save for the XO. But then, that's the XO's job.* Memories of Alistair King stabbed at her heart.

The ship seemed to be in reasonably good condition as well. *Belisarius* was a *Starbird*-class battlecruiser, as she'd guessed from the name. She'd caught a glimpse of it in the shuttle windows as they'd ridden away from Haven, studied it for any irregularities or identifying features. But to her eyes it looked much like any other *Starbird*: the large, long midsection with its quad engines to the aft; the swept-back wing structures, which if she recalled housed heat radiators and other devices best kept away from the crew compartments; and the long neck jutting out to the fore, which formed the linear accelerator portion of the ship's main gun. A graceful, powerful looking ship. She'd always liked the design, but it didn't tell her much about the vessel itself.

Inside, the ratings were going about their duties, and there were no obvious breaches of protocol in evidence—not that Mirra was intimately familiar with naval protocols. Despite the Naval Infantry Corps technically being a part of the Navy, she spent little time aboard their ships or installations. Her team's deployments had left them almost entirely in the isolated domain of Interstellar Special Operations Command.

"We're going to my stateroom," Hadrian said to Tsegaye. "I want the entire senior staff there as soon as we're underway and Bella's certain we're not being tracked."

"All stations, secure for Stardrive," the ship announced. "Repeat, all stations, secure for Stardrive."

"Tracked by *who*?"

Hadrian stopped for a moment. "Arno, as soon as we're underway. I promise you."

Tsegaye looked between Hadrian and Mirra. "Fine."

Hadrian clapped him on the arm and hustled on, keeping one hand on the wall-mounted rail. "Hope you don't mind zero-g."

"I'm a marine," Mirra said, not bothering to hide her pique.

When the ship's simulated gravity deactivated, neither of them missed a pace, stabilizing themselves on the handrails in the wall and ceiling and continuing on with something approaching grace until they reached Hadrian's stateroom.

Which was not what Mirra had expected. Her own squadron commander's office on the Fort was spartan in the extreme, but this was in large part because she almost never used it. The shore-based officers whose staterooms she had spent time in tended to also favor a minimalist, modernist style—save for the marines, who always seemed to have a penchant for the traditional.

Hadrian's style skewed heavily in that direction. The lights in the stateroom came up as they entered, revealing a preponderance of wooden furniture: the desk in the back of the room, next to a simulated window; several chairs, upholstered with what looked like leather; and two full-size bookcases taking up one entire wall. Mirra couldn't tell whether the volumes they bore were genuine, held in place by some unseen mechanism, or holographic. Somehow, she doubted the latter.

The walls and deck were still cool military metal, of course, but the earth-toned furniture and decorations—including what appeared to be an honest-to-god *painting* of a battlecruiser in flight —were prevented from clashing with it by the warm quality of the lighting. The scene gave Mirra pause, during which she realized she had never been in a naval captain's offices before. Perhaps they were all so charmingly anachronistic.

This, too, she doubted.

"Drink?" Hadrian said, floating over to a bar across from the sim-window.

Mirra floated over to the bookcases to test her theory. She spoke louder to match the rising Shepard tone of the ship's engines charging for Stardrive. "Depends."

"Bourbon."

Mirra glanced back. There was no label on the bottle Hadrian had retrieved, but the liquid floating within was a rich color. She nodded. The captain attached one of the two zero-g glasses in his other hand to the spout of the bottle, twisted to form a latch. The cup vacuumed in an acceptable measure of the bourbon, then detached.

Hadrian lightly tossed the filled cup across the room to her and repeated the process for himself. She caught the slowly tumbling glass in one hand and raised it to her lips as she examined one of the books: *The Gathering Storm*, the first in a six-volume series on Earth's Second World War. The author's name was Churchill; if she recalled correctly, he had been one of the national leaders in that conflict. All six seemed real enough. Like the bourbon tasted. She allowed herself to enjoy the latter for a moment. She'd needed a good drink since …

"Doesn't taste as good in zero-g," Hadrian said, rescuing her from an unwelcome reverie. "Must be the suction."

He rubbed his injured sternum, staring through the glass. He looked shaken. Probably just now coming down from what happened on the station. He had put up a good fight against his assailants, which meant he must have had training, but Mirra would bet anything it was the first time he'd ever had to do it for real. She sympathized, but the look in his eyes didn't fill her with confidence.

Hadrian seemed to find himself again once the rising tone of the engines stopped, indicating by its absence that the ship had started its FTL jump sequence. "When the staff gets here, I'm going to ask you to repeat what you told me on the shuttle. And then some. It's up to you if you want to tell them, but I think it'd be best if we all know what we're getting into."

"You trust them?" Mirra asked.

"I have to. Whatever we do next, we won't be able to do it alone."

I *might have,* Mirra thought. But this was the path she'd chosen, and it did no good to question that now. Fortunately she was spared that, too, when *Belisarius*'s senior officers started arriving after only a minute's awkward silence.

"Sorry for the short notice," Hadrian said once the officers had all arrived, in quick succession. "And for the secrecy, but that'll all make sense in a minute."

He turned to Mirra, then started introducing each of his officers in turn. "You already met Arno. This is *Belisarius*'s chief engineer, Commander Tsung Wei."

Tsung was a gruff, graying man with a hard, square jaw, and suspicious eyes that told Mirra he'd been through the gauntlet. His uniform sleeves were rolled up, and there were smudges on his collar and forearms. He greeted her with a nod, those suspicious eyes already probing hers for answers.

"This is our TacOps chief, Nasreen Hassani."

The young lieutenant gave Mirra a wide and seemingly genuine smile. She was strikingly beautiful, with an aquiline nose, thick but tidy eyebrows, and curled brown hair kept in a loose tail in accordance with regulations. Her almond, hazel eyes radiated promise. Mirra felt sorry for her.

"Our chief ECWO, Lieutenant Zevran."

Mirra had of course noticed the Citizen as soon as he'd entered the stateroom. Like most of his people, he was tall, with green-tinted skin and eyes, which were hypnotically large. Unlike most UCC, even military personnel, his light brown hair was buzzed short. But it was his bearing that most set him apart from the few other Citizens Mirra had known. Even floating in zero-g, he carried himself like a man exhausted. His large eyes told a story beyond simple tiredness; he looked on Mirra, and the world, like it had already failed him.

"And this is our chief surgeon, Doctor Stanisław Park."

"Pleasure to meet you," the doctor said with a broad smile, the only one to both speak to her and reach out across the room to shake her hand. He was a Free Worlder, Mirra saw, by his accent likely from Jayu. He was thin, with gray touching his black-brown hair at the temples. His narrow, blue eyes betrayed not a hint of guile.

"This," Hadrian said, turning once again to his officers, "is Commander Sorăna Mirra. LDRG."

Tsegaye frowned. "I thought you were down there meeting Special Warfare?"

"I was," Hadrian said. "Until they tried to kill me."

"What?" Hassani blurted out. The rest of the officers seemed stunned into silence.

"Now you see why I offered you all a drink," Hadrian said. "I'll let the commander tell her side of it."

Mirra scanned the strange faces floating before her—anxious, disbelieving, distrustful. Her instincts told her to keep her mouth shut.

You made your choice.

She began sharply, without preamble. "A few weeks ago, my

team was on an operation in Kyran space. We were compromised and ambushed. My entire team was either killed or captured. I alone escaped and returned to our rendezvous point."

She glanced at Hadrian. "Once there, like your captain, I was attacked. By my own recovery team. I managed to eliminate them and seize their ship. Its navigation logs showed it launched from Harrington's Haven, Military Berth 17-A. I proceeded there under cover, and set up a surveillance, hoping to discover who sold my team out, and why."

"Is it possible," the Citizen, Zevran, said, "that your team was simply ambushed by the *Kyrans*?"

Mirra stared hard at him. "I've been fighting the Kyrans for twenty-five years. They're not capable of doing what they did that night on their own. Someone told them we'd be there, and gave them the ability to penetrate our stealth and comms. And when I met with my recovery team, *they* fired first."

Zevran simply nodded, apparently unmoved by her best efforts at quiet intimidation.

"Wait a minute." Hassani raised her hand; her face was constricted. "You're saying ISOC's been infiltrated? Are these … Cipher simulants?"

"No," she said.

The thought had of course occurred to her. Especially if she was right that what happened on Baton had led directly to all of this. But somehow she doubted it. And in any case, there were certain things she wasn't ready to share with these people.

"We can't be certain," Hadrian corrected her. She gave no outward sign of her displeasure. "But so far, everyone we've encountered that's in on this thing has been legit. If they *were* simulants, they'd likely been in place for a very long time. Years."

"Jesus Christ," Tsegaye said. For a moment, he and Hadrian shared a knowing, worried look.

Mirra filed that away. "In any case, I observed Major Dayan

and his men for five days. Once your captain arrived, and I determined they were planning to make a move against him, I intervened."

"Meaning, she saved my ass," Hadrian said, "and blew her only lead in the process. Least I could do to return the favor is give her a new one."

"That's why we're heading back to the ignicite station?" Hassani asked.

Hadrian nodded. "Near as we can figure, the data we got from Doctor Narin was falsified. Either by Dayan, or Narin herself."

"But why?" Doctor Park asked. "Why lead us directly to them?"

Commander Tsung scoffed. "ISOC assholes love their fucking games. No offense."

Mirra dipped her head slightly in response.

"Before they jumped me," Hadrian said, "Dayan told me ISOC knew all about the ignicite, *and* its source, and had the situation under control. Best guess, they were hoping we'd buy that story and drop our investigation."

"Backup plan," Tsung added, "kill you, then take *us* out."

Park's eyes widened. "Destroy *Belisarius*? Surely you can't be serious."

"If they wanted to keep this secret—whatever it is—badly enough?" Tsegaye shrugged. "She's an older ship. Accidents happen."

Tsung glared at him. "Not on *Bella*."

"Would anyone else know that?" Tsegaye countered.

Tsung crossed his arms and grumbled.

"What secret could they *possibly* want to keep badly enough that they'd kill a Navy captain *and* a marine spec-ops team?" Hassani asked, bright eyes suddenly sunken. "Let alone trying to—"

"I don't know why my team was targeted," Mirra answered, too defensive. She felt she couldn't just leave it at that. *Half-truths make the best lies.* "Perhaps we saw something on a previous operation we weren't meant to. What that might have been, I have no idea."

Hadrian saved her from any potential follow-up questions. "One thing's certain: They already knew about the ignicite bombs. If I was to guess, I'd say they're the ones who've been smuggling them in."

"Based on what?" Zevran asked.

"A hunch." Another look between Hadrian and Tsegaye. "To what end, I don't know. One way or another, Doctor Narin's our best shot at finding some answers. Either she's involved in this, or there might be some information in that system that points us in the right direction. As of now, that's our mission priority."

"Do we report this to Admiral Singh?" Hassani asked.

"We don't know who's involved," Mirra said.

"Singh isn't." Hadrian gave her a look. "But either way, until we know how deep this thing goes, I don't want any connection to the networks, or any communications sent that have to pass through the Hub."

Mirra could see the fear caused by that realization in a few of the officers' faces. Entanglement-based communications were, on an individual level, a closed system. A QEC device was only capable of communicating directly with its entangled pair. That meant that in order to facilitate large-scale, interstellar FTL communications, a node-based hub system needed to be used. For a ship like *Belisarius* to communicate with its fleet HQ in a different star system, the transmission needed to be sent from the ship's QEC to its entangled pair in the Naval Communications Hub on Taranis; the Hub would then relay the communication through its internal network to the Hub-based QEC entangled with the relevant fleet HQ, which would then receive the message.

This *also* meant that, if the Hub were to be physically compromised, all those previously secure, uninterruptible communications might suddenly be blocked, redirected, or read by a hostile actor. Such a thing was unthinkable, and had never occurred in the history of the Compact. The Naval Hub, and its counterparts for the other services and the government, were the most securely guarded systems in the galaxy. But then, the Compact had never worried about protecting them from their own special forces.

"Look," Hadrian said. "I know this is a lot to take in. Believe me, I'm still coming to grips with it myself. But this is where we stand. Right now, we're the only ones that know about this conspiracy. It's up to us to untangle it, at least a little further, until we can get word up our chain of command *securely*. I know I can count on all of you to do what needs to be done. Whatever that might be."

Hadrian gave that a moment to land, then added, "Anybody want that drink *now*?"

The officers all smiled or chuckled, save Zevran, who seemed deep in thought. Mirra lowered her gaze.

"Maybe later," Hadrian said. "Okay. It's a half day ship's time back to the research station. I want everyone to finish up whatever's on their docket, then get some *rest*. I need my A-team in the CIC when we arrive at that station. Arno, fiddle with the watch schedule to make sure that happens."

"On it."

"All right. Any questions? Obviously, but any that need answering *now*? No? Good. Dismissed. Arno, hang back a minute."

"Right, Ian."

Mirra watched the officers float from the room. Only Zevran and Park gave her parting looks, entirely different in character.

"Thank you, Commander," Hadrian said once they were gone. "That can't have been easy."

"Quite all right," Mirra said.

"Our marine commander's quarters are empty. His possessions were removed a few days ago. You can stay in there, or if you're uncomfortable with that, there are guest—"

"The marine quarters will be fine. Thank you." She finished the bourbon that was left in her glass, then passed it to Hadrian. "And thank you for the drink. I'll make my way to the quarters now."

Hadrian nodded. "Bella'll show you the way. If you don't mind, I'd like you in the CIC when we get there as well."

"Of course."

I wouldn't miss it.

⁕

TRUE TO FORM, Tsegaye waited to take a drink—a big one—until everyone else had left. "Well. She's … interesting."

"Yeah." Hadrian took a suctioned sip of his second drink. "Put it this way, when she busted into that room, I didn't think she was there to *save* me."

Tsegaye shook his head. "LDRG … Special Warfare …"

"You thinking about Pyria *now*?"

"No kidding." Tsegaye floated over to the *Starbird* painting. "You don't think … I mean, you said if these are sims, they've probably been in place for years. What if it was *them*?"

Hadrian blew out a breath. "I almost hope it was. That'd tie everything up real nice, wouldn't it?"

Tsegaye's gaze fell. "I guess we're not that lucky."

"I wouldn't count on it."

But he *did* hope. Even as the bitter memories came back to him, he hoped.

EIGHTEEN

Hadrian couldn't sleep.

He was only surprised it had taken so long for the dreams to come to him, with everything that had happened. They were the same one's he'd had for a few months after the transfer, then every once in a while since. Dreams of fire, consuming, revealing. Of the screams he hadn't heard, and the laughter he had, of dead eyes and burned faces staring at him in silent judgment. Only this time, Mirra was there. Her voice, one of those laughing; her face, one of those scarred and judging.

He tried to keep up the charade until 0300 ship's time. Then he released the webbing on his bed and floated over to his dresser to change. A coffee-infused protein supplement and a short trip through the corridors later, he was in the officers' gym, alone. Since the ship was still under Stardrive, the gym was configured for zero-g. That made it a little more difficult for him to do his favored midnight exercise, but he could still manage.

After a warm-up and a little time on the resistance cycle, he strapped himself into the zero-g combat harness and started working the heavy bag. Naturally, it wasn't *heavy* at the moment, and the experience of throwing strikes with weightless limbs was different. But the equipment was able to compensate, and if one ever wanted to fight in zero or microgravity, one needed to get used to the feeling. Not that striking was the best way to fight in those environments, but Hadrian wasn't really here to train.

The faces of Dayan and his men flashed before Hadrian's eyes as he struck the bag. He tried to exorcise the images, and the feelings they conjured, with each hit.

What's the use?

Almost on cue, the hatch opened. Somehow Hadrian knew who would be drifting through it before he turned to look.

"Commander Mirra," he said. "Morning."

"Morning, Captain."

"Trouble sleeping too?"

"Not really." Mirra quickly scanned the equipment, then pushed herself off the doorframe toward the stretching harness. "I'd just gotten used to Haven time. As far as my body's concerned, it's oh-six hundred."

"Practically sleeping in, for a marine."

"Exactly."

Mirra hooked herself into the harness and started a personal warm-up routine. She was dressed in the full-body black skinsuit marines wore under their armor, which they also often trained in. She was well-muscled and wiry, rather than bulky like most marines Hadrian had shared a gym with. She had no obvious cybernetic enhancements—replacement limbs, that sort of thing—other than those her features made plain. Unlike many of her ISOC colleagues, particularly the Free Worlders, she seemed to prefer to take care of herself the old-fashioned way.

And she had no difficulty doing that, as Hadrian saw once she floated over to one of the resistance sets. She dialed it up to a setting Hadrian himself only rarely used, and started deadlifting with barely a sound of strain. Same when she transitioned to an overhead press.

"You ever box?" Hadrian asked once she finished a set.

She raised an eyebrow at him. "Pardon?"

"You know." Hadrian threw a couple punches. "Boxing."

Mirra looked almost sad, for a moment. "I've trained in unarmed combat. Not boxing, specifically."

"I used to compete." A few more strikes. "Just at the academy, but I enjoyed it."

"I understand it's popular in the Navy."

"Fought a few marines too. They were good."

"That stands to reason."

"Better than PAC guys."

"That *also* stands to reason."

Hadrian smiled. "I miss the ring, sometimes. Second favorite thing to do in SWOS."

"First being combat exercises?"

He turned to her, surprised. "How'd you know?"

"I read your service record before bed," Mirra said as she began another set. Hadrian couldn't tell whether to feel honored or violated. He shouldn't feel either, he supposed. "You seem to have had a knack for them."

More than a knack; he'd won the school-wide single-ship combat exercises all three years in a row, one of only five cadets in the history of Space Warfare Officer School to do so. And he'd been on the winning side of fleet-level exercises three-quarters of the time, due in no small part, his training officers said, to his own leadership and tactical initiative. The record had put him on the fast track to command and earned him a plum posting as gunnery officer on the cruiser *Kharkiv* for his final shipboard year of SWOS.

It was also a record he didn't like to talk about. Not anymore. True, he'd bragged about it with his classmates at the time, part of the atmosphere of friendly (and occasionally not-so-friendly) competition at the school. Afterward, though … it seemed trite to mention. That had been school. Games. Not reality. Something in the way Mirra had said it confirmed his distaste for discussing it.

"I enjoyed it, anyway." He threw a kick at the bag, floated back against the harness. It returned him to place. The bag didn't hit back. "Didn't do me much good, I guess. The boxing."

"You were up against three special forces assailants," Mirra said as she lifted, her voice tightening. "You had no chance. Considering that, you fought well."

"Thanks." Hadrian waited until she had finished her next set, then unhooked himself from his harness and floated over. "Speaking of which, I didn't properly thank you, for saving my life. I can't imagine it was an easy decision to go in there."

Mirra shrugged. "It was the logical choice. Surveilling Dayan had given me nothing for five days. You were my best chance at more intel."

"That's not what you said at the time," Hadrian said. Her brow knit. "You said you blew your only lead to save me. Even if it ended up taking you in the right direction, it didn't sound like you knew that'd happen."

Mirra considered silently for a few moments. Then she began another set. "I suppose I just had a hunch."

"Well, then. Thank you for saving my life on a hunch."

"Yes, sir," she said through an out-breath.

Hadrian floated silently before her for a moment, then pushed off to return to his exercise. Partway there, he grabbed the bar of another machine to stop himself. He hesitated to say what was on his mind, but ultimately, speaking won out. "We just met, so I might be misreading you, but … if I did something to offend you, I apologize."

Mirra finished her next set, then locked the exercise bar in place. She floated in her harness for a few seconds, seeming also to consider her words. "You're very familiar with your officers, Captain."

"I try to be." Hadrian waited for her to continue. When she didn't, her meaning became clearer. "I aim to create a collegial atmosphere. It's a legitimate command philosophy."

"For peacetime commanders, perhaps."

"You're concerned it won't hold up, if we get into combat?"

"I *know* that in war, it doesn't work. Commanders who try it find that out very quickly. Or, more often, they don't, and they get themselves and their people killed."

"That hasn't been my experience."

"War isn't an exercise, Captain."

That stung more than it should have. "Well, the war ended a long time ago."

"No, it didn't." Mirra finally looked at him, her eyes cold. "We just stopped calling it by its name."

Something about that rang painfully true for Hadrian. Memories of fire and unheard screams. *Still* ... "I know officers who have served in real combat that follow the same philosophy. Admiral Singh's one of them."

"Then he's become weak."

Hadrian shook his head. "You don't know him."

"I know this: Your officers are not your friends. You can ask your friends to do something unpleasant, and they'll do it because they like you. But you can't order your friends to their deaths."

"You *also* can't serve alongside people year after year and stay cool and detached the entire time." Hadrian waved at her. "Your team; you said it was together what, five, six years? You're telling me you never became familiar with any of them?"

"They're all dead."

Hadrian realized his mistake as he said it. He allowed the point to rest unchallenged, until Mirra turned her cold gaze away, started reconfiguring the resistance set.

"Okay," he said after a respectful pause. "You don't approve of the way I run my ship."

"It doesn't matter. It's your ship."

"Exactly."

Mirra turned back to him.

"I asked for your opinion," Hadrian said. "I'm not gonna complain that you gave it to me. But while you're onboard, you'll respect my command. Is that clear?"

"Perfectly," Mirra said without hesitation.

Hadrian nodded. It seemed the best understanding they could come to, at the moment. "Good. I was just finishing up. I'll leave you to it."

"Thank you, sir."

Hadrian toweled himself off and pushed off toward the exit as Mirra began a set of bar curls. He returned to his quarters under a cloud. He didn't know why the conflict should disturb him so much. Mirra was just a passenger on his ship, a temporary ally against ... whoever their enemy was. She was clearly going through her own struggle. Seemed like she had been for a long time.

It was the truth in what she said, he decided. He feared there was far more of it than he cared to admit.

NINETEEN

"All hands, prepare to secure from Stardrive. Secure from Stardrive, T-minus one minute."

Hadrian pushed off the HCI and floated over to strap himself into his acceleration seat. The ratings and section officers were already strapped into their own. Hadrian watched the point of bright, blue-shifted light in the center of deepest darkness on the viewer. One of the infinitesimal fragments of that light was their destination, and they were fast approaching it. The CIC was silent with anticipation.

"Deceleration in T-minus thirty seconds."

The main hatch on the upper deck opened. Hadrian didn't turn to see who might be entering so near to the deadline. Moments later, Mirra appeared beside him, floating into the guest acceleration seat and strapping herself in. She and Hadrian shared a curt, professional nod. They hadn't seen each other since their confrontation earlier that morning. In truth, Hadrian would prefer she not be here. But he'd wanted to retract her invitation less, and she might still be able to provide some useful insight, depending on how the situation developed.

"Deceleration in T-minus five seconds," Bella announced. "Four, three, two, one, mark."

The point of light on the main hardscreen expanded in an instant into a brilliant field of stars, one closer than the rest, the curve of a rocky world with a soupy atmosphere, and a tiny metallic mote reflecting all their light. A moment later, the feeling of weight returned, anchoring Hadrian to the deck of his ship once more.

"Secure from Stardrive."

Hadrian unclasped his restraints and rose from his seat, Tsegaye alongside him. The HCI projected a plot of the ignicite station in its orbit around the planet. "Full active scan, level three. Bella, raise Doctor Narin immediately."

Mirra appeared on the opposite side of the HCI a moment later. Hadrian kept his eyes on the plot.

"Passives show no unknown contacts in-system," Hassani reported. "Actives same, out to one million klicks."

"I have Doctor Narin on a voice-only channel, Captain."

Tsegaye raised an eyebrow. Hadrian shared the sentiment.

"Put her through."

"Captain Hadrian." Narin sounded surprised, but not suspiciously so. *"I didn't expect you back. Did our information prove useful?"*

"It may have, Doctor. In fact, I have some follow-up questions based on what we found on Haven. I'm hoping you can help us out just a little bit more."

"Of course, anything I can do. What do you need to know?"

"I'd prefer to come over to the station in person again. I'll be bringing a guest this time."

Mirra gave him a look. They hadn't discussed this.

"I'd be happy to host you again, Captain," Narin said. *"Unfortunately, we're having some technical issues at the moment."*

Hadrian's eyes darted up to the still-empty system plot, then to Hassani. She shook her head. "What sort of issues?"

"All sorts, it seems. We thought it was a software problem, but now we're concerned it may be some kind of virus. It's affecting our communications, our docking control systems, and our food processors. Maybe your engineers could be of some assistance?"

"Least we could do, Doctor." Hadrian snapped his fingers and pointed at the ECW station. Zevran nodded and got to work. "If we can figure out how to get over there without cutting through your hull, that is."

Narin laughed. *"I would rather avoid that."*

"Of course, if it *is* a software issue, maybe we could help you remotely. Can you give us access to your intranet?"

Hadrian glanced up at Zevran. He was still working away.

"I'll try, but with the issues we're having, it might be easier said than done."

Zevran finished, glanced back. *No sign of intrusion, no sign of faults,* he sent via text to Hadrian's implant.

"Can you give me a few minutes, Captain?"

"Of course. Take all the time you need." Hadrian swiped his fingers across his lips. Bella muted the channel. "Anything?"

"Still nothing," Hassani reported. "Out beyond twenty million klicks."

"Any local transmissions being sent?"

"Nothing, Captain," Zevran confirmed.

Hadrian leaned against the HCI but looked through the projection, at the hardscreen. The neutron star blazed brightly in the distance. The station twinkled like a star, and the planet churned below.

So peaceful.

At the thought, his hands clenched on the railing. A few more seconds ticked by before he spoke the decision he made in that moment. "Go full stealth."

At first, Tsegaye seemed not to have heard the softly spoken command. "Ian?"

"Now."

The tone in his voice snapped Tsegaye to. "Set stealth condition zero."

"Condition zero, aye," Zevran confirmed flatly. "All stealth systems to maximum."

"Sound general quarters," Hadrian said quietly. An instant later, an alarm began blaring.

"General quarters, general quarters," Bella announced. "All hands to battle stations. Set integrity condition alpha throughout the ship. Repeat, all hands to battle stations, integrity condition alpha, stealth condition zero."

Hadrian kept his hands on the railing, his eyes on the tactical projection, his face serious but relaxed. His heart was hammering so hard he could hear it. He struggled to keep his knuckles from turning white. He'd drilled general quarters hundreds of times, done it in combat exercises perhaps a hundred more. Though the sounds and procedures were all identical, this was different. He could feel it.

War isn't an exercise.

Despite himself, he glanced at Mirra. She was staring back at him, face unreadable.

"All hands report general quarters," Bella said. "Integrity condition alpha set, stealth condition zero active."

"Acknowledged," Hadrian said, and looked back up. The plot was still empty.

This better be for real.

*

MIRRA WATCHED HADRIAN take the ship to battle stations with surprise.

Not that she disagreed with the choice. Far from it; if anything, in his position she would have given the comparable order the moment they decelerated. She was surprised that he'd given it at all, and that his officers were carrying it out so calmly.

She supposed she wasn't giving Navy training enough credit. She had never paid much attention to the senior service's protocols and tactics, but what little she knew told her they drilled scenarios like these constantly. Of course, *this* was not the real test. What was to come would be.

As the minutes passed, she noted the tension among the CIC crew increasing. This was the hardest part of any engagement, in space or on the ground. From their apparent ages, she doubted any of them had seen real combat. The engineer, Tsung, likely had, and perhaps the doctor as well, in his own way. But they weren't here. And here was where skill and experience would make the most difference.

"Research station scanning for us with active sensors," Zevran reported. "No net penetration."

"Helm," Hadrian said, "set course zero-five-zero by two-zero-zero. Speed one quarter."

"Zero-five-zero by two-zero-zero, one quarter, aye."

The ship heaved slowly over. Mirra knew little about naval combat, but she knew they'd be operating on thrusters and inertia only while at full stealth. Firing up the ship's main engines would generate far too much thermal and other forms of radiation for the stealth systems to hide. That was something marine insertion vessels had to worry about too.

"Think they were buying time?" Tsegaye asked.

Hadrian nodded. "That's what I'd have done."

"I hope you're wrong."

Hadrian's eye twitched. "So do I."

Show some resolution, Mirra thought, but she kept her mouth shut. She could do no good now. She'd promised to respect his command, and so she would.

"Give it an hour," Hadrian said. "If there's still nothing, we—"

"Contact!" Hassani shouted. All eyes snapped toward her. *Jittery.* "Bearing … two-seven-four by zero-six-one. Range, three-point-zero-two light-seconds."

"Inside the horizon," Tsegaye said. Hadrian nodded. Mirra raised an eyebrow.

"IFF?" Hadrian asked.

"The stealth horizon," Tsegaye, seeing her expression, explained in a low voice. "We went condition zero three minutes ago."

"Negative IFF," Zevran reported.

"Working on an ID," Hassani added.

"If the contact had come in more than three light-minutes out," Tsegaye continued, "they'd have picked us up, then seen us go stealth. But that light's already past them. As far as they know, we were never here."

"Unless they pick up something with an active scan?" Mirra asked.

"Or unless someone on that station tells on us." Hadrian nodded up to the plot. "TacOps, what's the holdup on that ID?"

"I don't know, sir, I—Contact's gone stealth!"

The contact, which had appeared moments ago on the tactical plot, winked out. In its place, the HCI generated a translucent yellow probability sphere.

"Shit," Hadrian muttered. Mirra held her questions. "They ping us?"

"Negative," Zevran said. "No local transmissions detected."

"Then the station called 'em by QEC," Tsegaye concluded.

"Shit," Hadrian repeated. "Bring up the bogey. Let's see who we're dealing with."

"What the hell?" Tsegaye said when the ship appeared on the tactical display.

Mirra's brow knit. The ship had a similar basic shape to the *Starbird,* with radiator-style wings and a neck-section. But the wings were shorter, forward swept, closer to the hull. The neck was similarly stubby, harder-angled. If it housed a linear accelerator, like *Belisarius,* then it looked to be between the two angular protrusions at the nose. The ship was smaller than *Belisarius,* maybe the size of a light cruiser. It seemed to bear some similarities to ICN design philosophies, but the preternaturally smooth hull surface gave the impression of Cipher technology. But then, Mirra wasn't the expert. The real cause for concern was that the naval officers seemed just as confused as she was.

"The profile's got no hits in the database," Hassani said. "Pre-stealth emission signature's giving me nothing. Bella's never seen anything like it, and neither have I."

"Armed?" Hadrian asked.

"Looks that way, sir."

Hadrian breathed out slow and walked around the HCI to look up at the viewer. Mirra let her curiosity get the better of her and leaned toward Tsegaye. "Can we try to hail them?"

Tsegaye shook his head. "Any communication attempt gives away our position. In a naval duel, whoever hits first wins. Once we're both under full stealth, we've only got two choices."

Mirra didn't need to be told what those choices were. In an instant, the severity of their situation clarified. She understood why Hadrian had reacted the way he had when the unknown had engaged stealth, even if she condemned the outburst.

Charging up their Stardrive to run would give away their position too. If they wanted to flee, they could only hope they managed to get away before the hostile scored a direct hit with his main gun.

If it was a hostile. There was still the possibility, however slight, that this was all a misunderstanding. That Doctor Narin really had been having technical difficulties. That the unknown was some new class of ICN ship, or a foreign civilian vessel, uninvolved with the conspiracy, here by happenstance. That they simply couldn't ID her because *Belisarius* was disconnected from the networks, where the exonerating data might be sitting patiently, waiting to be accessed.

But there was no way for them to know without putting *Belisarius* in mortal danger. If they tried to communicate; if they tried to reconnect to the networks, and the conspirators detected them; if they tried to run. In each case, they might be blasted from space, dying with all hands.

On the other hand, if they fought, and they'd gotten it wrong …

And the longer we wait, the harder that will become. Mirra's eyes bored into the back of Hadrian's head.

"Designate the unknown as hostile," the captain said at last. "Find me a target."

TWENTY

The decision appeared in vivid color on the tactical projection above the HCI. The unknown's probability bubble turned red; a matching bubble in translucent blue appeared around *Belisarius*'s icon. It was that simple.

The hostile bubble was about a half light-second across, based on the time lag between when they'd engaged stealth, and when the light from that shift reached *Belisarius,* combined with how far they might have traveled in the intervening seconds. By contrast, *Belisarius*'s bubble was a full light-*minute* in diameter, which was a conservative estimate. She had gone stealth five minutes ago.

In theory, that meant this should be an easy fight. It should take their opponent a lot longer to shrink their probability sphere than it would take *Belisarius* to resolve theirs. But nobody ever won a battle by assuming it would be easy.

"Unknown hostile designated Echo-class," Hassani announced, excitement in her voice. "Showing target as Echo-1. Scanning visual data, running emissions analysis."

Zevran reported his own progress with little more than his

usual dispassion. "Searching for enemy network. Updating countermeasures."

"Helm," Hadrian said, "randomize course changes and intervals. Keep the center of the hostile bubble within a half second of firing arc. ECW, push our drone net out to range three, and hold."

"What happens now?" Mirra asked quietly as the stations acknowledged their orders.

"We try to get through their stealth," Tsegaye responded. "They try to get through ours. If we get lucky and find them, we can take a shot. If we find their drone net first, we can switch to active penetration protocols, try to breach their network."

"Won't that reveal us?"

"Drone net at range three," Zevran reported.

"Emissions trail goes cold," Hassani added. "They're buttoned up tight."

"It'll reveal *our* network," Tsegaye replied. "But at that point, we'll have a head start breaching theirs. Still puts us in the lead, and once we're past the first layer, we can use active defensive measures too. Confuse their breach attempts, scramble their targeting, that sort of thing."

On the tac projection, the hostile's bubble shrank fractionally.

"Bella," Hadrian said, "what can you tell me about their drones?"

"The hostile did not deploy drones before going to stealth."

Hadrian sucked his teeth.

"Playing it close to the chest," Tsegaye said.

That meant they'd probably be running a tight network, close in to the mothership. It'd hamper their own detection capabilities, but it'd make it harder for *Belisarius* to find them. That also meant that once *Belisarius* did find their network, they'd be a step closer to targeting the ship itself.

Maybe they're waiting for us to find their network, counting on their cyber capabilities to be better than ours. That might say something about who, or what, they are.

"Could they simply not be using drones?" Mirra asked.

"Not unless they're a lot more alien than they look," Tsegaye said. "A ship's drone net is half its combat capability, primarily defensive but absolutely vital. They can kick out EM interference, generate false signals, provide cyber offense and defense. As a last resort, once the ship is targeted, they anchor and help generate its defensive shield. Without them, you'd be a sitting duck."

Hadrian was surprised the marine seemed to know so little about naval combat. But then, his knowledge of ground combat tactics mostly came from history and was probably long out of date by now.

"What about armaments?" Hadrian asked. "What's he packing?"

"Not sure," Hassani replied. "That forward structure could be the linac for a UMAX, but analysis has zip on how powerful it might be. No idea on secondary weapons."

Hadrian nodded, though he didn't like the answer. Mirra had already been proven right in at least one way. All the drills and exercises they'd performed at the academy, and Hadrian had never simulated fighting an unknown opponent he had zero intelligence on, in a ship-to-ship duel, with no connection to the ICN networks.

"Visual analysis negative. Whatever active camo he's using, it's damn good." Hassani sounded disappointed.

Never mind that. A fight is a fight. Just find him before he finds you, and do what you have to. "Bella, go higher res. Comb that whole patch of space; we've got the time. Something's gotta pop up."

"Yes, Captain," Bella said. The red bubble shrank fractionally again, followed a moment later by the blue bubble, with a more significant contraction.

"Bella?" Hadrian asked.

"I've adjusted my projections based on the enemy's observed

defensive capabilities, assuming a similar level of offensive capability."

"Still got a big lead," Tsegaye said.

Yet as each second dragged past, the tension in the CIC increased. Of course, this was a new experience for each of them. But Hadrian felt there was more to it than that. A lack of confidence, in themselves. In him. Perhaps even in the ship.

You're just projecting, he hoped.

The red bubble contracted.

"All right," Hadrian said. "Keep this up, and we'll—"

An alert blared. *Belisarius*'s blue bubble flashed, then shrank to a tiny sphere a thousand kilometers across, comprising nothing but her own drone network, with her slightly off center.

"What?" Hassani blurted out. Hadrian barely managed to restrain his own outburst by baring his teeth.

"They're on our network," Zevran announced, some surprise finally creeping into his voice. "Switching to active countermeasures."

"How in the hell did they find us so fast?" Tsegaye asked, open-mouthed.

None of the words that came to Hadrian's mind would have been helpful. Now, a race was truly on. But by the time *Belisarius* realized it, the enemy had already lapped them. Put himself decisively, perhaps fatally, in the lead. If he'd been able to find their network that quickly, at such a major probability disadvantage, how quickly could he breach their network? Flood their targeting system with false positives, drown their sensors in noise, penetrate their stealth?

Too fast. All too fast.

"It doesn't matter," Hadrian said, to Tsegaye and himself. "He's on our network, we should be on his—where the hell is he?"

"Backtracing," Zevran said. A moment later, the hostile bubble flashed, then contracted drastically, shrinking from hundreds of thousands to mere hundreds of kilometers. "On it."

Bella would be straining now, fighting a silent battle to keep the enemy out of her own network while simultaneously trying to breach his. Zevran and his ECW crew, which made up more than half the ratings and junior officers in the CIC, would be adding their own talents and attentions to that fight, searching for intrusions and weaknesses, trying to spot bluffs and Trojans that an AI —one whose judgment was potentially compromised by an enemy counterpart—might miss.

The fate of the ship and its crew might well be decided by that invisible struggle. One there was nothing Hadrian could do to influence. He simply had to trust in his crew and his ship, and focus his energies on the parts of the fight where he *could* make a difference.

"Push the drones out to range four, randomize deployment. Give me a visual."

Bella threw up the optical sensor feed onto the hardscreen, so that Hadrian and Tsegaye could add their eyes to the search Hassani was already conducting. Now that the probability sphere had shrunk, there was a role for human eyes to play. Bella's visual analysis algorithms were far more advanced than human optical processing, but like the rest of her systems, once her network was under attack, they could be fooled. And the implant-augmented human visual cortex was nothing to sniff at. However slim, there was a chance that one of them might spot a momentary lapse in the enemy's active camouflage as their ship and its drones passed across the starfield. *Belisarius* might be able to use that to point their efforts in the right direction, give them a critical advantage that could keep them in this fight.

A lot of "mights."

Mirra leaned forward to add her own eyes to the search. In Hadrian's peripheral view, *Belisarius*'s sphere contracted yet again.

"They're through our first layer." Zevran was definitely frustrated now. He still didn't sound frightened though, more offended. "Engaging defensive isolation protocols."

"Any luck on their network?" Tsegaye asked.

"I'll report once I'm in."

Neither Hadrian nor Tsegaye bothered to chastise the ECWO for the protocol-breaching backtalk, when a simple "negative" would have sufficed. As long as he did his job, at this point, it hardly mattered.

None of it will matter in a few minutes.

Hadrian hated to think it, hated himself for thinking it. But it was true. There was optimism, and there was foolishness.

Belisarius was losing this fight. Only a few minutes in, not a shot yet fired, and she was losing. Whoever the enemy was, he had her completely outclassed in the stealth/detection part of the equation. Which meant that unless his gun was a lot weaker than it had any right to be, he had her outclassed, period.

Whoever. Hadrian looked up at the visual, empty save for the gentle curve of the planet, and the blazing neutron star beyond. *Or whatever.*

His mind had been racing through every book he'd ever read on naval warfare, every game he'd ever played, every exercise he'd ever run. It kept sticking on one thing, over and over. Every time, he pushed past it. Logic, and the enemy's capabilities, told him what they must be. And if that was right, then the play he kept landing on would be suicide.

But if logic was wrong, and his instincts were right, it might be the only chance they had.

"Bella," he said. "Get me Commander Tsung."

"Engineering here," Tsung's voice replied a few seconds later.

"Commander, I'm sending you a profile on the enemy ship we're engaged with. I want your opinion on him. Is he a Cipher?"

To his credit, the ornery engineer didn't question the request.

He simply went silent for a few seconds. *"There's some similarities. Given the shit-kicking his cyber's givin' us, I'd say probably."*

"That's not what I asked, Wei."

Mirra's gaze flicked toward him.

Tsung sighed. *"No. I don't think so. Doesn't feel right."*

Hadrian clapped his hands in spite of himself. *My thoughts exactly.* "Thank you, Commander. All right, here's what we do." He bounded up the steps to the upper deck as *Belisarius*'s sphere contracted yet again.

"Zevran, I want you to program this sequence into our drones." Hadrian reached over the ECWO's shoulder to tap out an energy pattern directly into his console. "On my mark, you're gonna execute it on the port-upper quadrant of our network. This energy sequence *exactly*, got that?"

Zevran peered at the console. "Yes, sir, but—"

"Helm." Hadrian was already turning away, "watch our energy grid. You see it doing *this*, you bring us down and starboard as hard as you can. Kick in the main engines, but *do not* let their energy curve get above point zero two. Then on my order, you swing us around and you get us in firing arc."

He moved over to TacOps as Keitel was acknowledging. "Hassani, once he sees this, he's gonna pop his shield. You keep on him. The instant it drops and you have a target, you fire. Don't wait for my order. Understood?"

Hassani looked up at him, nervous. "Yes, sir."

Hadrian patted her on the shoulder and returned to the HCI. "Wait for my mark."

Tsegaye leaned in close to him. "You sure about this?"

"Critical stealth penetration," Bella announced, as the blue sphere shrank one final time. "Enemy targeting imminent."

"I'm sure," he said. The look he gave his old friend told the truth, but it was one they both understood. Tsegaye nodded.

"Sequence programmed and ready," Zevran reported.

Hadrian took a deep breath. "Execute."

A cluster of drones in the upper-port quarter of *Belisarius*'s network drifted closer together on thrusters. Once they were in range of one another, they surged with power. They were designed to generate and anchor an enormously powerful magnetoplasma field, their mothership's last line of defense if she were targeted. The swarm of tiny craft used this energy now not for defense, but offense—at least, the *appearance* of offense, mimicking with preternatural accuracy the power curve of a charging ultra-relativistic mass-neutralized proton accelerator. Aimed directly at the center of the enemy's probability sphere.

Once the curve passed a predetermined point, Ensign Keitel heaved *Belisarius* down and starboard, pushing up her main engines, trying to keep them just below the rising wave of energy generated by the drones. Hadrian held his breath. This was the moment of decision, when he would learn whether he had just killed his ship and crew.

An instant later, the visual display came to life with a new point of blazing light. Hadrian flinched—but it was not the momentary spark before a UMAX was fired. It was the burning sphere of a magnetoplasma field activating.

Hadrian let his pent-up breath escape, waited one heartbeat, two, then—"Helm, now!"

Belisarius heaved back up, her nose swinging around to aim directly at the bubble burning brightly in space. Hadrian, Tsegaye, and Mirra gripped the railings of the HCI and leaned against the maneuver.

With near-perfect timing, *Belisarius*'s main cannon was brought to bear on target just as the enemy's shield collapsed, its drone network having burned itself out to generate the stellar energy required to deflect the apocalyptic shot that was now, truly, about to be fired.

Except it wasn't.

Hadrian glanced up at the tactical display. Bella's network had been penetrated enough that even after the enemy's shield collapsed, she couldn't resolve the enemy himself into a discrete point, the definite position of his ship in space. Instead, she was giving Hassani four possibles, each with a ranked probability rating marginally different from the next. It was up to the gunner to pick which target was the genuine article, and fire.

And she hesitated. Only for a moment. But that might be enough.

Without thinking, as if this really were just an exercise all those long years ago, Hadrian stabbed a finger at one of the targets on instinct. "Fire!"

Hassani must have pulled the trigger, for an instant later, power thrummed through *Belisarius*'s belly. Like the sound and feeling of her engines' prefire capacitors charging, but harsher, angrier. And briefer. Deep in the ship's core, her Higgs-Graviton exclusion field–equipped cyclotron was accelerating a stream of mass-neutralized protons up to near light speed.

An instant before she fired, the enemy beat her to the punch.

There was no time to tell what he fired. At this point, it didn't matter. All they saw was a flash of light, and then a stream of light-speed death was tearing space apart, straight for *Belisarius*.

Or rather, where the enemy thought *Belisarius* should be. The particle beam blasted through the burned-out quarter of her drone net, dead-center on the cluster Zevran had programmed to mimic a charging UMAX.

A fraction of a second later, *Belisarius* replied. The stream of protons raced down the linear accelerator terminal stage of her main weapon and erupted into space at the speed of light. Freed from the lightening grasp of the weapon's HGEF, the protons regained their considerable mass but lost none of their velocity. A concentrated beam of them carried more destructive energy than humanity had unleashed in the entirety of its Second World War.

It struck the enemy ship on its starboard wing, and a new sun blazed alongside the old.

The CIC erupted in a brief and violent cheer. Hadrian slapped the top of the HCI. "You got him, Hassani, nice shot!"

The TacOps officer didn't reply, or if she did, Hadrian didn't hear it. He and Tsegaye shook hands, clapped shoulders, both breathing hard. Even Mirra seemed relieved, though she was still peering at the hardscreen, and the fading bloom of destruction it displayed.

Hadrian checked the time. The whole encounter had lasted barely ten minutes. It had felt like hours. He breathed out, doing his best to keep his limbs from shaking with relief—both at having survived and the fact that the enemy's shot had at least proved he wasn't a wayward civilian ship.

Got you, you son of a bitch.

"Captain!" Hassani finally said. Hadrian's eyes swung up to her. "He's ... he's still out there, sir."

Hadrian spun back toward the display, fearful for a moment that another shot was about to rip through space and kill his ship. But Hassani's meaning became clear soon enough.

The enemy ship had indeed taken the hit. The massive gouge in his starboard side proved that. But he hadn't been destroyed, as a ship that size taking a hit that hard should have been. Instead, he was drifting through space, trailing gas and debris, power flickering and dying. Yet very much intact.

Hadrian's eyes narrowed. *Who in the hell* are *you?*

TWENTY-ONE

"Hostile is two hundred fifty meters in length, eighty-one in width amidships, thirty-seven in height. Tentatively classifying him as a light cruiser."

They had some breathing space, for the moment, and a good clear look at the ship they'd fought. As Hassani reported her findings, Hadrian, Tsegaye, and Mirra looked at the drifting wreck on the main hardscreen.

"Energy output for his shield network looks roughly equivalent to an Achilles Mk. III. Output from his main cannon shot …" Hassani paused. Hadrian glanced back; she had gone pale. "Equivalent to an Astra Mk. VII, at least."

"On a ship that size?" Tsegaye wondered.

Belisarius sported a Mk. VII herself, the same class of weapon on the fleet's massive battlecarriers. But the *Starbird* was a substantially bigger ship than this hostile, and it made use of overpowered reactors for its size in order to field the Mk. VII. For this cruiser-weight ship to have the same armament, it must have an even more power-heavy design.

Or be a lot more advanced than us, Hadrian thought. "You're sure of that, Lieutenant?"

"Positive, sir." Hassani swallowed. "If they'd hit us with that thing …"

"They didn't." Hadrian ascended to the upper deck, put a hand on Hassani's shoulder. "Zevran, what have you got on their ECW?"

"Still collating."

Hadrian squeezed Hassani's shoulder. "You made the shot, Hassani. You did good."

"Yes, sir." She smiled weakly up at him.

"Results are inconclusive," Zevran announced. Hadrian moved over to his station. "*Belisarius* is run by a Hopewell Type 15 adaptive neural network. Obviously, whatever the enemy was using is faster, better. That doesn't tell us very much. We're hardly top of the line."

"And how *would* it fare against top of the line?"

"According to my models, it most likely would have matched a Type 21, if not exceeded it."

Ciphers. But that didn't track, given the outcome of the fight. "Could they have been using some next-gen AI we're not aware of?"

"Very possible."

"Commander." Hadrian turned to the command pit. "You aware of anything at ISOC like that?"

Mirra thought for a moment. "As far as I know, the Type 21 is still state of the art. But I don't follow AI developments closely."

Hadrian leaned on the forward railing, next to Keitel's helm station, and stared at the mysterious ship. "How's his power curve? He trying to get back online?"

"Doesn't look that way," Hassani said. "He's still adrift. Power levels that low, must be running on batteries."

But if he's that advanced, it might not stay that way. "What about the research station?"

"No change since before the engagement."

"Bella." Hadrian returned to the HCI. "Open a channel to the station. Send: To whoever is occupying research station ... 47988-A, this is Captain Hadrian of the ICS *Belisarius*. We have reason to believe you conspired to attack this vessel. Respond immediately and explain yourselves, or we will be forced to take action against you."

"Think they'll reply?" Tsegaye asked.

Hadrian shook his head. "We'll have to try a more direct approach. Commanders, join me in the briefing room to discuss."

Mirra and Tsegaye nodded, the latter reluctantly. Hadrian turned to the upper deck. "Lieutenant Hassani, you have the conn. Keep us clear of that station, and if the hostile tries anything funny, you nail his ass again."

"Yes, sir," Hassani said.

Tsegaye and Mirra followed Hadrian into the briefing room via the hatch on the port side of the CIC. Bella gave them a tactical readout and visual of the disabled hostile, anticipating what they'd be discussing.

Hadrian leaned on the table and looked up at the projection. "We'll have to board him."

"Agreed," Mirra said.

Tsegaye looked between the two of them. "Okay, but we have no idea how many hostiles are still active aboard that ship."

"Can't be many. A UMAX hit like that, even active internal radiation shielding would have been overwhelmed," Hadrian said. Neutralized, relativistic protons passing through solid matter ionized atoms, knocked out subatomic particles, and released massive amounts of X-rays in a cascade of braking radiation. It was the insidious and deadly secondary effect of UMAX shots, aside from the devastating thermal and kinetic energy of the strike itself. "Most of the crew must be dead."

"If it *had* a biological crew," Tsegaye countered.

"It did. Of some kind. Besides, even Cipher combat platforms would get severely messed up by that much radiation. Should give us an advantage either way."

"True," Mirra said, "but the longer we wait, the more chance whatever resistance there is will have to recover. I should go now."

"You?" Tsegaye raised an eyebrow.

Mirra gave him a blank stare. "It's the only logical choice."

"She's right," Hadrian said. He'd have suggested it himself, much as he'd have preferred not to. "She's the only one with any real experience on an op like this."

"Granted, but given none of our ratings have even *met* her, shouldn't we have one of our own officers along too?"

"My thoughts exactly," Hadrian said before Mirra could object. "That's why I'm going too."

Now it was Mirra's turn to raise an eyebrow. *"You?"*

Hadrian returned the look.

"Actually," Tsegaye said, "I meant *me*."

"I figured, but—"

"Uh-uh." Tsegaye held up a finger. "That ship could come back online any minute. *More* hostiles could show up any minute, or that station might be hiding some surprises of its own. The captain needs to be in the CIC. However much he might want to get some answers in person."

Hadrian cut off his budding objection. He'd known Tsegaye would make that argument, and it was a good one. *Worth a shot.*

"Besides," Tsegaye continued, "you already told me next time it'd be my turn."

"I did not."

"You—"

"I *winked* at you. That's hardly a binding agreement."

Tsegaye crossed his arms. "Fine, but am I wrong?"

"You're not wrong."

"Okay then." Tsegaye gestured at Mirra. She had been observing the exchange with evident distaste.

"The captain should remain in command," she said.

"All right," Hadrian relented. "You can go. But Mirra will have tactical command."

"Wouldn't have it any other way," Tsegaye said.

"Nor I," Mirra added.

Hadrian smirked in spite of himself. "We still have some marine armor and weapons aboard, as well as the emergency defense kit for the crew. How many people do you need?"

"No more than ten or twelve," Mirra said. "Including the commander and myself."

"Bella," Hadrian said, "rank the crew by CQB exercise scores, exclude mission-essential personnel, then go down the list asking for volunteers. If we don't get enough, Arno can make some assignments."

"Works for me."

"I'll make use of the marine equipment and link some combat drones," Mirra said, "but your crew should use the kit they're most familiar with. Better gear won't matter if they're not comfortable using it."

"Good thinking," said Hadrian.

"Hang on," Tsegaye said. "Given that the station's clearly been compromised, there could be just as much useful intel there. What if we do a simultaneous boarding? Mirra can take the hostile, I'll take the station?"

Hadrian shook his head. "I don't like it. If these assholes are responsible for the bombings on Byas, it'd be just their MO to have that station wired to blow the second we set foot on it."

"In that case, the hostile could be wired too," Tsegaye suggested.

"Maybe, but I'm hoping they were planning to beat us the old-fashioned way," Hadrian said. "With their reactors down, they won't be able to trigger an overload. And if most of the crew was killed or disabled by the hit, they won't have time to set up conventional explosives. At least not yet."

"All the more reason to move quickly," Mirra said, an edge in her voice.

Hadrian gave her side-eye. "I'll send some autonomous units over to the station, see if they can trigger anything. If they don't, we may try and board it afterward. For now, you two need to get over to that ship. I want to know who these bastards are, how they got the edge on us, and what else they have planned."

"Roger that," Tsegaye said.

"Arno," Hadrian said as the two were turning to leave, "hang back for a second?"

"Meet you at the armory," Tsegaye told Mirra.

Hadrian waited until she was gone. "You sure about this?"

"I'm sure *you're* not going."

"That doesn't mean you have to." Hadrian jerked his chin at the door. "There's plenty other officers on this ship. We can find someone else."

"If that's true, why'd *you* volunteer?"

"Because it's my responsibility we're here. I followed this lead. I decided to fight that ship."

Tsegaye pointed an open hand at him. "I'm your XO—it's my responsibility too. I don't want to send someone else in our place. Besides, I told you, I'm itching to get off this tub."

"You also said I'm a better shot."

"With a pistol. I can shoot a rifle well enough."

Hadrian sighed. "Just be careful, all right?"

"Are you kidding?" Tsegaye nodded backward. "I'm letting *her* go first."

Hadrian's smile faded. "That's the other thing. Keep an eye on her."

"You don't think we can trust her?"

"I don't think she's with *them*. But she's got her own agenda. I'm not so sure it lines up with ours."

"What makes you say that?"

"Back on the station, the ISOC guys that were trying to take me? She killed 'em all. I'd have thought if she wanted more intel, she'd have at least *tried* to take one alive."

"What could that mean?" Tsegaye asked. Hadrian shrugged. "Well, if she's just out there to kill 'em all, I don't know if I can stop her."

"Just having you watching her might make her think twice. At least, you might see something gives us an idea if there's more going on with her than we realize."

"I can do that."

Fear for his friend's safety only really began to set in once Hadrian had given all his orders. Still, he didn't want to drag out a goodbye. It'd only make them both more nervous. And besides, the enemy ship had taken a brutal hit. If there was anyone left alive on it, they probably weren't in any shape to fight.

"Good luck," Hadrian ended up saying, and shook Tsegaye's hand.

Tsegaye smiled. "Keep the light on for me."

TWENTY-TWO

The ship's AI guided Mirra to the armory, near the launch bay. There was no guard posted outside; clearly the Navy personnel were content to leave the guarding to the AI. Mirra would not have been.

At least the equipment was in good shape. There was a full complement of repeater rifles, battle armor, and drones. The marines aboard had clearly been as fastidious about their gear as Mirra was. It hadn't been said, but she assumed it belonged to the marines who had been killed in the bombing. She gave a silent thanks to her fallen brothers and sisters for their diligence. It was the faces of her own men that flashed before her eyes as she did.

Soon, she told them. Though in truth, neither justice nor vengeance were promises she could keep.

She selected a suit of battle armor that looked about the right size for her—close enough that it would be able to mold itself to her without requiring modification. She had just stripped to her skinsuit when the armory door opened.

"Find something?" Tsegaye asked.

"Yes."

"Good." Tsegaye moved to the naval crew side of the armory, searched for a suit of the serviceable but less advanced combat armor he and his people would be wearing. "I'm sure Lieutenant Farris would be happy to see his gear put to good use."

Mirra didn't assess that the comment needed a response. She started setting up the battle armor in its sconce, readying it for her to step in.

"You been on many boarding actions?"

"Some," she said. "Mostly against Kyrans."

"That's gotta be tough."

Mirra nodded. "They're most dangerous at close quarters."

"Ever fought the Ciphers?"

"During the war."

"Who's worse?"

"They each have their own challenges." Mirra could have said more—that Cipher relentlessness in its own way equaled Kyran ferocity, that machine durability was ultimately a greater challenge than saurian savagery, that she *enjoyed* fighting the Kyrans more—but just then, she had a question of her own. "I'm curious about something."

"What's that?"

She turned around. "The stratagem Captain Hadrian employed. It worked perfectly, but he was reluctant to use it. It seemed his decision was contingent upon whether the enemy was Cipher or not."

Tsegaye nodded. "Well, he came up with that particular trick himself, back at SWOS. Helped him win the single-ship ladder his first year. Nobody ever saw it coming—their *first* time going up against him, at least. Once word got around, his opponents started to expect it. 'Course, by then he'd figured out how to use *that* to his advantage too."

"Then why hesitate to use it?"

Tsegaye gave a lopsided smile. "Because every time he or a

classmate tried it against an AI opponent, the computer saw straight through it. Even starting from a fresh instance, no data from previous sims or exercises."

"So logically, the Ciphers …" Mirra left the conclusion unsaid. Tsegaye nodded. "Quite a gamble, then."

"Yeah, no kidding. But it worked."

"Mmm." Mirra turned back to the armor rack.

"Can I ask *you* something?"

Mirra stepped into the armor, felt it close around her. She shut her eyes for a moment and savored the sensation. It had been weeks since she'd put full battle armor on. After being in her old suit throughout her ordeal on Lampshade, she had been glad for a break. By now, she'd once again started to miss the feeling of security, of power that came with it.

She turned to face Tsegaye, the armor's servos humming. He'd removed his outer uniform and was applying the torso piece of his own navy-blue armor. "Go ahead."

"You don't seem to like Ian very much."

Mirra selected a rifle. "Liking or disliking him hardly matters."

"Maybe not. But you don't *trust* him."

"I don't trust his abilities."

"Even after today?"

Mirra turned back to Tsegaye, checking the weapon without looking at it. "His indecision put the ship in jeopardy."

"I just explained that to you."

"*All* his decisions."

"If he hadn't gone stealth when he did—"

"He should have done it the moment we arrived." Satisfied with the check, Mirra slung the rifle on the magnetic latch on the armor's back. "Attempting to communicate with the station was a waste of time. It had clearly been compromised and should have been treated as hostile."

"Well, that's easy for *you* to say," Tsegaye rejoined. Mirra sighed and turned away again, this time to select a pistol. "No, no. You ISOC types, most of your ops are deep black. No oversight. Up here, we're actually held *accountable* for our actions. Most of the time."

Something in the way he said that caught Mirra's attention. She waited to put on her helmet. "Dealt with a lot of ISOC, have you?"

"More than I'd like. Ian too."

"Perhaps he could have learned a little more from us."

Tsegaye seemed to think for a moment, then holstered a sidearm and walked over to her side of the room. "Listen. I've known Ian a long time. We went through SWOS together. Both served on the *Kharkiv* in our final year, and another regular service after that. You couldn't pull us apart. Then I got transferred. We kept in touch, messages now and then. Met up on shore leave once, when they lined up. But more or less, we lost touch. That's what happens, right?"

Mirra nodded. That was the nature of military friendships. Something King had been trying to tell her himself, just before …

"Seven years go by," Tsegaye continued, rescuing her from the reverie. "He's a golden boy on the fast track, I'm slogging up the post-drawdown ladder. He gets assigned as Singh's XO on the *Spruance*, I figure I'll never see him again. Then one day, out of the blue, I get a transfer order. I'm assigned as XO on the destroyer *Marissa Tavukcu*. CO, Commander Ian Hadrian. I couldn't believe it. I was still a senior lieutenant. They had to promote me just to take the post. He could've tapped anyone for that spot, someone with connections, help his career. You know why he picked me?"

Mirra shook her head.

"Because he said he would." Tsegaye smiled. "*Ten* years earlier, when we were still snottie cadets at SWOS. We said, whoever got his own ship first, he'd tap the other to be his XO. That's it. That's the kind of man he is."

"Fine story," Mirra said. "But he should have picked the best officer for the job."

"You saying he didn't?"

"I can't make that judgment."

Tsegaye nodded, returned to his racks to select a rifle. "Well. Story's not quite done yet. Almost, then I promise I'll stop bothering you."

Somehow, Mirra doubted that, but she let him continue.

"That's the kind of man he is. Been like that long as I've known him. Quick with a smile, bend over backward to help you out, even if he barely knows you. But if you know anything about SWOS—or any other military academy—you know that an attitude like that can lead a certain type of person to underestimate you."

Mirra's attention was grabbed again, feeling the implied criticism.

"Maybe even push you around," Tsegaye said as he finished applying his armor. The joints whined when they sealed. "Now, Ian didn't mind. Sometimes these guys'd have a go at him, and he'd just let 'em. That only made them think less of him, of course. Then one time, one of these pricks—name of Thomas, I think—starts going after our friend Ryan. Ryan was a real quiet guy, smart as hell, but sometimes we wondered what the hell he was even doing in the Navy, you know?

"Anyway, Thomas smelled blood, started hounding the kid, making sexual remarks, that kind of thing. Ryan made it clear he wasn't interested, he had a boyfriend down on Sang-je. Thomas didn't let that stop him. Ian told him to back off, Thomas laughed it off. It seemed like things quieted down for a bit—then it came out that Thomas sexually assaulted Ryan."

Mirra's jaw tightened. She'd seen that sort of thing happen all too often herself.

"Ian found out, and ... he went *cold*. Never seen him like that. He walked right up to Thomas, told him he wanted to fight. Box, in the ring. All legit. Thomas laughed at that too." Tsegaye smiled, then it went dark. "Until they got in there, couple days later. Ian beat the living hell out of him. Kept hitting him after the ref called it, over and over. Never seen someone take a pounding like that. His face looked like a cut of meat. Only official censure Ian got. I think if he hadn't already been on the short list, he might've gotten expelled.

"Well, that and the fact that a couple hours after the fight, Ian and Ryan reported Thomas for the assault." Tsegaye shook his head. "They expelled the bastard and brought him up on charges while he was still in the infirmary. I would've liked to see the look on his face, if he still had one."

Mirra smiled at that, in spite of herself. Truthfully, she could think of one or two marines she wouldn't have minded giving the same treatment to.

"That's *also* the kind of man Ian is," Tsegaye said. "You know what I mean?"

That was a fine story too. It hardly proved that Hadrian was fit for combat command, but ...

"I understand," Mirra said. She suddenly wasn't in the mood to argue the point any longer.

"That's all I can ask," Tsegaye replied. A moment later the armory hatch opened again. Tsegaye smiled at the newcomers. "About time! You slackers didn't think we were going for shore leave, did you?"

"Hope not, XO." One of the newly arrived crewmembers, a chief petty officer by her uniform. She looked questioningly at Mirra.

"This is Commander Mirra," Tsegaye said. "She's a senior LDRG marine, so she's gonna be showing us fleeties what's what over there."

The CPO smiled. "CPO Rowley. Glad to have you, ma'am."

Mirra nodded, then put on her helmet to avoid further unnecessary conversation. Tsegaye, though, kept his off while the other volunteers streamed in, chatting with each of them while they put on their own equipment. The CPO aside, many of them looked nervous. As they should be. Tsegaye's simple conversation seemed to help put them at ease.

Perhaps Hadrian picked the right man for the job, after all.

TWENTY-THREE

Hadrian squinted against the exploding station. A moment earlier, the sensors on the drones breaching it had told them what was coming. It took a half second for the light to reach *Belisarius*. The explosion's destructive force had long since dissipated by the time it made the same journey.

"Antimatter detonation," Hassani reported. "Looks like a reactor containment shutdown. Probably set to trigger once the hatch was forcibly opened."

"Probably hoping we'd be closer when it did," Hadrian said, grimly satisfied. "You owe me one, Arno."

"Can the gloating wait until I get back?" Tsegaye replied, a second later. *"I'm a little busy right now."*

Hadrian smiled. "Bella, switch us over."

The tactical readout on the vaporized station changed to show the drifting enemy ship, and *Belisarius*'s shuttle decelerating as it approached its target. The main hardscreen switched to a dual image of armor camera feeds from Tsegaye and Mirra.

"Think there was anyone still on board?" Tsegaye asked.

"Drones showed one of the station's shuttles was missing," Hassani said. "Hasn't shown up in any of our system scans."

"My guess is, they bugged out after we left," Hadrian said. "Used an AI to simulate Doctor Narin and keep us busy, while it signaled that ship to jump in and take us by surprise."

"And if we'd tried to board, they'd have blown it," Mirra concluded.

"Speaking of which—Engineering, CIC. Commander, what's your read on the chances of that ship going boom?"

"Every antimatter reactor I've ever seen's been designed with the same fail-safe," Tsung replied. *"In a shutdown, all antimatter's shunted into magnetic bottles sustained by their own power supply. Impossible to open unless the reactor's brought back online. Usually inside a blast chamber you'd need a UMAX to crack open."*

"And you're reasonably sure that ship's got the same fail-safe?"

"Can't be sure *unless I get over there,"* Tsung said, annoyed. *"But the fact that it's still in one piece tells me yeah, it must have. Can't guarantee they won't find some* other *way to blow it to hell, but there you go."*

"Thanks, Wei. You catch that, guys?"

"Caught it," Tsegaye said. *"Should be good unless the power comes back on."*

"We can't count on that," Mirra added. *"Be on the lookout for explosive charges."*

Hadrian turned to the upper deck. "And Hassani, keep an eye on that power curve. It so much as twitches, you let me know."

"Yes, sir."

*

MIRRA LOOKED OVER the motley boarding team she'd assembled.

There were twelve of them, including Tsegaye and herself. As it turned out, they'd no shortage of volunteers from the crew. Her requirement had been met without having to go beyond the ratings and junior officers with the highest CQB scores. Many of them had likely wanted to put that training to the test. Others seemed eager for a chance to get a look at the mysterious ship they had so recently been locked in mortal combat with. And perhaps for a chance at some visceral release of the tension that short battle had built up.

The marine breaching shuttle had a capacity of twenty; eight of the spots were empty, giving the team a little room to breathe. Mirra would have had no trouble filling the extra slots with more volunteers, but she'd decided against it. Eager these might have been, but experienced they were not. As she'd told the captain, exercises—and training—were not war. She'd confirmed that she was the only one among them with any infantry combat experience.

The textbook play for a one-craft assault was to make or seize a breach point, then split into two squads of ten, one headed for the ship's primary or secondary control center, and the other for its main reactor. And if she'd had twenty marines, that's exactly what she would have done.

Under the circumstances, she had no intention of splitting her force. Lieutenant-Commander Tsegaye seemed a natural enough leader, but she wouldn't trust him to command a boarding assault on his own. That being the case, more than twelve inexperienced boarders would have become a hindrance rather than an asset, cramping the corridors through which they'd be fighting, more likely to get in one another's way than help.

She'd discussed the plan with Tsegaye on private suit comms, and he agreed. It made particular sense to stay together in this case, he said, since they did not know the layout of the enemy ship. Logical—another point in his favor. Mirra was almost beginning to like him.

"One minute to alignment," the shuttle pilot announced.

The external view was up on the hardscreen in the forward section of the crew compartment. The enemy ship was tumbling through space ahead of them, unmagnified. The shuttle had decelerated to a snail's pace; the hard part was matching its spin and attitude with the uncontrolled vessel so it could make safe contact.

The breach in its side through which they would ingress came periodically into view. The entirety of the ship's starboard wing had been vaporized, along with most of an engine. Blackened, twisted hull peeled away from the breach like charred flesh from a wound. Gasses still spilled weakly from the ship as it spun.

Yet terrible as the damage was, from Mirra's understanding of *Belisarius*'s firepower, it should have been greater. A ship this size should have at minimum been blasted in two, if not utterly destroyed by a direct, unshielded, full-power hit from an Astra Mk. VII. Whoever had built this thing had built it to last.

Let's hope its crew aren't as tough.

"Thirty seconds to alignment."

Mirra unlatched from her seat and floated into the center-fore of the compartment. "All right, listen up."

She turned around. Faces in armor stared back at her—dead faces. Contreras and Tchaikovsky, Demetriou and Yamada. Alistair King. Their faceplates up, their faces bloody, their eyes sunken and cloudy, gaping wounds in their throats. Their dead eyes looked on her with scorn, accusation.

Such as we are, they said, *you should be.*

Mirra blinked hard, breathed in sharp. The vision disappeared. She was in a different crew compartment. Different faces in different armor looked up at her. Not scornful but expectant. Trusting, or wanting to trust.

"We don't know what we're going to find on that ship," she said to the living. "The crew may already be dead, but we can't count on that. If any are still active, we should expect a fight. We need intelligence, but don't try to take any of them alive. If they're anything like the ones I've run into, they won't give you the chance. Defend yourselves by whatever means necessary."

Tsegaye looked at her strangely. She ignored him.

"Our objective is to locate and seize the ship's control center. With access to that, we can download their databases and get all the intel we need. We can also make use of it to secure the rest of the ship without fighting corridor by corridor." She didn't expound on that; they might be squeamish about the idea of venting fellow sailors out into space, or suffocating them in their own ship. She'd found fleeties strangely sentimental about that sort of thing. "I'll take point. Sensors show no simulated gravity fields active on the target vessel, so we'll be using zero-g protocols. Any questions?"

No hands went up. That was a good sign, or a bad one. Mirra chose uncharacteristic optimism. "Good. Check the weapons and gear of the sailor next to you."

"Ten seconds to alignment."

Mirra turned to watch the shuttle align with the enemy ship. For several disorienting seconds, their nose and the blasted hull spun past each other at high speed, over and over. Then the spinning of the enemy seemed to slow, and stop. The burned scar in the enemy ship was dead ahead, dim red light illuminating the exposed interior. Only the shifting shadows cast by the brilliant blue light of the distant neutron star told her they were still spinning, still tumbling. Only now, they did it in perfect tandem with the enemy ship. The pilot had done well.

"Aligned," he said. "Ready to move into contact on your order."

Mirra turned back. "Checked?"

Several of the volunteers nodded. Tsegaye spoke for them. "All good, Commander."

"Move into contact," Mirra ordered, then pushed off for the fore of the shuttle. "Follow me through."

As the shuttle moved into position and the crew cabin depressurized, Mirra activated her armor's auto-stabilizers and curled herself up into a ball in midair, her knees tucked into her chest.

She drew her rifle from her back and held it up in front of her. The attitude jets in her armor fired to keep her level. From now on, they'd respond to her intuitive commands, thrustering her through the enemy ship like a human drone.

At the same time, she deployed her actual drones. The marine armory had been stocked with a full complement of twenty Stiletto autonomous combat units. Less than half a meter long and only a few centimeters wide, the Stiletto was essentially a high-powered infantry maser with a suite of sensors, attitude jets, and low-grade mass-reduction and stealth systems. Technically, a Stiletto could be set to operate fully autonomously, seeking out and engaging hostile targets without any human intervention. Against Kyran opponents, they often were used just that way—and Mirra would have gladly employed all twenty Stilettos on this operation, to make up for the inexperience and small numbers of her boarding party.

But against the Ciphers, or another enemy with advanced cyberwarfare capabilities, naval regulations required human-on-the-loop operation of all autonomous systems. Too easy for the machines to turn against their masters otherwise. Given what they'd seen of *this* opponent so far, Mirra had no desire to serve them up a whole squadron of Stilettos to potentially compromise. Three was about the most she could handle on her own and still function at peak efficiency, so three she took. She had no intention of saddling inexperienced fleeties with drone ops they hadn't trained for just to take a few extra masers along.

Similarly, the naval armor the volunteers were wearing wasn't equipped with the reaction control system Mirra's employed. They'd have to move the old-fashioned way, with handholds and magnetized foot and palm pads. They were all perfectly capable in that department, as she'd seen while the ship was under Stardrive; nonetheless, this was one of the many reasons she would be the only one taking point. The thruster system, and her familiarity with it, would not only make her a smaller target but also give her superior maneuverability in the likely cramped confines of the hostile ship.

"Contact," the pilot said.

Mirra took a deep breath. The forward hatch receded, revealing the flickering red light and blasted open corridors of the enemy vessel, traversed by slashing shadows and harsh, flashing blue-white light.

"Breach," she said. Her Stilettos jetted into the dark, with Mirra close behind.

TWENTY-FOUR

As the team moved into the torn-open corridors of the enemy ship, the red light changed from flickering to rhythmic pulsing. The low-light filters in the boarding team's visors and cameras adapted in tandem with the pulses, so that in effect the light appeared to be pulsing from red to soft white. It was somewhat disorienting, at least for Hadrian back on *Belisarius*. He hoped that for the boarders, it was preferable to being left periodically in the dark.

For the first minute or two, the team moved silently. There was only one path they could take into the ship, the other route being blasted to pieces or fused shut by the immense heat of the UMAX strike. It was thus difficult to guess the internal layout. But Hadrian already sensed something strange about it. Much like the ship's exterior, it felt familiar and yet alien. Uncanny.

"Anything identifying yet?" Hadrian asked.

"Nothing matching existing databases," Bella replied. "Materials and design bear some similarity to Compact naval and civilian starship architecture."

Hadrian frowned. "Could it be melakeen? Or xirān?"

"Doubtful. Each species' ship designs have distinctive characteristics, none of which are present here."

"Stack up." On the camera feeds, Mirra approached a sealed double door. Tsegaye and the volunteers queued up behind her. She stabilized herself next to the door, reached out, and lightly depressed a raised section of wall to its right. The panel soundlessly clicked into the wall and slid down, revealing a glowing cluster of buttons.

"Looks like a standard emergency control surface." Mirra pointed at the large, L-shaped button at the bottom right. *"This should release the hatch once pressure's equalized."*

Further down the hall was a dead end. Behind them was the hull breach. Tsegaye pointed at the nearest junction in that direction. *"Set up the bubble—"*

"Belay that."

⁕

"SPLIT THE DOOR AND MAGNETIZE," Mirra ordered, gesturing with her rifle.

The sailors seemed confused by the order, but followed it, with more alacrity once Tsegaye urged them on. He took up a position to the left of the hatch. Mirra's Stilettos took up positions covering the hatch as she retrieved a set of paired breaching charges from her utility pack. She fixed the smaller of them to the exposed emergency panel, and the larger to the doors' center latch, then thrustered herself to the lead position on the right.

"Executing modified breach," she said, remembering belatedly the need to explain herself to her inexperienced team. "I go through first; the rest of you stay clear until decompression ends. Follow on my go-ahead. If any hostiles come through the hatch, watch your crossfire. Understood?"

"Roger that," Tsegaye confirmed for his crew.

Mirra drew her rifle, double-checked it was set to boarding mode. Its superfluid projectiles would be programmed for shallow material penetration: still able to defeat most personal armor before expanding, but not so punchy that they might pierce the ship's outer hull.

"Three," she counted, "two, one, breach."

She squeezed her left hand three times, rapidly. The paired charges exploded: first the smaller, then a split second later, the larger. The silent blasts reverberated through the hull. Unlatched and momentarily severed from its emergency control mechanism, the dual hatch slid open, as Mirra had hoped, releasing the atmosphere sealed up in the chamber beyond.

Two of Mirra's Stilettos jetted into the stream of violently escaping air, their thrusters firing to keep them stable. Their sensor data fed directly to Mirra's neural implant, with a visual projected onto her armor HUD.

The two occupants of the chamber had clearly not been prepared for the decompression. The black-clad, bipedal shapes were coming straight toward the hatch, carried along by the breeze even as the hatch on the opposite side of the room slammed shut, cutting off the flow of air from the rest of the ship. They had likely been hovering up near the corners of the room, waiting to unleash a crossfire on anyone who might come through the hatch in a more conventional fashion.

The decompression had destabilized them, but only for a moment. They were not flailing wildly as they tumbled through the escaping air. And they were still armed.

The Stilettos opened up as Mirra jetted forward to follow them into the room. Maser beams played across the heads and chests of the two hostiles, but the thin black suits must have been tougher than they looked—the beams didn't burn straight through them. One seemed injured or disoriented enough not to return fire, but the other was able to. His first shot hit one of the Stilettos and blasted it to pieces.

Mirra put a three-round burst into each hostile as she cleared the hatch. They jerked and twitched with the impact of the rounds, coming just as the rush of escaping air ended. The one on the right twisted off to the side to crash into the opposite wall of the room. The one on the left continued forward, his momentum carrying him out into the open corridor, trailing globules of red blood behind him.

"Hold fire!" Tsegaye ordered as the corpse came into view.

"Go," Mirra said as she pushed into the room, the two surviving Stilettos alongside her. She used the powered jets to twist her around as she entered, scanning every corner. Empty of threats.

And of most anything.

"What is this place?" CPO Rowley asked once the team was through. She took in the sparse surroundings of the mysterious chamber. It was empty, save for some closet-like sconces on each wall with clear doors. Also empty.

"It's almost like an inner airlock," Tsegaye observed. "Except it can't be. Too deep inside the ship."

"Check the body," Mirra said, jetting over to the room's only exit. She might concur with the confusion, but speculating would do no good. "And get the bubble set up over our ingress point."

"Aye-aye," Rowley confirmed.

Tsegaye headed for the enemy corpse still in the room with them while Mirra checked the controls on the exit. It was a single hatchway, with the same standard emergency controls. There was little point trying the decompression trick here. It was likely a corridor beyond, which would be less geometrically conducive. And if the two she'd already killed had been in communication with the rest of the crew, they'd probably be prepared for it now. Besides, she wanted to do something else, which she'd need the pressure in here equalized to attempt.

"What the hell?"

The tone of Tsegaye's voice caught Mirra's attention. She left the door panel and jetted over to join him by the enemy corpse. She hadn't taken in many details before—it had been holding a weapon in its hands, and this was a hostile ship. That was all that mattered. Now, she could examine it more closely.

What she saw froze her blood.

It was wearing a full-body black ... something. At first glance, it seemed to be formfitting, like her skinsuit. But, though largely featureless, it was bulkier, made from some kind of metal or hardened metamaterial, tough but flexible. A quick scan showed that her rifle rounds hadn't penetrated all the way through the target, likely expanding inside the body. That indicated that light as it looked, the suit's armor was at least as good as her own, hence why the Stilettos' masers also hadn't immediately burned through. The suit's helmet was almost formfitting too, like it had been molded onto the wearer's head. At first scan, Mirra couldn't see any way to remove it.

All that was odd, but there was more to Tsegaye's confusion.

"Look at this." He put his suited finger in one of the entry wounds on the chest. There was bloody red flesh there, very human—but when he pushed it aside, there was something else beneath. A glistening black surface, punctured by the bullet.

That completed the rush of sick recognition flooding into Mirra. For a moment, she was not floating in the derelict ship at all. She was back on Baton, standing in a blood-spattered chamber, looking down on an eerily similar corpse. And it wasn't Tsegaye probing at the wound she'd made in his chest, but Tchaikovsky.

Is this what he saw, too?

"It's artificial," Tsegaye said as he scanned the wound, snapping Mirra back to the present. "Some unknown composite. Looks like it runs underneath the entire ribcage, maybe further."

"Cipher simulant?" Hadrian asked over comms.

Yes, she wanted to say. As if somehow that would make it better, what had happened. But it didn't feel any more right now than it had then. "Doubtful. Unless it's some newer model."

"Designed for combat," Tsegaye suggested.

"It'd be less efficient than their existing platforms. And useless as an infiltrator."

"Agreed," Hadrian said. *"Not their style. Can you get that helmet off?"*

Mirra moved the body easily in the microgravity, hesitant as she was to touch it. Her suit's sensors didn't reveal any external controls that might release any part of the armor, let alone the helmet. "Not without cutting through it. We shouldn't delay that long."

"Your call. Try to bring one back with you, alive or otherwise."

"Understood," Mirra said. Part of her hoped she wouldn't get the chance. She didn't want to see what was under that armor.

"Bubble's up," Rowley reported from the breached hatch. "Pressure equalizing."

Mirra swallowed her building anxiety. She knew she should say something: that she had likely seen one of these things before; that there was a connection between these hostiles and the massacre of her men on Lampshade. But she told herself that now wasn't the time. Even as she knew she wouldn't say anything if it *were* the time. She still didn't trust these people enough to let them that far in. Besides, whatever connection the crew of this ship had to … what happened on Baton, and afterward, there would only be time to figure it out later *if* they got out of here alive.

To that end, she keyed her recon microdrones to execute a standard marine boarding protocol. The tiny spheres launched from her armor and spread through the room, seeking the air vents. Once inside the narrow ducts, they could use them as conduits to spread throughout the ship, providing vital intelligence on enemy positions.

Unless the ducts were sealed. Each of the microdrones ran into closed vents in the seams of the room. Mirra would have to cut through one of them to get an access point, but she suspected that if they were sealed here, they were sealed throughout the ship.

"Maybe they auto-sealed after the breach?" Rowley suggested.

Mirra recalled the drones into a tight pattern around her. "They did. They reopened when the bubble went up, otherwise the pressure wouldn't have equalized."

"So someone or something resealed them," Tsegaye said. "Meaning they know we're here."

Mirra nodded. "We'll stick together. I'll take point; Tsegaye, you take the rear. The drones will scout as far ahead and behind as possible, but expect an ambush. Split the hatch, Rowley on the left."

Mirra opened the control panel and uploaded a crack protocol. A few seconds later, her armor beeped and the door slid open. The same instant, Mirra's Stilettos and recon drones flowed through into the corridor beyond. Mirra braced herself.

The corridor was empty. To the left, it terminated in a door. To the right, it ended in a turn left, deeper into the ship. The longer corridor beyond the turn had two hatches on each side, and terminated in another. All were sealed.

"Go," she said, then jetted through the hatch and turned right. She kept an inset view to her rear in the corner of her vision, with an eye on that door at the end. The rest of the team filed out behind her after a brief delay. They moved well, taking advantage of the basic auto-stabilizers in their suits. Still, some of them clearly remembered their microgravity combat training better than others.

Fortunately, Tsegaye seemed to be one of the former. He kept a close watch on the door behind them as he came through, and Mirra rounded the corner up ahead. At any moment, it might slide open and reveal an ambush.

As might any of the doors in *this* hall. Like the exterior hull, the interior walls of the ship were opaque to most of her conventional sensors: infrared, microwave, lidar, the rest. She'd give her left trigger finger for an ENDAR drone to peer through the bulkheads, but entangled neutrino detection was still black tech. Only special forces had field access to it; the reg force marines on *Belisarius* hadn't had any stashed away.

Instead, the team would have to proceed methodically, opening each hatch as they went. But they'd only be able to take one path without diluting their force beyond effectiveness. And each hatch and corridor they left behind them would be another potential ambush point. This was why boarding actions were the most dangerous and stressful infantry operations in modern warfare. And why they were usually the exclusive province of marines, who were extensively trained and equipped for just these sorts of dangers. Sailors might be perfectly serviceable at defending against a boarding action, if they had to, but using them to *execute* one was a last resort. One Mirra had never been forced into until now.

They split the hall at the first pair of hatches. Mirra took the right door, Tsegaye the left. Opening them simultaneously was their best chance to avoid an ambush here. She would send her recon drones and two Stilettos through first, while Tsegaye's recon units watched their backs, with a reserve Stiletto she'd called up from the shuttle for fire support.

As she'd feared, each pair of hatches led to another empty corridor, ending in more sealed hatches. Each an avenue of attack they couldn't afford to clear. She'd have preferred ambush parties waiting within that they could have engaged. At least they'd have known where *some* of the opposition was. More emptiness just led them further into the dark, left her with more choices to make on less information.

"Seal them," she said, closing each hatch and heading to the end of the hall. Experience and her tactical algorithms told her that this direction, rather than either of the branches, was most likely to lead to a vital area. It would take them toward the center-aft of the ship, the logical place for a secondary control center or reactor. *If* there was any common sense to the internal layout of this ship.

There was no room to properly split the hatch at the end of the corridor, so the team lined the walls on either side leading up to it, with Mirra and Rowley flanking the hatch itself. Guessing another room, rather than more corridors, lay beyond, Mirra prepped a spread of stun grenades on her left-arm launcher before uploading the crack protocol to the control panel. If she was right, this would be the perfect place to set up a defensive position—pin the boarders down with heavy fire in a straight corridor with minimal cover, then hit them with a flanking force from behind, back near where they'd breached. It's how she would have defended this section of the ship.

Her armor beeped. The hatch opened. Her drones pushed inside, and she readied her grenade launcher.

She was half right. There was another room beyond the hatch, full of workstations and other cover. It was also empty. The two other hatches within, one leading toward the fore and the other to the starboard of the ship, were sealed. And no ambushers appeared behind them.

The silence gave her pause. *Where is everyone?*

"Ma'am?" Rowley asked.

"Go," Mirra replied, and jetted into the room. In the close quarters beyond, and with her drones kicking out high-density lidar and microwave pings, it should have been impossible for even advanced personal stealth systems to hide their operators for long. Still, she half expected to take fire from invisible assailants when she entered the chamber.

"Fan out," she said once most of the team was inside, and no fire materialized. "Cover each of the exits—breach and scout with drones on my command. Rowley, watch the rear. Tsegaye, on me."

"Awfully quiet," Tsegaye said on private comms. "Maybe the radiation burst got the rest of the crew after all?"

Mirra scanned the darkened consoles. "Maybe. But where are the bodies?"

"It stinks," Tsegaye agreed. "What do we do?"

"Where would you say we are?"

"A guess?" Tsegaye took in their surroundings. "Secondary command, maybe reactor control."

"Then try to get one of these consoles started up. We'll cover you."

"Roger that."

⁕

HADRIAN FOCUSED HIS ATTENTION to Tsegaye's view as the commander chose one of the control stations near the center of the room. Mirra moved off to the forward-facing exit hatch to scout for potential enemy ambush.

"Looks dead," Tsegaye said of the flat black surface. *"No analog controls. Touch or holographic interface. Might not run on battery power."*

Hadrian switched the CIC to a private channel with Tsegaye, so as not to interfere with Mirra's tactical command. "Maybe not a secondary command, then?"

"Or they deliberately shut it down, like with the vents. If so, maybe I can reactivate it."

"Commander," Zevran said, turning his seat toward the HCI, "look for a maintenance access panel on the underside of the console."

Tsegaye flipped himself upside down and lowered his head beneath the console. The design was strange, wholly unlike the stout, utilitarian control surfaces aboard *Belisarius* and other Navy ships. There was a slight curve to it, like it was meant to bend slightly around its operator. It was suspended above the deck by a single thin, tapered support strut, elegant rather than sturdy in appearance. Yet it must have been much stronger than it looked; the console, like the room itself, showed no sign of physical damage, despite the disabling hit the ship had taken.

There was an incongruity to the strange elegance of the control stations, clashing with the bare interiors of the ship.

"Got one. I think—yeah." Tsegaye depressed the panel, visible only thanks to a lidar scan by his suit. *"Woah."*

The panel revealed … something.

The internal architecture of ICN control and power systems tended to match their exteriors—highly analog, full of cables and physical circuitry. This was in stark contrast to almost exclusively wireless and, by outward appearances, far more advanced civilian technology.

In fact, the opposite was true. Compact military tech tended to be much more advanced than civilian, but analog systems, at least as backups, were a necessity to avoid critical failures during combat. Or worse, enemy infiltration of basic systems like lighting, life support, and control surfaces. The militaries of other powers tended to follow the same philosophy, for the same reasons.

What lay behind the maintenance panel in *this* console looked nothing like military or civilian tech. It was almost organic. But this wasn't Hadrian's area of expertise. "Zevran?"

The ECWO frowned more than usual and turned back toward his station. "It appears to be a solidified nanofluid, or nanogel. The circuitry is likely comprised of nanites suspended in the colloidal medium."

"Nanites … Are we in danger here?"

"It's unlikely the nanites are self-replicating, or even motile,"

Zevran replied. "In the proposals I've seen, they simply form a highly efficient distributed network with near-infinite redundancy. It's likely this gel is part of such a network that runs throughout the entire ship."

Hadrian turned to the upper deck. "Proposals? This technology doesn't exist yet?"

"Not that I'm aware of," Zevran confirmed. "Even working prototypes are a decade or more in the future."

"Would the Ciphers be capable of this?"

"Yes. But captured Cipher technology uses an entirely different architecture."

"As of twenty years ago," Tsegaye countered. *"Maybe they've upgraded."*

"Can we access it?" Hadrian asked.

"With some modified protocols, possibly," Zevran said. "Commander, network a materials probe with your remote systems infiltration module, then insert the probe into the medium. I'll take it from there."

"On it."

As Tsegaye worked, Hadrian checked the other feeds. Mirra had opened both other hatches and scouted beyond. No enemy outside the control room, at least as far as the next sets of sealed hatches. Rather than push further out, she'd set up a defensive perimeter inside the control room, with drones out in the corridors to watch for attackers.

Hadrian agreed with her and Tsegaye. This didn't feel right. But there was nothing he could do about that right now.

"Okay," Tsegaye said. *"Probe deployed."*

"Beginning infiltration," Zevran reported. Within seconds, a series of beeps emanated from the console.

"Hey, wait a minute." Tsegaye righted himself and floated above the console. The black surface had lit up. *"Looks like this thing's—"*

Tsegaye didn't finish his thought before the shooting started.

TWENTY-FIVE

At first, even Mirra didn't realize they were being shot at.

For one, the shot didn't sound like any weapon she'd ever heard, save the one time when they breached the ship. For another, it seemed to come from nowhere. One moment, the control room was silent and still, and the next, a small hole had been blasted in the fore-facing wall with a sharp, reverberating crack. For a second, even as her instincts told her what must be happening, she thought the ship might have been struck by a micrometeor, despite the absurd levels of kinetic energy a tiny space rock would need to punch through layers of armored hull that had not long ago absorbed a UMAX shot.

Fortunately, her instincts were faster than her mind.

"Cover!" she shouted just before the fusillade began.

The fore and starboard walls erupted with penetrating impacts, invisible forces tearing clean through the bulkheads. One struck a console on its way through the room; the control station shattered. Metal and polymer showered against Mirra's armor like hail. The mysterious gel that filled the consoles splattered against her and the wall behind. She curled herself up as tight as she could and jetted toward the ceiling.

A sailor tried to take cover behind one of the larger consoles. A shot blasted through the starboard wall, the console, the sailor, and the port wall behind him. The unfortunate sailor twitched and doubled over. His blood bubbled up out of the wound before his armor sealed it.

"High and low," Mirra said into squad comms, her voice loud but even. "High and low!"

The rest of the team belatedly took cover near the top and bottom of the room, flattening themselves to avoid the likely avenues of blind-fire near the center of the chamber. The shots kept coming. Judging from the minor decompression alarm flashing in her helmet, they were blasting clean through the ship and out into space. Her earlier thought about absurd levels of kinetic energy came back to bite her.

"*Belisarius*, Boarding Actual," she said. "Taking high-powered suppression fire from an unknown weapon. Armor and cover ineffective."

She checked her drone feeds for targets—nothing. Switching her rifle to maximum penetration and rate of fire, she let loose a long, whining burst, raking the starboard wall. Hundreds of superfluid projectiles punched through in response to the bigger, heavier punctures of the enemy weapon. Then she jetted to the right, turned, and fired a similar raking burst across the fore wall. A shot rent the air where she'd been, and after her second burst she thrustered down and away, avoiding another return shot.

That proved one thesis—the enemy either couldn't see them clearly, or they were terrible shots. Either worked for her.

"Hold fire!" she shouted when some of the sailors started similarly blind-firing, without first adjusting the penetration characteristics on their weapons. "Wait for targets!"

They didn't have to wait long. Seconds later, Mirra's recon

drones blared an alarm from their forward positions in the corridors beyond, just before they shorted out. At the same moment, Mirra's Stilettos opened up, bathing the enemy's approach vectors with maser fire. In her inset view, Mirra saw lanky black-clad figures flinching as the blazing blue-red energy fire burned against their armor, slowing their advance. The drones zipped randomly through the air after each burst, dodging return fire. But with only one drone in each corridor, they'd only last so long under a determined assault.

"Enemy incoming," she warned her team. "Displace after firing."

The feed from first one Stiletto, then the other, winked out of existence. Seconds later, black-clad figures appeared in each hatchway. They were torn apart by concentrated rifle fire, panicky shots continuing after the targets had been neutralized.

"Controlled bursts," she reminded the team, even as she fired another suppression series through the bulkheads, jinking randomly to avoid the return fire. "Rowley, take two men. Get back to the breach point and hold it."

"Yes, ma'am!"

That diluted her force in the control room, but with all this incoming fire, it was too crowded as it was. And the one Stiletto she'd left there wouldn't last any longer than its fellows had if the enemy tried to cut them off. They couldn't stay here.

Tsegaye clearly had the same thought. "Breaching this system, Commander. Just need a minute."

Mirra glanced at the XO in her rearview; he was hunched in front of the console, tapping away at it, right in the center of the room. A perfect target—proof that the enemy didn't have a clear view of them. *Nobody's* that *bad a shot.*

But if the enemy's fire kept up, it was only a matter of time before he was hit. She bared her teeth. "You have *one*."

"Roger that!"

*

Hadrian watched Tsegaye working and Mirra fighting, his hand obsessively rubbing at his beard. The skin beneath was getting raw. This was a brand-new experience for him, and he hated it. Everything in him cried out to get over there and help, or at least to pester the boarders with comms. Neither would help.

Try as he might, he couldn't stay completely silent. "Zevran, progress?"

"Minimal. Their system's a mess. No obvious logic to it. Function of the distributed network."

"Can't you just download their entire database?"

Zevran's frustration increased. "No. Not with this architecture. Neither of us can find the patterns without—Commander, I need you to operate the computer. Find systems or directories and activate them. That should give *Belisarius* and I something to work from."

"On it." Tsegaye's voice was remarkably calm, given the chaos erupting around him. *"But ... Damn, what the hell language is this? My implant's not translating it."*

The touchscreen panel was lit with buttons in odd shapes and layouts, each labeled with a seemingly random series of lines, hashes, and other markings.

Zevran spun around to look at the visual. His face was a scowling mask. "It's not a language, it's code. The crew must have the cipher programmed into their implants."

Hadrian's eye twitched at the use of the word "cipher." "Can you break it?"

"Not without reference points. Try pathways at random, Commander, until we come across something recognizable."

"You got it." Tsegaye tapped at controls, revealing new layouts of equally indecipherable buttons. *"Jesus Christ."*

They can't stay there.

*

As Mirra slapped another solid-state magazine into her rifle, the console below her took a direct hit and exploded. Her armor thrusters stabilized her against the force of the blast, and the shockwave the shot—whatever it was—had produced. The several enemy weapons now tumbling through the air with the dead bodies of their wielders must be responsible. Mirra couldn't spare a thought for what they might be, though the minor radiological alarm that beeped at the near miss gave her a clue.

Whatever they were, they were tearing through the ship and the boarding team with ease. Clearly, these guys didn't care what state the firefight left their vessel in, so long as it kept Mirra's boarding team from advancing any further.

Or from getting whatever data they could from the computer. Mirra clamped her teeth to keep from pestering Tsegaye. He and the CIC crew were working on the problem. She'd given him a minute. He had thirty seconds left.

And no more, she thought as another blind shot struck a sailor, this time in the shoulder. The crewman's arm was blown clear off, spinning away into the air. He screamed in pain and surprise, tumbled away—

Then the ship hummed with power anew.

Guessing what was about to happen, Mirra was able to get her feet beneath her and keep her footing when the simulated gravity came back online. The rest of the team wasn't quick enough, and they crashed with varying force against deck and consoles. Taking advantage of the presumed confusion, two more black-armored enemy came through each door. Mirra downed one with a quick burst, then sank into a crouch and spun toward the other. The second dying enemy got a shot off, blasting a hole in the deck at her feet and knocking her backward.

"Recover," she said, once again pouring suppressing fire into the two attack vectors. "Keep moving, displace! *Belisarius*, Boarding Actual. Main power's coming back online."

"We're reading that, Commander," Hadrian replied. *"Estimate ... four minutes until their weapons are online, or they reach criticality for containment breach. Can you get to reactor control?"*

Mirra didn't need to think about it. Even with her old team, in the time they had it would have been a tough proposition. "Negative. Resistance too heavy, no idea where reactor control is. We have to withdraw."

"Understood. Retreat to the shuttle at your—"

"Negative!" Tsegaye cut in. "We've got something here, just need another minute to get through!"

Mirra flinched away from another exploding console, rolled on the deck, and came up shooting at another black-clad attacker as he appeared in the starboard doorway.

Hadrian said what she was too busy to: *"You don't have a minute, Arno—get out of there!"*

"Thirty seconds!"

Mirra glanced at the XO huddled behind the main console for its illusory protection, tapping furiously at the mysterious touch-screen controls.

"Confirming that, Captain," a taciturn voice from the CIC added. *"Accessing some recognizable pathways. Should be able to download—"*

"Thirty seconds," Mirra said, against her better judgment. But the data in that computer might be her only way of tracking down the ringleaders of this conspiracy. The people responsible for killing her men.

That was worth thirty seconds.

*

HADRIAN WINCED as another crewman took a hit from the enemy's weapons, which Bella's analysis identified as handheld particle accelerators. This one took off the poor sailor's leg. She wailed, and Hadrian regretted his decision. The mission had to come first, he knew, and this was their mission. But at what cost? That was a question he'd never really had to ask himself, until now.

Not like this.

"You," Mirra said, pointing at an armored sailor. *"Take up the wounded and get the team back to the breach point. I'll cover you."*

The sailor didn't need to be told twice. Hadrian's thumb worked a divot in his jaw. He checked the clock. Twenty seconds left for Tsegaye. A little over three minutes until that ship either vaporized itself or Hassani had to do it for them.

Come on, Arno. Hadrian watched his friend stab at the strange control panel. Admittedly, a few of the directories did now look familiar. An image had popped up that might be the ship's reactor, another that vaguely suggested a filing system. It might be enough for Bella and Zevran to make sense of, but it was mostly nonsense to him. *God damn it all.*

"Downloading another directory," Zevran reported, a little less frustrated now. "Stand by."

The constant sound of repeater fire ebbed slightly as the other team members filed out of the control room, dragging the wounded and dead with them. Thankfully, the sailor who'd lost an arm earlier was back on his feet, fueled by painkillers and stims from his armor. Otherwise, they'd have had to leave the dead sailor behind. There wouldn't have been enough of them left to carry him.

In a moment, it was just Mirra and Tsegaye left in the control room. Hadrian didn't check the clock again before deciding enough was enough.

Mirra made the same decision. *"Time's up, Commander."*

"Just a little—"

"Now!"

"Leave the probe," Hadrian ordered. "Zevran'll get what he can. *You* get the hell out of there!"

"Roger that!" Tsegaye tapped one last control, then turned to crouch-run for the exit.

What happened next didn't register at first. There was a crunching, smashing sound from Tsegaye's audio feed, and he stopped in his tracks. A new hole appeared in the hull across from him. He swayed slightly. Hadrian was about to tell him to get moving.

Then Tsegaye looked down, and saw the gaping hole in the front of his armor.

"Arno!" Hadrian yelled, as his friend fell to the deck.

⁕

TSEGAYE TOOK THE SHOT in the center of his chest. Like the others, it blew clear through him, like he and his armor weren't there. It nearly took Mirra's head off too, if the blinding flash of light and the radiation alarm were any indication.

Through his faceplate, the XO looked shocked. Right before he pitched forward, making no effort to break his fall.

Shit. Mirra emptied the rest of her ammo block in a wide sweep across both fore and starboard walls, then took off at a low run toward the fallen officer, reloading as she went. Just before she reached him, she fired a spread of grenades from her arm launcher through each doorway.

There was no time to check him. As the grenades went off, she grabbed him by one of the handles on the back of his armor and hauled him away, walking backward in a crouch. She held her fire, not wanting to draw return shots when she couldn't dodge. Until more of the enemy started rushing through the doors, like they sensed her weakness. Like they had no care for their own lives.

She fired her rifle one-handed, downing two by the time she

reached the port hatch. Their shots blasted holes in the wall all around her. For a moment, she didn't think she'd make it.

Then she was through the door. She slung her rifle and lifted Tsegaye up over her back, armor servos whirring with effort.

"Get aboard the shuttle," she ordered on direct line to Rowley. She checked her clock. "Prep for emergency microjump, launch at T-minus thirty seconds."

"We're waiting on you, ma'am!"

"Launch at T-minus thirty, that's an order."

"... Yes, ma'am."

Mirra ducked from a near miss passing through the corridor over her head.

We'll make it.

⁎

TSEGAYE'S FEED WENT OUT shortly after he was hit. Mirra's followed after she ordered the shuttle to launch, with or without her. The last readout from Tsegaye's armor had said he was alive. Barely. Hadrian's knuckles were white on the HCI handrail.

"Thirty seconds to enemy reactor criticality," Bella announced.

"Astra locked on. Awaiting your order, sir."

Hassani's voice betrayed how little she wanted to be given that order. About as little as Hadrian wanted to give it.

The shuttle pushed clear of the enemy ship, a few seconds late. Hadrian hoped that was a good sign. Ten seconds of emergency acceleration later, it activated its Stardrive and leaped away faster than light.

Three seconds after that, the enemy ship exploded.

Hadrian reflectively shielded his eyes from the blast, though Bella dimmed the image to keep from burning out her crew's retinas. The miniature star it created was brighter and lasted longer than the death of the research station, but in time it, too, faded.

"Enemy ship destroyed," Hassani said. "Nothing left of it, sir."

Zevran's report was dispassionate. "I was able to download several databases before losing contact. Working on deciphering them now."

"Good work," Hadrian said in a hollow voice, as he stared up at the visual of the system, now empty of sentient presence, save *Belisarius* herself.

At what cost?

TWENTY-SIX

Tsegaye's deathly pale face stared up at Hadrian through the glass of the pod. His eyes were closed, his expression almost peaceful—except for a tightness around his eyes, his mouth. A tension that unconsciousness had not abated. He had not accepted death when it came for him. He had fought it, a brief but merciless struggle that this slight constriction was the last vestige of.

Good for you, Hadrian thought, and then—

"I'm sorry." Doctor Park finished Hadrian's thought. "He'd already been dead several minutes by the time he got here. There was nothing else I could do. Perhaps if he'd arrived sooner ..."

He couldn't have. Microjumping the shuttle had lengthened the recovery time. But if the boarding party hadn't done that, they'd have been vaporized when the enemy reactor went critical. Mirra had made the right call.

"Not your fault, Stanisław," Hadrian said. "What chance does he have?"

Park made a concerned face. "The wound was much more severe than it first appeared. Whatever that weapon was, despite the small entry and moderate exit wounds, it caused extensive burns both internal and external. Even if it hadn't severed his spinal column, the wound would have been fatal—he was suffering from radiation induced organ failure when he died. The other sailors who took hits had the same effects, I almost lost the two amputation patients even after we got them aboard. I've never seen anything like these wounds from an infantry weapon."

"Bella thinks it was a ..." Hadrian swallowed a surge of anger and fear. "Handheld particle accelerator of some kind."

Park's eyes widened. "Well, that would fit. In any case, Commander Tsegaye has been dead long enough that there's been significant brain damage in addition to the other wounds. The cryo will slow the degradation. If we can get him back to a fleet medical center or equivalent in the next week ... Sixty percent?"

Hadrian nodded.

"I'm sorry I don't have a different answer for you, sir."

"Sixty's better than zero." *If we get him back.* If *we get back.* "What about the others?"

Park momentarily brightened, turned toward the main area of the medbay. "Now that I've figured out the radiation effects, Jameson and Moretti will be all right. Off duty, of course, but they'll have their choice of bio or cybernetic limbs when we get back. In a month, you'll never know they were wounded. Phương, though ..."

Another for the tally, along with Lieutenant Farris and his marines. Hadrian suppressed his guilt and squeezed the doctor's shoulder. Park's sad smile spoke to the truth that he was taking the losses even more personally than Hadrian. The doctor didn't ask if it had been worth it. If whatever they'd retrieved from the enemy ship would justify Jameson and Moretti's limbs, Phương's life, and possibly Tsegaye's. He knew better.

Arno's dead face asked them both.

*

"WE SUCCESSFULLY DOWNLOADED portions of three databases before losing the connection. One relating to the ship's engines, another its comm system, and the third a library of some kind."

Zevran was leading the briefing in the captain's stateroom. Hadrian thought it would be easier here, where Arno's empty seat at the briefing room table wouldn't stand out like a gravestone.

He should have known this would be worse. He and Arno had spent many an hour here off watch over the last year, to say nothing of the time they'd spent in the much smaller, similarly appointed cabin aboard *Marissa Tavukcu*. There was no empty chair here, but Arno seemed to haunt the room itself, a specter just out of view, in Hadrian's peripheral. Like at any moment he might turn and see his friend standing there alive.

But perhaps the rest of the officers would take no note of him. The ghost at the feast, visible only to he who had killed him. Or in this case, sent him to his death.

I told you, I'm itching to get off this tub.

Zevran's briefing did little to dispel the heavy mood. The ECWO had reverted to the mean, just as aloof and dour now as if the battle had never happened. "*Belisarius* and I have deciphered portions of the library and comms databases, and a directory of the engine/reactor system. Progress is slow."

"Partially decoded?" Hassani said. "So you haven't figured out the cipher?"

Zevran cast a disapproving eye on the junior officer. "Ciph*ers*. Each system has its own—in fact, each sub-directory uses a variation on the system's cipher. They appear to be randomly generated, and the comm and engine systems have additional layers of security. The process will be a long one."

Tsung scoffed. "Damned inefficient way to run a ship."

"Not necessarily," Zevran said. "If the crew made use of extensive cybernetics, networked with the ship's systems, it would be no different from the way we interact with our computers. Perhaps *more* efficient."

"What have you found?" Hadrian asked.

Zevran brought up a holo of a directory. It looked unlike the strange view they'd gotten of the enemy computer—clearly the deciphered portions had been reformatted. "We've made the most progress on the library data. Most has little if any operational value. In fact, a great deal of it matches content in our own databases, particularly historical and general information. Which is in itself interesting."

"You're saying it's one of ours?" Mirra asked.

Zevran tilted his head. "The similarities suggest a common origin. But I haven't found any direct evidence of who built or crewed it."

"I may be able to shed some light on that." Doctor Park raised his hand from the arm of one of Hadrian's leather chairs. "Though that may only reveal more questions. If you'll permit a brief diversion?"

Hadrian gestured for him to go on. The doctor slid forward; Bella dutifully switched the holo at the center of the room to images of, and a medical readout on, the body Mirra's team had brought back from the enemy ship. As Park spoke, the wiry, black-clad corpse progressed through various stages of deconstruction.

"The autopsy I performed on our friend here was ... perplexing. The individual is human, or he was. Six feet tall, and despite his lanky appearance, 220 pounds. Killed by a series of projectile impacts to the abdomen, no surprises there. He shows no signs of being a simulant. This fellow was born, not grown. But sometime between birth and death, he received remarkably extensive genetic and cybernetic modifications."

"How extensive?" Mirra asked. She looked far more disturbed than Hadrian would have expected. Almost haunted.

Park stood, now in his element. The holo showed the enemy

revealed now, his thin black armor removed. The energy in the room changed, like an inaudible gasp. His skin had a strange, purplish hue, and ridges of metal ran underneath, or just bursting through, the skin all over his body, particularly his head.

"More than I've ever seen," Park said. "Cybernetically, most of his major organs have been replaced—lungs, liver, kidneys. All four limbs, both eyes. Significant neural augmentation, like our standard-issue implants, but far more advanced and integrated with his own nervous system.

"Genetically, some of his most fundamental characteristics have been altered. His skin can absorb various forms of radiation and process them as caloric energy—including X-rays. Along with the radiation shielding in their armor, and this subcutaneous layer here, this goes some way toward explaining how the crew survived the UMAX radiation burst. The skin may also have been capable of a minor adaptive camouflage effect, but I can't be certain. His metabolic system was more efficient than ours. His blood transmitted oxygen more effectively. And, the most perplexing thing of all ..."

The holo showed the body's revealed brain, with a matching diagram next to it. "His neuronal structure was altered via gene editing, in adulthood, to make it more receptive to cybernetic augmentation."

"I thought that sort of neuronal restructuring was impossible in adults," Hadrian said.

"Impossible?" Park said. "No. But it is only theoretical. As far as I'm aware, no process for that kind of editing has even reached the simulation stage, let alone human testing. Let alone *deployment*. I hardly believed it when I uncovered it, but it does explain how he was able to sustain and operate such extensive modifications and survive."

"Good God," Hassani said. "Was he even human anymore?"

"A fair question. If I was to compare him to anything, it would be a synthesis between the most extreme Free Worlder cybernetic and United Citizen genetic modifications, and then some, advanced by decades. With neural changes this comprehensive, he would certainly have been more mentally efficient than any of us. But beyond that, how he would think—what he would feel—would be impossible to predict."

"They threw themselves at us," Mirra said, eyes distant. "Cared nothing for their own lives. Just to hold us in place until the ship exploded."

"If you're suggesting they were remotely controlled, or had a hive consciousness," Park said, "I can't rule that out. But I also found no evidence to suggest that's the case."

"Either way, they're committed," Hadrian concluded. "Doctor; you said they were born, not grown. They're not simulants, but could that still be Cipher tech inside of them?"

"That's surprisingly difficult to say," Park admitted. "Cipher biotechnology usually possesses certain unmistakable hallmarks—energy usage, molecular structure, genetic code—none of which are present here. But given the extent and advanced nature of these modifications, and that I can't *positively* determine their origin, I can't rule it out."

Hassani crossed her arms. "There are stories about human populations in Cipher space. Descendants of abductees from the war, the Sukat Incident, even centuries ago on Earth. Those things could be breeding us out there. Breeding *this*."

Hadrian nodded gravely. "How about this guy's ancestry?"

"His genes have been too heavily modified," Park said. "Nothing conclusive."

"So." Hadrian stood. "We've got a natural-born human with more mods than a Unity Prime gene-chaser and Horizon borg-head combined, all functioning off a gene-editing tech that shouldn't exist yet, armed with some kind of handheld particle accelerator that *also* shouldn't exist, crewing a ship that *looks* almost like one of ours, except it's running off a computer technology that as far as anyone knows is still only a theory. That sound about right?"

Zevran nodded. Park said, "That sounds about right, Captain."

"Wonderful," Hadrian said.

"Black ops," Tsung offered. "Running beyond next-gen tech."

"Or someone wants it to look that way," Mirra suggested, perhaps the slightest bit defensive.

Wouldn't that be convenient for you? "Whichever it is, we know they've infiltrated ISOC, and maybe naval command too. We can't run this up the chain until we figure out how deep it goes. And we can't do that until we figure out what they're after, or at least what their next move is."

"We deciphered the ship's orders."

All eyes moved to the ECWO's taciturn face. Hadrian raised an eyebrow. "Burying the lede a little there, weren't you Zevran?"

Zevran shrugged. "It was necessary to provide context, to explain why we've recovered so little data. We don't know when or by whom the ship was launched, who sent these orders, or the broader strategic context into which they fit."

"Fuck's sake! Out with it, already," Tsung said.

"The orders were contained in the library system's short-term memory," Zevran said to grumbling from Tsung, "making them easier to decode. The crew must have accessed or received them recently. The ship, identified by an alphanumeric designation, was to proceed immediately to CAS 47988 on receipt of the orders. Once there, it was instructed to engage and destroy any ICN vessels present—namely, us."

The vindication that Hadrian had made the right choice was small comfort, given present circumstances. "And having done that?"

"After destroying *Belisarius,* it was to remain on station under stealth for several hours to ensure no other ICN vessels arrived.

Satisfied of that, it was to proceed … to Byas. There to rendezvous with two other ships which, based on their designations, *Belisarius* believes to be of a similar class."

Hadrian's mouth fell open.

"Byas?" Mirra asked.

Tsung's frown deepened. "What the hell for?"

"The orders say only that after the rendezvous, the three ships should remain under stealth and complete their previously assigned mission," Zevran said. "We haven't been able to locate or decode *those* orders yet."

A coldness spread through Hadrian's chest. "Based on the time this ship was ordered to depart, assuming a similar max Stardrive velocity to ours, when would this rendezvous have taken place?"

"Around fourteen hundred hours tomorrow, IST," Zevran said after a quick calculation.

"My God." The coldness gripped Hadrian's heart. "Singh."

It took a moment for the others to realize what he meant. Whispered curses followed. Mirra gave him a questioning look.

"Admiral Singh's escorting Defense Minister Reinhardt to Byas with a Fifth Fleet squadron for a surprise visit," Hadrian explained. "They're scheduled to arrive at fifteen hundred tomorrow."

Mirra leaned back as realization dawned. "An ambush."

"Like hell that's a coincidence," Tsung said.

Hadrian began to pace. "If they know the time of Singh's arrival, they probably know the coordinates too. They could set up under stealth just inside optimal UMAX range, blow the whole damn squadron out of space before they knew what hit them."

"They won't have a chance," Hassani breathed.

"We must warn them," Park said, horrified.

"We can't." Hadrian made himself stop, face his officers. "This was top secret info. Either these guys have highly placed people in the government, or Fifth Fleet, or they have the Naval Hub breached and they're reading all encrypted comms traffic. Hell, they might have read it off Singh's transmission to *me,* for all we know. We try to warn him, they'll know about it."

"Regardless," Park continued, "the admiral could call off the visit, avoid the trap."

Hadrian shook his head. "Or the enemy would *change* the trap. Wait to intercept them when they return to Ranak, or wherever the squadron diverts to. With access to fleet comms, there'd be nowhere they could hide."

"We can't just let them get away with this!" Hassani said. "There must be something we can do."

There is. When it came to him, the coldness gripping his heart melted away. A sense of incongruous peace washed over him. "Bella, if we leave immediately at max Stardrive, when would we arrive at Byas?"

"Approximately thirteen hundred hours tomorrow, IST."

"Then order the ship to secure for Stardrive. Helm, this is the Captain. Lay in a course for Byas, maximum velocity, execute on my order."

The meaning of his orders were clear. Hassani seemed energized; Tsung radiated a grim determination. Zevran, quiet resignation, the same as if he'd been ordered to conduct a routine diagnostic on the computer systems. Park looked worried, but said nothing.

Mirra frowned. "You're going to attack them?"

"We have the same advantage they'd have against Singh," Hadrian said, as he and his officers double-checked their surroundings for unsecured items and equipment. "We know where and when they're going to decel from Stardrive. We post up nearby and take 'em out."

"Except that we'd be one against three."

"Two," Hadrian countered, sharply. "We already destroyed one."

"Barely."

Hadrian's eye twitched. He gave himself a moment to breathe.

"Course confirmed for Byas, Captain," Ensign Keitel reported. *"Awaiting your order."*

"Stand by, Ensign." Hadrian turned from Mirra's impassive, disapproving stare to each of his officers. "This isn't gonna be easy. But our friends and comrades are sailing into a trap, and this is the only chance we have to save them. Besides that, our mission is still to defend Byas. Who knows what these sons of bitches plan to do after they wipe out Singh's squadron? If they're working for the Ciphers, they might glass the whole planet, or at least the parts of it they don't want to keep. In that case, we're also the only chance the byasians have."

"All stations report secure for Stardrive, Captain," Bella announced.

"Roger that. Helm, take us back to Byas."

"Yes, sir. Executing."

Hadrian and his officers floated up from the deck as the simulated gravity disengaged. The ship thrummed with building power. "I'll address the whole ship's complement before we get there, but for now, just remember this: We've got a job to do, we're gonna do it. And I know you're all up to it. I *know* it."

Park drew on some inner strength. Hassani nodded. "Yes, sir."

"Okay. We've got six hours ship's time until we get to Byas. Zevran, assign the best code-breaker on your staff—other than you—to work with Bella on deciphering more of that ship's orders. I want to know what else they're up to at Byas before we get there. I want *you* going over the data from the battle, see if you can figure out some way we can get an edge this time if we end up in another duel. Hassani, same goes for you.

"Wei, go over all the engineering data we got on that ship. Power output, speed, drones, hull—anything we might be able to use. Meanwhile, get your crews working on the Astra. I want to overclock our gun without blowing the whole ship up. I don't fancy winging the bastards again if we can avoid it."

“Don’t worry about that.” Tsung smiled grimly at Hassani. “I’ll give you the juice, kid. You just shoot it straight.”

A shadow of concern passed over Hassani’s face when she smiled. Hadrian made a note to follow up with her later. “Doc, you already know what to do.”

“Yes, sir.” Park’s smile was sad.

“Okay.” Hadrian looked at Mirra. “Dismissed.”

She seemed to understand. The other officers filed out one by one, leaving Hadrian and his passenger alone with the silence between them. That lingered for a moment, before it too departed.

“We had a deal,” Hadrian said.

TWENTY-SEVEN

"Did I break it?" Mirra said.

Hadrian stared darkly at her. "You said you'd respect my command."

"And I have."

"You just questioned my orders in front of my officers. I know you ISOC types play it loose with discipline, but I can't imagine even *you* stoop to that."

Mirra kept her frustration in check. With increasing difficulty. "We do if the orders are foolish."

"Foo—" Hadrian swallowed the word, then pushed off from his desk, floated over to one of his bookshelves. "What would you have us do, run and hide?"

"I would have us retreat to interstellar space to decipher more of the data we retrieved, at some cost, from the enemy ship. Enough to give us another lead."

"We deciphered enough to give us *this* lead." Hadrian turned back to her. "And I don't need you to tell me what the cost was."

Mirra let her eyes darken. "This is not a lead, it's a trap."

"So, what?" Hadrian shrugged. "We just let Admiral Singh, the minister of defense, and all those sailors die?"

"The alternative isn't saving them. The alternative is rushing into battle against a superior enemy, and watching them die regardless—"

"You don't know that."

"—while, in the process, we destroy the only ship and crew with any knowledge of this conspiracy, and with it the only chance of bringing its leaders to justice."

"Justice, or revenge?"

The dead faces of her men flashed behind her eyes. She knew what they cried out for. What they demanded. How thankless their task had been, how well-earned their rest—yet how could they rest, when they'd died as they had? Betrayed, and their betrayers free and living?

Finally, she let her anger slip free. "That's the problem."

"What?"

"Idealistic men like you who think there's a difference. Who think that what we do is in the service of some higher purpose." Mirra sneered. "We kill the enemy before they kill us. There's no great cause, no higher morality. The only people who think differently are … simulation soldiers like you, who don't know what it's really like out there."

Hadrian's eyes flared. "Don't I?"

"No. Fighting one battle and losing one friend doesn't mean you know."

Hadrian stared at her, silent, for a long time. She was surprised when it started to unnerve her. She almost looked away first.

Then he nodded.

"Did I tell you how I got *Belisarius*?" he said. "Did Arno?"

She shook her head.

"Couple years ago, I got my first real command: Destroyer, *Marissa*

Tavukcu. She was old, small, out of date. I loved her. We both did. She was all we'd ever wanted." Hadrian seemed to catch on his next words; his eyes finally left hers, drifted downward. He pushed off for his bar, poured himself a sealed bourbon. This time, he didn't offer her one.

"She was posted to Pyria, with Twelfth Fleet. Easy job, for the most part. Orbital recon, fire support. Hunting for Cipher smugglers, never finding any." He took a long drink. "One day, this fire support request comes in. Priority Alpha, Special Warfare unit."

Hadrian looked at her, accusatory. She was Naval Infantry, not SWB, but ISOC tended to find themselves painted with the same brush regardless of which service they belonged to. She was used to it. And the concatenation was not always unjustified.

"They're in this village in League territory," Hadrian went on, "and they're taking heavy fire. I can hear it over comms, sounds bad. But I can't see anything. Literally—forest canopy's too thick in that region for visuals, and none of my sensors have a thing. I can see the team's beacons, but no thermals, no movement, no EM. Nothing. Team leader says the enemy's got a Cipher disruptor active, but he'll paint their positions on the map."

Another long swig. "Thing is. ROE says I can't shoot without confirmation of the target. Not in League territory. But I *have* confirmation, right? Guy on the ground is right there, painting the targets for me. I can hear him taking fire. 'We're dying down here,' he says. Seems like he means it."

In spite of everything, Mirra found herself drawn in. "What'd you do?"

"I ordered the shoot." Hadrian's eyes took on a distant, haunted cast Mirra was all too familiar with. "Good shots. Dead on. But … there's no insurgents in that village. No Bloc troops. No weapons. There *are* over three hundred civilians. Or there were. I can see them, once the canopy burns away. Through the fire. What's left of them. And I can *hear* the Special Warfare officer, laughing. 'Nice shooting,' he says. Then—"

Hadrian sliced his hand across his throat. Transmission dead. His lips curled down in disgust. "I don't know if they'd already massacred the village, wanted us to cover their tracks. Maybe they wanted *us* to do it for them, and most of those villagers were still alive when I fired. That's the one that … Either way, I don't know why. For fun? Revenge?" Hadrian turned his disgust on her. "What's the difference, right?"

Mirra ignored the accusation.

"After that, I did what you're supposed to do." Hadrian scoffed. "Ran it up to my squadron CO. He took it to the admiral. Nakatomi called me over to the *Manaan* the next day. Told me that it was a good shoot. That there *had* been weapons, and a Cipher disruptor. That all the seemingly civilian bodies—the *children*—were in fact insurgents. Making this one of the most effective fire support missions of the entire deployment."

Hadrian shook his head. "I said that couldn't be. He said it *was*. I said I'd take it over his head, to theater command, or to Admiral Singh. He said if I did that, evidence would be released … which would show that Arno and I had ordered the strike on our own initiative, *knowing* there were no insurgents in the village. That there hadn't even been a Special Warfare team there. That our crew had carried it out, knowing that. That my squadron CO had authorized it, knowing that. And that my ship's logs would reflect those *facts* and show that we had conspired to fabricate the evidence of weapons afterward. Since the evidence actually *had* been fabricated, that part wouldn't have been too hard."

Mirra wasn't shocked by what Hadrian told her—except, perhaps, by how much it reminded her, once again, of the mission on Baton. And before that, of New Eden. But it *had* clearly shocked Hadrian. She wanted to resent him for that … But then, there was a time, long ago, when she felt the same.

"Even if the story leaked to the press," Hadrian said, "and they couldn't prove who leaked it, all of that would come out. We'd all be finished. Arno and I would have ended up in prison. And *they* still would have gotten away with it."

He finished the last of his drink, then let the cup drift through the air, watching it with regretful eyes. "So we kept our mouths shut. They gave us promotions, pinned medals on us. I burned mine. Then they gave us *Belisarius*. Put us out here, out of the way. Sometimes I still wish I'd come clean, even if it wouldn't have made a difference. Just to get it off my chest. But it's the times I don't, the times I love *this* ship, that I feel the worst."

Hadrian took a deep breath, then turned his gaze on her again. Some anger had returned to it, but tempered, measured. "I haven't been in the shit like you have, but I know what your kind are capable of. And I *know* what the Navy's capable of."

Mirra felt the atavistic urge to leap to her service's defense. Instead, she said, "And after all that, after the last few days, you still think there's more to what we do?"

"I have to," Hadrian said without hesitation. The words seemed to give him strength, somehow. Push out some of the anger, the bitterness, and the guilt.

Mirra couldn't imagine why. "I don't."

If Hadrian was disappointed by her answer, he did a decent job of hiding it. "That's up to you. You're not under my command, I can't order you to do anything. If there was somewhere along the way we could drop you off, I would. There isn't. So you're going with us."

"Understood."

"But." Hadrian retrieved his drifting glass. "You did save my life. And Arno's … for now, at least. That's got to be worth something. So when we get to Byas, I'll give you one of our shuttles, a rifle, and a suit of marine armor. You can have the data Zevran's decoded. You can go where you like. I won't force you to die on a fool's errand."

The gesture was unexpected. Somehow, it stung her. "Thank you."

Hadrian held her gaze for a moment, as if expecting her to say more. Or expecting to say it himself. Then he nodded at the door. "You can go. I've got work to do."

Rather than repeat her thanks, she floated through the hatch and left the captain alone. Outside in the corridor, she found herself alone too. Despite the sailors deftly drifting past her as they prepared their ship for another battle. Part of her felt compelled to join them, somehow. The part of her honed by decades of training and experience. It couldn't bear to be still at a time like this.

But that was a mindless part. These people were all going to their deaths. To meaningless deaths. Like the ones her men had died. Only this time, there would be no lone survivor to bring them justice. Vengeance.

Yes, she thought as she made her way silently past the damned, *there will be.*

TWENTY-EIGHT

The lift door opened before Hadrian realized it had stopped. If that hadn't snapped him out of his introspective spiral, the noise of the Engineering section might have. Failing *that*, the crewman who nearly crashed into him when he floated out of the lift would have done the job.

The engineer did a double take, his eyes widening when he realized who he'd almost collided with. He let go of the heavy piece of equipment he was carrying to salute the captain—then panicked as it continued through the air ahead of him. He barely managed to grab hold of it and hook his foot into a railing to arrest the object's flight before it careened into someone or something valuable.

Hadrian smiled. A dozen more engineers were working just as hard, if a little more carefully, within sight of the lift. Support drones hovered around them, assiduously avoiding the sailors' movements. Despite being one of the largest single compartments in the ship, Engineering always felt cramped and crowded. The two massive, sloped housings toward the rear of the main chamber radiated the low, permeating hum felt throughout the ship, adding to the sense of ceaseless work.

Then there were the cables. It was one thing to know that a Navy ship's systems had analog cores, for security and reliability reasons. It was quite another to see the bundles of insulated wires and filaments spilling out of maintenance hatches, or lying severed on the floor pending replacement. There was something perverse about it, like seeing a person's intestines.

Still, Hadrian had always liked it down here. Some command officers seemed uncomfortable with the incongruity, the disparity between the well-ordered and clean upper decks and the controlled chaos of the lower. Hadrian felt the opposite. Somehow, it was comforting to him to know that the precise, hypermodern warship he commanded still had this hive of messy, human activity at its heart. Even so, he didn't get down here as often as he might have liked. Whoever else worked down here, this was the domain of one man alone.

"Damn it to hell, Rodriguez! Are you *trying* to kill yourself? 'Cause I got a sidearm'll do the job a lot quicker!"

An engineer pulled back from the console she'd been working on, held her hands up as she drifted slowly away. Her support drone hovered back with her. "Sorry, sir!"

"Don't apologize," the pair of legs sticking out from under the same console said. "Make up your damn mind. If I have to find a replacement for you, I'd rather start now."

"No, sir!"

"Then get back in there and do it *properly*."

"Yes, sir!" Rodriguez tilted forward and returned her hands to the console. A few seconds of tinkering later, and the tenor of the hum in the room changed slightly.

"Finally." Commander Tsung floated out from under the console. The sleeves of his dull blue work uniform were rolled up.

Sweat beaded on his brow. He wiped it away with his forearm, leaving a slight smear of lubricant behind. The blushing engineer continued working as Tsung deftly pushed off the deck with his toes, righting himself to look over her shoulder. "Good. Now the rest."

Rodriguez visibly relaxed. "Yes, sir."

Tsung patted her on the shoulder, then caught sight of Hadrian as he twisted to survey his crews at work. He nodded at the captain, but instead of coming over to greet him, pushed off toward the next task on his list. Hadrian followed him to a bundle of cables spilling out of one of the huge reactor housings. "Cap'n."

"Commander," Hadrian replied.

"Don't see you down here too often." Tsung examined the cables. Hadrian noted that no support drones followed the chief around as they did the rest of the Engineering crew. "Come to check on us?"

"Just making the rounds."

Tsung grunted, started detaching one of the cable bundles. "Well, don't need to worry about us. Everything's on track. Hassani'll get her big gun overcharged without blowing us all to hell or lighting us up like a nova. Least on account of my reactors."

"I have no doubt. What about the study of the enemy ship?"

"Finished. Not much to—son of a *bitch*." The panel sparked. Tsung tossed a detached bundle of cables behind him. A drone swooped in to pluck it from the air. "Not much to say. Hell of a cannon packed into that little frame. Must have a hell of a reactor to go with it. Durable as a mother too. If our girl was built like that, I wouldn't mind so much when that idiot helmsman bounces us off a gravity well."

Hadrian moved back to give the engineer's elbows some room. "Heavily armored?"

"Not just that. Thing could take stress that'd crush any ship in the Navy. Every compartment, bulkhead, and millimeter of the bitch was micro-engineered to withstand stress. I'm talking gravitational, now." Tsung looked up at Hadrian. "She could've slammed right into a planetary well and survived. Wouldn't've been pleasant, but she'd have survived. Probably could have dived right down a black hole's throat, if she'd wanted to. I could sell her structural designs at Hyperion and retire."

"What would you do with retirement?"

"None of your damn business, that's what." Tsung returned a fraction of Hadrian's smirk. "Anyway. Direct hit from a UMAX'd still blast the thing to pieces, so just make sure Hassani shoots straight next time."

"I'll pass that along."

"Something else bothering you?" Tsung asked when Hadrian didn't excuse himself.

Is there? "Like I said, just making the rounds. How's your crew?"

Tsung jerked his head in the general direction of a few hustling engineers as he secured the replacement cables. "Keeping busy. That's the important thing, time like this."

"Good." Still, Hadrian didn't leave. "And they're … confident?"

Tsung sealed the panel, stared silently at it for a moment. Hadrian feared he might be about to get one of the chief's famous tongue-lashings for wasting his time, commanding officer or no. That would have created an awkward situation, requiring discipline that now would have been the worst possible time to dispense.

"I was in the Terrible Tenth, back in '84," he said eventually. "At Embra. First combat posting, the *Sunderland*. Tender, converted carrier. Machine bastards just kept comin', week after week. Kept us working round the clock. Sending us over to ships, bringing ships to us. That was the first time I saw Bella."

Hadrian's eyes widened. *Jesus, were the stories true?*

Tsung thumped a bulkhead with his fist, gently. "Brand new, back then. She was in a bad way when they brought her to us.

Took a glancing hit from a positron lance, sheared half her starboard wing clean off. She shot back and killed the son of a bitch, but nobody thought she'd make it. Back then especially, the Mark IIs packed a punch, but they'd come apart if you tapped 'em hard enough. We worked on her for a week. Two, three times we thought she was gonna blow, take us with her."

"Why didn't they send her back to dry dock?" Hadrian asked.

"Couldn't get her Stardrive online without killin' her. Besides, if there was any chance we could get her running again, we needed the firepower. The Tenth was hanging by a thread." Tsung scoffed at the memory. "We got her reactors stabilized, running. The 'nids fabbed a replacement wing. Tell you what, she looked like hell with that ugly bug contraption fused to her, but ..."

Tsung looked around at the bulkheads, the ceiling, the exposed wiring, as if it were a beloved childhood home. Or a beloved child. "When I watched her fly away at the end of that week, ready to fight, I knew there was no other ship in the fleet I wanted to serve on. And if they ever gave her to me, I'd never let her go." He turned to Hadrian. "Bella's got no give-up in her. Not a bit of it. Whatever you need, she'll give it to you. I promise you that."

Hadrian saw the confidence he had been looking for in the engineer's eyes. And now, he felt it all around him too. "I have no doubt."

Tsung nodded curtly. "Now get out of my way so I can get some real work done."

"Roger that, Chief."

"Cap'n."

Hadrian's smile only faded when he approached the lift, and a call made the next stop on his rounds obvious. "Go ahead, ECWO."

"We've deciphered more of the enemy's orders," Zevran reported. *"You'd better come take a look."*

*

Belisarius's Electronic and Cyberwarfare section was rarely fully staffed. Its officers and ratings were commonly stationed in the CIC while the ship was in operation, making up nearly half of the Command Information Center's crew at any given time. The rest could be found at secondary stations distributed throughout the ship during combat, in case the CIC was compromised or damaged.

The central ECW section was primarily used for signals and data analysis and decryption, as was the case today. Hadrian had instructed Zevran to delegate the task of deciphering the enemy's data to his subordinates, and there were indeed two of them working on *something* in separate corners of the section. Each of them was using privacy equipment, helping them focus on their task.

Zevran had decided on his own initiative to continue the decryption of the ship's library database himself. Under the circumstances, Hadrian was glad he had, and glad that his two officers wouldn't be able to hear their conversation in the low-lit, quiet room.

"I wasn't able to decode more of the ship's orders," Zevran explained, as they both floated over his console. "Rather, *related* orders, also stored in short-term memory."

"Related how?"

"They detail what I believe to be a subsidiary, or backup plan for this operation at Byas." Zevran brought the orders up on the hardscreen, text-only. "Like the ship's orders, they're vague, but the implications are clear."

Hadrian read the first few lines. His eyes widened. "A *ground* operation?"

"And the target is explicit."

The bottom fell out of Hadrian's stomach as he read. A last-minute reception had apparently been planned to welcome the VIPs to Byas. Likely, Singh had signaled ahead to the planet, giving them a day's notice to set it up. Probably would have signaled *Belisarius,* too, if they'd still been connected to the network.

Whoever wrote these orders had clearly been connected all along. From the looks of it, they'd somehow known ahead of time that a reception would be planned, even if they couldn't be certain of the details.

But one thing *was* certain.

"Everyone's gonna be there," Hadrian said. "All the olans, from every district. Their households and councils. The ICRA leadership."

Jack.

"Perfect target for a decapitation strike," Zevran said.

"Plant a big enough bomb, they could blow them all to hell." *Damn it.* "Or, storm the place, take as many of the VIPs as possible hostage. With the squadron in space wiped out, the leadership destroyed or in disarray, Cipher-loyal insurgents could take over the whole planet. Then use the hostages as shields when Compact reinforcements show up."

"That seems a logical conclusion."

Hadrian shook his head. "With the recent bombings, there'll be added security. They'd need a pretty strong force with some heavy firepower to storm it."

"No roster or order of battle is provided, but based on the data we have, *Belisarius* projects a likely combination of local insurgent forces with infiltrated combatants. Possibly of the same type we encountered on the enemy ship."

"With those weapons, they'd tear through local security." Hadrian blew out a long breath. "If we're right, this is all keyed to help the insurgents take over. That begs the question: Are we dealing with the Ciphers? Some new variation, a breakaway faction maybe, if they even have those?"

Zevran breathed deeply. "That's the other thing I've uncovered."

He checked behind them to make sure his officers weren't watching. The unusual behavior from his ECWO put Hadrian's hackles up.

"In the comms and reactor systems," he explained, bringing more data up on the hardscreen, "there are elements of Cipher code. It doesn't match exactly anything we've seen before, but that in itself doesn't mean anything. They modify their code frequently. The unusual thing is what it's been modified *with*."

Zevran tapped a few more controls, and a set of code came up on the screen. Hadrian squinted. "What am I looking at?"

"This." Zevran tapped the highlighted lines. "It's UCC code."

It took a moment for the significance to sink in. "You're sure?"

"I recognize it," Zevran said, a hint of pique. "I used it myself, before …"

"How are they even compatible?" Hadrian asked.

"The Cipher code seems to have been written specifically to interact with it. Now, the types of code we're seeing here, and the purpose they serve, suggest that the reactor is of combined Cipher-UCC *design*."

"On a *war*ship? That can't be," Hadrian said. Zevran gestured at the screen. "But … how would the Ciphers get a hold of UCC technology, if they're the ones behind this? I can't imagine the councils would willingly help the Ciphers get control of any planet, even if they oppose the Protectorates."

Hadrian thought he detected the hint of a sardonic sneer on Zevran's face before he said, "Nor I."

"And the conspirators we've run into so far have all been special forces. Hardly an arm of UCC policy."

"Indeed, but the evidence is clear. UCC technology is being used, combined with Cipher technology. For what purpose, neither *Belisarius* nor I can speculate."

Hadrian peered down at the screen again. "Could it be that

someone wants it to *look* this way? Create the impression that there's cooperation between the UCC, ISOC, and the Ciphers?"

"That is a possibility. Without more data …"

Hadrian nodded. "Well. You were right to keep this to yourself, for now. If you find anything else, bring it to me directly. I'll brief the senior officers on it before we arrive."

TWENTY-NINE

"Damn it to hell!"

The outburst that greeted Mirra when she entered helped convince her that she must have taken a wrong turn in her wanderings about the ship. It looked as though she had just drifted straight into the CIC: There was the glowing HCI, in the command pit to her right, with the big hardscreen on the fore wall; before her were the upper deck crew and officer stations, ECW on her immediate left, helm a little ahead on her right, and directly in front of her, TacOps.

Two clues told her she hadn't wandered into the ship's control center. For one, TacOps was the only station occupied by an officer. For the other, Mirra was fairly certain *Belisarius* hadn't just been destroyed by an enemy UMAX strike.

The combat simulator room's lone occupant slumped in her seat, evidently having taken no notice of Mirra or the entry alert that must have heralded her arrival. It would have been a simple thing for Mirra to push off from the doorframe, float back out into the corridor, and leave without ever having been noticed. If the officer ever took notice of the alert, she could check who had entered—and probably be glad of the speedy departure.

"I apologize for the interruption," Mirra said.

Lieutenant Hassani spun her chair around. Embarrassment flushed her cheeks as she waved the simulation away. The CIC disappeared, leaving a bare, low-lit room ringed with dark consoles and seats in its wake.

"That's all right, ma'am," Hassani said. "I was just … Can I help you with something?"

Mirra pushed off into the room, letting the door close behind her. "I was hoping to get in a sim or two before we arrive at Byas."

"Oh, you'll want the infantry combat simulator. That's a deck down."

"My mistake. I'm sure this one sees a fair bit more use."

Hassani nodded. "I can, uh, show you down there if you'd like?"

"I'm sure I can find it on my own." Mirra drifted forward. "I take it you're having trouble sleeping?"

Hassani smiled tiredly. "Captain gave first watch the evening off so we can be on when we get to Byas, but … Yeah, don't think I could sleep right now. This seemed like a better use of time."

That depends. "May I see? I've never watched a naval combat simulator in action."

"Sure," Hassani said after a moment's hesitation. She gestured for the sim to reactivate, and the empty CIC appeared all around them, the room suddenly seeming twice as large. Hassani turned her seat back toward her now-lit console. "I don't think the tech's changed much since the war, except the holosomatics are a bit more advanced—but I guess you're familiar with that anyway, using the infantry version."

Mirra touched the illusory railing of the upper deck, felt the dull haptic feedback. The fragment of the ship's AI managing the illusion had interfaced automatically with her neural implants and was feeding the sensation directly to her. It was almost, but not quite, as if the object were really there.

"It looked like you were simulating the battle over the ignicite moon again," Mirra said.

"Not quite," Hassani said through a breath. "Similar parameters. Since we expect to face the same class of ship at Byas. Two of them, rather."

She brought up the program she had been running, reset to the beginning. The enemy ship's probability sphere appeared over the HCI, surrounded by tactical readouts. The sphere had already shrunk, and targeting alerts were frozen in the process of flashing. Hassani's program cut to the chase, to the point of the engagement at which her role was becoming paramount. There was little she could do during the long stretch when the sensors and ECW sections of the two ships were dueling, trying to shrink that sphere.

Second mistake, Mirra thought.

The simulation stayed frozen. Clearly, Hassani was only willing to show so much. Mirra didn't blame her. *She* would've been reluctant to show even this.

And what does that say about you? "It didn't appear to be going very well."

"No," Hassani said.

"It did in reality."

A longer pause. "Did it?"

"We survived."

Hassani nodded slowly. Mirra hoped she'd finally pushed enough of the younger woman's buttons.

"I started out running the captain's trick," Hassani said at last. "Bella caught it every time, so I programmed her not to expect it. Then it worked, most of the time. Other times I don't use it. Other times I try my own tricks. Almost every time, the same thing happens."

Hassani let the program run. The dueling probability spheres shrank. She put her hand on the firing controls. The enemy sphere resolved into a cluster of possible targets. Hassani chose one and fired.

The shot sailed harmlessly through space. The enemy's simulated return fire slammed into *Belisarius*. The simulation froze once again, now with a red *DEFEAT—SHIP LOST* readout over the HCI. Red light bathed the simulated room.

"You choose the wrong target," Mirra said.

"Or I'm too slow. Or my shot hits their shield, theirs hits ours, but their gun recharges faster. Or there's a *second* ship." Hassani shook her head. "A lot of different ways to get to the same damn place."

Mirra let the silence speak for her.

Hassani stared bitterly up at the sign of her defeat. "You know, back at the academy … I outshot everyone in my class. Outshot the computer. I was fast, but that's not enough. I was fast and *right*. Somehow I just always knew."

She stabbed blindly at the hardscreen of her console. "Same thing with shipboard sims and exercises. I always thought that'd translate, but …"

Hassani turned to Mirra. "This is a good posting. She's an old ship—some officers call postings like this dead-end billets. Maybe that's true for them, but me? I only made lieutenant a year and a half ago. TacOps chief on a battlecruiser …"

"Now you're doubting that confidence."

"How could I not?" Hassani waved at her console. "I froze. When the targets came up, I *froze*. I've *never* frozen. My first time in the hot seat back at the academy, everyone watching me, I didn't freeze."

"Hesitations happen, particularly the first time in combat."

"Not to Captain Hadrian. It was his first battle too, and he knew what to do."

Mirra could have said something about that. "And what did he tell you?"

Hassani hung her head. "Just what you did. We survived. Hesitations happen. I did good; next time I'll do better."

Mirra nodded.

"You know what I didn't tell him, though? The worst part?" Hassani scoffed. "I'm *glad* I froze. Because I was wrong. I knew which target I thought it was, I was *sure* it was, but I was wrong. If I *had* trusted my instincts, we'd all be dead. How the hell am I supposed to move on from that?"

"You're right." Mirra pointed at the defeat condition. "You failed. You need to own that."

Hassani's brow knit. "Isn't that what I'm doing?"

"No. You're letting *it* own *you*."

Hassani seemed to think for a moment, then turned to the defeat indicator. "So how do I do one and not the other?"

"By accepting your failure. You keep running the same simulation over and over, trying to change the result. How many times have you?"

"Three," Hassani said. "Out of twenty."

"And how many times out of twenty would you have been satisfied with?" Mirra asked. It was obvious what the answer was. "You wouldn't have been. You'd have launched a twenty-first sim, and when you failed, *that* would've been the only one that mattered."

Mirra drifted into Hassani's eyeline. "You're trying to erase your failure with successes. Except you can't. You know that, but you're trying anyway. No matter how many times you do better, you won't be able to erase the fact that *that* time, you failed. That if it had been up to you ..."

The faces of her men flashed before her eyes, dead and pleading. "That all your comrades would be dead. And you with them. That's a terrible feeling. Even worse when you've actually done it."

Hassani's eyes changed. Perhaps she'd made the connection Mirra just had. Mirra hoped not ... and hoped *so*.

Hypocrite, she thought. What would she honestly have been doing in the combat sim? Would she not have been running Lampshade over and over, as many times as she could? Just to see if there was any way she could have done better, any way she could have saved King, or Tchaikovsky, or any one of her men? Just *one*?

Maybe that's why she'd stopped here instead of floating away unseen. She'd known what Hassani was doing, instinctively. After all, it was in her too.

"It's the easiest thing in the world for something like that to own you," Mirra said, "if you let it. And nothing, no amount of success, real or simulated, can ever erase it."

No amount of revenge.

"What does?" Hassani asked.

"Nothing. You have to embrace it. Make it a part of you, and not one you're ashamed of. *Own* it. You failed. You weren't good enough. But that's the only way we can get stronger. By knowing our weaknesses."

"Okay," Hassani said at length. "Okay, I will. And I'll keep trying."

"That's the other thing." Mirra waved around them. "*This* isn't real. This emptiness. It's a fantasy. One where everything's on you, alone. But you were right—if that were true, we wouldn't be here. What you do, you do for them, *and* with them."

"That's a lot of responsibility," Hassani said.

"It is."

Hassani nodded. "Thank you, Commander. I think I'll try another one."

Mirra patted her on the shoulder, then pushed off for the door. As she left, the simulated CIC came to life with simulated officers and crew, buzzing with all the activity it should rightly have. Mirra couldn't see enough data to be certain, but she'd have bet the engagement parameters had been changed too.

Out in the relative dark of the corridor, the faces of her men came back to her again. She thought she might have gotten them wrong. They demanded justice, yes—but perhaps their plea was for something else too. Something *for* her, as well as from her.

She just wasn't sure it was something she could accept.

THIRTY

Hadrian didn't see Mirra again until they met in the launch bay, less than an hour ship's time before arriving at Byas.

He had checked in on her once during his rounds. Bella told him she, too, was wandering the ship, though avoiding the main crew stations rather than seeking them out. She had spent a little time in the combat simulator with Hassani, which was odd. But he didn't intend to ask her what she had been doing. He didn't want her to know he'd been checking up on her, petty as that was.

Mirra had arrived at the bay before him. She was floating there now, unanchored near the shuttle he'd promised her, staring at it. She looked different, somehow, apart from the borrowed twilight-blue marine uniform she was wearing. Quiet, as she'd been since he met her, but less cold. Hadrian got the sense of introspection from her, which was about the last thing he'd have expected. It gave him pause.

She noticed him before he could announce himself. The sense of introspection vanished when she turned to him, but in so doing, proved it had existed. "Captain."

"Commander." Hadrian moved along handholds toward her. "All set?"

"I have what I need."

"What about your civilian clothes?"

"Recycle them."

Hadrian smiled briefly at the memory of her bursting into the little room and killing all three conspirators, wearing her incongruous civvy outfit. In retrospect, it suited her even less well than it had seemed to at the time. "The armor and weapons I promised are on board. Fuel, water systems, and food synthesizer are stocked, should have no trouble getting you to the next port."

"Good." Mirra glanced at the shuttle; a little of the introspection returned. "When do I launch?"

"As soon as we arrive. Provided the enemy isn't already there. If we fly into a fight, you'll have to stay aboard. I'm sorry, but—"

"Of course. Is the system still clear?"

"Bella's scanning Byas every microjump. The last one's plotted less than a light-hour from our arrival coordinates. If the enemy's already there at that point, she'll cancel the last jump and we'll reassess."

"Perfect, provided the enemy didn't arrive in that hour."

"That's physics for you." There was a pause. "Where are you planning to go?"

Mirra seemed to consider whether to answer. "Back into the core. Haven't decided where yet."

"Clock's ticking."

"Always."

Hadrian paused again, as if a better opportunity would somehow present itself. *Ah, hell with it.* "I need to ask you for something."

Mirra turned back to him.

"Zevran uncovered more of the enemy's orders," Hadrian said.

"It looks like there's a ground component to this operation, targeting the planetary leadership."

Mirra's eyes narrowed. "With what forces?"

"Unclear, but we suspect a combination of infiltrated ... Whoever the hell you fought on that ship, and local Cipher-loyal insurgents."

"Suggesting it *is* the Ciphers we've been fighting."

"*Or* they want it to look that way, to gain the allegiance of the insurgents—point is," Hadrian said, anticipating a counterargument, "we know what they're going after. VIP gathering to welcome Singh and Reinhardt. All the pack and district leaders will be there, along with ICRA administration."

Mirra nodded. "Kill or capture?"

"Also unclear, but I'd bet they'd prefer the latter."

"Use the VIPs as hostages."

"Exactly."

"And whoever they can't capture, they'll kill."

Hadrian bit his cheek. "That's why I need your help. I have people down there I know I can trust, but I can't warn them via comms without alerting the conspirators. And with the timing, and the odds we'll be facing, I can't afford to send any of my officers down there to carry a personal message."

Mirra's gaze drifted toward the deck.

"Look, I know it's my duty, not yours," Hadrian said. *And I'm not sure you'd care if it* was *yours.* "But I'm not asking you to go down there and fight them off on your own. I just want you to carry the message. Then you can jet off to wherever—"

"I'll do it."

Hadrian tripped over his arguments. There was a risk to her, of course, even though he wasn't asking her to fight. The delay might mean she'd get caught on the planet when the enemy ships arrived. If *Belisarius* failed to take them out, she'd be trapped down there with everyone else. Possibly doomed to die in an orbital bombardment or insurgent attack. Either way, unable to pursue her quest for vengeance.

"Thank you," he said eventually.

"It's the least I can do."

"It's a bit more than that."

She winced. "I didn't … I may have saved your life, but my trail would have gone cold without your help. Even if I'd found out about the ignicite mine, if I made it there, I'd more than likely have been killed or captured when that ship showed up. So. Least I can do."

"Fair enough," Hadrian said.

"Who should I make contact with on the surface?"

Hadrian's urgency returned. "The shuttle's IFF and your marine creds should get you into the capital area. Find the ICRA chief administrator. She's a virgonid named Jack. I'm downloading everything we have to you. Give it to her, and tell her I sent you."

Mirra's eyes unfocused as she scanned the data he sent to her implant. "I can't provide a proper encryption key. Why should she believe me?"

Hadrian smiled. "Ask her how Pericles is doing. She'll understand."

Mirra's brow knit. "The Athenian statesman?"

"The …" Hadrian blinked. "Yeah."

"Why would that convince her?"

"I gave her my copy of *The Peloponnesian War* before we left. She's been reading it."

Mirra nodded. "Good thinking."

Did she look it up? No. Couldn't have. We're disconnected from the networks. Hadrian shook his head. "Yeah. Um. A couple of our marines are still down there, and her ICRA security teams aren't bad. If she knows what's coming, hopefully they can at least hold the bad guys off until reinforcements get down there."

"I'll make sure she understands the situation."

"Again … Thank you."

"Not necessary."

"Fifteen minutes to arrival at Byas," Bella announced.

Hadrian breathed deep. "I've gotta get to the CIC."

Mirra nodded, then made for the shuttle.

That's it? Even a few hours ago, he would have been eager to see her leave his ship, with or without a final word. Now …

"You know," he said. She turned. "I do hope you find what you're looking for out there."

Mirra hesitated. "So do I."

"If you do," Hadrian said, "and we don't make it … Give 'em hell for us."

Mirra's eyes tightened. "I will. You do the same."

Suddenly, for the first time, Hadrian felt sorry for her. "You got it."

"Good luck," she said after a too-long silence. Then she pushed off toward the shuttle, entered it without hesitation or a backward glance.

"You too," Hadrian said after her.

THIRTY-ONE

"Arriving at Byas in three ... two ... one."

As *Belisarius* dropped to sublight, the tactical projection above the HCI came to life with passive data. The first thing Hadrian noticed was that they'd actually arrived *at* Byas, on station near the planet, not a billion or more kilometers away as they would have if Bella had canceled their final microjump. That meant that an hour ago, there had still been no enemy ships in the system.

And now ...

"No enemy or unknown contacts," Hassani reported. "Plot is clear."

Hadrian breathed easier. "Friendlies?"

"Captain Martin's fighters are on station, closer in to Byas than we left them. Probably waiting for the admiral to show. No civilian traffic detected."

"Keeping the skies clear," Hadrian said. *Good. That'll make this easier.* "All right. Bella, clear *Sparrow Two* to launch. As soon as she's away, secure from Stardrive and go full stealth."

"Aye, Captain."

⁂

"SPARROW TWO IS CLEARED to depart. Engaging automatic launch protocols."

No sooner had the launch bay doors opened than the shuttle was catapulted through them. Mirra felt nothing. The craft was still in the embrace of its mothership's Stardrive field; mass and inertia meant nothing to it. Mirra didn't even need the straps holding her into the pilot's seat. By the time the shuttle cleared the field, the acceleration had stopped. She was already going as fast as she'd need to, to get to her first stop.

The planet Byas came into view a moment later. It was an unremarkable blue-green world glowing in the dark, like so many others Mirra had seen from space in her long career. The sight had long since ceased to hold any wonder for her, if it ever had.

The war had never brought her to Byas. During the final campaigns against the Ciphers, she had fought primarily on Sukat, a gray and heavily urbanized world, many of whose cities had already been blasted from space by the time she arrived, giving the impression that the whole planet was a ball of rubble. Some of her comrades had fought on Byas, and while the combat there had been brutal, they'd described the world as beautiful, pastoral. If the view from above was any indication, it still was.

For now.

An indicator on the flight console beeped. Mirra switched the hardscreen to magnified aft view, just in time to see the receding *Belisarius* shimmer, then fade out of visible existence. A moment later, she disappeared from the shuttle's sensors too. With both vessels disconnected from the naval network, the standard feed of tactical information that would have linked them was silent. All that indicated to her that the battlecruiser was still out there was a simple quantum locator beacon, entangled directly between shuttle and mothership, capable of passing only the most basic information.

If not for that, *Belisarius* might as well not exist.

In a few hours, it won't.

"Automatic launch protocols complete," the shuttle announced. "Releasing manual control."

Mirra's eyes flitted back to Byas. Really ... what now was keeping her here? She'd said she owed Hadrian, for helping her get this far, but did she really? What point was there in staying? *Belisarius* would more than likely be destroyed—she was going into battle against a numerically and technologically superior enemy, with only the brief advantage of surprise in her column. That being the case, nothing that happened on the planet would matter. Why should Mirra risk her life, her mission, just to warn people she didn't know who were doomed regardless?

Because you said you would. You gave your word, to a fellow officer.

Mirra's eye twitched. *And is that still worth anything?*

Even if nothing else is.

Mirra sighed. The black of space called.

*

"*Sparrow Two* is turning for Byas," Helmsman Keitel reported. "Estimate landing in twenty-four minutes."

"Thank you," Hadrian said, to his officer and to the blip of the shuttle on the tactical plot. "Set a course for Target Coordinates Alpha, best possible stealth speed."

"Aye-aye, sir, best possible stealth. ETA ... thirty-six minutes."

Hadrian checked his clock. *Cutting it close. Nothing for it.*

He looked into the empty space next to the HCI where Arno should have been standing. It was wrong, not having him here. Especially at a time like this. Hadrian would have given anything to be able to lean on him, even silently, to share the burden of command just that little bit, as he and their ship sailed toward their greatest, perhaps their final, test.

It pained him to picture Arno frozen down in medbay, his death becoming permanent in slow-marching increments. Pained him even more than *knowing* he was dead and gone would have. For he still might not survive, even if the ship did. Still might not make it back to a full medical facility in time to revive him. And if he didn't, that would all be on Hadrian.

One more burden he couldn't share.

"Captain," Bella said, snapping him from his reverie. "Group Captain Martin is attempting to hail us via broadcast, asking why we have activated stealth protocols. We are also picking up check-in requests from planetary administration."

Come on, Ian, Arno would say if he were here. *You gonna feel sorry for yourself, or you gonna get this done?*

"Ignore them," Hadrian said. "The enemy might have lurker drones nearby. We can't risk giving away our position."

"Yes, Captain."

Hadrian regretted the necessity. He and Martin had never been the best of friends, but the fighter commander was still a fellow officer. Hadrian hated leaving him in the dark like this. But Martin's aging Uhlan interceptors would be able to play no meaningful part in the battle to come. Best if they stayed close to the planet, where they might be able to swoop down and provide air support if things down there got too intense.

Thinking of Jack, Sithelius, and the others, Hadrian glanced at the plot of Mirra's shuttle one final time.

Thank you, he thought to her.

"Time to target, three-zero minutes."

THIRTY-TWO

Mirra would have missed the Byasian capital had the shuttle's nav system not guided her there.

The "city" looked like nothing more than a landscape of rolling hills in a wide, green valley with mountain ranges to the north, an ocean to the east, and plains to the south and west. The only notable thing was the great number of those hills, and how many of them appeared to be rather small.

Only as the shuttle descended did Mirra take note of the clear signs of civilization: flying and ground-based vehicles, landing pads, roads and paths connecting the little hills together. Even these latter seemed almost camouflaged, blending into the landscape until the shuttle was making its final descent. She'd known the byasians were semisubterranean, but she'd still expected more ... *more* above ground. She wondered if perhaps what appeared to be camouflage *was* camouflage, a holdover from their centuries of domination by the Ciphers—a vain attempt to hide from their machine oppressors, or from more mundane enemies among their own kind.

In scope, too, the field of hills that comprised the planetary capital was much smaller and less active than she'd expected. That must reflect the distributed structure of the local government, with most power being exercised at the district level, at least according to the brief she'd read en route to the system. Then again, with all the district leadership apparently here to welcome the visiting dignitaries, this must be about as busy as the capital ever got. If that was the case, ordinarily it must be something of a ghost town.

Mirra put the shuttle down at a landing pad about a kilometer from the site where the ceremony was to take place. She'd have preferred to land at the site itself, but this was as close as landing control would let her get, even with her marine credentials—which, she was gratified to find, the conspirators hadn't managed to get canceled or flagged.

At least, she *hoped* they hadn't been flagged. The fact that there wasn't a party of armed ICRA security waiting for her on the pad suggested that hope wasn't in vain. She left her weapons, including her sidearm, in the shuttle and jogged toward the ceremony site in her uniform. Given the circumstances, she was loath to go unarmed and unarmored, but any complications entering the site itself would only cause a delay she couldn't afford.

The small, scurrying byasians seemed to pay her no mind as they went about the business of the day. Even the few human and virgonid ICRA staff moving about didn't give her a second glance. That was good. A jogging marine wouldn't raise any alarm bells on a day like this, particularly given the short notice with which this assembly must have been called.

As she moved through the low buildings, many of them shorter than her, Mirra was struck by a sudden surreality. She was unarmed, and unarmored; she was on a lush and verdant planet, with a moderate and comfortable gravity; she was jogging at an almost leisurely pace, with the sun and a pleasant breeze on her face. To some people, the feeling might be the most natural thing in the world. She couldn't remember the last time she had experienced it.

If it hadn't been for the looming violence only she knew about, she could almost have enjoyed it.

Then her destination came into view. A collection of standard Compact prefab structures had been erected behind a security perimeter near the edge of the city. Two marines in battle armor stood guard at the main entrance, rifles low, faceplates retracted. Each eyed her with passive suspicion as she came around the corner. She slowed to a brisk walk.

"Help you, ma'am?" the marine on her left, a petty officer, third class, asked. Mirra was wearing a reg force marine lieutenant's uniform, with printed commander's rank insignia attached.

"Petty Officer." She stopped a few meters away. "Commander Mirra, LDRG."

The PO3's eyes narrowed, then flitted as he studied the ID burst she'd sent him. It must have checked out, as he nodded. "On mission, ma'am?"

"From Captain Hadrian direct. I need to speak to the ICRA chief administrator immediately."

At the mention of the captain, the two marines shared a glance.

"One moment, ma'am." The PO3 held up a finger. Then after a brief and silent exchange, his demeanor relaxed. Slightly. "This way, please. Hodge, keep watch."

"You got it, boss."

"Administrator's at the ceremony site," the PO3 said. "Just this way."

Mirra followed him into the buzzing temporary village. There was a more even mix of locals and ICRA here, with far more virgonids than she was used to seeing in one place. Those that joined the military tended to serve in their own units, due to their unique physiologies, while they were conversely overrepresented in the ICRA and similar organizations.

Their abundance helped her notice a conspicuous absence. "You're short-staffed, PO."

"Yes, ma'am." His bitterness was evident. "Took heavy losses in a bombing last week. Four marines left. I'm ranking."

"Your name?"

"Ryu, ma'am."

"How are the ICRA security, Ryu?"

"Not bad." Ryu gave a slight shrug. "Not marines."

"Understood."

The ceremony site didn't come into view until they'd virtually cleared the temporary village. Reason being, it was *also* half underground—rather, it was a wide open-air dugout, with stadium-style benches descending toward a stage at the bottom, where structures were being erected. It would provide the crowd an excellent view, and force the VIPs to speak up, rather than down, creating a sense of humility.

It was also a defensive nightmare.

"Should we be expecting to need them, ma'am?" Ryu asked, probably thinking the same thing she was.

Instinctively, Mirra wanted to explain everything to him. Make sure his marines would be prepared for what was coming. But she still didn't know who she could trust down here. "I wouldn't expect *not* to."

"... Understood."

They descended into the pit. Mirra spied a virgonid locked in an evidently heated conversation between two knots of byasians. The virgonid was the only calm participant; she was visibly pregnant, with a large and likely near-mature egg sac on her back. Mirra and Ryu slowed just short of the stage to wait for the confrontation to end.

"Outrageous!" one of the byasians said, to hisses from the opposing knot. "The mountain district has every right to be represented at these proceedings!"

"To what end?" replied the leader of the opposite party. "Compromising its security so that your insurgents can attack—"

The mountainer leader growled. The virgonid made a plaintive gesture. "Olan Sithelius, as you are well aware, Olan Ghar and his party have been cleared by security."

Sithelius chittered. "How convenient! But I will stipulate they do not represent a *direct* threat. I am forced to wonder, though, why we should allow those who question the legitimacy of the Protectorate to participate in a *Protectorate* ceremony, hmm?"

"Typical," Olan Ghar said, "of the oceaners to selectively apply the rights afforded to us in the Articles of Protectorship—"

"Typical of *mountainers* to exploit those rights in order to see them destroyed!"

"Olans, please," Jack said. Her mellifluous, androgynous voice somehow smothered the building rage of the opposing parties. "Has this not been held as a place of peace since the defeat of the Ciphers?"

At the mention of the machines, the byasians in Sithelius's party spat on the ground and flicked their tails.

"It has," Ghar admitted, watching the spitting ritual with evident distaste.

"Indeed," Sithelius agreed. "In defiance of the violence committed against us by—"

"And as such," Jack interjected, "it must also be a place of *respect*. Disagreement, yes, but respect."

Ghar flicked his tail. "Wisely said."

"Agreed." Sithelius bowed. "Thank you, Administrator. Those of us who are loyal to the Compact will keep watch on our … *neighbors*, with the utmost respect."

"Thank you," Jack said, as Ghar sneered. "Now, I'm certain you both have other duties to attend to?"

Ryu waved at Jack as the two parties of byasians reluctantly departed, eyeing each other over their shoulders. "Madam Administrator?"

Jack's many eyes regarded them with an alien curiosity that was also, somehow, comforting. "Mister Ryu—is this our visitor?"

"Yes, ma'am. She's clean."

The virgonid met Mirra as she walked up the steps onto the main platform. "Pleasure to meet you, Commander. I'm Jack."

"Mirra." After a moment's hesitation, she took the virgonid's proffered appendage, shaking it like a human hand. It didn't feel as strange as she'd have expected. "I'm sorry to intrude, but this is an urgent and sensitive issue."

Jack's head drew back slightly. "I see. And ... Captain Hadrian sent you?"

"He did. He apologizes he couldn't come down or contact you himself. But he did tell me to ask you how Pericles is doing."

Jack laughed; for a moment, the eight-foot-tall arthropod's body language seemed decidedly human. "Not very well at the moment. He's just died of plague."

Mirra relaxed a little at the effective countersign. "A great tragedy for Athens."

"It must have been." Jack walked toward the empty center of the stage. "So, what is this urgent issue, Commander?"

Mirra lowered her voice. "There's a significant security threat against this ceremony. If you'll grant me direct access, I'll forward you everything we have on it."

"Of course."

A few gestures later, Mirra was able to upload their decoded intelligence to the virgonid's implant. "Bottom line: We believe a force of unknown size, consisting of local insurgents and advanced, infiltrated operatives, intends to attack the ceremony. Likely hoping to seize you and the local leadership as hostages. Failing that, to kill you."

"Where did you get this information?" Jack asked as she studied the intel.

"An unknown hostile vessel we encountered in CAS 47988. We believe at least two more such vessels are en route here now, intending to intercept and destroy Admiral Singh's squadron when it decelerates from Stardrive. *Belisarius* is up there under stealth waiting to intercept the hostiles. That's why Hadrian can't contact you."

Jack's head snapped toward her. "Ian's going to fight them alone?"

Her concern gave Mirra pause. "His intent is to ... disrupt their ambush and hold them until the admiral arrives. Then the squadron should be able to deal with them easily."

It wasn't entirely true, but it seemed to mollify Jack. In part. Mirra got the sense she *knew* it was a softening of the truth. Still, the virgonid drew herself up, pushed her obvious concern for her friend to the side. "Well. We'll just have to do our part down here. Do you have any idea when this attack is to begin?"

"Likely around the same time as the ambush in space. Within the hour."

"Then I'll have to—"

Mirra raised her hand. "One other thing. We've encountered several officers in the ICDF that are involved in this somehow."

"Surely not."

Jack's innocence lit a spark of resentment in Mirra, as Hadrian's had. This one, though, guttered out as soon as it flared. "Several of these officers already tried to kill or capture myself and Captain Hadrian. They may be Cipher infiltrators, or otherwise connected with the machines. We don't know. But in any case, there is a conspiracy within the Compact of which this attack plays some part. We don't know who we can trust."

"That may be," Jack said, shock receding quickly, "but all we can do now is rely on our people."

Mirra nodded. "I just wanted you to be aware of the facts."

"I appreciate that, Commander. Will you be returning to *Belisarius?*"

Mirra braced herself for the request she would have to refuse. "No, my ... I have an important mission that takes me elsewhere."

"Then you should leave immediately, before you're trapped here." Jack extended her appendage again. "Thank you, Commander. You risked yourself and your mission to come here and warn us, and I appreciate that."

Mirra shook her hand reluctantly. She had been expecting to have to fend off pleas to stay and fight. "Not at all."

"I'll brief my security team—if you could fill in Petty Officer Ryu on your way out, I'd be very grateful."

"Of course."

"Good luck, Commander. And if you see Ian again before I do, tell him ... Just tell him thank you."

"I will. And good luck to you."

Mirra left the stage. Ryu had waited for her partway up the stairs out of the pit. At least she'd be able to give in to her commander's instincts and brief the marine about the coming storm. Maybe give him a chance of getting his marines and their charges through it alive, even if she couldn't stay to help them.

She looked back once as she ascended the stairs. Jack was once again hard at work, preparing for real battle as calmly as she'd defused the petty political argument.

THIRTY-THREE

"T-plus two-zero minutes," Hassani reported. "Plot clear."

Hadrian could see that for himself. "Admiral Singh's ETA?"

"ETA … thirty-two minutes," Helmsman Keitel answered.

In theory, every minute the enemy didn't show up was to their benefit. But minute by minute, the tension in the CIC increased. Every moment that passed was a moment that a battle could begin. You could only take so much of that before the dam burst.

At least Group Captain Martin had given up trying to contact them. Or, Bella had given up telling Hadrian when he did.

"What's the situation on the surface?" he asked, in case there was anything else the ship might be keeping from him.

"Unchanged," Bella told him. "Commander Mirra has landed and reached the ceremony site."

That's something. "Good. Keep me updated."

"Yes, sir."

There was nothing else he or his people could do but wait. The demand for action ground like metal on metal in his mind. Chattering away would only increase everyone's anxiety, though, even if it alleviated his own. He had to go on projecting a calm that he didn't feel.

Too bad. This is what you always wanted.

Is it?

He had always thought so. As a youth, nothing had seemed more exciting than commanding a starship. He'd grown up on stories, historical and fictional, of dashing commanders leading their ships through peace and war, through danger and challenge, and he had imagined that he could do it just as well as they had.

The academy had done nothing to disabuse him of that notion. He'd never felt more fulfilled than he had in the command exercises, his classmates working with him like a real crew, pulling off feats few other cadets could match. He had known in his bones that he'd chosen the right path.

And then? Pyria, and this. He had tasted real battle, and though he and his ship had survived, he *had* been found wanting. And there had been a cost.

Now, facing an even greater test, he had never been *less* sure of himself. It was *his* decisions, and his alone, that had brought his ship and crew here. It was by his order that they waited, minute after agonizing minute, to face an enemy that outmatched them in almost every way. And if his ship was destroyed, if his crew died out here, far from home, it would all be because of him.

There were moments where the command of a starship lived up to the romantic image he'd once had, but at its core was this: to bear the burden of all those lives, those hopes and dreams and fears, on your shoulders. And to do it silently, with a straight back, and a calm expression on your face, even while doubt and anxiety churned your insides to mulch.

This was what it really meant, to be the captain. He saw that now.

And seeing that ...

The alerts blared and the tactical plot lit up just before

Hassani's voice caught up. "Contact—*Three* hostile contacts! Hull and armaments match Echo-class—Sir, what do we do?"

Three.

They'd planned for two. Two, they could handle. Take out one in a surprise strike, duel the other like they had before, hope for the best.

They had moments before the enemy went stealth. The range was good; they'd set up their ambush perfectly. They could still take the shot. But they'd barely survived the last fight. Even if they destroyed one, what chance did they have against the other *two*? Their only chance at survival might be to run, *now*.

Is this still *what you want?*

⁕

THE FIRST EXPLOSION hit as Mirra entered the shuttle.

She recognized it instantly. It was perhaps a kilometer or two off, deeper into the city. Not too powerful. Certainly no threat to her ship. She barely felt it reverberate through the ground. It still stopped her in her tracks.

The shuttle's nose was facing into the city. She activated the hardscreen on external feed just as a second, then a third explosion tore through the little city. Plumes of dirt rose into the air. Underground bombs, planted in some of the semisubterranean buildings, likely well ahead of time by local insurgents. Ignicite, if she was placing a bet, smuggled through security before anyone was wise to its existence.

Familiar screams wafted into the shuttle on the breeze. Shocked and frightened. A fourth explosion temporarily drowned them out. Deeper still into the city.

It's starting.

This was just a distraction. A few bombs to draw attention, and perhaps some security personnel, away from the ceremony site.

Any minute now, other explosions, the rattle of rifles, and the hiss of maser fire would roll and crash much closer by. The shuttle might well be caught in it.

Time to go.

She'd done her part. Warned Jack and the marines. They wouldn't be fooled by this distraction. They'd be ready when the real attack came, and they'd fight it off.

Or they'll be overwhelmed.

Is that my problem?

Hadrian had talked of duty. She knew what hers was. She was the last survivor of the 2/5. However temporary her residence there, she would also be the last survivor of *Belisarius,* after it was destroyed in its doomed fight above. Once that happened, nothing that occurred down here would make a difference. Effective resistance would only buy these people a few minutes or hours of life and freedom.

Her duty was to see that they, and her men, got justice. Revenge. Whatever they were owed. To do that, she had to leave. *Now.*

A fifth explosion rocked the shuttle. Closer. Another terrified scream followed it.

Mirra's eyes sought first the pilot's seat, then the battle armor hanging on the rack next to her.

*

"FIRE!" HADRIAN SAID.

Hassani pulled the trigger as the enemy's drone swarms were still deploying. *Belisarius*'s overcharged reactors hummed with immense power, then her Astra spat it all forth in a concentrated stream of hyper-accelerated protons. The lead cruiser in the diamond formation took the beam full-on amidships. For a moment, it disappeared behind the nova burst of the UMAX shot.

Hadrian held his breath.

The two other enemy ships veered off as their leader's reactors went critical, narrowly avoiding the expanding bubble of energy and shattered hull fragments—more and larger fragments than Hadrian would have expected, but fragments nonetheless. It had been a perfect shot. Ultradurable next-gen tech or no, the unprepared cruiser hadn't stood a chance.

"Direct hit!" Hassani yelled. "Target destroyed!"

There was no spontaneous cheer from the CIC crew. This time, they knew the worst was still ahead of them.

"Helm," Hadrian said before the explosion had dissipated, "Evasive Protocol Epsilon. Bella, reestablish full stealth."

"Yes—"

Enemy UMAX fire blazed in the fading light, once, twice. The first shot tore through space where *Belisarius* had been when she fired. The second scraped by less than a thousand kilometers off her dorsal quarter, following them through their first evasive maneuver. Close enough to trigger her shield net—but they'd disabled the automatic shield protocols for just that reason. Hadrian had manual control himself.

"Full stealth reestablished," Bella announced.

"Helm, switch to Evasive Bravo. TacOps—"

"Enemy's gone stealth," Hassani said. "I have no shot."

Damn. They'd have been lucky to recharge the Astra before the enemy was able to vanish. "Plot it."

Three probability bubbles appeared on the tactical plot above the HCI. Two red, one blue. All in the critical phase. Each ship had fired a shot already. No hiding in the big empty, letting passives do the work at long range.

"It's a knife fight," Hadrian said. "Zevran, start cracking those sons of bitches."

"Yes, sir."

The drones were out. ECW suites were battering against one

another. If the enemy came out on top, *Belisarius* would be destroyed.

The real question was what *Belisarius* could do if *she* cracked the enemy's defenses first. Without being destroyed by the return fire.

Luck would've been nice. *Just have to settle for being better.*

The blue probability bubble contracted.

THIRTY-FOUR

What have you gotten yourself into now, Sorăna?

Mirra moved through the increasing chaos of the city with her father's voice echoing in her head. He'd had countless causes to say those words to her when she was a child. She'd always had a way of finding trouble back then, when it refused to find her. The polar opposite of her brothers, who'd given her no end of grief for it.

But her father had always had a faint, wry smile on his face when he'd said that to her, tired or exasperated as his voice might have sounded. Fleet Captain Mirra had loved and been proud of all his children, but there had been a special place in his heart for his daughter's mischief, unspoken though it might have gone.

The ghost of that pride helped keep her going now, even as she realized she hadn't felt its spark in her chest for a very long time. And she needed it now. This idyllic pastoral city was going to hell. Fast.

Mirra navigated the winding earthen streets under full stealth. The streets had already largely emptied, panicking civilians scurrying underground. Other than scattered bodies, there was little sign of them. Most of those who remained above were combatants.

She pressed herself against a sloping wall now as one ran past her—a lone byasian in a security uniform, firing a projectile pistol backward as he went. Rifle fire churned the earth after him. He ran straight past Mirra, unseeing. She let him go, uncertain which side he was on. She'd already passed one knot of byasians shooting at each other, both wearing security uniforms and armed with standard-issue weapons.

An explosion shook the earth behind her. Her rear sensors and drones saw no threat, so she kept moving. Changed direction, climbed up a low rise in front of her—the roof of a semisubterranean shop, by the looks of the sign outside. She got her bearings; there was the ceremony site, a few hundred meters away. Weapons fire flashed in the temporary village. She might already be too late.

A hundred meters or so to her right, another firefight. She zoomed in. A mixed force of ICRA and local security looked to have barricaded themselves in a larger mound building, with a good number of firing positions. They were surrounded by a large force of insurgents, taking losses but advancing on the structure. Much more clear cut. From this vantage, she could easily take out a few of the hostiles, give them a hand.

No. She gritted her teeth. *Don't give away your position. You don't know who else is out there. Stay focused.*

She left the security personnel to their fate and hustled toward the ceremony site, moving over rooftops when she could, relying on her stealth systems to keep her hidden until she got closer. None of the byasians or the ICRA would have any chance of detecting her.

Once there was only one large building between her and the gates she'd passed through not so long ago, she ran half up the side, then dropped prone and crawled the rest of the way. Stealth systems or no, some old-fashioned concealment never hurt.

She sent her recon drones up over the lip of the mound ahead of her. The picture clarified. The temporary village was in abject chaos. Several of the structures were burning. Another exploded before her eyes, about halfway in toward the main site. Grenade, probably. Screams wafted out of the hellscape: dignitaries and civilians of three species with no underground hideout to run to. Mirra—

Rolled to the side as a burst of projectiles tore through the earth to her left. She scrambled partway down the hill, switched to penetrating sensors. If someone had spotted her …

But no more rounds came in toward her. A few more smacked into the side of the building, the ground around it. Strays. Slowly, she crawled back up to the lip to take the read.

She saw where the rounds had likely come from. Her passive IFF systems picked up pings from four marines in battle armor, commanded by Petty Officer Ryu, spread out in prepared firing positions just inside the perimeter. Her armor's onboard AI filled out a silhouette of each marine on her HUD, based on the ping's location and other context clues. A burst of repeater fire would rattle from one, followed by a quick displacement, then another burst. The marines were backed up by a handful of Stilettos darting back and forth and lancing out with maser fire, and two larger, four-legged Arachne combat units, laying down suppressing fire with their repeater cannons. Three other Arachnes had already been destroyed, their smoking remains lying strewn across the fighting position.

The squads of skittering, screeching byasian insurgents streaming toward the village, shooting wildly, stood little chance against even this lone fireteam. Just a few meters to Mirra's left, a pair of insurgents carrying some kind of rocket launcher crept up the side street, only to be torn to bloody bits by repeater rounds before they had a chance to aim. The marine had likely tracked them from beyond visual with a combination of recon drones and penetrating sensors. If this was all the enemy had to throw at the site, the defenders didn't even need Mirra's help.

But it wasn't. Still as she could remain, she scanned the streets, the fields beyond. The enhanced infiltrators, whoever they were, would be moving under stealth, next-gen or better. But Mirra might still have a chance at spotting them. She'd fed all the data they'd collected from the firefight on the ship, and from the body they'd bought back, into her implants' onboard tactical AI. She had her own suite of next-gen detection soft and hardware, courtesy of ISOC. Interfacing that with the battle armor's standard systems, she hoped, would give her the chance of spotting *something*, provided she knew where to look.

She got the clue she needed, but not the way she'd hoped. Calm and collected, Ryu's marines kept shooting and displacing, holding off the insurgent attack—until one of them, halfway between two firing positions, took an invisible hit and staggered. A second later, the sound from the shot reached Mirra's audio sensors. It triggered a painful recognition in her—the same brutal, reverberating crack of a handheld particle accelerator of unknown, incredibly advanced design.

The marine fell to one knee, his stealth systems flickering in and out, and turned in the direction he thought the shot had come from—only for another to blast his armored head from his shoulders.

Mirra grimaced and followed the line from which the shot had come. Nothing. She activated her passive comms receivers, set to decode standard marine tactical transmissions.

"Weber's down! Where'd the goddamn shot come from?"

"Stay in cover!" She recognized Ryu's voice. *"Put up extra recon. Hold your fire until you have a target!"*

Good thinking, but it wouldn't do them any good. Mirra'd bet anything the enemy was tracking the marines the same way *she* was. The same way her team had been tracked on Lampshade.

Sure enough, another trio of particle blasts came in. One blew a Stiletto out of the sky; another struck a marine fully in cover, punching clean through armor and barricade to kill her.

"Son of a bitch!" The unknown voice.

Mirra followed the trail of the latest burst.

"Displace, displace!"

Two faint ripples against the side of a building, fifty meters ahead and to her left, already inside the village perimeter. Working backward from their particle beam shots, her AI filled in the bipedal shapes, crouching but not bothering to cover, firing at the marines they could easily see, thanks to their supposedly secure IFF beacons.

I see you. Mirra flipped her rifle to full armor-piercing and fired.

Her first burst took the closest enemy in the side. His armor splintered and his camo wavered, then he slumped over. His comrade spun instantly toward Mirra, drawing a bead on her. Her second shot caught him in the chest, and her third tore his helmet apart. Red blood splattered across the earthen mound behind him.

Got you, you—

Rounds tore the earth all about her. She rolled down the back side of the building, armor-piercing slugs chasing her all the way. Growling, she took a chance and flipped her friendly comms to receive/transmit. "Marines, check fire, check fire, friendly to your front!"

The incoming fire stopped, but it was another few seconds before Ryu responded. *"What friendly? Who the hell is this?"*

"Commander Mirra." She rose to a crouch and scanned the avenues around her. "I'm speaking to PO3 Ryu."

"Turn on your goddamn IFF—"

"Negative, deactivate *your* IFF. The enemy is tracking you. Repeat, IFF has been compromised by an advanced hostile force."

The silence told her he was considering it. There wasn't any time for that. More of the mystery hostiles must be inbound, if not already here.

"I'm coming out to rendezvous. Hold your fire on the gate."

"... Roger that," Ryu confirmed, but Mirra was already moving.

Almost the moment she had rounded the corner, another particle shot blasted through the building where she'd been standing. Dirt and rock sprayed out from the strike. She threw herself to the side, narrowly avoiding a second shot, and launched the two Stilettos she'd been carrying on her armor. The drones returned fire, then one immediately shattered under a third shot.

"Suppressing fire, suppressing fire!"

The shots must've finished what her warning started. Ryu ran toward her, homing in on her comms, firing the same direction she was. The other marine and the Arachnes laid down a base of fire. Mirra got to her feet, still shooting, and hustled into the village beside Ryu. Particle shots followed them.

"Cover's no good," Mirra said. "I can upload a detection protocol, help you track them. Then we've gotta go after them."

"Roger that, Commander. Hodge, displace and suppress!"

"You got it, boss!" The other marine launched a spread of grenades in a high arc, then hustled to a new position as they exploded, shattering another temporary structure. Mirra noted he and Ryu had deactivated their IFFs and those of their drones; her armor was tracking them now based on learned patterns and suit comms. But it was imperfect; and if it worked for her ...

"Maintain passive stealth, but switch off visual camo," she told Ryu. "They've got a read on us—all we'll end up doing is shooting each other in the back."

"Yes, ma'am."

"And no more transmissions—vocal comms and hand signals only, roger?"

"Roger."

"Move!"

She and Ryu took off at a low run, particle fire still coming in, downing another Stiletto. Hodgman fired a burst over and between them, then hustled after them. The Arachnes and Stilettos stayed at the gate to lay down suppression and draw fire. She braced herself for flanking fire to come in from as-yet unseen enemies, but so far they were lucky. These two teams might be the only infiltrators in this area, for now.

She and Ryu held their fire. No reason to give the enemy more data to go on until they had a clean shot. The enemy didn't seem to feel the same way. Mirra thanked them silently for it.

Civilians who had been hiding among the buildings scattered, screaming as the firing intensified. One human took a particle shot as he ran from cover. He exploded at the waist, falling in two halves to either side. Mirra hoped her wild firing hadn't hit any of the cowering bystanders earlier. She threaded between the runners.

Her AI guided her toward the likely position of one of the shooters, tracking the shots as he displaced and fired. Only a handful of light structures between them now. She might have a shot through them, but if there were civvies still hiding there …

She waited for the clean kill, and got it a few seconds later. The stealthed bastard was shimmering just a few meters from her when she rounded the last corner. He turned toward her, and she held down the trigger, pumping full-auto, partial armor pierce into his chest. The first rounds cracked his chest plate, then the rest punched through, expanding inside him and smacking against the inside surface of his armor on the other side. The lanky hostile twitched and flailed, then crashed backward, blood leaking over still half-invisible armor plate. Her barrel followed him down—

Then a hostile alert flared on the right of her HUD. She spun toward it, just in time to reach out and grab the barrel of a particle rifle, yank it away as it fired. The shot reverberated through her skull, blurred her vision. Her implant raced to clear it. She tried to bring her rifle to bear, but the enemy was in too close. He wrenched at his own weapon, fired it again, reached for her helmet.

She dropped her rifle, drew her sidearm, and fired full-power into his gut.

The maser beam burned against his armor, not getting through. But the blaze of blue-red light and searing heat gave the enhanced hostile pause. He drew back a space—just enough. Mirra kicked him in the chest, then held down the trigger again. The beam cut up across him, his neck, his head, melting the helmet to slag as he fell. She kept firing until he stopped twitching.

"Clear here," Ryu announced.

Mirra holstered her pistol and retrieved her rifle. "Fall back, head on a swivel."

"Yes, ma'am."

They made their way back through the burned and shattered prefabs. Ryu slashed his hand in the direction of the stadium once, twice. Hodgman took point. Mirra brought up the rear, walking backward. Sporadic fire grew louder as they approached.

When they were short of the lip of the stadium, Mirra felt a rap on the back of her helmet. She half-turned. Ryu and Hodgman had stopped. By hand signal, the petty officer told her Hodgman had spotted hostiles advancing on friendlies ahead—multiple byasians, if she interpreted the scurrying gesture correctly, and three under stealth.

She nodded, and gave the signals to set up an ambush. Ryu confirmed. She silently thanked the deceased Lieutenant Farris for keeping his marines up on hand signals. Not all officers made the effort these days.

The three of them split up, moving quiet and low to the edge of the stadium. She was right about it being a defensive hell. ICRA security had set up a perimeter around the main stage as best they could, where the VIPs were sheltering. She saw a number of bodies on the stage, but none virgonid. A dozen or more dead insurgents littered the seats and steps, while still more tried to advance.

The ICRA were holding them off, helped by the fact that the hostiles clearly wanted them alive. But the three enhanced hostiles moving slowly and invisibly down the main walkways toward them would seal their fate soon enough. Once they were close enough, they could take out the whole security team without fear of hitting the VIPs. Game over.

Not this time. Mirra gave Hodgman and Ryu the signal to select targets closest to them and fire on her shot, then drew a bead on the center of the fuzzy sensor ghost advancing just below her.

A split second after Mirra fired, the other marines dropped their targets. The enemy didn't even have the chance to turn around.

With their advanced backup down, and fire now coming from two sides, the insurgents panicked and fled. None of them made it out of the stadium bowl alive. For an eerie moment, the firing died down to nothing, save the more distant echoing booms and rattles from their drones back at the gate, and from the city beyond.

"Marines?" a tentative voice called up from below.

Mirra raised her hand. "Clear. Coming down." She turned to Ryu. "Hold up here until I bring them up. Then we get the hell out of here."

"Where to?"

"Landing site, klick and a half away." She uploaded him the coordinates. "My shuttle should fit about twenty."

"Roger that."

Mirra jogged down the aisle, stepping over shattered enemy corpses. An ICRA security officer with a maser rifle stood up from behind cover to greet her.

"Holy shit, it's good to see you," he said.

Mirra raised her visor. "Where's Jack?"

"Here." The virgonid stepped out from backstage, where the

frightened dignitaries were sheltering. "Commander. It *is* good to see you."

Better late than never, Mirra thought with some self-recrimination. "This position is indefensible—we've got to move."

"We have wounded," Jack said. "Some quite badly. I don't think we can move them."

Mirra set her jaw. "They'll have to be left behind. If we stay here, we all die."

"Very well." Jack nodded in the human fashion. "Chief Constable, gather up all who can walk, and any who can be moved, and go with the commander to safety. I'll remain here with the rest."

The constable blanched. "Ma'am—"

"That's an order," Jack said. "Go, now."

The officer, though worried, seemed disinclined to further resistance. He started gathering up his people and their charges.

Mirra leaned in to the virgonid. "Administrator, you can't stay here."

"I can't leave these people to die alone. They're in my care."

Mirra glanced at the maturing child on the virgonid's back. "Captain Hadrian—"

"—will understand." Jack's mandibles clicked in a smile. "Eventually. Now go. Get these people to safety."

Jack moved toward the grievously wounded. Mirra couldn't take her eyes from her, until the constable forced her to.

"Ready, Commander." He had a ragged group of security and civilians behind him. All looked terrified.

Mirra glanced up the hill, where Ryu and Hodgman were waiting. *Job done. Get moving.*

She breathed out, slow and steady. "Rendezvous with those marines up there. They'll take you to a shuttle."

The constable nodded, and hustled his charges up the hill. Mirra gave a hand signal. Ryu acknowledged. He'd get them out, if he could.

And what about you?

Mirra headed toward the backstage refuge.

"Olan," Jack said, "you must go, now."

One of the abrasive Byasians Mirra remembered from earlier, Sithelius, looked up at the towering arthropod. "And surrender the care of my people to you? These are my kin, Administrator. I should never be allowed in my beloved home again, if I abandoned them now."

"Olan Ghar has gone."

Sithelius chittered. "And so proved the cowardice of the mountaineers for all time. As if more proof were needed. I'll see to my own; tend the others, Administrator. You and your marine."

Sithelius nodded toward Mirra. Jack's carriage drooped when she realized who was standing behind her. "Commander, you don't have to—"

Mirra held up one finger.

Jack's voice synthesizer sighed. "Thank you."

Mirra nodded, and turned to watch the upper perimeter. Ryu gave her a salute before he led the civilians out of sight.

Me?

She saluted him back.

I'm where I belong.

THIRTY-FIVE

"Zevran, tell me you've got something."

Even looking at the back of his head, Hadrian could see the dark expression on Zevran's face. "The updates are helping, but it's not enough. We're trying to fend of simultaneous penetrations and breach a system faster and more adaptable than ours at the same time. It's not possible."

"Not even for you?"

"No. All I can do is hold them off, and not for long."

Belisarius's bubble contracted again. So did the red one designated Echo-3—for the first time. Hadrian had placed high hopes on the updates Zevran had made to their cyberwarfare suite based on the captured data and systems architecture from the enemy ship, using an algorithm he'd designed himself. But if that was having an effect, it was only to delay the inevitable.

Hadrian turned to his next best bet. "Hassani, anything on that tailpipe?"

"They're buttoned up tight, sir." Hassani winced. "I didn't even detect any emissions when they were out of stealth."

"Everyone leaves something behind."

Hassani turned to him. "Not these guys, Captain. I'm sorry."

As before, this was a race they were going to lose. Fighting dirty was the only shot they had. Hadrian needed to pull another trick out of the bag, and fast.

But what? As before, a two-on-one duel against a technologically superior opponent wasn't something they'd thought to wargame at SWOS. There was nothing in the book for this.

Hell with the book. The book's for the other guy. What do you *have?*

Hadrian stared through the tactical plot. *Missile minefield might have worked—no time to set it up. They'd see if I launched now.*

Can't send the drones after them. Two-on-one, we're gonna need that shield. Martin's fighters are too far away to pull a pressure wave.

Scoot n' shoot? Hadrian smiled faintly at Arno's voice in his head.

Need a couple light-seconds' distance to pull that off. This close, they'd actually hit us. And oh yeah, there's two *of 'em.*

Well, Arno would have said, *that simplifies things, doesn't it?*

Always looking on the bright side, aren't you?

"Sir?"

Hassani's eyes were on her console. Other eyes were on him. NCOs and junior officers at stations around the CIC. He knew all their names, if little else in some cases.

Kawasaki, in ECW—he sings. Badly, but he loves it. His bunkmates never complain. Olmstead in TacOps; she plays chess. Never against the computer, on principle. Halvarsson, in Engineering—just a name and a face.

One hundred twenty-seven names and faces. One hundred twenty, now, with the ones already dead. The living all looked to him, wherever their eyes happened to be pointed at the moment. Hundreds more in Singh's squadron. Millions on the planet below. All counting on him to know what to do. Counting on the other one hundred twenty of them to pull it off. But on *him* to know.

"I can only give us a few more minutes," Zevran said.

Hadrian's heartbeat slowed. "That's all we'll need. Zevran, Hassani, bring up the drone controls. We're faking 'em out again."

There was a moment's silence before Zevran spoke. "Captain, if the hostiles were observing the battle at—"

"If they were, they'll have something else to think about." Hadrian moved to the upper deck. "Push the drone net out to range two-point-five. Program sectors A *and* F to simulate an overcharged Astra buildup. One for each of the bastards."

Zevran nodded. Hassani turned her chair toward Hadrian. "They'll think one's a decoy and one's real."

"And they won't know which is which." Hadrian leaned over her console. "We get real lucky, they both pop their shields. Less lucky, one pops, the other tries to shoot us. We take out the unshielded one, then it's a straight duel. One-on-one. All we'll have to do is hold them off until the admiral gets here."

"Sounds good to me."

"But you have to make that shot." Hadrian gripped her shoulder. "You'll get one chance. *Make* that shot."

A battle was fought behind Hassani's eyes. One side claimed victory. Peace came over her. "Yes, sir. I will."

He gave her shoulder a pat, then headed back down to the HCI. "Bella, keep the shield under my control."

"Yes, Captain."

"Drone net ready," Zevran reported. "Awaiting your order."

The eyes were still on him.

"Execute," he said.

Two clusters of defensive drones around *Belisarius* flared to life, each mimicking exactly the power curve of an overcharged Astra Mk. VII UMAX cannon charging up. Each appeared to be aimed at one of the two shrinking enemy probability bubbles.

Hadrian watched the tactical plot, tensed. *Come on, you sons of—*

Echo-3's probability bubble shrank to nothing as its shield popped, a sphere of blue-white light surrounding a still-unseen central point. Hadrian's eyes flitted to Echo-4, hoping for the same, and when it didn't come, hoping for the shot that would equally reveal the enemy's position if not leave him defenseless. If it was coming, it would come ...

Now.

As Echo-3's shield began to dissipate, Echo-4's remained dormant. He was playing it smart. Waiting. But *Belisarius*—Hadrian—had no choice. Their gamble had been made. There was only one way to play it out.

Echo-3's shield bubble faded, revealing three likely target points beneath it, the best estimate *Belisarius* could give them.

Hadrian's fist clenched. "Fire!"

Hassani pulled the trigger while space still glowed with Echo-3's dissipating defense shield. The overcharged UMAX shot blazed in the night.

Echo-3 blew apart.

"Direct hit," Hassani shouted. "Target destroyed!"

This time there was a cheer, pent-up tension breaking free as the molten remnants of the enemy ship streaked off into space like meteors in the night sky.

Then, Echo-4 fired.

*

THE LIP OF THE STADIUM pit erupted with fire. Micro-particle beams blasted clear through the earth and stone, lancing down toward the stage and leaving trails of whizzing debris in their wake. Rocks pelted Mirra's armor, but none of the shots struck home. Yet.

She could play that game too, if not quite so well. Streams of superfluid projectiles blasted back through the earthen rampart at each unseen shooter, but she had no way of knowing if she hit any of them.

"Get back!" she yelled to her charges, for all the good it would do. "Huddle in the center!"

She darted back and forth on the stage, launched the few microdrones she'd saved. The little automatons zipped off toward the sources of the shots. One was blasted out of midair before it crested the ridge, but she was gratified by the handful of explosions that followed after the rest were out of sight.

Must've gotten a couple of them at least.

Not enough. She turned round and round, constantly moving and firing—first chasing shots, then at targets as they began to present. The nimble infiltrators were charging down the pit under cover fire now. Much as that put the pressure on, it was likely the only thing keeping Mirra and her charges from being blasted to pieces right then and there.

The enemy still wanted the VIPs alive.

Not at all costs, it seemed. As Mirra dropped one of the charging enemy with a quick burst, a blind shot ripped through dirt, rock, and the roof of the stage to blow one of the huddling byasian delegates apart. Blood, fur, and fabric showered his wounded compatriots. Mirra sprayed the rest of her magazine in the direction the shot had come from, then darted to the side to reload as the VIPs warbled in terror.

Won't last much longer.

"Commander!" Jack shouted. "Behind—"

Mirra spun just in time to see the virgonid take a particle shot to the right side. Both her legs on that side disappeared into a cloud of hemolymph and exoskeleton. She tipped over and crashed onto the stage, more life-fluid spilling out beneath her as she struggled to keep herself upright, to scramble for the illusory cover of the backstage area. Sithelius scurried out to help drag her back, but she proved too heavy for the brave little politician.

Mirra finished her turn, slapped her new magazine in, and held down the trigger on the enemy who'd shot Jack, only a few meters away and charging toward them. Her full-auto burst sawed him in half. His torso fell into her; she batted it aside with her rifle, spun toward the next charging target.

The infiltrator leaped into her, taking them both down to the deck. He pressed Mirra's arms down, held her legs in place. Inside his stealth field, she could see him clearly. His black-carapaced helmet stared impassively down at her.

She struggled to bring her rifle up, to free her legs, to no avail. If he tried to go for his own weapon, or strike her, it might create an opening she could use—but he did nothing. Just resisted her every move.

It was all he needed to do. She rolled her head right. Two more semi-visible infiltrators were coming down the stadium steps toward the stage. She couldn't quite bring her pinned rifle to bear on them. They'd be down here in seconds. They could put a shot through her head and massacre or carry off the wounded. There'd be nothing she could do.

She looked back up at the faceless mask of her attacker, but there was nothing there, no hostile visage for her to draw strength from. Reflexively, she tried to engage her arm blade, but she didn't have one. This was standard-issue battle armor, not her custom special forces rig. *That* armor was long gone. Like her team. Like she was about to be.

I'm sorry, she thought. *I failed you.*

The black mask stared down at her.

Not yet.

She bared her teeth and growled, strained, and fought, to the last.

*

HADRIAN BARELY MANAGED to trigger *Belisarius*'s shield before Echo-4's shot struck home.

The universe disappeared behind a wall of glowing energy.

Then the wall flared with impossible brightness as the UMAX beam slammed into it. The plasma field polarized the beam, then the magnetic field surged against the attack, fractionally deflecting it. Enough energy to vaporize a mountain range was pushed away by a barely greater force, weakened by the ruse the drones had just performed. The beam burned through space less than a hundred kilometers off *Belisarius*'s port quarter. The shock of its passing set off radiation alarms and rattled the battlecruiser violently, sending Hadrian crashing into the HCI.

Belisarius's drone net couldn't handle that much power more than once. As a body they died, burned out in their final act of preservation, the ship's last and most desperate line of defense.

Gone.

The enemy had revealed himself by firing. They had him—but he'd yet to expend his own shield. *Belisarius* just had. And so the enemy had them too.

"Astra recharged in fifteen seconds!" Hassani announced, hands white on her controls.

Hadrian looked at the tactical plot. Bella estimated the enemy's weapon would be recharged in less than *ten* seconds.

Another race they couldn't win. And this time, they'd already played their final card.

The eyes were on Hadrian again.

Is this still what you want?

The enemy turned his weapon on them. Hadrian looked death and defeat in the eye.

Yes.

It is.

"New contacts," Hassani reported.

Hadrian closed his eyes.

"Friendlies!" Hassani's voice cracked. "Six of them, bearing zero-four-four by—"

Hadrian's eyes snapped open. "Helm, evasive maneuvers. Bella, reactivate IFF!"

Belisarius dove and weaved through space, hoping that the surprise of the new arrivals might throw off the enemy gunner's aim just enough for a dodge to be effective.

It did better than that. The seconds ticked by, up to the enemy's estimated recharge time, and past it. Faced with the sudden arrival of a full squadron from Admiral Rohan Singh's Fifth Fleet a mere twenty thousand kilometers to his rear, the enemy held his fire. Maybe he planned to turn his gun on one of the new threats; maybe he was hoping to go undetected by them—they hadn't seen his previous shot, so had no idea where he was.

Either way, Hadrian didn't intend to give him the chance.

"Astra charged!" Hassani said.

Hadrian gripped the HCI railing. "Bring us about and fire."

Keitel swung *Belisarius* around in a tight turn, bringing her nose to bear on the hesitating enemy ship. The moment her cannon was in arc, Hassani pulled the trigger.

The shot didn't need to be a direct hit—but it would have been. Hadrian knew it. The enemy had no choice but to activate his shield or be destroyed. The magnetoplasma field deflected the UMAX shot at nearly a right angle, so that for a moment it appeared as two separate beams propagating in different directions.

The shield faded. The enemy ship was still intact, his gun was still charged, and he was now bringing his own nose down toward *Belisarius*.

They'd done all they could. Hadrian had done all he could. It was out of their hands now.

*

It took a few seconds for Mirra to realize what happened to the infiltrator pinning her down. By then it was all over.

At first, all she knew was that he reared up and away from her, contracting toward his right side. Something appeared to have pierced his armor at the hip, and blood was pouring from the wound, spurting on to her.

She didn't ask questions. She wrenched her right arm from his loosening grip, held her rifle up one-handed, and fired a long armor-piercing burst into the two enemies that had just climbed up onto the stage. While they were still falling, she freed her left arm, pushed her attacker up, and pressed the muzzle of her rifle into his chest. The burst she fired blew his back apart like an exploding grenade.

Mirra shoved the corpse off her and came up on one knee, spinning around to track the other threats she knew were out there. Another particle shot came in, blasting a gouge in the stage next to her and knocking her off balance. She yelled—

And the sound of rifle fire followed, muffled and half-distant. She regained her balance and kept turning, but held her own fire. One by one, the blind-firing particle shots stopped coming in. Then the rifle fire, too, stopped. Mirra held position.

"Clear up!"

The voice came over Mirra's local comms. A moment later, two blue IFF pings briefly flashed on her faceplate, showing a position just behind the crest of the stadium pit. "Clear up!"

"Clear down," Mirra replied after standing and doing another quick sweep. "We need medics, now."

"Roger that," Ryu replied. "On the way."

She hadn't ordered him to come back. She didn't know where he'd left the other VIPs. Even so, she wasn't about to reprimand him.

Particularly after she took stock of her charges, and saw who had saved her.

*

HADRIAN HAD NEVER seen a single ship pummeled by a squadron of UMAX shots before, even in holos. Under other circumstances, he might have found it distasteful overkill. Here and now, he broke into a grin.

Five of the six shots hit, one after the other in the space of two seconds. A seventh shot flared out as the ship was dying—underpowered, abortive, the cannon severed from its power source even as it fired. The shot that would have killed *Belisarius*, a mere second too late. Time slowed with the realization, and he saw it all. The enemy ship shattered like a glass smashed by a half-dozen hammers. Then the containment on its antimatter reactor failed, and the whole disintegrating mess vaporized in a white-hot nova.

Hadrian's ears were ringing so decisively with relief, he barely noticed the cheer that had gone up from the CIC crew. This one was raucous, enduring. Like they couldn't believe they'd survived.

Told you, Arno's voice said. Hadrian smiled.

"Captain," Bella said, her tone incongruously calm. "We are receiving urgent hails from Admiral Singh's flagship, and—"

Shit. "Reactivate local comms, send sitreps. Get me on with Admiral Singh. And pipe down, everyone—don't want to spook the old man."

The relieved laughter had died down by the time Singh appeared on the hardscreen, standing at the HCI on his flagship *Raymond Spruance* with his equally concerned-looking staff. "Ian, what in the hell is going on? I'd better damned well have just destroyed an *enemy* ship."

Hadrian grinned. "You did, sir. We're forwarding our intel to you now, and I'll explain everything myself soon, but right now we have an urgent situation on the surface."

"God's name," Singh said as his eyes scanned an unseen intel report. "It's chaos down there. Who are the hostiles?"

"We're not exactly sure. Everything's in Bella's report, but their target is the capital and the VIPs gathered there."

Singh grimaced to stifle a curse. "I'll send down all the marines I've got."

Marines.

"Once the situation's secure," Singh continued, "I want you over here *immediately* to explain this mess. Can we expect any more hostile ships to arrive?"

Hadrian held up a hand. "Unknown. We should stay at general quarters. I'm sorry, sir, but I have personnel in the combat zone on the surface. I need to get in contact with them."

"Do what you have to, son. Singh out."

"Bella," Hadrian said the moment Singh's image disappeared, "can you get in touch with Jack, or ... Who was the ranking marine we left down there? Ryu?"

"I was attempting to inform you earlier, Captain," Bella replied. "We are receiving an urgent comms request from Commander Mirra."

Hadrian's eyes widened. "She's still down there?"

"Yes, sir. Shall I put her through?"

"Right away."

Hadrian turned back to the hardscreen. A moment later, it came to life, but not with Mirra's face. Instead, it showed a first-person view from her helmet sensors. Hadrian's breath caught in his throat.

She was in the stadium pit in the capital district; Hadrian remembered it from his own arrival at Byas a year ago, the small but still somehow overwrought ceremony the olans had put on to welcome him. Where he'd first met Jack, Sithelius, and the others he'd worked with for the last year.

It had been almost completely destroyed. The stage was blasted and broken. Craters and scars marred the earth and stone of the stadium itself. Broken and bloodied bodies littered the stage, the steps, the seats. Some byasian, some human, others black-armored cyborg infiltrators. The sight left Hadrian speechless.

"Mirra?" he said at last.

"Captain," she replied. "You succeeded?"

"We're alive. As are you." *And what are you still* doing *there?*

"We've taken heavy casualties, but the attacking force is dead or in retreat. We need large-scale medical support, air cover, and reinforcements."

"It's all on its way to you now." Hadrian swallowed. *Casualties.* "Who's with you?"

Mirra hesitated before she turned to show him.

No.

THIRTY-SIX

It was Jack who had saved Mirra. In so doing, she had spent her own life.

Somehow, the badly wounded virgonid had dragged herself across the stage, trailing viscera behind her, to the spot where Mirra had been fighting with the infiltrator. She'd used what little strength she had left to rear up and crash down on the hostile, piercing him at the hip with a razor-sharp talon Mirra hadn't even known virgonids had. Then she'd collapsed, dying. She lay there still, breathing heavily and slowly.

Mirra sank onto her haunches next to Jack, pointing her rifle skyward, and retracted her visor. She studied the virgonid's wound, even more grievous now that it had previously seemed. Mirra had a basic medkit in her armor, but she didn't know where to start with virgonid physiology.

"What can I do?" she asked.

Jack looked up at her, then pointed behind her with a wavering hand. "They … know."

Mirra turned, kept her rifle from swinging down toward the approaching virgonids. She didn't know where the aliens had come from, if they'd received the call for medics, or if some signal from Jack herself had summoned them. There were three of them, and they converged on their fallen sister silently, gracefully.

Mirra stood and stepped back, giving them room. Sithelius approached slowly from where the byasian wounded lay, stood beside her. He looked on the fallen virgonid with an expression Mirra couldn't read. But he too was completely silent.

The three other virgonids knelt over Jack, gingerly examined her from each side. They paid almost no attention to her wound. Instead, they were focused on the egg sac on her back. After a few seconds, one of them bowed its head next to hers and made a chittering, cooing sound.

The moment she heard it, Jack relaxed. Only then did Mirra realize she had been tense, anxious. Her mannerisms were so alien, and yet somehow so human. Mirra felt she could even read her facial expressions, though she had no face in the human sense. It was uncanny. It made her feel the moment all the more.

Jack nodded. One of the virgonids stepped back, and the other two moved around behind her, began gently massaging the sack with their feeler appendages. With effort, Jack looked up at Mirra.

"Commander," she said. "Thank you."

Mirra shook her head. "Thank *you*."

Jack laughed, coughed. "Did *Belisarius* survive?"

"Mirra," Hadrian said in her ear.

"Yes," Mirra said. "Captain Hadrian's on comms with me."

"May I ... see him?"

"Put me on."

Mirra gave some commands to her armor's comms unit. A moment later, a hologram of Captain Hadrian appeared beside her. His face was grave as he knelt beside Jack.

*

THERE WAS LITTLE DECORUM in what Hadrian was doing. He didn't care.

Bella projected a holo of Jack and the virgonids tending to her onto the deck of the CIC, just below the hardscreen. Hadrian knelt next to it, like she was really there. It was what she'd see too. He hoped that'd bring her some comfort. The CIC crew watched them silently.

"Jack," he said. "You're not looking so good."

"Same as … always, then?"

Hadrian smiled, for a moment. He glanced at her caregivers, then her terrible wound. He could only look on it for a second. "What are they … Can't they do anything?"

"Not for me," she said. Hadrian winced. "But … I'm sorry, Ian. I was somewhat closer to term than I let on."

Her child. Hadrian looked up at the sac on her back. The other virgonids were prompting it to hatch. They were saving her child.

Tears sprang into Hadrian's eyes. He smiled.

"I didn't want … I didn't want you to fear …"

Hadrian shook his head. "I'm happy. I mean it."

"I know."

The virgonid midwives began making a harmonic cooing noise. The sac shuddered in response.

Hadrian sniffed. "You, uh, thought of a name?"

"Several." Jack coughed. "At first, I thought perhaps Ian, but … I didn't want people to become confused. Since you two will be spending a great deal of time together."

"Oh, well. You don't have to worry about that. People can just call me Hadrian. Little Ian?"

"I thought of a more elegant … solution. Xenophon."

Hadrian laughed. "Xeno? If he plans on spending much time with humans, I hope he's got a sense of humor."

"He will."

"He'll have yours."

Jack nodded.

"Jack. This last year …" *With everything that came before. Things I never even told her about, yet somehow …* "You don't know what your friendship's meant to me."

"Yes, I do. And so will my son."

And then, he was there. The two virgonids caught the new life as it slid from its cocoon, squeaking and clicking. Jack seemed to deflate further as it did, but in relief, a laying down of burdens rather than a surrender. Hadrian stared at the fragile young creature in wonder, hardly believing it would one day grow into one of the huge, terrifying, gentle beings that now cradled it in their strong but delicate hands.

He rose and stepped back as one passed the child to the other, and that one came around before the mother, held her offspring low before her. Jack took up the harmonic coo now, though she had barely enough strength left to make it. She raised one trembling hand before her, the long appendages humans called fingers waving weakly, seeking connection.

By instinct, one of the child's tiny, matching hands rose up to meet it, and they twined together. The pairs of alien eyes locked together, and when Jack smiled, her child smiled back. *He* smiled back. For a moment, if only a moment, all of Hadrian's sadness at the death of his friend was swept away. It was a miracle, what he was witnessing. Something no human would ever truly understand, yet something each could feel, on a level deeper than understanding.

"He's beautiful," Jack whispered.

"Yes," Hadrian said. "He is."

Then the mother's hand drifted down, its last strength failing. And Jack was gone.

Xeno's hand still grasped for it, not understanding and yet knowing, feeling. He turned his infant head toward the strange light glowing beside him, looked up into Hadrian's holographic face, the tears that fell on *Belisarius*'s deck but to him must be vanishing into thin air. And he raised his grasping fingers toward it.

Hadrian smiled, and extended his own hand. Hadrian felt the illusory touch of the tiny being's fingers on his own, a holosomatic projection from his neural implants into his mind. Xeno, emerging into the world, would feel nothing. Even so, Hadrian knew the infant would understand the gesture, and its meaning. He would feel it.

Then the virgonid cradling the child stood back. The other two moved forward to tend to Jack's body. Hadrian turned away; more holograms rendered before him as he moved. Sithelius standing with his head bowed in prayer, his wounded retainers behind him. And Mirra, her rifle slung, looking down on the scene with an expression he had never seen on her face.

Peace.

He caught her eye. They looked at each other a long moment. Hadrian knew what he wanted to ask, what he wanted to say, but no words would come. He simply nodded.

She nodded back.

THIRTY-SEVEN

Smoke still rose from extinguished fires and destroyed buildings when Hadrian reached the surface.

The devastation was concentrated on the ceremony site, but not limited to it. A battle had taken place in the capital city, far smaller than the ones that had raged across the planet's surface during the war, yet dwarfing the minor clashes and bombings that had thus far characterized the insurgency. Intel estimated that twenty to thirty cyber-enhanced infiltrators and upward of four hundred byasian insurgents had conducted the attack. Added to the dozens of ambushes and bombings that had occurred simultaneously in the other districts, thousands of local guerrillas had been coordinated to pull this off. Thousands more might still be waiting in the hills and tunnels of Byas.

Capital security forces had rallied after driving off the attack and had now been reinforced by some three hundred fully equipped marines from Admiral Singh's squadron. Hadrian watched a squad of them now, patrolling the new perimeter of the ceremony site, with recon drones buzzing high overhead and semiautonomous heavy weapons deployed alongside them. Unless there was also a much larger force of infiltrators waiting in the wings, any attack against *this* force would have been suicide.

As, in reality, the last one had been. The bodies were still being cleared away, but several hundred of the local insurgents had been killed in the attack. Less than a hundred had escaped into the surrounding hills, and many of these had already been captured or killed by pursuing marines. Hadrian walked past a row of the dead now; pity clawed at his heart as he looked on their small, furry, broken bodies. It was hard to imagine that creatures such as these had caused so much wanton destruction and death just a few hours ago. Their weapons taken away, the only thing that marked them out from their civilian or security counterparts were the red tattoos permanently dyed onto the fur of their faces: a stylized gear-like sigil, indicating their enduring loyalty to their old machine overlords. The Ciphers.

Was it you? Hadrian asked silently. Somehow, he didn't think so. Even if the evidence was beginning to pile up. And, he had no doubt, the rumors were already beginning to spread, among the locals and the Compact personnel.

The bodies of the infiltrators had already been cleared away—those that were still intact. Most were on their way up to Byas Station for closer analysis, away from prying eyes. Hadrian doubted they would learn much more than Zevran and Doctor Park already had, but there was always the possibility.

Without thinking, Hadrian had come to the lip of the stadium pit. He looked down at the ruined stage, the spot where Jack had died, where her son Xeno had been born. Hadrian's heart was still a roiling sea of emotion at the memory, just a few hours old. He wanted to meet the little one, but he also didn't think he could bear it. Not yet.

Admiral Singh and Minister Reinhardt were down there now with a heavy marine guard, surveying the damage. Hadrian had been against Singh coming down, and Singh against Reinhardt accompanying him, but in the end, both men's superiors could not be swayed. In neither case had Hadrian been surprised. But he *was* surprised that there were no media drones hovering over the scene to record the minister bravely striding among the wreckage, posing for whatever effect his media team decided they wanted to achieve—empathy, indignation, a promise of vengeance. That alone made Hadrian respect the politician at least a little more.

"Captain Hadrian."

Speaking of. Hadrian turned and looked down. "Olan Sithelius."

The little byasian leader had approached him alone, his denuded retinue waiting a few meters away along with his bodyguard. Sithelius's fur and clothing were still stained with dirt and blood. Several of his household, Hadrian knew, had been killed right next to him. He had stayed with Jack and the wounded, and thus nearly died himself. Yet he held his little head as high as he always had, and with as much pride.

Always knew there was more to you than met the eye.

"I'm gratified to see you survived," Sithelius said.

"You too."

"And to hear that you defeated the servants of the machines in space." Sithelius hissed and flicked his tail. "Despite being badly outnumbered. A glorious victory."

"Thank you, but we don't know for certain the Ciphers were involved."

Sithelius's nose wrinkled. "Who else could it have been? No living beings would commit such savagery."

Hadrian could easily have quibbled with that, but he didn't have it in him. "In any case, your people didn't do too badly down here either."

"We were taken by surprise." Sithelius looked away. "We would all have been taken or killed, if not for Commander Mirra. And Jack."

Hadrian bowed his head.

"I did not appreciate his style of argument," Sithelius continued, using Jack's birth gender. "He was far too accommodating. At first, I interpreted this as weakness. But I was wrong. He was a most worthy representative of your people, Captain. His sacrifice on behalf of mine will long be remembered."

Hadrian smiled. "I know she'd appreciate that very much. She really did care for your world."

Sithelius gazed out at the hills on the horizon. "I hope his replacement has as much integrity and clarity of sight. Will *you* be remaining at Byas, Captain?"

"I don't know," Hadrian answered truthfully. "It's possible *Belisarius* will be reassigned."

Sithelius seemed to think for a moment. "If you are to leave us as well, then I make the same prayer for your replacement. It has been an honor to argue with you, Captain Hadrian." Sithelius extended his little hand up.

"An honor," Hadrian said, bending down to take it in his own, "and a pleasure, Olan Sithelius."

Hadrian felt a twinge of guilt as the byasian took his leave. He had come to feel responsible for this world and its people during his time here. He had known, of course, that it would not be a permanent posting—no posting in the Navy ever was—but given the circumstances of his arrival, and how long *Belisarius* had already been on station here, he'd expected to remain for a long time. Now that he had actually fought, and his sailors and marines had spilled their blood, to defend this place, he felt an even greater sense of duty toward it. Even as the truth was becoming clearer to him.

"Meet me at the temporary headquarters in ten minutes."

Hadrian glanced down into the stadium pit as the text-only message came in to his implant. Admiral Singh was looking up at him, expression serious. Hadrian gave him a furtive salute.

I'm ready to leave.

*

Admiral Rohan Singh stood with hands on hips, staring out the window of the temp HQ for at least a minute in silence.

Mirra had never met the man before today. Heard little about him, save for his exemplary war record. Still, despite the lack of red flags, and Hadrian's obvious trust in him—perhaps, in some small part, *because* of that trust—she had been reluctant to tell him everything. Even though Hadrian had insisted they had little choice, and all logic and reason had agreed with him.

The hardest thing to come clean about had been Baton. She had wrestled with whether to tell Hadrian, and by extension Singh, from the end of the fight until now. In the end, she had decided she had nothing to gain any longer by keeping it hidden. Revealing to them that she and her team had seen one of these enhanced infiltrators before—and that she suspected this was why her men had been killed—provided them with potentially crucial information about the extent of the conspiracy. At the same time, it didn't meaningfully expose her any more than the rest of what she'd said did.

Still, it had been hard for her to relate even the basic facts of that mission. It had felt like a betrayal of her men, somehow.

So far, the admiral's reaction was doing little to dispel her concerns. She glanced at Hadrian; he gave her a thin but reassuring smile. Clearly *he* had no such concerns, or he was doing a good job of hiding them. That too did little to reassure her. They hadn't left things on the best terms aboard *Belisarius*, and aside from the comm right after the battle, they hadn't had much chance to speak since then. She felt there was a lot to say. Little as that appealed to her.

"This is all quite hard to credit," Singh finally said. He turned slowly, and looked at Hadrian. "Truth be told, if it were anyone but *you* telling me this, I'd be inclined to think the evidence had been fabricated. As it is …" Singh shook his head.

Mirra prepared herself to fight for the truth, even if it was against a flag officer.

There's one positive: Don't have to worry about killing my career anymore.

"I don't know what to hope for," Singh continued. "That these conspirators *are* Cipher infiltrators, or that they aren't."

"I know what you mean," Hadrian said. "If they *aren't,* then someone within the Compact wants to make it look like the Ciphers just tried to seize control of a Protectorate world."

Only when Singh nodded at that did Mirra finally begin to relax.

"And if they are, then they just *did.*" Singh's gaze flitted to Mirra. "If what you've told me is true, Commander—and if Ian's telling me the truth, I have no reason to doubt you—then they're likely also working with one or more Kyran clans. I don't think I need to tell you two, of all people, how bad an alliance like that would be for the Compact right now."

Mirra said what didn't need saying. "We're not prepared for war."

"Not on two fronts. *Three.* Even the Navy is stretched thin dealing with the Pyrian civil war and the Protectorate insurgencies. That's just the military situation—the less said about the political, the better. It's hard to imagine something like this coming at a worse time."

"I doubt that's a coincidence," Mirra said.

"No." Singh sighed. "I'm not looking forward to reporting this back to NGHQ."

Hadrian glanced at Mirra, for the first time in the conversation looking a little concerned. "Sir … what exactly are you going to report back?"

"Good question." Singh smiled ruefully. "The cat's at least half out of the bag. But until we know how far this goes, is there anything I should try to keep back? Would it do any good if I did?"

"Choices I don't envy, sir," Hadrian said.

"Particularly as you've both just made them?" Singh walked toward them. "I appreciate you coming clean with me. That can't have been easy—especially for you, Commander, given your circumstances. I want to thank you for that, and for remaining here to defend the capital. As far as I'm concerned, you've gone above and beyond."

Mirra was momentarily struck silent. Belatedly, she shook the admiral's proffered hand. "Thank you, sir."

"You too, Ian." Singh clapped Hadrian on the arm. "Regardless of everything else, I plan to put you and your crew up for commendations. I wish I could offer you the same, Commander, but ..."

"Quite all right, Admiral," Mirra said. She noticed Hadrian's demeanor sour when the topic of medals was raised. "We're used to fighting in the dark."

Singh smiled. "Now, I'll have to think about all this. Why don't you both return to *Belisarius*? I'll come up myself once I've made a decision."

"Actually, sir." Hadrian glanced at Mirra again. "There was something else I wanted to discuss with you. In private."

"Of course," Singh said.

Mirra saluted and made her exit. She was fairly certain what Hadrian wanted to talk about.

*

DESPITE WHO HE was telling it to, it was easier to get the whole story out this time. Unleashing it on Mirra first had dispelled the terror of it. That, and the battles in between, had helped put things in perspective.

Even so, it was painful to see the disappointment on Singh's face. The only consolation was that it hurt less than seeing the pride when he *didn't* know the truth had.

"I knew there was something off about that mission," Singh finally said, once Hadrian had finished. "But … Damn it all, Ian. What did I say about things coming at a worse time?"

Hadrian smiled sadly. "I should have told you sooner. When it happened."

"Yes. You should have." Singh leaned back in his chair, sighed heavily. "I can't believe—Admiral Nakatomi actually said that to you? Threatened to fabricate evidence, blame it all on your crew?" Hadrian nodded. "God damn him. What the hell was he thinking? What's he *involved* with?"

Hadrian shifted uncomfortably. "I was under the impression he just wanted to avoid bad publicity at a time when—"

"No." Singh shook his head to belabor the point. "Not him. I've known Jim Nakatomi since the war. We were never the best of friends, but … it's hard to accept he did this at all. There's no *way* he would have done it just to sweep an embarrassment under the rug. If he stooped that low, he thought he was doing it for a higher purpose. There must be more to this than you realized. What that is, I can't imagine."

Somehow, that didn't sit well with Hadrian. Like he wanted it to have been nothing more than simple skulduggery and ass-covering. "Whatever it is, this has gone on long enough. After everything that's happened, let them say what they want. I'll go to NGHQ or ICGS—or if they won't listen, parliament, the media, whoever."

"Hmm." Singh brooded for a moment. "I don't think we can."

Hadrian's stomach churned. "All due respect, sir, it's not your burden to bear."

"It is now. Think about the implications of this. You're talking about a fleet admiral threatening his own officers with prosecution based off falsified evidence, to keep quiet a massacre committed by a rogue ISOC team. Right after you finished telling me about a conspiracy within the ICDF involving rogue ISOC elements. *And* we just fought off an attempted massacre committed by those elements. We can't ignore the possibility that they're connected."

Hadrian's frown deepened. He *did* want them to be connected. That was what bothered him. "To what end, what … what could slaughtering a peaceful village on Pyria have to do with this?"

"Maybe those villagers saw something they shouldn't have—maybe even the same thing Commander Mirra's team did. Maybe something was being tested on them. Ian …" Singh stood, took his shoulder. "I'm not saying for certain there's a connection, but we can't rule it out. And until we know more, coming clean with this might only make things worse. We'd have to go public with *everything,* and it's too soon for that. At the very least, they could use this fabricated evidence to discredit you, kill the whole story. We need to find out who's really behind this, and what their objectives are."

Hadrian opened his mouth to protest, then slowly nodded.

Singh patted him on the shoulder. "I'm sorry, son. I know you want to come clean, let this go. You'll just have to wait a little longer."

"Yes, sir."

"Speaking of which—you've somehow given me even *more* to think about, so thank you for that. Get back up to your ship. I'll be along as soon as I can. Hopefully with some orders for you."

THIRTY-EIGHT

Orders.

It wasn't the resolution Hadrian had hoped for. Singh was right; he had wanted to face the music for what he'd done. Not just the failure in judgment that had resulted in the village's destruction, but the worse one of agreeing to keep it quiet. In giving the order to fire, he'd acted on the best information available to him at the time. Perhaps he should have been less trusting, but ... They hadn't trained him to expect that kind of betrayal.

They *had* trained him to tell the truth. And it shouldn't have mattered that his superiors had ordered him not to; it shouldn't have mattered that they had fabricated evidence to pin it all on him and his officers—he should have gone straight to Singh anyway, or over their heads, damn the consequences. It would have been the right thing to do.

Why didn't you? Really?

The door alert chime was a relief, despite who was behind it.

"Drink?" Hadrian offered her.

"Thank you," Mirra said.

He poured them both a stiff bourbon. They stood in silence for a moment before he raised his glass. "To absent friends."

"Absent friends."

After they drank, Mirra turned away. Hadrian knew there was more to say. A lot more. He didn't know where to start, and apparently he wasn't alone. She walked over to his bookcases, studied them as she sipped on the bourbon.

He half-smiled. "How did you know who Pericles was?"

"My father," Mirra said after a moment's silence. "He saw to it I was schooled in ancient history."

"From the source?"

She nodded. "The epic poems, the histories."

I'll be damned. Hadrian shook his head. "So who's better, Herodotus or Thucydides?"

"Thucydides, obviously," Mirra said. Hadrian chuckled. "Truth be told, my favorite was Ammianus Marcellinus."

Hadrian's brow knit. "Oh?"

"Later Roman Empire." Mirra peered at the section of the shelves dedicated to the period. "Chronicles a time of resurgence just before the final collapse of the West. Describes several battles and sieges he personally participated in, quite a unique perspective."

"Ah. Of course."

"He's rather obscure. I'm not surprised you haven't heard of him."

"I—" Hadrian swallowed his pique. "I've *heard* of him. I just don't happen to have a copy."

"Mmm." Mirra pulled a book off the shelf. "May I borrow this? It's been a long time."

Hadrian moved closer. It was his copy of Xenophon's *Anabasis*. He smiled sadly.

"... Of course, I can pull it up off the network if you'd—"

"No, no." Hadrian pushed it toward her. "Please."

"Thank you. I do prefer the genuine articles."

"Me too."

They stood in silence a little longer.

"Can I ask you something?" Hadrian said. Mirra nodded. "Why'd you go back? To fight, on Byas?"

Mirra seemed to search for the answer in her glass. "Jack."

"She asked you to?"

"She *didn't*," Mirra said. Hadrian smiled. "Neither did you."

"That was all it took?"

"I thought about …" Mirra finished her drink. "Since they were killed, all I've been able to think about is my men. How I could avenge them. Jack, and you, made me think about what they would have *done*. If they'd still been alive. They wouldn't have run off in the middle of a fight while those people needed them. Not for anything."

"Neither would you, as it turns out."

Mirra almost smiled. "I haven't given up on getting justice for them."

"Nor should you."

She studied the cover of *Anabasis*.

"In any case," Hadrian said, "thank you. For everything."

"May I ask *you* something?"

"Of course."

"What did Admiral Singh say? When you told him about Pyria?"

Hadrian sighed. He had wanted her to ask, and dreaded it. "I told him I wanted to come clean. Go public. He said now isn't the time."

"The conspiracy."

Hadrian nodded. "I don't know how to feel about that."

"You've been silent all this time," Mirra said. "Why should now be different?"

Hadrian let the implied judgment lie. It was fair. "I was asking myself that before you came in."

"And?"

It was hard to believe Mirra was the one driving the conversation. Hadrian was glad for it. "I told myself I stayed silent to protect my people. I couldn't bear the thought of them—of Arno—going down for something they didn't do, while the bastards actually responsible sailed away unpunished."

"That wasn't true?"

"It was, but there was more to it." Now it was Hadrian's turn to finish his drink in one swig. "Bitterness. If our superiors were going to betray everything the uniform stood for, why should we fall on our swords to preserve it?"

Mirra said nothing, but he knew she understood that. All too well. It would have made it easy to leave it at that.

"And," he said, "commanding a ship was all I'd ever wanted. Since I was kid. The truth would have taken it away from me."

He felt Mirra looking at him. He couldn't face her just yet. Instead, he stared into the space beyond his bookshelves.

"So I kept my mouth shut and my dream alive. But I think that's why she never really felt *mine*." He placed a hand on the nearest bulkhead. "*Belisarius*. Not like *Marissa* did, before ... I knew I only had her because of a lie."

"And now?" Mirra said after a pause.

"Now? After yesterday ... Yeah. She does feel like mine. Like I proved myself, like I ... scrubbed away some part of the stain."

Mirra took his glass alongside her own and went to the bar to refill them.

"And it's only after that, I feel like I'm ready to do what I should have done all along," Hadrian said. "Come clean, and lose her. Lose everything I always wanted, maybe forever."

"It's no small thing," Mirra said, handing him the refilled glass, "to give that up."

"And now they won't let me. Of course ... I *could* still do it: Go to the media, or parliament. Maybe Singh's order is just an excuse."

"You told him," Mirra said, "believing the consequences would be what you'd feared."

Hadrian shook his head. "What does it mean, though, that I was only willing to once I finally, really *had* it? Once I thought it was real?"

"Perhaps that you're a better man than you think." Hadrian looked up at her, surprised. "If not as good as you'd *like* to be."

Hadrian laughed. "I guess I can live with that."

"We should all be so lucky."

After their final toast, the door chime sounded again. They looked at each other in surprise for a moment, only then remembering what they'd been waiting here for.

"Come," Hadrian said.

Admiral Singh said nothing, even when he took the drink Hadrian offered him. Instead, he took it over to the holographic window, stared out at Byas and the glittering motes of his squadron orbiting above it. Hadrian and Mirra shared a glance after a minute passed without change.

"You know," the admiral said then, "you two put me in quite a bind by saving my life."

Hadrian smiled. "I'll keep that in mind next time, sir."

"Yes, well. I've been selective with my report to NGHQ. Based on your recommendations, there are aspects I'll wait to report in person. But that still leaves the question of what to do with you."

For a moment, against his higher judgment, Hadrian's hackles raised. "Sir?"

Singh turned. "You, Commander. I don't think you realize what a precarious situation you've placed yourself in by staying."

"I do, sir," Mirra said, unfazed. Hadrian looked at her.

"I've come up with a rather unorthodox solution," Singh said. "But it'll only work if you're willing. Both of you."

THIRTY-NINE

"First of all," Hadrian said, "Arno's going to make it."

The mood in the briefing room lightened. After the elation of victory and survival had ebbed, concern for Arno had descended in its place. Hadrian was ashamed that it hadn't in him, to the same extent; there had simply been too many other things on his mind.

"Doctor Park can fill you in on the details," he said.

"Indeed." Park leaned forward. "As you all know, I transported Commander Tsegaye to Byas Station personally. While the station lacks the medical facilities to effect his full recovery, they were—under my supervision—able to stabilize his condition, sufficient that he could be placed back into stasis for transport to Ranak. The full fleet medical facility there should have no trouble reviving him."

"How long will he be out of action?" Hassani asked.

Park made a noncommittal gesture. "He could be conscious again in as little as three weeks, but full recovery … three or four months? He was physically dead for quite some time, sadly. Neural reconstruction is a delicate process, and there was also extensive spinal and radiation damage. Nonetheless, I'm confident he will eventually be good as new. Or, as good as thirty-five."

Hadrian and Hassani shared in the doctor's chuckle. "Whenever he does wake up, I know he'll be immensely proud of you all, and what you accomplished here. So's Admiral Singh—he's planning to address the entire crew before we head for Ranak, but in the meantime, he asked me to extend his thanks to you for saving his squadron, and Byas. He also told me he intends to put the entire ship up for an Executive Unit Citation."

Only Hassani seemed to truly take pride at that. Zevran, of course, did not react; Tsung simply grunted; and Park smiled as though he'd been offered a discount at his favorite shop. The crew would doubtless appreciate it, assuming they received it. Hadrian had no doubt Singh would pull whatever strings he had to, to make sure they did.

"If Commander Tsegaye is going to be off duty for several months," Zevran said, "who'll be serving as executive officer?"

Thought I'd have more time. Hadrian cleared his throat. "Right. About that ... You know, I think it'll be simpler if she just introduces herself."

Hadrian flicked a finger toward the door. A woman wearing a Navy commander's uniform entered, came to attention at the far end of the briefing table.

"Commander Mirra reporting as ordered, sir."

*

"AT EASE, COMMANDER," Hadrian said. "Please have a seat."

The officers' reactions varied as Mirra took her seat at the opposite end of the table from the captain. The Citizen, Zevran, seemed unsurprised. She wondered if he were capable of any emotions other than frustration and disdain; she supposed that now she'd have the opportunity to find out.

The doctor's smile was polite and confused. The engineer, Tsung, was clearly unimpressed. She wondered if he was salty at having been passed over for the post himself, being senior—but no. If her read on the man was anywhere close to accurate, he had no interest in a command position. Just a *personal* distaste, then. She could handle that.

Only the young woman, Hassani, seemed equally surprised and pleased. She gave Mirra a subtle but welcoming smile. Mirra gave her an equally subtle nod in return. She wondered if their conversation in the training room before the battle had had any impact on the lieutenant. The fact that they were all still here might indicate that it did.

"I can see you're all confused," Hadrian said. "Here's the situation."

Mirra remained silent and impassive, projecting confidence. She had wanted to explain things herself; Hadrian had convinced her to let him handle the first part. That would make it clear to the officers that he was on board with the plan, rather than having it foisted upon him by the admiral.

"Commander Mirra technically holds a naval rank," Hadrian continued. "She also has a fleet officer's identity, for clandestine ops purposes. She'll be assuming that identity, and taking on the role of a replacement XO for *Belisarius,* now that her real ISOC identity is dead."

Doctor Park frowned. "Dead?"

"As far as ISOC is concerned, at least officially, my LDRG team was wiped out in an ambush on Lampshade," Mirra said. "Myself included. The only people who know any different are involved in this conspiracy. They can't reveal that they know I'm alive without *also* revealing their involvement."

"Which creates an opportunity for us," Hadrian added.

"Are we being reassigned to investigate this conspiracy?" Hassani asked.

"Yes and no," Hadrian said. "For the time being, *Belisarius* is being reassigned to Ranak to join Admiral Singh. Whatever posting we get after that will be on the books, regular force. But, in addition to our reg force mission, Admiral Singh is personally assigning us to root this thing out."

"On our own?" Zevran asked.

Hadrian shook his head. "He's going back to Concord to report to ICGS and the Executive in person, in case these guys have compromised the Hub. He expects they'll assign additional resources to tackle this—but it'll have to be small scale, under the table. At least until we figure out the reach this thing has. He wants us to be his eyes and ears in the fleet, and his arm, if need be. Commander Mirra's assignment to *Belisarius* helps us do that."

"Yeah." Tsung raised a hand. "She doesn't have any training as a fleet officer. What the hell use is she gonna be as an exec?"

Mirra gave him her best implacable glare. He returned it with his own.

"That's the thing," Hadrian said, keeping his cool. "Given our new covert mission, we're going to need additional capabilities. Our marine detachment is being reinforced and made permanent, to tackle small-scale ops. They'll be under Mirra's direct command. She can provide expert advice on that front, ISOC, and covert ops in general. Besides which, she's already shown she has good judgment—*and* that she's willing to go toe-to-toe with me when she thinks I'm wrong. What more do you need from an XO?"

Hassani smiled. Tsung shrugged and looked away. Likely the best she was going to get from him.

"I want to assure you all, I didn't take this decision lightly," she said. All eyes turned to her. "Nor do I take the responsibility lightly. As much as I appreciate Captain Hadrian's vote of confidence, I have to admit that I may have been ... overzealous in my commitment to certain courses of action over the last week."

It was hard for her to say. Hadrian knew that, but she hoped the others couldn't tell just how hard. She'd had to practice the little speech before the meeting. "I offer no excuses. I can only say that I know what I don't know. In as much as I'm here to offer my expertise in certain areas, I will need to rely on *your* expertise when it comes to the running of this vessel. Which, events have proven, is significant."

Outwardly, it was not the most glowing praise. But it was a lot, coming from her. She hoped they could see that.

"All right?" Hadrian said after a sufficient pause. "Good. Then let me officially welcome Commander Mirra, ICN, as our new executive officer. Now, Commander, if you'd continue the briefing?"

Mirra stood. "Thank you, Captain. Our analysis of the remains of the enemy ships, and their personnel on the surface, has revealed some troubling facts. In the main, the admiral's intel team's findings conformed with our own—with one notable exception."

A quantum code fragment appeared above the briefing table. Zevran's eyes narrowed. "That's Cipher code."

"It is," Mirra said.

There was the frustration, again. "That wasn't in the data I studied."

"No," Mirra confirmed. "The admiral's team went over our recovered intel and found no trace of it. Similarly, obvious Cipher technology was found in the bodies of the infiltrators on the surface, while none was found on the body from 47988."

"There were some enhancements which appeared to have been influenced by Cipher technology," Doctor Park offered.

"As did the code Lieutenant Zevran discovered in the enemy database," Mirra said. "But where those connections were implicit, these are explicit. And not very difficult to find."

Hassani leaned forward. "Are you saying someone wanted to make it *look* like the Ciphers were responsible for this attack?"

"That's my assessment," Mirra said. "The admiral agrees. However, that does not mean the Ciphers were *not* responsible. They have conducted equally convoluted information ops in the past, for motives just as obscure. It may be that they wanted us to find evidence of their involvement here, but remain uncertain as to the level and nature of that involvement."

"That being said, if the Ciphers are a part of this, I don't think they're the whole story," Hadrian said. "Cipher ships would have seen right through the tricks we pulled on them. And there's no evidence those rogue ISOC agents were simulants."

"So it could be Compact traitors working with the Ciphers *and* the Kyrans, trying to start a war?" Hassani asked. "Why would any human do that?"

"Why do some byasians still worship the metal bastards?" Tsung said.

"That's different," Hassani retorted. "They were brainwashed by centuries of occupation. We haven't been."

"No accounting for stupid."

"The point is," Hadrian said, "we don't know. We can't even make an educated guess. All we *do* know is that a conspiracy is festering in the heart of the Compact military. Whatever they want, they're willing to murder their fellow sailors and marines, and massacre civilians, to get it. That means they're our enemies, whatever uniform they happen to be wearing. And right now, we're among the few who know they exist."

Hadrian looked meaningfully around the table. "That number'll grow over time, but while it does, we've got to stay alert. Trust no one who doesn't already know. That being said, we can't lose sight of why we're doing this. Why we fought here."

It was clear the other officers knew what he meant. So did Mirra. They were ideas for which, she realized, she had long since ceased to hold reverence. Even before Baton, and the ambush on Lampshade, had pushed her into outright bitterness, right to the edge of nihilism. Duty. Honor. The defense of those who can't defend themselves, of the liberty and freedom of those who don't appreciate them. The higher ideals that the Interstellar Compact was founded upon, which it so rarely, if ever, fully lived up to.

Had she found those higher ideals within herself once again?

No. Twenty years of fighting in the shadows, of being the dagger in the Compact's underhand, couldn't be erased by a single act of selflessness, or by a few high-minded speeches from an idealist. Even one she had come, however grudgingly, to respect.

But perhaps, she thought as she looked at the officers around her, she had found something else. Something she'd lost much more recently. Perhaps the rest could, someday, grow from that.

"We can't forget who we are," she said.

Hadrian smiled.

FORTY

We can't forget who we are.

Mirra's words are ringing in my head as we prepare to leave Byas. Did I forget who I was, after Pyria? At the time, I didn't think so. I told myself there was nothing else I could have done—that they'd tied my hands. There was no point ruining your career, and mine, and getting us sent to prison over something someone else did. One injustice wouldn't correct another.

I see things differently now. I see that the truth matters, even when justice can't be done. It matters in and of itself; maybe nothing matters more. It demands we live up to it, and when we don't, it lets us know, every single day. That's why it hurts to live a lie deep in your soul. Like I was for the last year. Living the lie that the truth didn't matter.

Now, I know that, and ... I'm asked to live another lie. The same lie, on the surface. That's why it was hard for me to accept when Singh asked me to do it. But I see that differently now too. This new lie is only for the world. The old lie is the one I told myself, and you. That's the big lie, the most pernicious and destructive one. Now that the old lie's been overcome, the new one doesn't feel so heavy. And like the old one, it won't survive forever.

I feel like we were all living a lie, of a kind. Maybe it was just that we understood our place, our purpose, the reason why we got up and worked every single day. The reason we did it out here, on an old ship orbiting an alien world in deep space, instead of back home, with family, friends, the people who love us.

We understand that purpose now. In spite of everything we know, the dire straits we're in, there's an unmistakable energy. I can see it on their faces, feel it in the way they walk the ship. Seeing it has made me feel young again. The ship feels younger too, even though she's almost as old as I am. So does her crew—even old Tsung seems to be putting a bit more vinegar in his coffee. Got a real spring in his step when he chews people out now.

Doc Park still smiles all the time, but there's a little less tightness around his eyes. Hassani holds her head higher; she always had pride, but now she looks like she's earned it. And she has.

Zevran ... Well, he's Zevran. But I swear his dourness seems a little lighter, somehow. That Ensign Coleridge is even poking his head out of his lab from time to time. I actually saw him eating in the mess hall with the other officers yesterday. Didn't look like he was saying much, but hey, it's a start.

You would be happy. Will be happy, when you wake up.

Then there's Mirra. In some ways, I can't believe how well she's fitting in already. She's taken to the role of XO with almost distressing relish. As great as you and I are together, I have to admit that we're two of a kind. When I think back, nearly all of the best Captain–XO teams I've known have been two sides of a coin, each balancing the other out. That being true, if I'm the collegial one, maybe my XO should be a laser-cut hardass. Whatever else I can say about Mirra, no one fits that bill better. The crew have already gotten over their confusion and awkwardness at her assignment. She doesn't even have to raise her voice: One glare from her and they snap to faster than I've ever seen.

As to the rest of it, I still don't know how to feel about her. We've come to an understanding, but will that last? Are we too different? When the chips are down, will our priorities, our beliefs clash again? Stupid question—of course they will—but will that help us, or hurt us?

Only time will tell. But even on that front, as on the others, I feel a sense of undeniable optimism. Belisarius *is one hell of a ship. I know I'm biased—we're biased—but I think Tsung was right. I don't think I've ever served on a ship that would have brought us through the battles we fought to get here. I know I've never served with a crew that would have done better. I may have come by them dishonestly, but that's not how I'm going to keep them.*

I don't know when you'll get to read this. I don't know if you'll ever come back to Belisarius, *but I know this: after everything we've been through together, whatever happens next, we'll still be friends. Brothers.*

And, as I order our ship to leave the posting she's held for the last five years, I can say that I have one thing back that I thought I'd lost.

Hope.

To: Arno Tsegaye, Ranak Fleet Base Medical Center
From: Captain Ian Hadrian, ICS *Belisarius*
March 14, 2507

EPILOGUE

"Why do we fight?"

Professor Thierry van Alden let the question hang in the classically appointed lecture hall for a moment; just long enough that some students would consider how to answer it, not so long that any of them would get the chance.

"Given that this is the History of Warfare," Van Alden said, pacing slowly, "I might suggest you focus your thoughts on that level of conflict, but you can take it to mean what you like. Why do individuals fight with one another, or sports teams, or political parties? Is there one cause, or many?"

This time, he let the question hang a little longer. Several students put up their hands; the dynamic holoprojection brought their representations into focus nearer the front of the class. Van Alden indicated one of them, a young, hairless woman with bluish skin.

"There are any number of reasons," she said. "Jealousy, fear, bigotry—"

Van Alden nodded. "There are many *proximate* causes. But there is one *root* cause, from which all others spring. Anyone care to hazard a guess as to what it might be?"

This time, more hands went up. Van Alden selected a young man with the more typical green-tinted skin of a Citizen. "Greed? The nature of property and possession?"

"Closer," Van Alden said, "but not deep enough."

He next selected the student whose personality profile suggested they would give the answer he was looking for. They were largely unmodified, almost Terran in appearance, though their profile indicated they too were a Citizen. "Human nature?"

Van Alden smiled. "Human nature. I'm sure we've all heard that explanation before. It's certainly easy to give, and just as easy to let lie. It doesn't require any further investigation, does it? 'Oh well, it's just human nature,' you can say, and shrug, and go about your business. There's no changing human nature, is there?"

The class, even the unfortunate student who was the indirect target of the mockery, chuckled at that.

"I, for one, do not hold to that," Van Alden continued. "Eight hundred years ago, a great thinker said, 'Man is born free, yet he is everywhere in chains.' We might just as easily say, 'Man is born at peace, yet he is everywhere at war.' What does that mean?"

Again, Van Alden preempted the answers. "It means that like slavery, war is not a natural condition of humankind. Instead, it has been thrust upon us. But by who, by what? Different explanations have been offered throughout the ages: gods, diseases, scarcity, ideology. Today, we can blame aliens, machines. The truth, as I alluded to earlier, lies much deeper than that."

Van Alden brought up a hologram he'd designed himself, a visualization of the spread of humanity from Africa, across the Earth, then out into the stars. "Look at the development of human civilization. War has been the engine that drives it all throughout our long and bloody history on Earth, even to the present day."

The student who'd provided his convenient answer raised their hand again. Van Alden considered brushing past the question—the other students' subjective projections wouldn't show the raised hand unless he allowed it—but the interruption might prove useful again.

"But the Age of Expansion wasn't violent," the student, Andra, said. "We made peace with the virgonids, and only colonized uninhabited planets. Conflicts didn't arise until Frontier and the other Free Worlds encountered the Kyrans. Until then it was peaceful."

Thank you again. "Was it? *Why* did humanity feel the need to expand beyond Earth? It was the pressures caused by the slow recovery following the Third World War. Why did Venturestar and the other corporations found their own private colonies instead of participating in the joint Terran initiatives? It was greed, competition with one another, which eventually turned violent. The same is true of those who founded the so-called Free Worlds —they refused to abide by the common rules set on Earth, insisted on forging their own path. In the process, they encountered and antagonized the Kyrans, leading once again to war."

As Van Alden hoped, this alone failed to cow Andra. "If that's true, then couldn't the argument be made that war has been a positive force in human history, at least partially? If it's driven us to explore and settle space?"

"Indeed it could," Van Alden allowed, smiling. He'd have to keep an eye on this one; they might prove a star pupil someday, if their more prosaic instincts could be corrected. "And it has been argued. But we must look critically at that too: the idea that human expansion into space has been a positive thing at all."

That caused just the sort of stir he'd hoped it would. He pressed on with full confidence. "Look at what we have done, everywhere we have 'explored.' We have made war against the Kyrans, against the Ciphers, against each other. Even the aliens we have allied with, we have done so only in order to fight against others. The species we have 'liberated' from Cipher oppression—*have* we, or have we simply forced them to exchange machine oppression for human?

"Indeed, leave interstate conflict aside. Nature itself, we have warred against. Every planet we come to, we change to fit our needs. Even now, geoengineers ravage a world in the Concord system to make it fit for human habitation, just so our politicians can have a more pleasant place to argue. We have destroyed entire *stars,* feeding them into black holes to feed our own endless hunger for antimatter—which fuels our relentless pursuit of war. Do you see the connection?"

At this, Andra was finally silent, though Van Alden could see they were not entirely happy with the explanation. No matter. Most of the others were clearly swayed, which meant Andra and others like them soon would be too.

"For thousands of years," Van Alden went on, "human civilization has developed with one goal in mind—however it is framed, in whatever language it is cloaked: to dominate others by force. This permeates every level of those civilizations. It is the reason individuals fight, the reason states go to war, and the reason entire species strive to exterminate one another. And it is *wholly* unnatural."

Van Alden let that hang for quite some time. There were no interruptions, no comments. *Perfect.*

"Now, what can be done about this?" Van Alden smiled. "I'm afraid that's outside the purview of a simple history course, even at the graduate level." An appropriate peal of laughter. "I'm sure the topic will come up in the course of our discussions this year, but it won't be our focus. Instead, we will study the ways in which war has shaped and been shaped by human civilization; how the development of civilization is inextricably linked to war, and why uncoupling those two things is so difficult, even here in the nominally pacifist UCC. Now, we have a few minutes left. Any questions before we depart?"

Van Alden gave one of the hitherto silent students the chance to speak. As he did, a news alert came through onto his neural implant. He had "do not disturb" toggled on during class, of course, but this alert triggered a number of his high priority search protocols. He read it while half-listening to the student's question.

His blood ran cold. It was a struggle to keep it from his face.

"An excellent point," he said once the student had finished speaking, though it hadn't been. "One we'll certainly be returning to very soon. Now, I do apologize, but I may have been somewhat overzealous in my estimate of our remaining time. Fantastic first session, everyone. For next class, make sure you've reviewed all the week one materials outlined in your personal syllabi, and complete the assignment it generates for you. I look forward to seeing you all again. Good day."

Van Alden cut the class transmission somewhat hastily, before any students could interject or request a personal meeting. The subjective lecture hall went abruptly dark and shrank to its true form, Van Alden's spacious office and seminar room, just large enough for a half-dozen students and himself to sit comfortably.

He stood in the dark for a moment, then circled to his desk and opened up the news feeds. It was all over them. He skimmed through headlines and summaries. *Near disaster on Byas ... Dozens of civilians killed, hundreds injured ... Attack on an ICN squadron ... ICS* Belisarius *prevents total destruction ... Does this mean another war with the Ciphers?*

Van Alden slammed his hand down on his desk. He left it there, fuming, focusing on the pain radiating up his arm. Then he made his decision. He flicked his wrist, activating the military-grade privacy screen embedded in his desk, then bent down to retrieve the small spherical device hidden beneath it. He stared at it for a moment, swallowed the hint of fear that always crept up when he did so, and activated it.

Almost instantaneously, an unnerving disembodied voice filled the room. *"What is your purpose?"*

Van Alden's eye twitched. "Was it us?"

The voice didn't need to be told what he meant. *"It was."*

"Damn it all," Van Alden muttered. "This was a major operation. Why wasn't I informed?"

"Your participation was not necessary."

"And if it had succeeded?"

"Your participation would *not have been necessary."*

"I suppose we'll never know," Van Alden said, piqued. "Since it failed."

"Failure was not unanticipated."

Van Alden frowned. "You … intended for it to fail?"

"It was not unanticipated. Contingencies were prepared."

"And will any of *those* require my participation?"

"You are already performing your required function." There might have been a hint of annoyance in the voice. Or it was only Van Alden projecting. *"When the time comes for that function to be advanced, you will be informed. You are already aware of what will then be required."*

"What it will require is preparation. I won't have time to *do* that if I don't know when the next phase is beginning."

"You will receive adequate warning."

"Based on *your* definition of adequate?"

"Yes."

Something in the way the voice said it gave Van Alden pause. He swallowed hard.

"You will be contacted with further instructions," the voice said. *"Do not contact us again except in exigency."*

"Fine," Van Alden said, but the voice had already cut the

connection. The professor sat behind his desk, holding the little device for a while. He left the privacy screen active. He wondered, not for the first time, if he was making the right choice.

Man is born at peace, he thought.

"Yet he is everywhere at war."

APPENDIX

OFFICERS OF THE ICS *BELISARIUS*

Captain Ian Hadrian, Commanding Officer (Eos, Hyperion System, Terran Interstellar Union)
Lieutenant-Commander Arno Tsegaye, Executive Officer (Earth, Sol System, TIU)
Commander Tsung Wei, Chief Engineering Officer (Zheng He, Xihe System, TIU)
Lieutenant-Commander Stanisław Park, Chief Medical Officer (Jayu, Sang-je System, Free Worlds Republic)
Senior Lieutenant Zevran, Chief Electromagnetic and Cyber Warfare Officer (Revolution, February System, United Citizens' Councils)
Junior Lieutenant Nasreen Hassani, Chief Tactical Operations Officer (Earth, Sol System, TIU)
Ensign Samuel Coleridge, Astrophysics Advisor (Luna, Sol System, TIU)

SENIOR OFFICERS, INTERSTELLAR COMPACT NAVY (ICN)

Vice Admiral Rohan Singh, Commanding Officer, ICN Fifth Fleet (Rāma, Vālmīki System, TIU)
Rear Admiral James Nakatomi, Commanding Officer, ICN Twelfth Fleet (Homestead, Beacon System, FWR)

OPERATIVES OF THE 2ND SQUADRON, 5TH DETACHMENT, LONG DISTANCE RECONNAISSANCE GROUP (LDRG)

Commander Sorăna Mirra, Commanding Officer (Freedom, Frontier System, FWR)
Senior Lieutenant Alistair King, Executive Officer (Taranis, Helvetios System, TIU)
Junior Lieutenant Horatio Contreras (Freedom, Frontier System, FWR)
Warrant Officer Volodymyr Tchaikovsky, ECWO (Zemlya, Perun System, TIU)
Petty Officer Grant Demetriou (Horizon, Dawn System, FWR)
Petty Officer Saito Yamada (New Eden, Hollandia System, FWR)

TECHNOLOGY

ADAPTIVE NEURAL NETWORKS

The core artificial intelligence (AI) technology used by the Interstellar Compact military. ANNs, sometimes colloquially referred to as "simulated intelligences," are not truly unshackled artificial general intelligences (AGI), in that they do not possess true sapience or self awareness. Instead, ANNs possess all the other capabilities of a sapient being, with reaction times, data storage, and information processing capabilities orders of magnitude beyond even the most heavily augmented biological mind.

ANNs are indispensable to the cyberwarfare operations of naval ships; only they possess the processing power, speed, and adaptability necessary to go toe-to-toe with Cipher cyberwarfare systems, including managing the adjustments necessary to maintain a ship's stealth screen. They are also the only systems capable of making the constant picosecond-scale calculations required by the Stardrive.

In addition, with the help of drones, ANNs handle the majority of the basic functions of running a starship or military installation which would once have required human crew, such as routine maintenance and communications. This results in the crews of modern warships being a fraction the size of vessels in earlier eras, even when of comparable or greater size and mission capability.

ANTIMATTER REACTORS

Modern naval vessels require enormous amounts of power to function; in the case of larger vessels, their power requirements exceed the output of the entire planet Earth in the early twentieth century. Most larger vessels employ a number of high-efficiency antimatter catalyzed fusion reactors to generate power for everyday operation and basic systems.

However, only matter–antimatter reactions can provide the titanic power necessary to operate a naval vessel's two primary combat systems: the UMAX particle weapon, and the magneto-plasma shield system. A ship's matter–antimatter reactor powers only these systems, in order to preserve precious antimatter fuel and generation capability for combat.

Matter–antimatter reactions approach 100 percent efficiency and are extraordinarily stable once begun, provided they remain within a powerful magnetic bottle to ensure a matter annihilation cascade does not occur. However, the catastrophic potential of such a cascade means that M–A reactor operations are highly delicate and require a reliable secondary power source, usually provided by fusion reactors, to function.

The potential for catastrophic failure also makes significant safety measures necessary. For instance, Compact and Cipher M–A reactors employ a similar fail-safe which, in the event of shutdown, shunts all antimatter into magnetic vaults with their own internal nuclear power supplies. The design of the reactors will physically prevent the antimatter being removed from these vaults until the main reactor reaches a certain minimum power level, making it necessary for the supporting fusion reactors to come online before the antimatter reactor can be activated.

Kyran reactors rarely employ such a fail-safe, making catastrophic failure a near certainty in the event of a ship being disabled; this also makes it easier for Kyran crews to scuttle their vessels to avoid capture or to strike a final blow against their enemies.

ENTANGLED NEUTRINO DETECTION AND RANGING (ENDAR)

An experimental form of quantum radar using entangled neutrino pairs, rather than photons as in traditional quantum radar (see "Lidar"). An ENDAR set generates and sends out waves of sensor neutrinos. When these neutrinos interact with an object, their minute disturbances are instantaneously reflected in the entangled idler neutrinos contained within the ENDAR set. Since neutrino interactions are incredibly weak, the detectors assigned to observe the idler neutrinos must be extremely sensitive.

These weak interactions also mean that unlike with traditional lidar or radar, there is no data collection from a bounce-back or return of the sensor beams. Data can only be collected from the entanglement effect, making ENDAR scans substantially lower resolution than those possible with traditional quantum radar. Other major limitations of ENDAR in its current form are the high energy requirement and the rapid expending of source material for neutron generation, meaning sets can only be operated for a short time before needing to be recharged.

However, the great advantage of ENDAR is that neutrinos are able to pass through almost all matter. This allows an ENDAR set to generate a complete, if low-resolution, scan of an entire area and all the objects within it, regardless of any intervening terrain or other obstructions. This capability is extraordinarily valuable in a military context, particularly in ground or boarding operations—for example, by mapping the entire interior of a vessel or building and all the hostiles moving within it.

Neutrinos' weak interactions also make it much more difficult for the subject of the scan to detect its source, potentially making it more useful as an active scan option during stealth combat situations. Currently, the technology remains in the field-testing stage, in which capacity it has reportedly been deployed by some special forces units.

HIGGS-GRAVITON EXCLUSION FIELD

The basis of mass neutralization, HGEF technology was independently invented several times in known galactic history, the most notable being by the joint human–virgonid Project Stardrive in TSY 2095. Virgonids had invented generators capable of producing the Higgs anti-boson centuries earlier, allowing them to significantly reduce the mass of their ships and enable relatively practical sublight interstellar travel. After the project's discovery of the graviton in TSY 2090, it was a relatively simple matter to adapt these generators to produce anti-gravitons—not true anti-particles, but engineered tensor excitations that locally cancel space-time curvature—as well.

This combined anti-Higgs/anti-graviton field is able to effectively neutralize the mass of an object and isolate it from the effects of gravity. This, in turn, enables the decoupling of said object from the "baseframe" and recoupling it to the "metaframe," the preferred foliation of space-time (see "Metaframe / Baseframe"). Scaling this paired technology up eventually allowed faster-than-light travel using the Stardrive, but the HGEF serves numerous more mundane functions as well, from increasing carrying capacity at the personal and industrial level to reducing thrust requirements for take-off and landing.

The ability of an HGEF to neutralize an object's mass scales with that mass, and its ability to nullify the effects of gravity scales logarithmically with the strength of the gravity currently acting upon the object. This means that an HGEF generator on, say, a human-sized object in 1g of gravity, is able to operate at only 20 percent of capacity. The HGEF on a cruiser-sized vessel in close orbit of an Earth-gravity planet is able to operate at only 0.5 percent capacity, and so on.

This effectively limits the ability of HGEFs to operate inside gravity wells, whether natural or artificially generated. Practically, this means that significant thrust is still required to escape gravity wells, that Stardrives cannot be operated too deep inside gravity wells (the "gravitic threshold"), and so on. This creates opportunities for interdiction of Stardrive-capable vessels, for example, and also provides a simple defense against HGEF-equipped projectiles or suicide vehicles; an HGEF generator operating at or near full capacity that runs into a more powerful gravity source will invariably either shut down or overload. In the case of superluminal or near-superluminal projectiles and vehicles, even a controlled, sudden shutdown can be catastrophic.

HOLOSOMATICS

An innovative technology originating in the UCC which interfaces ultra-high-resolution holographic projections with neural implants to create holograms which can be physically interacted with. Holosomatic systems transmit information in real-time directly to the subject's brain, creating near-perfect impressions of sensory experiences such as smell, taste, and touch.

Commercial holosomatic systems are designed not to create perfect representations of sensory experiences to avoid abuse. However, many people who have tested unrestricted holosomatics still report an indefinable sensation that the projections are not "real," even in double-blind experiments; the mechanism behind this sensation is not currently understood.

LIDAR (LIGHT DETECTION AND RANGING)/QUANTUM RADAR

Traditional quantum radar (colloquially known as lidar, or "light detection and ranging,") is a sensor technology which relies on entangled pairs of photons to make detections. The lidar set generates and sends out sensor photons; when these interact with an object, the lidar set is able to determine physical information about the object, such as size, shape, and distance, using data both from the bounce-back or return of the photon beams/waves, and the minute disturbance of the sensor particles themselves, which is instantaneously reflected in the entangled idler photons contained in the detector itself.

The latter form of quantum detection occurs the moment the sensor photons interact with the object, regardless of distance, in some cases greatly reducing the time lag of a detection by the operator of the lidar set. However, the resolution of scans combining both return (which propagates back at the speed of light) and quantum detection data is greater.

Lidar scans can be mitigated or even defeated by advanced visual camouflage systems. Since lidar is also a form of active scanning, which may reveal the location of the sensor and its operator, it is rarely used in stealth-based combat situations.

MAGNETOPLASMA SHIELD

Every naval ship's last, most powerful, and most desperate line of defense. A ship's drone screen serves as a conducting medium and generation network for a dual-layered high-energy plasma and magnetic field which can be used to vaporize incoming projectiles, absorb relatively low-energy maser and laser weaponry, and its primary purpose: deflect ultra-relativistic particle beam weapons.

Given the enormous destructive potential of UMAX-style weapons, a ship's first and best defense is not to be detected at all, then to avoid being targeted. If these lines of defense fail, surviving a UMAX shot becomes extremely difficult. There is no known artificial force powerful enough to absorb such a shot; a ship's only hope at survival is to deflect it.

With the unique nature of UMAX shots, even this proves difficult. A UMAX particle beam is neutralized before it leaves the weapon, meaning it cannot be deflected by even the most powerful magnetic field. As such, any defense must first impart a charge to the shot before it can be deflected. This is where the dual nature of the magnetoplasma shield comes in. The primary purpose of the plasma field generated by the drone network is to impart a charge to the incoming beam so that the magnetic field can deflect it.

The deflection itself, however, presents a problem, given the extreme power of a UMAX shot. An even greater degree of power is required to deflect it, which even a massive drone network is not capable of producing. Instead, the drones serve as a conducting network for the energy output of the ship's main matter–antimatter reactors, which, by adding the drones' own internal nuclear power generation, are the only source capable of exceeding the power of the shot and deflecting it. Doing so, however, invariably burns out the drone network, rendering it useless after a single deployment of the shield. This makes the decision of when to activate the shield one of the most vital choices a commander must make in the heat of combat; the survival of their ship often depends upon it.

Only larger ships such as ICN battle carriers have backup drone networks that can be deployed, allowing for additional uses of the shield; even in these cases, several minutes are usually required, at minimum, to deploy the shield, resulting in a window of vulnerability after it is initially deployed. The relative power output of the two ships in combat also determines a shield's deflection potential: for example, a destroyer-class vessel's shield simply cannot produce enough power to deflect a full-power shot from a battle carrier's UMAX.

MASERS

Directed energy weapons based on electromagnetic waves at the microwave frequency or below. Modern masers employ a combination of multiple energy frequencies to increase effect on target. Handheld masers are typically employed as sidearms by ICDF personnel due to ease of use, high capacity, and high accuracy, even though their effectiveness does not compare to superfluid-based weaponry.

Similarly, naval vessels tend to employ masers as point defense and close-in weapons, primarily for the purpose of shooting down incoming projectiles, drones, and fighter craft. Higher-output masers are also employed in Orbital Fire Support roles by dedicated OFS platforms such as refurbished *Pinatubo II*-class battleships, and OFS mission-typed ships like *Darius Benson*-class destroyers.

METAFRAME / BASEFRAME

The metaframe is the preferred foliation of space-time, a universal aether-field at which space-time is directionally agnostic but temporally ordered. The metaframe's enforced universal time direction prevents any violation of causality and sidesteps Lorentz symmetry—meaning that *c* no longer applies as a universal speed limit.

Particles and objects which are decoupled from the "baseframe" —the space-time which normal matter inhabits—by bombardment with Higgs anti-bosons and anti-gravitons (see "Higgs-Graviton Exclusion Field") can be recoupled to the metaframe by these same particles, theoretically allowing superluminal travel at almost no energy cost. In practice, perfect decoupling of macro-scale objects is impossible, and an infinitesimal amount of bleedthrough to the baseframe persists. As a result, ultrahigh energy levels are required to break Lorentz symmetry and enable superluminal velocity even after an object has been metaframe-coupled.

The preferred space-time foliation was first theorized in the Einstein-Aether modifications of special relativity on Earth in the early 21st century. Its existence was proven by Project Stardrive's chief engineers, the human Dr. Chandra Vaughan and the virgonid genealogy collectively known as Karl, in the 2090s, shortly after they discovered the graviton; the official Compact name for the phenomenon is the Vaughan-Karl Metaframe.

NEURAL IMPLANTS

Networks of cybernetic implants designed to interface directly with the subject's brain and nervous system. While neural implants of varying sophistication are fairly common in the Compact civilian market, extensive neural systems are standard issue for all ICDF military personnel.

Military-grade neural implants serve a number of critical functions, including interpersonal communication, interfacing with AI-powered systems—such as a ship's ANN, or a marine squad's automated weapon platforms—and enhanced data storage and information processing. Implants also perform passive functions, such as improving reaction times and fine motor skills.

While some higher-end civilian implants can be controlled by thought alone, military-grade neural implants are typically controlled by voice commands and gestures. This is a security restriction, designed to prevent a hostile actor from gaining remote control of a neural implant, or worse, reversing its thought-control mechanism to influence the operator's subconscious mind. Military neural implants' control mechanisms rely on physical connection to the operator's relevant brain areas and neuronal pathways, making them much more difficult to spoof.

This security comes at only a minimal cost in operating efficiency; for example, the verbal commands do not need to be spoken aloud to be interpreted. With practice, an operator can form the words in their verbal cortex but not express them physically or audibly, so that the implant will receive the command without the operator presenting any outward indication of having given it. Similarly, physical gestures do not actually require the full movement of the limb or digit to transmit, only a minimal activation of the associated neurons in the predetermined pattern.

SIMULANTS

Artificially grown humanoids of Cipher design, simulants are outwardly indistinguishable from human beings. Only a detailed molecular or genetic analysis is capable of identifying a simulant by certain hallmarks of artificiality, or by known simulant genetic lineages.

Simulants first began to appear in the latter half of the Galactic War, serving as spies, disinformation agents, and leave-behind operatives in Cipher-occupied Compact territory, later on appearing as infiltrators in free Compact systems. The first simulants were exact copies of humans captured by the Ciphers, in some cases centuries earlier; later "models" are typically unique individuals, though many appear to be iterations based on combinations of the genetic material of previously abducted individuals, like future generations of natural human breeding pairings.

Despite advanced modern methods for detecting simulants, they remain a significant threat to Compact security, as they too continue to increase in sophistication. Certain theories persist that simulants are, in effect, a distraction; the real Cipher infiltrators are naturally bred humans derived from entire captured populations and brainwashed by a lifetime under machine control. To date, however, no such individuals have been positively identified.

STARDRIVE

The system that allows FTL travel through a combination of HGEF technology; advanced AI processing; and ultra-long-range, ultra-high-resolution sensors. Only the combination of all three of these elements allows safe and effective faster-than-light, interstellar travel.

Like the HGEF, Stardrive seems to have been independently developed at least three times in galactic history. The Ciphers and the ara' each invented a Stardrive analogue at some unknown point in the last several thousand years, if not earlier. The Yu-Nee Consortium invented a less efficient light-speed–capable Stardrive analogue circa TSY 2250, subsequently sharing it with the other members of the future Association of Non-Aligned Systems. Other than these, the only known invention of the Stardrive occurred in the late twenty-first century in the Sol system, the product of a joint human–virgonid engineering project. The first superluminal Stardrive test occurred in TSY 2095.

Other species and factions now possessing the Stardrive—the melakeen, the xirān, the uthal, and the Kyrans—all acquired it by various means from virgonids or humans.

The first component of the Stardrive is the HGEF, which effectively reduces the mass of the ship to zero and prevents gravity from acting upon it. This allows the ship to be decoupled from the "baseframe" inhabited by normal matter, and recoupled to the "metaframe," on which superluminal travel is possible without violating causality (see "Metaframe / Baseframe"). Once metaframe-coupled, sufficiently powerful engines can propel the ship at, and beyond, the speed of light. Navigation is extremely important; as discussed in the relevant entry, even scraping too close to a powerful enough gravity well could cause catastrophic HGEF failure, and the likely disabling or destruction of the ship.

However, the problem, as early Project Stardrive engineers quickly discovered, is much more acute than that. At such incredible velocities, gravity wells are not the only threat to a ship. While a ship coupled to the metaframe can essentially "pass through" microscopic and submicroscopic particles, given the small amount of bleedthrough to the baseframe something as small as a pebble-sized piece of space dust, at relative superluminal velocities, is imparted with titanic destructive force. At the same time, its inherent gravity is nowhere near strong enough to cause HGEF shutdown or collapse. A ship impacting such a pebble while under Stardrive is likely to be destroyed instantly.

The only way to prevent such a catastrophic collision is to sweep the ship's path with ultra-high-resolution sensors and make course corrections to avoid even small particles of dust. As such, a ship under Stardrive does not constantly travel at superluminal velocities; instead, it makes dozens of superluminal microjumps every second, each time dropping to sublight to scan the path ahead to the maximum range its sensors can achieve the required resolution, and making any required course corrections before jumping forward again.

This means that the effective velocity of a Stardrive-capable ship is limited not by the power of its engines or HGEF generators but by the resolution of its sensors and the processing speed of its navigational AIs, the only systems fast enough to process the vast sensor data and make the necessary calculations without sacrificing any speed advantage the microjumps confer. On average, a ship at Stardrive spends 50 percent of each second FTL-jumping and 50 percent scanning ahead. This also has the effect of halving the time dilation effects of long-range FTL travel.

STEALTH SYSTEMS

An array of interlinked active and passive stealth systems are the first line of defense for Compact space and ground forces. These include AI-managed adaptive visual camouflage, heat and other emissions management systems, electromagnetic interference, physical and signals-based decoys, and extensive cyberwarfare suites. These systems combine to make Compact vessels, vehicles, and personnel extremely difficult to detect, and challenging to effectively target even once detected.

The high kill-potential of weaponry in the early twenty-sixth century makes effective stealth systems essential for survival in a combat environment, be it a fleet-level space battle or a squad-level infantry engagement. The invention of QEC in the late twenty-fourth century eventually allowed for a quantum leap in the practical and widespread use of stealth in combat. QEC allows Compact units to maintain constant, untraceable, uninterruptible communications and positioning with one another without breaching stealth, drastically reducing the possibility of friendly fire incidents and lack of cohesion that in previous eras might have resulted from such extensive, individual-level use of stealth systems.

SUPERFLUID REPEATER RIFLE

The standard primary infantry weapon of the ICDF. Repeaters are essentially an ultra-high-tech iteration on old chemical-reaction based projectile weapons, which for all their advanced capabilities are mechanically simpler than the firearms of the twentieth and twenty-first centuries.

For ammunition, repeaters use a solid block of a tungsten-derived metamaterial, loaded into the weapon much as magazines were in earlier firearms. The operator can program the weapon to fire shots of varying caliber at rates ranging from single fire to one hundred plus rounds per second. The magnetic extractor is paired with a laser, which shaves each programmed mass from the solid block before feeding it into the preparation chamber, where it is flash heated into a superfluid state.

This superfluid is a highly programmable metastate, allowing the firing chamber to imbue each round with set characteristics, from the shape of the round to the depth and density of material it should penetrate before expanding and stopping. This makes the SRR an ideal multi-purpose infantry weapon, equally effective at engaging single or area targets, armored or unarmored infantry, or light armored vehicles, and for engagements in high-collateral damage potential environments, such as in civilian areas or aboard light-skinned space vessels.

Special forces variants of the SRR may be fitted with additional modules, such as DEW (maser or plasma), missile, and anti-stealth.

QUANTUM ENTANGLEMENT COMMUNICATIONS (QEC)

The foundation of modern Compact civil and military communications and interstellar coordination, QEC were pioneered by scientists in the United Citizens' Councils, based on technology recovered from the Ciphers during the Second Cipher War (2374–2379). Prior to the advent of QEC, practical interstellar communications were only possible through the use of Stardrive-equipped courier ships and drones, meaning messages might take weeks or months to travel from one end of human and allied space to the other.

Once perfected and disseminated, QEC technology allowed for instantaneous, uninterruptible, and uninterceptible communications across any distance. This vastly increased the potential for interstellar coordination and was one of the crucial developments which made the foundation of the Interstellar Compact possible.

Each QEC unit contains a core of compressed hydrogen separated into compartments. Each compartment represents a quantum bit. Each hydrogen atom in this core is paired with an atom in the corresponding qubit compartment of a twin core, entangled together during construction of the units. When one of these atoms—say, representing the number 1—is activated by observation by the originating QEC unit, the spin of the entangled particle in the receiving unit is instantaneously resolved. This resolution is detected by the receiving unit and interpreted as the number 1. Detecting this resolution without first observing the particle in the receiving unit is achieved by use of a Discrete Eigenstate Filter, which maintains the integrity of each particle's superposition until it is intentionally observed. The DEF was the missing piece of the puzzle which captured Cipher technology revealed, finally allowing existing theoretical models for QECs to be put to the test in the late twenty-fourth century.

Communications between two entangled units can be carried on until the paired cores are exhausted of unobserved atoms. At this point, the cores must be exchanged for fresh entangled pairs. This makes quantum bandwidth an important factor in interstellar communications. Text-only comms consume less bandwidth than audio, which consumes less than visual, which consumes less than full holographic.

Most QEC units are not directly linked to one another, however. Facilitating practical, widespread interstellar communications requires the use of several QEC hubs spread throughout Compact space. A typical QEC unit's entangled pair is located at one of these hubs. When a transmission is sent from an originating unit, it is received by the hub-pair; the AI managing the hub then locates the hub-pair of the transmission's intended recipient and relays the messages back and forth by this method.

While direct-entangled comms cannot be intercepted or jammed in any way, hub-based comms could be, in theory, if the hub itself were physically or digitally compromised. This makes QEC hubs among the most closely guarded sites in the galaxy, with physical access strictly controlled, no connection to non-QEC networks of any kind, and numerous safeguards set up to prevent the introduction of Trojan programs via authorized entangled communications.

ULTRA-RELATIVISTIC MASS-NEUTRALIZED PROTON ACCELERATOR (UMAX)

The primary armament of most ICN vessels, the UMAX is a weapon of unparalleled destructive power. Derived from earlier Ultra-Relativistic Electron Beam (UREB) weapons, which are still employed by many Kyran ships, the UMAX makes use of advanced Compact HGEF-based mass neutralization technology to create an even more devastating and effective weapon.

Capital-class UMAXes employ a two-stage system. The preparation stage is a cyclotron particle accelerator, which draws power directly from the ship's M–A reactor to generate and repeatedly accelerate a beam of high-energy protons along a circular path until they reach a significant fraction of the speed of light, usually 0.6–0.75c.

The terminal stage is a linear accelerator (linac) with a built-in HGEF generator. The HGEF neutralizes the mass of the proton beam, allowing the linac to accelerate it up slightly above the speed of light. Once the proton beam leaves the linac and the effect of the HGEF, it regains its mass but loses only a fraction of its velocity, resulting in a full-mass proton beam propagating at the speed of light.

At this velocity, relativistic effects act upon the beam, vastly increasing its effective range by slowing the rate at which bloom occurs from an outside perspective. The beam imparts titanic levels of thermal and kinetic energy, rendering conventional armor effectively useless. The beam also generates enough x-ray radiation when striking its target to create a braking radiation cascade; this typically results in massive casualties among the crew of a ship, even if the beam strike itself is not sufficient to destroy the vessel.

Other than not being shot at, the only known defense against a UMAX is a magnetoplasma shield of sufficient power to charge and then deflect the beam, though this approach carries significant limitations with current technology (see "Magnetoplasma Shield").

UMAX weapons are most commonly employed in space combat; while highly effective at saturation bombardment of ground targets from orbit, their use in this role is heavily restricted by the Interstellar Code of Armed Conflict, an originally internal Compact legal code to which the Association of Non-Aligned Systems are now signatory. The ICAC prohibits the use of UMAX weapons against targets in or near biological population centers in all but the most exigent circumstances, due to the massive potential for collateral damage. Typically, the ICDF only employs UMAX weapons in orbital bombardment of Cipher worlds and installations. Notable exceptions include the bombardment campaign against the Kyran clan home worlds from 2482–2484, which remains controversial to this day.

SPECIES

An enigmatic amphibianoid species first encountered by the virgonid in 2295, the ara' are one of the few civilizations known to have independently developed FTL technology. Contacts between the Compact races and the ara' have always been peaceful, but the ara' have also shown little interest in deepening connections with other powers.

The ara' possess highly advanced technology, the extent of which remains unknown. As well as a Stardrive analogue, observation suggests they are capable of some form of FTL communication and make extensive use of sophisticated AIs, possibly integrated with their own consciousnesses in some way. The nature of ara' weapon and defensive technology is unclear.

For reasons unknown, the Ciphers seem never to have interfered with the ara', at least since the Compact races became aware of them. Given that the ara' transmitted a significant amount of data on the Ciphers to the pre-Compact Alliance in 2316, however, it seems likely that the two peoples had some form of contact in the distant past.

BYASIANS

The Compact name for the sapient mammalianoid species native to the planet Byas. For a complex sapient species, the byasians are significantly smaller than the galactic average, rarely more than one meter in length including tail. Physically, byasians resemble a combination between a number of Earth species, sharing many traits with squirrels and raccoons. The basic unit of byasian society is the pack, a loose kin-grouping similar to an old Earth clan.

Oral histories suggest that the byasians had in general reached something akin to an Earth Bronze Age level of technological and social organization by when the Ciphers arrived, around TSY 2000. The machines took complete control of the planet and divided the byasian packs into seemingly arbitrary geographical groupings called districts. Within these districts, the Ciphers enforced varying forms of social organization, economics, and cultural and religious practices. The Ciphers permitted low-level conflict to occur between these district groupings, but rarely within them. Alliances and enmities formed during this long period of interdistrict conflict persist to this day.

The scars of Cipher occupation run deep in byasian societies. Some districts still revere the machines as gods and pray—or even fight—to bring about their return. Others loathe their former overlords, and their fellow byasians who long for them to come back. Suspicion and distrust are endemic in almost all byasian societies, having been so frequently pitted against one another and betrayal by Cipher-loyal informants having been a fact of daily life for centuries.

Another near-universal byasian cultural trait is a love of argumentation and debate. In addition to the pressures of manufactured conflict, byasians had to become adept at choosing their words carefully in order to survive. Now, liberated from Cipher domination, educated byasians are free to let loose all the rhetorical skills they have cultivated under restriction for generations. This can be intimidating, even infuriating, for humans and others whose cultures may not place such high value on open, constant, and apparently hostile verbal sparring.

CIPHERS

A highly advanced, fully artificial civilization, the Ciphers are one of the great mysteries of the galaxy. Though first knowingly encountered by human explorers from the Corporate Worlds in the late twenty-third century, evidence suggests the Ciphers had been covertly observing the development of humans, virgonids, and other species for hundred or thousands of years previously. Compact scientists today believe that some of the reports of so-called UFOs and UAPs, endemic to Earth in the twentieth and early twenty-first centuries, were likely these Cipher probes, and that some small number of even older reports may represent the same phenomenon.

The origin of the Ciphers is wholly unknown. Logic suggests they or their antecedents must have been created by a biological intelligence at some point in the distant past. However, no information about this species, and whether that creation was intentional or accidental, has yet been uncovered. While the Ciphers have frequently communicated with the Compact and other races, they have never shared any such information.

Similarly, the precise nature of Cipher consciousness remains unknown—for example, it is unclear whether each physical Cipher platform possesses a discrete consciousness, or a network of multiple consciousness, *or* if all Ciphers are animated by a single hive consciousness. Despite great leaps in the field over the last few centuries, Compact and allied scientists have never succeeded in creating a fully conscious, sapient AI, certainly not in the way that the Ciphers evidently possess these traits. Captured Cipher ships, drones, simulants, and combat units reveal little in their physical architecture that could answer this great question.

The true level of Cipher technological advancement is another topic of debate within the Compact. At each stage of contact and conflict with the machines, their military technology at least seems to have been roughly on par with, or slightly ahead of, their biological adversaries. Given the now two-century history of conflict between the Ciphers and the Compact races, that would suggest that Cipher technology has advanced at roughly the same rate as, for example, humans, despite beginning with a massive head start.

The great unlikelihood of this being coincidental has resulted in a number of theories. The first, most commonly accepted, is that before encountering and warring with humans, the Ciphers had reached a technological plateau beyond which they saw no logical reason to advance. Since then, lacking imagination and innovation in the biological sense, Cipher advancement has been tied to that of humans and their allies, in some cases directly as a result of reverse engineering.

Another, less comforting theory suggests that the Ciphers have either deliberately restricted their technological development, or appeared to do so, in order to keep pace with their biological adversaries. Why they would do this, and thus expose themselves to potential defeat, is unclear—but given the Ciphers' apparent penchant for enigmatic experimentation on the populations under their control, it cannot be ruled out.

HUMANS

Having now spread from their home world to dozens of stars across thousands of light-years, humans in the twenty-sixth century are more diverse and varied than they ever were on Earth—and yet, thanks to the Compact and QEC technology, they are in some ways more connected than they have been since their interstellar diaspora first began in the early twenty-second century.

Many of Earth's myriad cultures survived their journey to the stars, while others evolved and intermixed to create entirely new cultures native to the colony worlds they now inhabit. Biologically, while four hundred years is not enough time in human terms for natural evolution to make a significant course change, exposure to alien environments and long-term habitation in space has led to changes among some populations relative to their Earth-bound ancestors.

The much greater changes have come by human hands, either as a result of genetic manipulation or cybernetic augmentation. Anti-transhumanism laws and a general culture of conservatism following Earth's Third World War led to a drastic slowing in the pace of the technologies, but as humanity spread further from the home world and its violent past, these restrictions began to loosen. Today, while most humans remain recognizably human, significant genetic and cybernetic modification is common across the species.

Indeed, a number of cultural and national groupings have adopted such widespread and consistent forms of modification that some anthropologists suggest they should soon, if not now, be classified as human subspecies—the largest of these being the people of the Free Worlds Republic and the United Citizens' Councils, whose median modifications can usually mark them out at a glance to members of other groups.

KYRANS

In fact a group of several related species, "Kyran" is simply a Compact designation for the biological/sociocultural grouping of these species. The name is derived from a transliteration of the name given by Kyrans for their origin: Kyr. It is not known if Kyr is a planet, a star, a star cluster, or even an ancestor species or concept. Cryptic explanations from Kyrans themselves have at times suggested any or all of these definitions.

The known Kyran species are thought to be members of a single clade, most analogous to the dinosaurs of prehistoric Earth, and similar species discovered in the fossil record of the melakeen home world Nalak. Kyran social organization seems based in large part on species, such that members of each species appear to play designated roles in their respective societies, with examples of individuals straying from these roles vanishingly rare. The Kyran names for these species and their roles are not known; Compact designations are derived from their observed social roles.

The four confirmed Kyran species are the pterochids, stepharchids, both a ruler/warrior caste; the argotids, a soldier caste; and the ischeronids, a worker caste. Three species believed to be from the same clade as the other Kyrans are the smergonids and sklekarids, possible additional worker castes, and the epheuronids, which may be an engineer or scientist caste.

MELAKEEN

A mammalianoid species originating on the planet Nalak, first encountered by human explorers in TSY 2289. The melakeen are quadrupedal and, like humans, now largely hairless save for patches on their backs and inside certain joints. Melakeen are trigender, with a complex method of sexual reproduction unknown in large Earth mammals. Aside from these stark biological differences, and the effects of the three-parent family structure on melakeen cultures, their social and political development has more closely mirrored that of humanity than any other species encountered to date.

This close mirroring—after a period of initial uneasiness caused by a mutually uncanny appearance—helped foster close relations between the two species. Peaceful trade rapidly evolved into military cooperation under the threat of the Ciphers. Today, the melakeen are one of the associate member races of the Interstellar Compact, their fierce independence holding them back from full integration.

VIRGONIDS

A technologically advanced arthropoid species first encountered by humans in the Sol system. The virgonid language is based on a combination of pheromones and sounds which humans cannot reproduce, and is thus not transliterable; their human name is derived from their star system of origin, Ross 128, located in the constellation Virgo.

The virgonids are the only sapient insectoid species in the known galaxy and possess a unique life cycle. Each virgonid is born male, in which capacity he may serve as the "contributor-parent" in sexual reproduction; later in life, he may transition to female, at which point she will be able to serve as a "bearer-parent," carrying a number of fertilized eggs to maturity. This process results in the death of the bearer-parent, usually within hours of successfully giving birth. The individual virgonid lifespan averages only three to five Terran years.

Virgonids were able to develop and maintain a complex, technological civilization despite these extremely short lifespans only after evolving an incredible ability: near-perfect genetic memory transfer from bearer-parent to offspring. This ability, combined with renowned virgonid selflessness, allows multigenerational training for complex skills, which can then be passed down generation to generation, each one gaining new experience and knowledge. Today, virgonid genealogies, or "dynasties," often dominate the highest ranks of science and engineering professions.

An individual bearer-parent is able to control the number of eggs she brings to maturity, which may be anywhere from one to around twenty. This allows virgonids to easily maintain sustainable populations in established colonies, on long-term space missions and the like, while also permitting "population bomb" scenarios to occur, such as when a new virgonid colony or outpost is being established. In these multiple-offspring births, each receives the full memories of the bearer-parent; however, each child soon develops his own personality during the rapid early maturation stage, resulting in a clutch of discrete, if similar, individuals.

This ability for relatively small numbers of virgonid to rapidly produce geometrically increasing numbers of offspring, combined with their high level of engineering knowledge and skill, gives the virgonids, as a species, military potential paralleled only by that of the self-replicating Ciphers. Historically, though, this potential has been almost entirely unrealized. The virgonids are naturally a peaceful and inquisitive people, being roused to war only by the greatest necessity. Even during the Galactic War (2477–2485), the virgonid contribution, while essential to the ultimate Compact victory, was largely limited to engineering and manufacturing support, with most virgonids eschewing combat roles.

Virgonids are almost universally seen as friendly, inquisitive, and quick-witted, both as individuals and as a group. They bond easily with humans, who for their part—provided they can get past the atavistic fear engendered by massive, talking insects—can find in virgonid genealogies a series of lifelong, steadfastly loyal friends. Virgonids who interact with other races regularly take human names rather than attempting to transliterate their monikers in their own unique language, so closely do they identify with humans.

XIRĀN

A cetaceanoid species first encountered by humans in the early twenty-fourth century, the xirān are the only intelligent aquatic species in the known galaxy to have developed a technological civilization. Like the virgonids, the xirān independently developed mass manipulation technology, without which escaping the gravity well of their home world in heavy, water-filled spacecraft would have been impossible. However, they too fell short of discovering the graviton, restricting them to sublight interplanetary and interstellar travel until their contact with humans and virgonids.

Due to their unique evolution, xirānite technology is different compared to the varied but similar technologies developed by air-breathing species. Xirānite social organization is also unique: each xirān is typically highly individualistic, and yet they possess a strong sense of community from small groups all the way up to the species as a whole. There seems to be little tension between these two social poles, as there tends to be in human cultures.

The xirān have shown great interest in peaceful coexistence and cooperation with other galactic species, culminating in their association status within the Interstellar Compact. However, their unique environmental and technological requirements make full side-by-side coexistence with air-breathing species difficult. As such, it seems likely that there will always be a level of separation between the xirān and the other Compact races. The xirān, for their part, seem comfortable with this.

FACTIONS

CIPHER EMPIRE

The Compact name given to the polity controlled by the machine race known as the Ciphers. The extent of this empire is unknown; during the negotiations for the Treaty of Omega Serpentis, the Cipher representative provided the Compact with evidence of dozens of transformed machine world-based systems elsewhere in the galaxy, whose locations, if they exist, are unknown. To date, two such machine world systems, each time falsely believed to have been the Cipher capital or home system, have been destroyed by the Compact races, at the conclusion of the First Cipher War in 2314, and at the end of the Galactic War in 2485.

In addition to their machine worlds, the Ciphers control an unknown number of worlds bearing indigenous organic civilizations. Several of these were liberated during the Galactic War and now fall under Compact jurisdiction under the Articles of Protectorship. At least four more such worlds are known to exist and given the estimated interstellar scope of Cipher influence. Many more may remain undiscovered.

The Ciphers seem not to possess a government in the traditional sense, and, depending on the nature of Cipher consciousness, may not require one (see "Ciphers"). There is also little pattern to the manner in which they rule over their subject species. Each of these biological civilizations is kept at a different level of social and technological development. Some, like Byas, were maintained at an Earth Bronze Age-equivalent level, while others, like Sukat, were permitted to retain an industrial civilization. In some cases, the Ciphers seem to have used a relatively light hand, merely observing and intervening to prevent any developments they deem unacceptable, while in others, the machines interfere almost constantly and at every level, experimenting with different forms of social and cultural order, conflict, and even biology.

Ciphers have performed similar experiments on captured populations of humans and other Compact races during their wars, often with horrifying results. Populations on Cipher-occupied worlds have been culled seemingly at random, while individuals and small groups have endured everything from vivisection to forced breeding, to psychological torment by means of virtual reality environments. In other cases, as at Rāma in 2313 and Zevka in 2375, entire worlds have been wiped out. The purpose of these experiments and seemingly random massacres has never been ascertained.

Similarly, the reason for Cipher vacillation between extreme belligerence and peaceful coexistence has yet to be determined. It is now believed that, given the resources of their empire, the Ciphers were fully capable of wiping humanity from existence during the First Cipher War (2312–2314), without much difficulty. Evidently, they chose not to, instead accepting a limited defeat at the hands of the human–virgonid alliance. Why remains a mystery and has defied all preexisting human expectations regarding the behavior of a potential artificial civilization, largely based on the concept that a machine intelligence would be entirely rational. But if the machines saw humans as an existential threat, why would they not eliminate us? And if they did not, then what logical reason would they have to fight us at all, given that they precipitated the war?

The Compact may never be able to answer these questions, but many experts on the Ciphers now believe that all their conflicts with us have been one massive, interstellar experiment of some kind. Like the others, its purpose is unknown, and we are left to wonder: What happens when it is over? Will the Ciphers disappear and leave us to our own devices, or will we finally witness the full extent of their power—and if the latter, even with all the advances we have made over the last five centuries, will we have any hope of survival?

FREE WORLDS REPUBLIC (FWR)

A human interstellar polity centered to antispinward of Earth, the FWR began as a group of fiercely independent and unauthorized wildcat colonies, first founded between 2225 and 2260 in an effort to escape the restrictive policies of the Earth-governed Terran Interstellar Union. Contact and conflict with the nearby Kyran clans prompted these colonies, led by the Frontier system, to form a military alliance against the hostile aliens. Shortly after the allied victory over the Kyrans at the Battle of Frontier in 2272, the alliance was formalized as the Coalition of Free Worlds (CFW), which would then evolve into the more unified FWR in 2320.

The Coalition was described by its first commander in chief, legendary Admiral Rance "Starbird" Wolfe, as "diverse worlds united by a single spirit," and the same largely holds true today. The Republic is governed by an elected bicameral legislature and a popularly elected president, with an independent judiciary. Even in the era of the Compact, the FWR maintains a loose federal structure, with each of the member worlds or system-states retaining a wide latitude in domestic affairs. Similarly, each of the larger worlds, such as Freedom, Beacon, and Jayu, are split into multiple smaller provinces and states, each of which retains significant control over local affairs, and so on down, in some cases, to the municipal level.

Mandatory service is perhaps the most salient federal law

enforced by the FWR. At the age of twenty-one, all citizens must choose between two years of military or community/civil service. Most choose the latter, resulting in a lower degree of automation in the FWR compared to the other human polities. However, a significant portion (around 25 percent in peacetime) choose military service of some kind. Most often, these individuals choose to serve in their local Planetary Defense Forces, but service in the ICDF also counts toward the two-year quota. Individuals who refuse either military or community service lose the right to vote in federal elections or run for federal office; only on some worlds, such as Freedom and Horizon, do they also lose this right at the local level.

Free Worlders tend to guard their liberty zealously and are renowned for their bluntness and their openness regarding political issues and debates, leading to a reputation for being argumentative. While in-utero elimination of various diseases and conditions is common in the FWR, most forms of post-birth gene editing are prohibited. Conversely, cybernetic augmentation is only loosely regulated at the federal level, resulting in a much higher degree of adoption throughout the FWR relative to the TIU or the UCC.

INTERSTELLAR COMPACT

A loose federal system uniting all three major human powers with the Virgonid Greater Hive, the Interstellar Compact has its roots in the military alliance between the TIU, the VGH, and the CFW, secretly signed in June 2313 in response to the growing Cipher threat. In 2340, the alliance was formalized and expanded to include the new UCC, as well as associate members the melakeen, the xirān, and the uthal.

Continuing conflict with both the Ciphers and the Kyrans led to closer ties and increased cooperation between the allied powers.

In the contentious Monocerotis Summits, annual negotiations occurring at V616 Monocerotis between 2390 and 2400, the Articles of Compact were ultimately agreed upon, and the Interstellar Compact was formally inaugurated following the first interstellar elections in December 2401. The full members of the Compact are the Terran Interstellar Union, the FWR, the United Citizens' Councils, and the Virgonid Greater Hive. The melakeen and the xirān maintain a status as associate members, essentially permanent military allies of the Compact with special trading and migration rights.

The Compact's remit is almost entirely limited to military and foreign affairs, as well as trade and monetary policy. The Articles guarantee certain basic political rights, in order to ensure equal participation in the Compact electoral process, but otherwise domestic affairs are left entirely up to the member state governments. The Compact is governed by two primary branches: the Interstellar Parliament and the Interstellar Executive.

The Parliament is divided equally, with twenty-five seats going to each of the four full member states. The electoral process for these representatives is determined by the member states themselves: in the UCC and the TIU, they are chosen directly by the electorate; in the FWR they are elected by the planetary legislatures; while in the VGH, they are selected by random lot. Parliament is tasked with passing laws, setting taxes, and declaring war.

The Interstellar Executive is led by the Executor, who serves as the Compact head of state and commander in chief. As with Parliament, the method of the Executor's election varies by member state. The TIU and UCC vote directly, while the FWR and the VGH send electors to a convention, the former chosen by election, the latter by random lot. The Executor conducts foreign policy, serves as commander in chief of the military, and breaks deadlocks in Parliament. They appoint an Executive Cabinet, with ministers of state, the economy, the Navy, communications, and foreign affairs. These ministers must be approved by Parliament before they take up their duties.

By far the two biggest draws on the Compact budget are the Interstellar Compact Defense Forces (ICDF), in particular the Interstellar Compact Navy, and the Interstellar Compact Reconstruction Authority (ICRA), which is tasked with administering the Protectorate worlds liberated from the Ciphers at the end of the Galactic War.

KYRAN CLANS

The highest known level of Kyran social and political organization is referred to as the clan in Compact nomenclature, though this label is somewhat inappropriate in its traditional definition. Kyran clans may comprise millions or billions of individuals, and most members appear to have no kin relationship to one another. However, the ruling castes of each clan *are* closely kin-related, and it is from these ruling families or houses that the clans derive their names. Each known ruling house seems to be comprised exclusively of members of one or the other ruling species, either pterochid or stepharchid—Clan Harag is ruled by pterochids, Clan Rhyllok by stepharchids, for example. Cooperation between clans ruled by opposite species is extremely rare; constant warfare is more the norm.

Indeed, warfare has been nearly the only form of interaction between the Compact races and the Kyrans since humans first encountered them in the mid twenty-third century. The continued survival and relative technological sophistication of the Kyran species make it clear that warfare cannot possibly be their sole cultural and political occupation, however central it clearly is to their dominant cultures and belief systems. However, like a cosmic inverse of the reclusive ara', they seem completely uninterested in peaceful coexistence with aliens, or even other Kyran clans, instead pursuing violent confrontation of varying degrees whenever possible. Only vague cultural and pseudo-religious explanations for this behavior have been offered by the Kyrans themselves, leaving the Compact races, particularly the FWR, to grapple constantly but blindly with the Kyran threat.

Much of the Kyrans' most advanced technology seems to have been pilfered or otherwise derived from that of other species they have conquered or warred with over the centuries. Indeed, Stardrive was only acquired from humans after several border conflicts with the FWR; prior to that, and unique in known galactic history, the Kyrans pursued the conquest of neighboring stars and alien peoples solely through the use of sublight generation ships, displaying an extraordinary commitment to warfare and conquest.

Thanks to their inability to match the technological development of their Compact adversaries, the Kyrans remain a constant, but manageable, threat to galactic peace. Given their vast numbers and apparently inveterate aggression, many analysts fear that were all or most of the Kyran clans to unite under a single ruler, they would become an existential threat to the Compact. However, constant internecine warfare among the Kyrans suggests this possibility is remote.

TERRAN INTERSTELLAR UNION (TIU)

Centered on Earth, the TIU is a massive federal parliamentary democracy encompassing humanity's original colony worlds, mostly settled during the twenty-second century. The TIU has its roots in the Global Union State, declared in the aftermath of Earth's Third World War in 2063. After the conclusion of the First Contact Crisis (2081) and the signing of the Treaty of Mars (2104) brought the GUS and the Virgonid Greater Hive into close cooperation, Earth's government used the jointly developed Stardrive to launch several officially sanctioned colonization efforts to nearby habitable planets.

Initially, these colonies were de jure ruled directly from Earth, while being de facto independent due to the lack of effective interstellar communication. When the TIU was established in 2204, creating a parliamentary system in which each colony would participate in an overarching interstellar legislature as well as their own, in practice little changed—except that planetary legislatures now had more of a vested interest in obeying Earth's dictates.

In response to the exodus from Earth and the colonies of wildcat settlers that would eventually form the CFW, and the growth of independent corporate colonies in the twenty-third century, the Earth government loosened its hold on the established colonies. By the advent of QEC in the late twenty-fourth century, this equilibrium was well-established enough to resist new Earth government attempts to develop stronger controls.

Nonetheless, the TIU federal government remains stronger than that of the FWR, and the TIU tends to be more culturally homogeneous. The TIU is also more conservative in the field of transhumanism than either the FWR or the UCC, in part a relic of the backlash against both cybernetic and genetic augmentation following Earth's Third World War. While still employing both technologies today, in both the military sphere and the civilian market, citizens of the TIU tend to be more similar in appearance and capability to the humans of old Earth in the twenty-first century than their counterparts in the other powers. Culturally, they are often seen as being polite and friendly, more eager to find common ground than to argue with or impose their views on others.

UNITED CITIZENS' COUNCILS (UCC)

One of the main Compact member states, the UCC began life as the Organization of Interstellar Growth and Development, colloquially known as the Corporate Worlds (2300–2314). The OIGD itself was an amalgamation of the colonies founded by the Big Four private space corporations since 2208, which retained their independence from the TIU.

In the course of the Corporate Worlds War (2312–2314), a number of revolutionary groups rose up against the OIGD government, angered by years of increasingly totalitarian surveillance, rapacious economic policies, and the war itself, particularly the use of the Ciphers against the other human powers. The governing boards of the OIGD were overthrown, and a number of Citizens' Councils set up in their place, which immediately made peace with the Alliance.

The Citizens' Constitution of 2315 established a unique form of government in the new UCC, a two-house representative democracy with no specific leader or head of state. The upper chamber is the Citizens' High Council, a body of thirteen members elected directly by the populace across the UCC. The chairperson of the high chamber is chosen on a random, rotating basis every 4.6 months, to ensure that each member chairs once during a five-year term.

The lower house is the Assembly, a larger body with hundreds of members, also elected every five years. Since there is no means of equally sharing the responsibility of leading the Assembly, the task is left to an AI speaker. Programmed to be completely impartial, the non-voting AI's only task is to prevent the Assembly from descending into bickering and chaos—which, occasionally, happens regardless. Should the Assembly deadlock, the issue is sent up to the High Council for a decision.

The local governments of worlds and municipalities within the

UCC follow a similar pattern, with Citizens' Councils serving as an upper chamber; however, there is a wide variance in the structure of the lower Assemblies. In some cases, the entire populace (in theory) serves as this body.

In contrast to the FWR, cybernetic augmentation is largely forbidden in the UCC, while genetic modification is widespread and almost completely unregulated. This results in the widest variance in the basic human form among United Citizens, many of which resemble depictions of humanoid aliens from twentieth and early twenty-first century Earth fiction. That being said, the basic modifications which nearly all citizens receive from birth create a recognizable "typical" United Citizen, much as standard cybernetics do in the Republic. This basic suite of genetic enhancements means that despite having the widest variance in appearance and other surface characteristics, the UCC populace has the lowest variance in general ability.

The UCC government provides its citizens with an extremely generous universal basic income and relies heavily on automation to fill most non-creative jobs. This is in part a dividend of the UCC's constitutionally enshrined pacifism, engendering resentment in certain other corners of the Compact, particularly the FWR; it is charged that the UCC can only provide such a decadent life for its citizens because it relies on the military protection of the other Compact member states against threats such as the Ciphers and the Kyrans.

VIRGONID GREATER HIVE

Another human-style label applied to an essentially untranslatable virgonid term, the Greater Hive concept refers to the virgonid interstellar state, the body of the entire species, *and* to the long-standing alliance between virgonids and humanity. While outsiders instinctually try to distinguish between these three concepts, the virgonid themselves find no distinction necessary.

The political embodiment of the Greater Hive is the only pure direct democracy in the known galaxy. All decisions are reached by scaled consensus; a decision to declare war is voted on by the entire adult virgonid population, to found a new settlement by the population of the world in question, to levy a new tax by the population that will be affected, and so on. By the standards of other species, such mass consensus is astonishingly easy to reach. Genuine political disagreements are vanishingly rare. Even most ships and space installations are governed by consensus rather than having a human-style command structure; only military vessels have a designated captain, though he or she is also chosen by the consensus of the crew.

The original Greater Hive concept dates back to around 9000 BTSY. Like humans, virgonids spread across their home world from a single point of origin, before being fractured by environmental factors around the time they attained sapience, roughly two million years ago. The virgonids' short generations mean they can evolve quickly; by the time the local hives that expanded from these colonies came back into contact over the succeeding millennia, they had changed so much biologically that they invariably regarded each other as existential threats.

The planet gradually descended into a state of near-constant total war, each hive trying to wipe out the others with which it was in contact, sparing none. Many hives were annihilated or absorbed, until a handful of super-hives dominated the habitable zone of their home world, a ring along the tidally locked planet's terminator line. The war between these hives continued for centuries, until several of the hives began developing a theory of science.

These scientist-genealogies quickly determined that the planet's resources were growing scarce; if unrestricted wartime breeding and devastation continued for a mere few decades more, they would be depleted, and the entire species would inevitably go extinct. The only solution was for the hives to unite and restrict their birth rates until the planet's environment had a chance to replenish itself.

Once this Hive Unification concept was disseminated, it was adopted with extraordinary rapidity; thousands of years of warfare were set aside in a matter of months. The disparate virgonid peoples joined together and interbred, keeping their numbers in check. In the space of a century, the planet's environment indeed recovered, and the modern virgonid physiology still known to us today was established.

ASTROGRAPHY

JOINT INTERSTELLAR COMPACT SYSTEMS

Concord—IC Capital
Concord Station–Initial Construction Completed TSY 2401
Compact Prime–Terraforming Begun 2429 (Incomplete c. 2507)

V616 Monocerotis
Gargantua Mine–Constructed 2372
Monocerotis Shipyards–Constructed 2378

MAJOR TERRAN INTERSTELLAR UNION SYSTEMS

Sol–TIU Capital
Earth–Unification 2083; Capital, New York City
Luna–Founded 2049; Capital, Armstrong
Mars–Founded 2086; Capital, Janssen
Enceladus–Founded 2093; Capital, Sharma

Hyperion (Gilese 357)
Eos–Founded 2132; Capital, Neo Athens
Astraeus–Founded 2219; Capital, Astropolis

Helvetios (51 Pegasi)
Taranis–Founded 2150; Capital, New Berlin
Sequana–Founded 2211; Capital, Rivièreville

Vālmīki (HR 8799)
Rāma–Founded 2165; Destroyed 2315; Refounded 2325; Capital, New Kolkata
Sita–Founded 2350; Capital, Brahmana

Xihe (Kepler-10)
Zheng He–Founded 2181; Capital, Kāishǐ
Shujun–Founded 2202; Capital, New Taipei

Perun
Zemlya–Founded 2354; Capital, Novyy Kyiv

Theȉyw
B̂ān ȟım̀–Founded 2385; Capital, Nakhon

MAJOR FREE WORLDS REPUBLIC SYSTEMS

Frontier (HD 197027)–FWR Capital
Freedom–Founded 2225; Capital, Freedom's Landing

Dawn
Horizon–Founded 2241; Capital, Ellis

Beacon
Homestead–Founded 2259; Capital, Traveler's Rest
Hearth–2301; Capital, Wolfeburg

Sang-je
Jayu–Founded 2279; Capital, New Seoul

Hollandia
New Eden–Founded 2287; Capital, Elysium

MAJOR UNITED CITIZENS' COUNCILS SYSTEMS

Progress (Formerly Venture [Kepler-186])–UCC Capital
Unity Prime (Formerly Opportunity)–Founded 2208; Capital, Council Prime
Equality (Formerly Synergy)–Founded 2291; Capital, Bell City

Justice (Formerly Surya)
Ngayo (Formerly Hua)–Founded 2209; Capital, Nyaaya

February (Formerly Market)
Revolution (Formerly Capital)–Founded 2217; Capital, Revolutionary City
Restitution–Founded 2338; Capital, Xolani

Shokunin (Formerly Seisan)
Kyōyū (Formerly Rieki)–Founded 2228; Capital, Nakamura City
Fukushi–Founded 2329; Capital, Neo Kyoto

Denklik (Formerly Ticaret)
Zevka (Formerly Anlaşma)–Founded 2239; Destroyed 2375 (Not refounded)

MAJOR VIRGONID GREATER HIVE SYSTEMS

Virgon (Ross 128)
Virgon (Ross B)–Unification ~9000 BTSY
Ross D–Founded 801 BTSY

Luyten
Luyten B–Founded TSY 1425
Luyten C–Founded 1591

Wolf 1061
Wolf B–Founded 2141
Wolf C–Founded 2165

MAJOR PROTECTORATE WORLDS

Byas
Ranak
Sukat

ABRIDGED TIMELINE OF HUMAN HISTORY, 2061–2507

FIRST CONTACT AND EARLY EXPLORATION: 2061–2205

2061—Earth's Third World War ends in total victory for the Global Democratic Alliance.
2081—*Destiny* mission to Mars rescued from disaster by virgonid ship. First Contact Crisis ends peacefully; human–virgonid relations established.
2087—Joint human–virgonid colony established on Mars. Project Stardrive begins, working toward a mass-reduction/neutralization based interstellar drive.
2090—Project Stardrive discovers the graviton.
2095—Project Stardrive builds working prototype of Higgs-Graviton Exclusion Field generator. First FTL capable Stardrive tested.
2100—First manned FTL Stardrive flight.
2104—Treaty of Mars establishes formal diplomatic and economic ties between Earth and Virgon; first interplanetary alliance in known galactic history.
2132—First permanent human extrasolar colony established in Gilese 357. Star is rechristened Hyperion, the third planet Eos.
2133—Hyperion Panic follows increase in Unidentified Aerospace Craft (UAC) sightings on and around Eos. Similar sightings had occurred on Earth and Virgon for centuries.
2141—Joint human–virgonid antimatter mine at neutron star PSR J0108-1431 comes online. Virgonids colonize Wolf 1061 system.

2194—4 Dra CVS successfully collapsed into singularity, creating first artificial microquasar. System rechristened Ouroboros.
2204—Centennial of Treaty of Mars. TIU established, uniting Earth, Eos, and its other colonies in a single representative government. First permanent antimatter mine comes online at Ouroboros, opening way for longer-range Stardrive expeditions.

SCRAMBLE FOR THE STARS: 2205–2312

2208—Venturestar establishes first independent colony in Kepler-186; star rechristened Venture, fifth planet, Opportunity.
2225—First successful wildcat colony established in HD 197027; the third planet is called Freedom, the star rechristened Frontier.
2248—Wildcat colony on planet Locke disappears.
2250—Human galactic population reaches twenty-five billion, spread across dozens of colony worlds, mostly within a five-hundred-light-year radius of Earth.
2270—First acknowledged contact with Kyrans results in war. Wildcat colonies form Alliance of Free Worlds to resist Kyran invasion.
2272—Frontier military leader Rance Wolfe, "the Starbird," defeats the Kyrans at the Battle of Frontier.
2279—The Alliance is formalized as the CFW, a loose federal republic.
2289—TIU explorers make contact with the melakeen.
2291—Corporate colonies make unacknowledged first contact with the Ciphers.
2295—Virgonid explorers make contact with the ara'.
2300—Venturestar and Surya Offworld merge to form a new corporate-political entity called the Organization of Interstellar Growth and Cooperation (OIGC), colloquially known as the Corporate Worlds.

2306—Corporate Worlds scouts make contact with the xirān.
2311–2312—Attacks by UACs begin throughout human space, escalating and prompting fears of an alien invasion.
2312—Joint OIGC–Cipher attack against the TIU launched. TIU legislature votes to declare war on the OIGC.

CONFLICT AND CONTACT: 2312–2379

2313—Massacre of Rāma by Ciphers; OIGC–Cipher fleet defeated by joint TIU, FWC, and virgonid fleet at the Battle of Hyperion.
2314—Corporate Worlds War/First Cipher War ends. OIGC falls to internal revolution; replaced by UCC. Assumed Cipher home world destroyed.
2317—Virgonid explorers discover the planet Pyria, home to an early industrial mammalian civilization. Allies agree not to interfere in its development.
2320—FWC further formalized as the FWR.
2339—Tannhauser Incident; miscommunication results in battle between Free Worlds Navy and United Citizens' Defense Forces squadrons scouting the Tannhauser system.
2340–2342—Partially in response to the Incident, the wartime alliance is formalized in a series of negotiations. The new Alliance of Interstellar Civilizations, colloquially the Organic Alliance, includes the TIU, the VGH, the FWR, and the UCC as full members, with the xirān, the melakeen, and the recently discovered reptilian uthal as associate members.
2348–2350—Allied explorers discover Ranak, Byas, and Embra, each home to a sapient species at a different level of pre-spacefaring technological development. All are found to be under control of the Ciphers.
2358—FWR launches massive invasion of Kyran space, intending to end the threat once and for all.

2359–2360—Soaring civilian casualties on Kyran worlds prompt backlash from Alliance partners, particularly in the UCC.
2374—The Sukat Incident; Allied expedition to newly discovered civilization captured by Ciphers. Second Cipher War begins.
2375—Massacre of Zevka; UCC world completely destroyed by Ciphers, over 100 million dead.
2377—UCC scientists pioneer quantum entanglement communication after studying captured Cipher technology. Several Kyran clans launch an attack against the FWR and occupied systems.
2379—Second Cipher War ends with *status quo ante* agreement.

THE ROAD TO COMPACT: 2380–2401

2380—Discussions of a federal union between the three human powers and the virgonids begin.
2381—New UCC constitution officially enshrines pacifism. Entire military demobilized.
2390—First annual summit on federalization begins at V616 Monocerotis, site of a new joint Allied antimatter mining facility far from both Kyran and Cipher space.
2395—Melakeen and xirān agree to become associate members of any future federal government at Sixth Monocerotis Summit; uthal withdraw from negotiations.
2398—Compromise of 2398 reached at Ninth Summit. UCC will maintain pacifist constitution but will not have veto power over use of military force by the future federal state.
2400—Compromise of 2400 reached at Eleventh Summit. UCC citizens will be permitted to join the federal military, but in so doing will be stripped of their UCC citizenship and permitted to return home only after service, renouncing the use of violence, pledging renewed loyalty to the constitution and ideals of the UCC, and completing a reeducation program. First Interstellar

Constitution signed at conclusion of summit. Interstellar Compact Navy officially comes into being on December 10.
2401—Elections for Interstellar Parliament and Executive held. Interstellar Compact officially comes into being on December 10, under the leadership of Indira Magnúsdóttir.

GROWING PAINS & GALACTIC WAR: 2402–2485

2402—Planetary Assault Corps, Interstellar Compact Trade Organization, and Interstellar Compact Central Bank officially come into being.
2407—Treaty negotiated with the neutral Yu-Nee Consortium outlining resource and colonization rights in border systems.
2411—Virgonid "Angus" Administration comes to power in second Compact general elections.
2418—Cybernetic Compromise reached between the FWR and UCC over military and social engineering uses of cybernetics, bifurcating the IC's cybernetics and AI industries.
2423—IHC ruling on genetic enhancement technology creates the Genetic Addendum to the 2418 Cybernetic Compromise.
2426–2476—"Age of Peace" sees unprecedented prosperity and calm in human affairs.
2474—Under covert influence by the Ciphers, Pyrian World War erupts between the democratic Raelan League and the authoritarian Lamian Bloc.
2477—Interstellar Parliament votes to intervene and prevent conquest of Pyria by the Ciphers. Third Cipher War begins. Ciphers make early gains, conquering significant Compact territory.
2478—Third Battle of Pyria ends in Compact defeat. Kyran clans Harag, Rhyllok, and Shahak launch coordinated invasions of the FWR.

2479—Kyrans attack the Alliance of Non-Aligned Systems, bringing them into the war.
2480—Twin offensives against Hollandia and Pyria launched.
2481—Fourth Battle of Hollandia strands tens of thousands of Compact sailors and marines on occupied New Eden.
2482—ICN Third Fleet destroys Kyrans in Fifth Battle of Hollandia, finally relieving ground forces trapped on New Eden for eight months. Massive Compact offensives liberate Kyran- and Cipher-occupied planets.
2483—ICS *Belisarius* launched.
2484—Offensive into Cipher territory liberates future Protectorate worlds.
2485—Last combatant Kyran clans surrender. Compact offensive destroys the system designated Cipher Prime, but the Cipher Empire endures. War ends with the Treaty of Omega Serpentis.

RECONSTRUCTION: 2485–PRESENT

2485—ICRA established, initially to aid Pyria and Association worlds' recovery after enemy occupation.
2486—Articles of Protectorship passed and signed, creating the Protectorates of Byas, Embra, Sukat, and Ranak.
2487—ICRA's remit expands to the Protectorates, the goal being to aid them in reaching independence after centuries, or millennia, of Cipher dominion and experimentation.
2491—Executor Clarke's second term ends; Executor Sapkowski elected on promise of peace and economic stability through graduated military reductions.
2500—ICRA operations on Pyria end on schedule; ICDF drawdown begins.
2501—Interstellar Compact centennial. Executor Sapkowski reelected.

2502—Pro-Cipher insurgent movements begin in the Protectorates.
2503—Pyrian Civil War begins.
2504—ICDF military assistance mission to Pyria authorized.
2505—Increasing commitment of ICDF and ICRA security forces to counterinsurgency operations in the Protectorates prompts growing calls from the UCC and their parliamentary allies that the Compact should withdraw from the Protectorates.
2506—Captain Ian Hadrian assigned to the ICS *Belisarius* at Byas.
2507—UCC-led calls to end of the military support mission in Pyria and grant the Protectorates independence increase. Opposed FWR-led calls to increase military support for Pyria and the Protectorates grow in strength.

ACKNOWLEDGMENTS

The Si Vis Astra universe began life as an eighth-grade creative writing assignment. Tasked with writing a two-page short story based on an original idea, twelve-year-old me wove together an exciting (and, in retrospect, somewhat convoluted) tale about a murder on a spaceship—involving spies, world-weary war veterans, double agents, rebellious colonies, and more. "The Sukat Incident" eventually came in at an epic twenty-one pages, and from that moment on, I knew in my heart I wanted to be a writer.

I continued working on that universe all through high school and university, often when I should have been paying more attention in class. I wrote an embryonic version of *Lessons of War*—titled *Time Is the Fire*—which featured many of the same characters, but in a very different universe, and told a story that was just a little too overcrowded and a little too derivative to make it to publication.

Years later, after publishing *Oblivion's Cloak,* I tried to retune *Time Is the Fire,* but I was unhappy with the results. After finishing the rest of the Oblivion's Galaxy trilogy, I decided to do a full revamp of the universe in which the story was set—what became Si Vis Astra—and then do a page-one rewrite of the first book in that universe, which became the book you're holding in your hands right now.

That means *Lessons of War*'s journey here took somewhere north of twenty years. And that means there are a lot more people to thank—and to thank more deeply—than one ordinarily would with the first book in an author's second series.

Many people supported or encouraged my pursuit of writing over those long, long years. First among them, of course, is my mother, who's read everything I've ever written and loved it—even when it wasn't all that lovely. But she's also provided honest and thoughtful feedback over the years that's helped make me a better writer, in addition to making me a better man. For that, I am ever grateful.

Then there are my friends, many of whom I've had since those high school days, or even earlier. In particular, I give thanks to Jake Davis, who even loved the original version of this story, and helped develop the redesign of this universe—and to Derek Kent, who provided an eager sounding board for many of the cooler ideas in this book, and who was also the very first person to back the book's Kickstarter campaign when it launched.

As always, my editor, Katherine Kirk, has done a fabulous job. She helps shape my stories and words far more deftly than I thought an editor could—particularly in this case, as she also did the lovely formatting work you're looking at now.

Then there are my wonderful beta readers, without whom this book, like my others, would be far poorer. In particular, I would like to thank Dan Loving and Lisa Hunt for their input, as well as Rick Moltzon, Christian Meyer, and Adam McDonough, who also gave their backing to the Kickstarter campaign and thus helped bring this book to life even more than they otherwise would have.

But the book you're holding wouldn't exist without the dozens of other incredibly generous people who backed it on Kickstarter. I'd never run a campaign before, and I wasn't sure what to expect when I put it together. The results were better than I could have hoped for, and they provided me with everything I needed to make this book the best it could be.

Thank you to all those wonderful people who made this possible—especially those of you who are holding one of the limited edition paperbacks in your hands right now: Collin Sult,

Donna H., E.M. Middel, Duncan Wilcox, Paul S., Kelly McMahon, Dan Martinez, Kurt Beyerl, Ryan S., Morthis Redknight, Kress Beckler, Javier Vega, Ken Checinski, Mdtommyd, Brian Potter, Phil C.—as well as beta readers Christian Meyer and Adam McDonough, who really went above and beyond. I was truly blown away by your generosity and support for this project. This special edition was a joy to produce; having a high-quality print of a book I've been trying to make for decades is a dream come true, and I couldn't have done it without you.

Then there are my friends and family who also backed the project. Anyone who says you can always count on your people to support your creative endeavors hasn't tried it for real. The ones who are really willing to give you concrete support—whether it's on Kickstarter or in some other way—are rare and precious birds. I already mentioned my great friend Derek, but among those who also backed the project are Jim Cassels, the Spence Family, Linda Black, Craig & Marjorie McFadyen, and of course, my mother. I am truly and eternally grateful for your support.

Finally, as always, I give thanks to (and for) my wife, Victoria—that rarest of partners, whose support is true and genuine, whose patience and selflessness are without equal, and whose love is boundless. This last year has been a wonderful and challenging one for us both, and I can never thank you—nor love you—enough for all you have done for our family.

Thank you, once more, to you all. I hope this book serves as a fitting testament to your support.

Dylan McFadyen

ABOUT THE AUTHOR

Dylan has been writing science fiction stories since he was old enough to write, and original science fiction stories—discounting admittedly awesome, fully illustrated *Star Trek* and *Star Wars* fan fiction—since he was twelve. His first novel, *Oblivion's Cloak,* took first place in the Space Opera category at the 2023 CYGNUS Book Awards, a division of the Chanticleer International Book Awards.

Other than sci-fi and storytelling, Dylan loves history; he has a master's degree in international relations and conflict, and to this day spends as much time reading history as anything else.

When not reading or writing, Dylan enjoys spending time with his lovely wife, Victoria, and their son, William, particularly watching yet more stories, from brilliant favorites like *Battlestar Galactica* and *The Expanse* to joyously terrible films like *Miami Connection* and *Samurai Cop*. Of course, William is too young to watch these himself, but he does make very approving noises when Dylan explains the plots to him.

He also has a *Lord of the Rings* tattoo, which in a way tells you everything else you need to know.

www.ingramcontent.com/pod-product-compliance
Lightning Source LLC
LaVergne TN
LVHW041059080826
845145LV00007B/1638

* 9 7 8 1 7 3 8 3 1 4 3 1 7 *